SARAH STUDIED HIM FOR AN INSTANT, THEN LOOKED AWAY,

her cheeks growing pink. "Colin, I know not what to do. Lord Nicholson has a way of twisting the meaning behind words. I cannot turn him away without appearing surly. Just last night, he took me for a walk into the garden…" She trailed off, her hand fluttering to her throat.

Colin felt heat invade his gut. God knew he'd seduced his share of females, and the thought of Lord Nicholson seducing Sarah made him want to plant a fist into the other man's finely chiseled mouth. "What did he do to you?"

"Nothing objectionable. And yet, I felt so flustered. I suspected he wanted to…kiss me. At home, I might have aimed a kick at him, but here, everything is so different. The daughter of a duke wouldn't kick."

Silently Colin wished he hadn't been so successful at making a lady of her. "Lord Nicholson is a rake. He's well practiced in getting what he wants."

"I know that, but how do I send him away without seeming ill-bred?"

Colin drew her close, knowing with something close to despair that he wasn't at all different from Lord Nicholson, at least when it came to Sarah. He'd wanted her for so long that the mere brush of her hair against his chin nearly drew a groan from him. "We need to begin some new lessons. Now."

FORBIDDEN GARDEN
A *Romantic Times* Top Pick for March 2000

"Exciting, inventive, spellbinding; Tracy Fobes once more ventures out of the ordinary in *Forbidden Garden*. The added presence of Darwin and Huxley as characters provides a strong sense of the historical backdrop, as does Anne's need to be accepted in a male-dominated world. To this, add a touch of the paranormal and you have a book to truly savor."

—*Romantic Times*

"You'd better set aside plenty of time to read *Forbidden Garden* to the finish, since once you start this you are in for the duration because it grabs you and doesn't let go. I couldn't even think of putting this book down. A not-to-be missed novel by the very talented Tracy Fobes, a woman who comes up with something different and innovative with each book she writes. Brava!"

—*The Belles & Beaux of Romance*

"With novels like *Heart of the Dove* and *Touch Not the Cat*, Tracy Fobes is gaining a reputation for exciting historical romances with a twist of the supernatural. Her latest novel, *Forbidden Garden*, will enhance her prominence. Ms. Fobes has written a winner."

—*Affaire de Coeur*

"This exquisite and sensual romance is definitely out of this world! I couldn't put this book down until I'd read the entire thing. For something different, don't miss this one or Ms. Fobes' first two works, *Touch Not the Cat* and *Heart of the Dove*. I can hardly wait to see what her next theme will be. Bravo, Tracy!"

—*Old Book Barn Gazette*

Books by Tracy Fobes

Touch Not the Cat
Heart of the Dove
Forbidden Garden
Daughter of Destiny
To Tame a Wild Heart

Published by Pocket Books

TRACY FOBES

TO TAME A WILD HEART

SONNET BOOKS
New York London Toronto Sydney Singapore

This book is a work of fiction. Names, characters, places and incidents are products of the author's imagination or are used fictitiously. Any resemblance to actual events or locales or persons, living or dead, is entirely coincidental.

An *Original* Publication of POCKET BOOKS

 A Sonnet Book published by
POCKET BOOKS, a division of Simon & Schuster, Inc.
1230 Avenue of the Americas, New York, NY 10020

Copyright © 2001 by Tracy Fobes

All rights reserved, including the right to reproduce
this book or portions thereof in any form whatsoever.
For information address Pocket Books, 1230 Avenue
of the Americas, New York, NY 10020

ISBN: 0-7434-1278-8

First Sonnet Books printing August 2001

10 9 8 7 6 5 4 3 2 1

SONNET Books and colophon are registered trademarks of
Simon & Schuster, Inc.

Front cover illustration by Steven Assel

Printed in the U.S.A.

Thank you to my mom and dad, who always believed in me and encouraged me to fly; and to my editor, Caroline Tolley of Pocket Books, whose genius for knowing exactly what a story needs is without compare.

Author's Note

Although the Duke of Argyll is an old and revered Scottish title, and the Scottish town of Inveraray forms the Argyll family seat, Edward, Duke of Argyll is a wholly fictitious character invented for the purposes of this story only.

TO TAME A
WILD HEART

✤ Prologue ✤

Scottish Highlands, 1796

Phineas Graham was a very proper man who had one chief task: to insure that his employer, His Grace, the Duke of Argyll, lived comfortably and graciously. Renowned for his knowledge on the ceremonies of life, manners, entertaining, household management, and official etiquette, Phineas enjoyed his position as the duke's most valuable retainer and viewed all of his duties with the utmost gravity.

But he didn't always take pleasure in them.

This last week's effort to escort Her Grace, the Duchess of Argyll, to Dunrobin Castle definitely fell into the category of duties he didn't like.

Phineas shifted upon his bench atop the landau, his gaze drifting past the primroses and heather that grew in untamed clumps along the edge of the road, to settle upon the cliff edge some twenty feet away. Far below, foaming sprays of water leaped upward along the rocks, battering the shore with a roaring sound, as though the sea were reaching upward to draw the carriage over the edge. And there, deep in the waters of Moray Firth, a ship sailed along the trading route to Inverness. Dutch, by the look of it, Phineas thought idly.

As far as he was concerned, the driver, who sat next to him on the bench, drove far too close to the edge of the cliff. Ocean spray from below mixed with the dust they'd churned up on the road to create a fine paste that was slowly turning Phineas's navy livery brown. Bumps and ridges on the road had conspired to send the landau repeatedly into the air and given him a backache. Overall, he didn't like traveling and suffered it for the duke's sake only.

This entire journey had proven particularly vexing. With her constant complaints and questioning, the duchess had been a thorn in Phineas's side from the very start. She'd demanded they ride at a devilish speed and moaned over every stop they made. A more leisurely pace would have made the journey easier for all, especially the horses. He thanked the good Lord that they'd likely reach Dunrobin Castle before nightfall.

Despite his pains, Phineas lifted his chin and endured. He winced only slightly when the carriage hit another pothole and a tremendous thud rocked the carriage. Still, when vicious pounding from the carriage compartment sounded beneath his feet, he permitted himself a small sigh.

"Pull to the side," a shrill voice commanded from within, "and open this door."

The driver, his bearded face as dusty as his livery, steered the carriage to a halt next to a clump of heather. "The awd bitch's at it again."

"Mind your language, sir," Phineas warned.

The driver shrugged. "If we keep buggering about like this, we'll never get tae Dunrobin Castle."

Wearily acknowledging his point with a nod, Phineas climbed down from the box. "I'll speak to her." He grasped the latch and opened the carriage door.

A barrage of cool and imperious tones preceded the duchess. She stuck her head out of the door, forcing him to rear back quickly lest they bang foreheads. The rest of her followed in a cloud of perfume that left Phineas sneezing.

He offered her a smart bow.

"You, man." She poked his surcoat with vigor. "You drive without thought. Indeed, I've begun to suspect you aim for every bump and ridge you can find, although for what reason, I cannot say. I'd have a better ride on a swaybacked nag."

Phineas didn't bother to remind her that he wasn't driving the carriage, but serving as escort. And while he would have liked to tell her that one couldn't avoid all potholes while driving at the speed she insisted upon, instead, he simply nodded. "My apologies, Your Grace."

She studied him with narrowed eyes. Moisture dotted her lily-white brow and two spots of burning pink had bloomed in her cheeks. Phineas braced himself for the onslaught. But when it came, it hadn't nearly the force he'd been expecting. Apparently their journey had worn her out, too.

"I am going to be lenient with you, Phineas Graham, because you're my husband's most trustworthy retainer. From now on, see that my ride is as smooth as glass."

"Yes, Your Grace."

She gave a satisfied nod. A moment later, two little faces peered at him from the interior of the landau with the wide, delighted gazes of four-year-olds who've had the tedium of their day interrupted by the unexpected. Phineas, who'd always had a soft spot for children, allowed his lips to twitch upward.

Lady Sarah, the duke and duchess's daughter, had none of her mother's damnable ill humor and was, in fact, a sweet-natured little thing whose deportment and manners well befit her station. The other child, Nellie, was the maid's daughter. Throughout the journey, the maid had attended to the duchess, and little Nellie to Lady Sarah.

The duchess sighed sharply. "Come out of the carriage, Sarah. Since Graham has forced us to take this break, we might as well stretch our legs."

Phineas held out a hand to help the children alight, but the duchess turned such a black frown upon him that he dared not take another step. He climbed back onto the bench and watched them out of the corner of his eye.

One by one, a harried-looking crew descended, the two little girls looking only slightly fresher than their wilted mothers. Still, the open air and fine Scottish sunshine quickly worked its magic on them, for within minutes they were hopping and laughing about, Lady Sarah's voice trilling like a robin's.

The child sang about riding a cockhorse to Banbury Cross, and then asked her mother question after question about the lady with rings on her fingers and bells on her toes, much to Phineas's amusement. Nearly pop-eyed, the duchess ripped an emerald ring from her own finger. She shoved it into her daughter's hand, told her to play with it, and directed Phineas to drive on before the journey killed her.

Huddled together, the two girls disappeared back into the carriage, the ring passing back and forth between them as each admired the stunning, heart-shaped emerald on their own little fingers. The duchess and her maid brought up the rear. Phineas, weary himself, nodded to the driver, who slapped the reins against the horses' rumps.

They were off again.

The duchess's warning riding high in his mind, Phineas kept a sharp lookout for bumps and ridges, and pointed them out to the driver. Somehow they managed to keep the ride smooth and the next few miles passed uneventfully. Just after he began fantasizing about pulling up the carriageway to Dunrobin Castle, however, he heard something.

Hoofbeats.

Many of them. Moving quickly.

Behind them, but coming closer.

Phineas craned his neck and saw a great cloud of dust following behind several men atop horses. Alarm flickered through him. The road they were traveling on led to only one place: Dunrobin Castle. Had some great catastrophe occurred? Or had the group of men a more sinister purpose? The dour part of his nature insisted upon the second option.

The Highlands, Phineas knew, had been unsettled for many years now. Clan chieftains were routing their clansmen from their ancestral homes to provide more grazing land for sheep, because sheep made more of a profit than farmers. The Countess of Sutherland, for whom they were bound to visit, had cleared more land of its tenants than any other aristocrat, earning the eternal hatred of most Highlanders. Indeed, they were currently traveling over

Sutherland lands. Were these men who were following them a band of Highlanders, intent on revenge against the countess?

Their pursuers drew closer. Sackcloths covered their faces. Only their eyes were visible. The alarm in Phineas hardened into fear.

"Do you have a pistol?" he shouted into the driver's ear.

"Nay, sir, I didna bring one." The driver urged the horses into a faster pace.

At first, they began to outdistance the highwaymen. But their victory was short-lived. Phineas risked a glance backward and watched the lead brigand draw a pistol from his belt. Moments later, the sound of a shot cracked across the moors.

The carriage surged forward, then began to sway back and forth at mad angles. The sound of that pistol shot, Phineas realized, had whipped their horses into a frenzy. His hands began to shake and he acknowledged that they were hip deep in trouble.

The driver struggled with the reins, trying to regain control of the horses, but he might as well try to harness a whirlwind. The horses dragged them over a giant pothole. Their carriage flew into the air before settling down again. Phineas heard the duchess's shrill cry over the sound of the pounding hooves and the carriage's creaking timbers.

He squeezed his eyes shut, and then opened them. They were in God's hands now.

The highwaymen drew abreast on either side of the carriage. Phineas saw their mean clothes, their worn tack, and the pistols they'd shoved into their belts. Tattered plaid sashes declared their alliance to the Sutherland clan, the people who had suffered clearances the most. Their eyes held the grim light of vengeance.

The largest man had a gray beard that flowed like dirty snow from under the sackcloth. He yanked a pistol from beneath his plaid and motioned for Phineas to stop the carriage. At the same time, the road turned toward the left, moving dangerously close to the cliff edge. The driver heaved mightily on the reins, trying to halt their momentum.

The horses had other ideas. They refused to obey. The carriage veered crazily toward the edge of the cliff, and for a second Phineas thought they would go over. Instead, they righted themselves and barreled down the road, hitting another bump and taking to the air before slamming down again.

His heart in his throat, Phineas saw that the road curved to the left again. He knew the horses couldn't navigate the curve safely...the carriage was moving too fast. In seconds it would become a coffin. Thinking of the two little girls trapped within its leather squabs, he grabbed the reins along with the driver and helped him pull.

He was too late.

Just as the carriage hurtled over the edge of the cliff, Phineas threw himself off the driver's bench. He had a sensation of sailing through the air. When he hit the ground, it was as though God himself had sent a giant hand into his midsection, driving the air from his lungs, stunning him with one mighty blow.

He lay there groaning, eyes closed.

The highwaymen drew up beside him with a great cloud of dust and volley of hoofbeats.

"Holy Mother," one of them muttered. "We've done it now."

"We were just supposed tae stop them and deliver a warning," another voice cried.

"The countess won't rest until she's hung every one o' us," a third man said.

"Do ye think any o' them are alive?"

"Are ye daft? Who could survive a fall like that?"

"Should we check?"

Phineas, his head ringing, struggled to pull air into his lungs.

A few seconds later, the sound of a low whistle broke the quiet. "They must have tried tae jump from the carriage. Look at her, just laying there."

"Aye, she's dead. Both o' them are dead. The sea will take the bodies."

"What about 'im?"

Phineas sensed rather than saw them move to his side. One of them grabbed his shirtfront, lifted him, and then dropped him again. His head banged against the ground, rousing a fresh wave of pain.

"He's only half dead. We don't want any witnesses. Finish the job, Angus."

Phineas heard shuffling and low conversation. Someone stooped close to him and rolled him toward the edge of the cliff. Suddenly, the earth beneath him disappeared. He tumbled downward like a rag doll. Rocks and boulders smashed into him. Just as he began to lose consciousness, his back slammed into something very hard.

The air puffing from his lungs, he stopped tumbling.

He risked opening one eye.

He'd landed on a ledge.

Above him, bushes thrust their scraggly trunks out of the cliff. He couldn't see the edge that he'd fallen from or the Highlanders. And if he couldn't see them, then they couldn't see him. Would they look for him, to make sure he was dead? Sweat popped out on his brow. His neck aching, he scanned the ledge for a crevice to hide in.

A few seconds later, the sound of hooves dancing upon the road split the silence, answering his question. The Highlanders were leaving. He stopped worrying about his own survival and turned his thoughts to the duchess and the others.

Were they still alive?

Groaning, he rolled onto his stomach and dug his fingernails into the dirt. Inch by inch, he pulled himself toward the edge of the narrow embankment which had saved his life. When he felt the land fall away beneath his hand, he lifted his head to peered downward.

What he saw on the shore a hundred feet below nearly made him cry out.

The landau had broken in two, its leather-wrapped interior exposed like fractured bones. The driver's body had tangled in one of the carriage wheels, his neck at an impossible angle. Her Grace, the Duchess of Argyll, and her maid lay nearby, sprawled in the sand like two broken dolls. Tidewater had begun to come in and lapped gently at their dresses.

Phineas moaned softly.

They were all dead.

For the first time, he realized that something was very wrong with his left leg. He couldn't feel his foot. In fact, pains that grew sharper with every passing second were flickering through his midsection.

He was going to die, too.

Darkness began to close in on him, one of the

soul as well as the mind. He had failed to keep the duchess safe. He had failed his employer, who trusted and relied upon him more than any other member of his staff. He deserved to die.

Just as he let his head drop to the ground, a glimmer of movement near the door of the carriage caught his attention. Drawing on his last bit of strength, he lifted himself onto one elbow and looked again.

A little head moved in the crack separating the two halves of the carriage.

Blood matted her hair, obscuring its color.

Phineas exhaled sharply. He fixed his attention on her, as the edges of his vision grew blurred, then contracted until he could see only a single point of white. As he passed into unconsciousness, he wondered who had survived the crash—Lady Sarah or Nellie—but then decided it didn't matter. What chance had a hurt little girl against the North Sea, which was slowly climbing toward high tide and would soon bury her in a watery grave?

❖ 1 ❖

The Scottish Highlands, 1813

Wild, insistent knocking awoke Sarah Murphy from a sound sleep. Yawning, she pulled the shawl covering her legs off, struggled out of her rocking chair and walked to the door. A glance out the window revealed old Liam Porter on her porch, standing in the rain with his hat in his hand.

Dismay filled her. She'd had a tough day working with Mr. Whitney's sick cows and had nearly fallen asleep on her feet while dosing them with a draught of herbs. Even so, she swung the door open, allowing a bitter wind to sweep inside her small croft. Just as soon as Liam's feet touched the kitchen mat, she closed the door behind him. "Mr. Porter. What's wrong?"

" 'Tis Mary," he gasped. "She's lambing and one of them is stuck."

Thunder pounded off in the distance, adding to the clamor of the first real summer storm since May had arrived. She looked doubtfully out the window. "Are ye certain the ewe's not just tired? Ye can give her a little help by tying a rope around the lamb's front legs and easing it out—"

"I've tried everything. Nothing helps. Ye know she's my best Cheviot. I spent my savings on her."

Sarah frowned. The Porter family had gambled everything they owned on Mary, this sheep whose lambs would demand huge sums once they'd successfully entered the world. If she didn't help and Mary died, God forbid, they'd go under. She was going to have to brave the storm, and just after she'd managed to build a decent fire in her hearth, too.

Patting her pocket to make sure her panflute still nestled within, she hurried over to the hearth and poured just enough water on the fire to turn it to embers. "How long has the ewe been straining?"

"Bless you, Miss Sarah," Mr. Porter said, his eyes shining. "Mary's been at it for hours. These big mitts of mine can't squeeze in there tae bring the lamb out. I need yer lady's hands."

She glanced around her neat little home, with its homespun curtains and larder stocked with food, to make certain she'd left nothing burning, then yanked a shawl around her shoulders. She grabbed her satchel on her way out. Liam was already standing on the porch, waiting for her. She followed him into the driving rain and wind that seemed to want to turn her to ice.

When she saw his pony cart, she groaned. Apparently they would have no shelter on the entire ride to his farm. Still, she knew how important Mary was to his family, so she kept her silence. Mud sucked at her shoes and worked its way into her stockings as she crossed the yard and climbed into the cart.

Liam slapped the reins against the pony's rump

and off they went, moving far too slowly for Sarah's comfort. The trip to Porter's farm, which was a tricky affair, required that they travel down into town and back up into the Highlands on the other side. Sarah held on to the sides of the box as they bounced and jolted their way along the lane, stopping several times for the fences and gates that intersected the moors.

"Are ye doing well, Miss Sarah?" he asked as they sped along. "Have ye all that ye need? We worry about ye, the missus and I."

"I'm fine, Mr. Porter. Please don't concern yourself over me."

And it was true. Her ability to tend sick animals and bring them back to health where others failed had brought her renown even beyond Beannach, the village where she lived. The farmers she assisted were infallibly generous, not only giving her coins for her help, but also insisting she accept bread, cheese, meat, and other household necessities. She had everything she could possibly need.

Nevertheless, they worried about her. They just couldn't accept the idea that a woman of one and twenty years would prefer to live alone, rather than find a husband to care for her. In fact, she'd dodged so many attempts at matchmaking that she'd become quite skilled at it.

But sometimes, in the darkest hours of the night, she found herself lying awake and feeling so terribly lonely. Years had passed since she'd moved into her own croft, and it had been longer since anyone had touched or hugged her. Once, she'd lain in bed for hours, with a pillow in her arms, and wondered if she were real. Lately, though, she'd been thinking a lot about what it would feel like to be kissed...by a man.

Bright morning light always banished such yearnings. She enjoyed her independence and, quite frankly, preferred animals to men. Animals didn't demand fine dinners and drink whiskey and throw stinking socks on the floor for others to wash. And animals couldn't get a woman with child. They hadn't an ounce of malice in their bodies, and were creatures of pure love.

"And the Murphys, Miss Sarah? How are they?"

"Very well, thank you. They've just purchased a few longhorn cattle, and Mr. Murphy is trying to mate them with the cows he keeps in the high pasture..." Sarah rattled on about farm matters, her thoughts only half on what she was saying.

The Murphys had found her wandering the Highlands when she was just a child of four years, and given her their name, but little else. Her next fifteen years had passed in a blur of household chores, which included washing Mr. Murphy's horrible socks and shepherding his flock of ragtag sheep. She'd enjoyed tending the sheep the most, and her care for them had shown in their fine wool coats and lack of illnesses. Indeed, word of the fine Murphy flock had slowly spread through Beannach and, soon, Sarah had found herself consulting with other farmers on the condition of their flocks and ways to improve them.

Almost before she knew it, Sarah had become the most popular person in the village, entertaining visits from farmers with sick animals at all hours of the day and night. Mr. Murphy hadn't approved of her activities, though, declaring that they interrupted his sleep and invaded his privacy. Sarah suspected they'd also made him feel less of a man, after repeatedly watching his face fall when farmers came asking for her advice rather than his.

Whatever the case, when she turned eighteen, Mr. Murphy had asked Sarah to move into the abandoned croft across the Murphy farmyard, so he could sleep without interruption and not be bothered with constant visits from his neighbors. Sarah had quite happily complied with his wishes, eager to be away from that stifling household and Mr. Murphy's constant disapproval.

Now, she paid the Murphys a nominal fee each month to rent her croft, and shopped in the Beannach general store, and visited the Murphys at least once a week, out of both respect and a desire to pacify them. After all, she did live in their croft and entertained all sorts of woolly creatures in her parlor. Beyond that, though, she focused her time almost exclusively on her patients. And despite the farmers' wives who kept trying to marry her off, she liked it that way. In her experience, a "family" had nothing to do with love; it simply meant more work. Her animals were the only kind of family she ever wanted to know.

Drenched right to the skin, Sarah finally arrived at Mr. Porter's farm. He drove past the farmhouse, which looked invitingly warm and bright, and went straight to a crumbling, ancient byre that reminded Sarah of a stone cairn. Deep, incessant baaing echoed from behind the barn door, coupled with a lamb's high-pitched cry. They sounded in serious straits indeed, fellow sufferers in a stormy night that seemed determined to offer only discomfort.

Sarah jumped from the pony cart and, Liam following close behind, hurried into the byre.

"We'll need hot water, clean sheets, soap," she instructed, but Liam, who'd lambed more than his share, was already heading out the barn door, having confirmed that the ewe hadn't progressed on her own.

Sarah knelt by the ewe and assessed the situation. A newborn was bawling on the hay at her hooves, but the ewe took no notice of him. Head hanging low, she was shaking with strain. Sarah noticed two hooves slip outward, then slip back in as the ewe stopped straining. She wondered why the ewe, a healthy, wide-hipped animal, wasn't able to birth the other lamb on her own.

Sarah placed the panflute against her lips and blew several calming notes, her fingers dancing nimbly across the wood, from hole to hole. Frequencies, most beyond the range of normal human hearing, vibrated across the moors. She blended them with more familiar, audible musical notes to create a harmony that the sheep, specifically, would understand.

People who'd listened in on her music said it sounded like two flutes playing—one normal and the other slightly guttural. They'd described the effect as strange, yet subtle. But to Sarah, it was a language far older than civilization, from a time when wild and tame had no meaning.

Taking no notice of Sarah's melody, the ewe rolled her eyes until the whites showed all around. Feeling more than her own share of anxiety, Sarah took off her shawl. Lambing was dirty, if rewarding, work. She was rolling up her sleeves when Liam arrived shortly afterward with a bucket of warm water and soap.

Quickly she soaped up her arms and, just as she pushed the ewe's tail aside to discover why the lamb refused to be born, Liam stuck his head next to hers for a look.

He shook his head at the ewe's bulging, abused posterior. "She's in terrible shape."

"She's not too bad," she insisted, listening to the ewe's low bleats and watching her footwork. The ewe was speaking to her as sure as Liam spoke, and many years in the company of sheep, along with a bit of magic, had taught her how to translate. "She's hungry, and any ewe that can think of food is a ewe with a lot of fight left in her."

"Are ye certain?"

She shrugged. "There's no doubt."

He let out a prolonged sigh. "Thank goodness ye've come tae help me, Sarah Murphy. Ye're a wonder."

"I won't be a wonder until I have a newborn lamb in my arms."

He opened his mouth to say something, closed it, and then opened it again. His cheeks grew red. "Aren't ye going tae play that flute of yours for her again?"

Sarah observed him with a touch of amusement. Like all of the farmers, he suspected her flute lay at the heart of her ability to heal, and would badger her mercilessly to play it. And he was right, though not in the way he thought. While he assumed her music somehow drove the illness out, in truth, she used the flute to talk to animals and diagnose their illnesses.

The flute was part of her earliest memories. When the Murphys found her wandering the moors all of those years ago, it had been her only possession. Its trilling warble had delighted her and she'd taken to playing it for animals almost from the start. The flute had allowed her to communicate with her only friends, the creatures of the moors, and she'd talked to them endlessly, learning more from their replies than any school could teach her.

At first, she'd thought everyone could talk to animals in this way. On trips to the general store in Beannach, she'd occasionally told the villagers what their sheep thought of them or where a pet dog had buried his master's shoe. Often she told Mrs. Murphy that her cats wouldn't mind a scrap or two of beef, earning a chuckle from her. But then, rumors about her strangeness had developed, and Mr. Murphy had begun cuffing her on the side of the head every time she mentioned what an animal had said. She quickly learned to keep her mouth shut tight on the subject. As she grew, she discovered that not everyone had her skill, and even as she wondered at it, she understood that things would go more easily for her if she just pretended to be like everyone else.

Still, once she'd started healing the villagers' animals, which were often the lifeblood of a farm and whose loss could bring total devastation, opinions on her skills had changed—for the better.

"I already played for the ewe," Sarah reminded Liam.

"Maybe ye ought tae give her one more song," the farmer coaxed.

Knowing better than to argue with him, Sarah sighed and took her panflute out. She reassured the ewe again, who baaed loudly in response, then began to strain.

Sarah shoved the panflute back into her pocket. Two hooves slipped out about an inch or so. She forgot Liam as she maneuvered her hand into the ewe and felt around for the lamb's head. A single set of legs and arms greeted her fingers, and a hard little lump that didn't feel at all like a head—

Because the *lump* is a *rump*, she realized triumphantly.

"Mr. Porter," she breathed, buried elbow deep inside the ewe. "We have one more lamb tae go, and I'm afraid we've a breech presentation on our hands."

"Ye mean arse first?"

"Aye."

"That's a fine piece of news," he grumbled.

The ewe tightened her muscles around Sarah's arm in an agonizing grip. Sarah took quick little breaths as her arm slowly went numb, and fumbled around until she managed to find the lamb's head. The lamb gave a quick jerk when she touched its mouth—at least it was still alive. In any event, she could see why Mr. Porter had suffered so much difficulty. While the ewe was wide hipped, the lamb was unusually big, not leaving much room in the passage for both it and his large hands.

"We have tae turn it around," she gasped, and began to maneuver the lamb's small body into a better position. It trembled within the ewe, and she could imagine how terrible it must have felt, being pushed back in after an eternity of being pushed out.

Nearly an hour had passed before she had the lamb positioned head and front feet first, enduring each of the ewe's bone-cracking contractions with grimaces that become more unguarded as time went on. She felt Liam's gaze on her, but she didn't care *what* he saw. Birthing was an exhausting business, and she was feeling every moment of it. When at last the lamb began its journey down the passage again, and its hooves peeped out of the ewe, she grabbed them almost joyfully and pulled its small body into the world.

The lamb plopped into her skirt. Mist rose off its body. It didn't seem to be breathing. She held him upside down until he had coughed up a good deal of fluid and then settled him back into her lap, rejoicing in the way he took a few snuffling breaths before breathing easily. He began to wriggle in her arms, practically knock-kneed in his need to get to the ewe, and she laughed softly as she rubbed him down with the sheet.

"He's a fine lamb." She gave Liam a brilliant smile. "A real beauty. And sprightly, too. Ye'll have yer hands full with him."

"Ah, lassie, ye are a wonder." Liam nodded in contentment, then pulled a pipe from his waistcoat and lit up.

Sarah regarded him with something between dumb wonder and weariness. Here she lay, battered and bruised, covered in muck and filth, and he was going to smoke a pipe? Then again, such was the way with Highland farmers. A nasty piece of work like this was a part of daily life. Not much fazed them.

"Mr. Porter, I should be going now. Will ye take me home?"

"Oh, I almost forgot, lass. I saw Mr. Murphy in town just before I came tae get ye. He's been looking for ye. They've got visitors up at the farm who want tae meet ye."

Sarah sat up straighter. "Do ye mean that while I've been laboring away on yer ewe, Mr. Murphy and his guests have been waiting for me?"

"Aye, lass. Don't ye think the ewe was more important?"

"I suppose she was." She climbed to her feet and used a handful of hay to wipe herself off. "Ye'd better take me over to the Murphy farm right now. Ye know what kind of temper Mr. Murphy has, especially when he's been intae the whiskey."

"Aye, I do."

Together, they left the ewe, who was now contentedly slurping up water from the trough, and went out into the night again. The storm hadn't slackened at all, and Sarah was alternately blown to bits and hammered with rain as they zigzagged back through the Highlands and to the Murphy farm.

As soon as they reached the rough dirt lane that led up to the farmhouse, Liam stopped the cart and let her out. He thanked her and promised that she'd find a nice side of beef on her doorstep tomorrow. Wind slapping her tangled hair against her cheeks, she sent him on his way and hurried up the lane.

As soon as she rounded the barn, which blocked sight of the farmhouse from the lane, she discovered a very fine, high-sprung carriage sitting in the farmyard, next to the Murphy's dilapidated little gig and several broken buckets that needed mending.

Startled, she paused. She studied the carriage, wondering who had come to visit, and why. A curious gold emblem decorated the carriage's door. It looked like a shield. Something about the shield seemed familiar. For some reason, it frightened her. The fact that her fear was utterly groundless frightened her even more.

Self-consciously she glanced downward. Muck formed a dark brown stain around the hem of her dress. Fluid of an unknown variety decorated her bodice with splotches. Her hair lay matted against her head like an old hag's and she hadn't the slightest doubt that mud freckled her face.

She wasn't exactly in the best of condition.

Her stomach tightening, she raced back to her own little croft. The kitchen was warm and inviting, and for a moment she was tempted to stay within the familiar, safe walls. But she knew she couldn't. Mr. Murphy got a trifle mean when kept waiting too long, and she wouldn't be the cause of Mrs. Murphy's suffering.

Sarah plunged a cloth into a bucket of water near the front door and scrubbed at her face and hands. That done, she dragged a comb through her hair and managed to twist it into a fairly circumspect bun. She slung a clean plaid shawl over her shoulders to hide the worst of the stains on the gown's bodice. For the finishing touch, she yanked a clean plaid skirt off a shelf and drew it on over her gown, so that it might mask the mud stains at the hem. While she looked a bit bulky, at least she was presentable.

Her courage bolstered, she hiked up her skirts and dashed out the door, across the farmyard, and to the Murphys' front door. Before she could knock, however, a hushed yelp and a flash of red that looked almost gray in the darkness caught her attention. *Sionnach.*

Comforted only slightly, she made a cradle of her arms and called to him. The fox's hair bristled as he slunk into the open from beneath the steps, and then jumped into her arms. She ran a gentle hand across his head, and then withdrew her panflute from her pocket.

Softly she trilled a few notes, asking him who had come to visit.

Sionnach's reply, delivered in a growl deep in his

throat, coupled with a complex paw maneuver, left her far from satisfied. He didn't know the identity of the visitor, and could only suggest she use diplomacy.

Use diplomacy? Whatever did he mean by that?

With a few more trilling notes, she pressed him for further details, but the fox growled no more. His dark eyes remained expressionless.

Frowning now, Sarah returned the panflute to her lips, knowing Sionnach wouldn't like her next question. Still, she had to know. A tiny bud of hope unfurling inside her, she asked him if he'd had any news of the white beast.

This time, the melody she'd blown on the panflute had a poignant quality. The fox's answer, however, had nothing emotional about it. He growled, clearly annoyed, and told her that he hadn't heard of the white beast because there was no such thing, and that she should forget the creature and live in the present.

Disappointment coursed through her. For years she'd been trying to find the white beast that haunted her dreams. And while she'd heard snippets of his existence from the birds who stopped to roost in the Highlands, and the mice and voles who built nests in the heather, she had never been able to find him.

"The white beast *does* exist," she told him softly, in human language, and the look in his dark eyes told her that while he might not comprehend her syllables, he knew exactly what she'd said. He let out a gravelly sigh that suggested his patience with her was thinning.

Sparing Sionnach a frustrated glance, she turned the doorknob and stepped into the kitchen. Although the fox thought her obsessed with the white beast and lately had refused to cooperate with her, he still remained her dearest friend. Over the years, she'd grown to trust his counsel and admire his cunning ways. Some of his methods she'd even adopted as her own. And yet, at times she found him the most aggravating animal she'd ever had the misfortune to encounter. She told him so frequently, much to his obvious amusement.

Sionnach wasn't amused now, though. The two old men standing in the middle of the kitchen floor had thoroughly captured his attention. His small body tensed in her arms.

Sarah froze, too, her eyes wide.

As if one, the two men turned toward her.

Silence filled the kitchen. It seemed to last an eternity.

Bewildered, she stared at them. The older man had a wealth of gray hair that hung nearly to his shoulder. A plaid tam o' shanter topped his head, much in the manner of days gone by. She estimated his age at well past fifty.

His garb, she realized, was very rich, and much finer than his companion's. An olive-colored coat of heavy wool cloth, with a deep collar and several shoulder capes, wreathed his thin form. His waistcoat was again of wool and his neck cloth was loosely tied. Highly polished, tasseled boots drew her eye away from his sticklike legs, encased in fawn-colored breeches.

Still, his eyes bothered her the most. Although they were very kind, she thought she saw a strange sort of hunger hidden behind his gaze. He'd locked his attention on her as though watching her would offer him insight into the mysteries of life and death.

That strange sense of familiarity washed over her again. She thought that she might have seen this man before. Inexplicably, she trembled.

She turned to stare at the richly dressed man's companion, who was studying her inch by inch just as she was examining him. His gray hair and wrinkled countenance marked him as well past fifty years of age, too. Though fine, his dress was much more severe, consisting of black coat and breeches, black shoes, and white stockings.

Their gazes locked. He assessed her with cold indifference, like a farmer contemplating a cow for purchase. At length, he winced and refocused on his companion. "I see no obvious resemblance."

Sarah raised an eyebrow. Uneasiness coiled in her stomach. Whatever did he mean?

"Sarah Murphy, where have ye been?" a male voice bellowed. His ponderous belly preceding him into the kitchen, Mr. Murphy clasped a whiskey glass tightly in his hand. Square of forehead, with thick eyebrows and mouth pursed disagreeably, he was a flabby and sour-looking man who kept his cellar well stocked with ale, rather than fruits and vegetables. "Christ, lass, ye look a mess," he declared.

"I've been helping Mr. Porter with his Cheviot," she replied calmly. "I only found out a half an hour ago that ye wanted tae see me." Her gaze fell to his feet, clad only in wool socks that had, as usual, begun to stink quite badly. She couldn't prevent a grimace of distaste.

An abrupt movement in the corner caught her attention. Eyes imploring, Mrs. Murphy was making a bending motion with her hand. With a spurt of dismay at her own lack of manners, Sarah realized what the older woman wanted. Forgetting about Sionnach, she began to bend into a curtsy. The fox dropped awkwardly from her arms and, with an angry yelp, ran beneath the curtain to the sleeping quarters.

Eyes narrowed, the richly dressed man grimaced and rubbed his chin with two fingers, as though he'd just witnessed something that had given him a turn.

His partner shook his head sadly. "I tell you most respectfully, Your Grace, that while the fabric *may* be very fine, it has been fashioned into a peasant's dress, cut and sewn in such a way that it can never be refashioned into a ball gown."

The sound of the man's cultured accents, though no surprise given the fancy carriage, reminded Sarah that she stood before some very wealthy gentlemen indeed. She forced her lips upward into what was no doubt a sickly smile and finished the curtsy.

The richly dressed man coughed. His companion frowned. Clearly she had disappointed them. Disgusted them, even. Why would they feel they needed to stand in judgment of her? Remembering the clearances that had plagued the Highlands for decades, she wondered if they'd come to turn them all out of their houses. She fought back an urge to sprint back to her croft, bar the door, and take up what puny arms she possessed.

"Sarah," Mrs. Murphy breathed, the pinched look on her face made more obvious by her widened eyes. "His Grace has been waiting for you."

"His...Grace?"

"Aye, His Grace," Mr. Murphy confirmed, a gleam

entering his eyes, one that immediately put Sarah on alert. The old farmer's gaze never sparkled like that unless he stood to gain something.

The severely dressed man took a step forward. "May I present His Grace, the Duke of Argyll."

Sarah stifled a gasp. Completely flustered, she curtsyed again. How could she have ever felt, even for a second, familiarity upon seeing him? "I'm very pleased tae meet ye," she managed.

At the sound of her voice, the duke's eyebrows drew together. His companion shuddered. The pair exchanged concerned glances.

"I am Phineas Graham, His Grace's man of business," the duke's companion went on to say. "We are here to investigate certain claims."

"Claims?" Her gaze never leaving the visitors, Sarah moved to Mrs. Murphy's side and took her hands. She wasn't surprised to discover that the older woman's hands trembled. Still, Sarah saw that her eyes were clear and alight with a serenity that came from facing years of marriage to a man like Mr. Murphy.

"Aye, claims," Mr. Murphy echoed. He tipped the glass of whiskey to his lips, took a long pull, and then set it on the kitchen table, empty. "This is the lass we found on the moors, just like we told the baron in town."

The duke glanced around their small stone kitchen, his attention sweeping past the butter churn and stoneware to settle upon a few chairs gathered around the open-hearth fireplace. "Why don't we all sit down, Mr. Murphy?"

"Of course, Yer Grace. Forgive me for not suggesting it sooner," Mrs. Murphy replied for her husband, and set herself to the unfamiliar task of serving a duke.

Sarah ushered their visitors toward the old rocking chair and straight-backed chairs that formed a half circle around the fireplace. Embers glowed within the grate, remnants of an earlier fire used to make green dye. They gave the room a cozy feeling without overheating the air. But Sarah felt cold. She tried to understand the secret she saw hidden in the depths of Mr. Murphy's eyes.

Claims?

The duke watched her closely as he moved to a straight-backed chair. She selected a seat as far away from him as possible. Phineas Graham sat nearest the fire and, after serving them all cups of tea, her mother perched on the rocking chair.

"Show her the ring," the duke commanded.

Graham fished in his pocket and brought out a heart-shaped emerald ring. He held it up for all to see. Although only a single lantern lit the kitchen, the ring sparkled with green fire.

Recognition made Sarah stiffen. "My ring."

"It's *my* ring," Mr. Murphy corrected her. "I sold it tae the baron tae pay for my new longhorn cattle."

Sarah bristled. "But that ring was my only link tae my true past—"

"It was mine, lassie, payment for taking ye in and feeding ye all those years."

Mr. Graham cleared his throat. "The Baron of Beannach brought your ring to Edinburgh. He sold it to a fine jewelry collector, whom the Earl of Cawdor routinely patronizes. The earl, who is distantly related to His Grace, recognized the ring while selecting a few pieces from the jeweler. He bought the ring and returned it to His Grace."

Sarah's throat had gone almost entirely dry. She felt a strange tension in the room, the same kind that directly preceded a birth...or death. "Why does my ring interest ye, Yer Grace?"

"First tell me where you found it," the duke commanded.

"'Tis just as I told the baron," Mrs. Murphy answered for Sarah, a trifle frostily. "Sarah was wearing it on her thumb when we found her wandering the moors, all of those years ago. An orphan, she was, thin tae the point of starvation and dressed in rags. My husband and I took her in."

"When was that?"

Mrs. Murphy paused, her forehead wrinkling. "It was a long time ago. I recall the weather being very hot. June, perhaps. Mr. Murphy was herding our sheep through grazing lands when he came across Sarah. A little bundle of rags, he called her, and brought her home in his arms. She almost died. I had tae nurse her night and day for nearly a month."

"How old was she when you found her?"

"Three, maybe four years old."

The duke sat forward in his seat, his eyes narrowed. "Why did you call her Sarah?"

"When we were nursing her back tae health, she said 'Sarah' over and over again. We figured Sarah was her name."

"And you say you found her with this ring."

"Aye, we did," Mr. Murphy chimed in, his eyes growing more bloodshot with each passing minute.

The duke looked at his man of business. "This

young lady was found dressed in rags. My little Sarah wore only the finest of gowns."

Sarah stifled a gasp. *His little Sarah?*

"After a week or so of wandering the moors," Graham replied, "the finest gown might well be nothing but rags."

The duke nodded. "It could be her, Phineas. It damned well could be."

Her hand at her throat, Sarah stared at them. "It could be *who?*"

Ignoring her question, Graham focused on Mrs. Murphy. "Do you still have the clothes you found your daughter in?"

"They weren't even fit for dusting the tabletops. I burned them long ago."

Graham frowned. "Did you find any bumps or bruises on her?"

"She had a large goose egg on her head," Sarah's mother offered. "Her hair was bloodied."

"Was she carrying anything other than the ring?"

"She had a panflute made of reeds."

Sarah clasped the panflute in her pocket protectively.

The duke's eyes narrowed. "A panflute?"

"Aye."

He turned to Sarah. "Do you remember where you found the panflute?"

"Nay, I don't," Sarah lied. In fact, she had a hazy memory of the white beast giving her the panflute—as a gift. Still, she wasn't about to discuss the white beast now. People invariably thought her daft when she did.

Ignoring everyone but his man of business, the

duke murmured, "The panflute was probably a toy she played with. It *is* she."

"The ring proves little." Graham's voice had a warning tone to it. "She could have come by it in many ways."

"Don't forget," the duke insisted, "this young lady calls herself Sarah."

Graham frowned. "Perhaps she was having nightmares and calling out to her good friend Sarah."

He and the duke exchanged a long glance.

At length, the duke's lips tightened. "It *is* she. I know it. I feel it in my gut."

Another long moment passed, and when the duke finally spoke again, he sounded choked with emotion. "God has been merciful to me."

Sarah pressed a hand against her heart. Panic was mounting in her, along with a strange sort of wonder.

After a moment, Graham turned to Mr. Murphy. "Why didn't you report this child you found to someone?"

"We did." The old farmer lifted his feet closer to the fire crackling away in the hearth, renewing the stink of rotten wool in the room. "We told a few people in town. No one cared much."

"But the girl had an obviously expensive ring," the duke pointed out. "Didn't you wonder where she had come from?"

"Aye, I thought hard about it. I decided she must have been the child of some whore," Mr. Murphy stated baldly, "who'd birthed Sarah, then abandoned her on the moors when she started getting in the way of business. She probably gave Sarah the ring tae ease her conscience."

"An eminently reasonable explanation," the duke

agreed, his face tight. "But I'm afraid it's completely wrong."

Utter quiet descended upon the Murphy farm kitchen. Her gaze flitting between her mother and the duke, Sarah's stomach churned into a tight coil. "I know ye, don't I?" she whispered.

The duke looked at her for one long moment that, for Sarah, seemed to last hours. Then, suddenly, he smiled. "You are my daughter."

Sarah felt her face drain of all warmth.

A long pause ensued. She tried to understand what he'd said, but his words had jumbled together in her mind. Cold rivulets of shock seeped through her, making her shiver. Her mouth dry, she stared with haunted eyes at this man, with his fancy clothes and smooth, cultured attitude, and eyes that wanted to own her. "It canna be true."

"My dear, I've been searching for you. You *are* my daughter."

"Ye're his daughter," Mr. Murphy added truculently from his corner of the room. "Don't ye deny it, lass."

Sarah forced herself to look at the duke again. Her throat growing tight, she marked the raw hunger in his gaze. She saw a different sort of hunger in Mr. Murphy's eyes and understood in that moment that the old farmer wanted to sell her to the duke. He thought she owed him and only needed her cooperation to close the deal.

"Sarah," the duke continued tentatively, "I want to bring you home with me. To Inveraray, where you belong."

Sarah jumped up from her chair and faced the duke. Did he really think that she would willingly trade the moonlight and the warm sheep smell of the stable for his gold? "How can ye be sae sure I'm yer daughter?"

Mr. Murphy moved close to Sarah and raised his hand in a threatening gesture. "Don't ye question it a second longer," he hissed close to her ear. "I'll see ye turned out of that old croft, and I'll make sure no one brings ye their animals. Ye're his daughter and tae his home ye're going. If ye stay here, ye'll starve."

Her voice equally low, she spat, "How much whiskey did the duke's money buy ye?"

"A damned good amount. Now pack yer things, and go."

Tears brimming in her eyes, Sarah looked at Mrs. Murphy. The older woman had to help her. If she lost her croft, her animals, and the friendship of a few farmers, she'd lose everything of value in her life.

The older woman shrugged. "I'm sorry, lass. I'll miss yer company sorely."

❖ 2 ❖

Colin Murray, Earl of Cawdor, settled himself on the bench of his navy blue phaeton and studied the woman next to him. Lady Helmsgate was the perfect lover for him—a bored society beauty who'd married a much older man and sought a younger lover to slake her desires. He hadn't yet buried himself in the softness between her thighs, but he knew that moment wasn't far away.

She cast a negligent gaze at the ruins he'd directed his phaeton through, her lips opened in a seductive pout that Colin found very effective. A white bombazine gown trimmed with swans down along the bodice, cuffs, and hemline made her look very young, but Cawdor knew she'd reached her birthday of five and twenty; he'd attended the ceremony himself.

"Do you see those fallen stones, Amelia?" he asked, pointing toward an old fort that had crumbled eons ago. Waning sunlight painted it with a peach glow, while wild tulips along its base swayed in the light spring breeze. "Long ago, they held garrisons of Roman soldiers."

A tremor in her answer betrayed her excitement. She buried her hands deeper into her white fox muff, the one he'd bought her for her birthday. " 'Tis an exceedingly remote site."

"Do you wish me to turn around and return to London?"

"No, not yet. Cawdor, do you have another for me?" she asked softly, her gaze slipping to his coat pocket.

"Another what?"

"Another poem to match the one you gave me last night."

Reluctantly he dug around in his coat pocket, looking for the small piece of parchment. "I hope you find my poor effort acceptable. Most of my morning was lost to its creation, I'm embarrassed to admit."

She held out her hand, the gesture oddly reminding him of a wife demanding her husband's gambling winnings. Cursing Lord Byron for starting this poetry craze with his *Childe Harold's Pilgrimage*, he drew the parchment from his pocket and placed it in her palm.

Eyes narrowed, she read aloud the lines he'd cooked up:

Love is a draught of pleasure,
Love is a taste of pain,
A shining light, sparkling bright,
Or sometimes a dark and bitter rain.

"Very nice, Cawdor," she purred, even as he shuddered at the inanity of his own verse.

He prayed that his cronies at White's never caught wind of his poetry writing. "Remember,

Amelia, these poems are for you and you alone. Don't share them with anyone."

"I'll keep them with the other two you've written me."

"Two?"

"Don't you remember, the night we were introduced, you gave me my first poem?"

Colin grunted, mercifully having forgotten that piece of frivolity he'd written, one praising her beauty or some such nonsense. The damnable thing of it was, he had actually enjoyed writing the poem, even if he hadn't an ounce of talent for it. Rarely had he faced a more formidable challenge than deciding on lines which would best press his advantage while making the words rhyme.

She tucked her newest poem into her muff, then placed a warm little palm against his sleeve. "You must write me another."

Colin covered it with his own. "Come with me to Lady Delham's soiree tonight. You know of Lady Delham, no?"

"I've heard she's a bit...fast."

"Fast, but well respected even by Lady Cowper and her fellow dragons. There, we can relax, and enjoy ourselves as we could never do at Almack's."

Her blue eyes darkened and her lips opened a little more. With a jolt of pleasure, he realized he could have her here and now, if he so desired. But he didn't want her now. He preferred to sip rather than gulp, to savor the moment when he had poised himself above her sprawled body, her legs open to accept him.

She rubbed her cheek against the fox muff.

"Would you please show me more of the ruins, Cawdor?"

"If you wish." He directed his matched bays toward a more secluded area of the ruins, where a grove of birch trees provided shade and intimacy.

At some point over the last ten years, Colin had become a man of charm, taste, and impeccable manners in a society where manners and civilized living were all. At the same time, he was a dedicated hedonist and gambler whose dalliances were the stuff of legend. Style, sensuality, and intellect were the words he lived by. Considering the stalk, rather than the kill, the true hunting pleasure, he attracted women into his bed and men to his side as a candle gathered moths.

At two and thirty years, he had acquired the notorious status of rakehell. Colin took pride in his achievement and had every intention of continuing to pursue a lifestyle of refined carnality, for which he displayed an unquestionable talent. And yet, he had to admit that lately, his lifestyle had seemed a touch colorless to him. Nothing he did, no new adventure helped. Was this what people meant when they said they had grown old? If so, then God help him, he'd be using a cane and hobbling around by the time he reached forty.

He maneuvered the carriage around a stone cairn. The birch trees beside them shivered in the breeze, making a rustling sound, and far in the distance, a cow bellowed. They were quite alone. And Lady Helmsgate, her lips parted and her blue eyes very wide, kept playing with her muff in a way that was making him rock hard.

Without warning, the sound of distant hoofbeats

intruded on their tête-à-tête. Colin narrowed his eyes.

The hoofbeats grew louder. Someone was heading straight for the ruins. He muttered an oath. Christ, what luck. He'd brought her here specifically because no one ever came to these old stone forts. Lord Helmsgate wouldn't appreciate gossip that turned him into a cuckold. Discretion, after all, was the key to any affair.

Lady Helmsgate groaned. "Make him go away."

"Put your bonnet back on, and draw the brim low. Keep your head lowered as well," he counseled. "I'll start back toward the inn, so that we may collect your maid. Don't worry, Amelia. We won't be discovered."

"Cawdor—" she whispered, an edge to her voice.

"Shh." He pressed a finger against her lips and muttered another oath. He'd told no one but Higgins, his valet, of his intended location. Perhaps some farmer was passing by...

The figure rode into sight. Dressed in somber black, the man's eyebrows were drawn together in an expression of anxiety. As soon as Colin recognized his identity, he relaxed, though he couldn't quite suppress a spurt of annoyance.

"It's only my valet, Higgins," he told her. "We can rely completely on his discretion."

Her mouth turned downward. "I hope so."

The valet wasted no time in riding up to Colin. His gaze averted from Lady Helmsgate, he slipped a hand into his jacket and drew out a letter. "My lord, my apologies for interrupting your jaunt, but this letter arrived from the Duke of Argyll an hour ago."

At the word *duke*, Colin stilled. "The Duke of Argyll, you say?"

"Indeed, my lord."

Frowning, Colin accepted the letter from his valet. The duke was his mentor, his confessor, and a stand-in father after his parents had left him with the duke and moved to the Continent. Those ten years he'd spent at Inveraray Castle with the duke were his brief and only connection with practicality and self-sacrifice; the rest of his life he'd spent in a more civilized manner.

And if Colin had learned one thing during his long association with His Grace, it was that he almost never wrote letters. The duke complained that anything written down might eventually return to haunt the writer. Indeed, the last time Colin had received a formal missive from the duke, his entire life had turned upside down.

He handed the reins to his valet and jumped down from the phaeton. Then, leaving Higgins in charge, he walked a few paces away from Lady Helmsgate, opened the letter and began to read:

My dear Colin,

I have very good news for you. Do you recall the emerald ring you found in Edinburgh, the one belonging at one time to my wife? Phineas Graham, my man of business, has discreetly investigated its origins on a farm in the Highlands, near Dunrobin Castle. He discovered a gem much more precious than any emerald ring. It seems my daughter survived the carriage accident after all!

I have met the young lady, and she is returning to Inveraray with me within the next few days. 'Tis my wish that you also travel to Inveraray,

immediately. I will need your assistance in pol-
ishing her into the lady she was born to be.

  While you may announce Sarah's recovery,
please remain quiet regarding the details of her
past, until I have decided how best to present
them. As you are family, I know I can count on
your discretion.

Your good cousin,
Edward, Duke of Argyll

Colin nearly allowed the letter to drop from his
nerveless fingers. The duke's daughter, found at last?
Impossible! The child had died almost seventeen
years ago.

A frown twisted his mouth. He folded the letter
and slipped it into a pocket in his coat.

"Cawdor, are you well?" Lady Helmsgate asked,
her voice breathless.

Striving for an indifferent demeanor, Colin nodded.

"Did something happen to the duke?"

"No, he's quite well." He fixed his gaze on a distant tree, but didn't really see it. A fog seemed to
have invaded his mind, obscuring everything but the
words he'd read in that letter:

It seems my daughter survived the carriage acci-
dent after all!

How in hell, he wondered, could the girl have survived? They'd found the carriage in pieces along the
shore, almost a mile away from the place they'd
found evidence of its trip over the cliff. Clearly it had
tumbled end-over-end down the hill and broken into
pieces before being swept out to sea. And when the
duchess's and maid's bodies had washed ashore,

they'd been twisted and bruised nearly beyond recognition. Of the two girl's bodies, they'd never found anything.

She hadn't survived, he thought suddenly.

The notion had an unpleasant ring to it, a truthfulness that sliced through him like a knife blade. Some greedy-guts was preying on an old man's grief and loneliness. He could easily imagine the duke grasping at straws, wishing so much to believe that the daughter he still longed and grieved for had survived.

"Cawdor, you simply must tell me what is wrong," Lady Helmsgate prodded. "My husband is one of the duke's oldest and dearest friends. He'll want to know if anything has happened to the duke."

Colin forced himself to focus on his companion. "Nothing is wrong. In fact, everything is very much *right*. The duke has found his long-lost daughter."

"What?" Lady Helmsgate lapsed into a wide-eyed stare.

"His daughter has been recovered."

"Didn't she die in a carriage accident, many years ago?"

"We thought so. But we were mistaken. She is alive, and well."

"I cannot believe it."

Neither can I, Colin almost found himself saying. He managed to choke the words back down as one by one, the implications of the duke's "find" struck him between the eyes.

Until now, he'd been the next in line to inherit the Argyll dukedom. Even though he and the duke were only distantly related, through the cousins of second cousins, he nevertheless remained the duke's closest living relative. He didn't actually *need* the dukedom, of course. He'd inherited the earldom of Cawdor and everything else that went along with the title, outside of Cawdor Castle, which his parents had sold.

But he wanted the dukedom. In particular, he wanted Inveraray Castle, the gem of the Highlands. And if this girl convinced the duke that she was his daughter, she stood to inherit all. It didn't matter that she was female...Scottish law was different from English law. There were no barriers to women inheriting a title, the Countess of Sutherland being the most recent example.

"What will you do?" Lady Helmsgate asked, interrupting his train of thought yet again.

Colin suspected she was referring to the fact that the duke's daughter would usurp his inheritance. "I'll welcome his daughter back, of course."

"Where has she been all of these years?"

"I have no details."

"Oh, you must get them." Her features sharpened. "What is her name?"

"Lady Sarah."

"Hmm. Lady Sarah." Lady Helmsgate became quiet again, evidently mulling the situation over.

Colin took advantage of her distraction and returned to thinking about the implications of Lady Sarah's recovery. At Inveraray Castle, the Argyll family seat, he'd learned how to appreciate the wild beauty of the moors. When he'd turned sixteen, he'd embarked on an arduous effort to improve the estate's profitability, under the duke's approving eye. He'd invested a lot of time in that estate and forged deep ties with the servants and tenants.

He paused, remembering. Deep ties. Ties that he'd broken some ten years ago, when he'd come to London at the duke's request, to 'gain some polish.' That request had also come in the form of a missive, the duke's first life-altering letter that had thrown Colin into the vast playground some called society.

City life, Colin acknowledged, had easily seduced him. Women, games of chance, and the intrigues of the *ton*...he'd found them very amusing, and at some point he'd decided he wasn't cut out for a bucolic existence. Too soon, Inveraray had become nothing more than a memory.

He hadn't understood how much he missed Inveraray Castle until now. Even if he convinced the rich banker who had bought Cawdor Castle to sell it back, Colin knew his family seat could never replace Inveraray.

Colin fought an urge to rub his face with both hands. The jumble of emotion inside him had transformed to something approaching weariness, tinged with a strange sort of confusion. For the first time, he realized he'd lost something, but he didn't have the damnedest notion what that something was.

Completely unsettled, he nevertheless came to one indisputable resolution. Yes, he would obey the duke's summons and return to Inveraray. When the duke arrived with his "long-lost daughter," he would polish her. But he'd also do his damnedest to confirm the chit's story, and God help her if she was *anything* but the duke's daughter.

"Cawdor?" Lady Helmsgate's voice had taken on a nagging quality.

Colin took a deep breath, turned, and took the reins from the valet. "Find Mr. Cooper for me, Higgins," he murmured, low enough so that Lady Helmsgate couldn't overhear. "He's that Bow Street runner everyone has been talking about: the finest bloodhound in England, or something similar."

"I know of him, my lord."

"See if he is free to take on an assignment for me. Tell him I'll pay well, and ask him to come to Inveraray Castle in Scotland to meet me."

The valet nodded, then asked, "Shall I prepare your trunks?"

"Yes. We leave in the morning."

His countenance betraying not the slightest hint of curiosity, the valet offered him a bow before remounting his horse and riding off in the general direction of London.

"Where is your servant going, Cawdor?" Lady Helmsgate eyed Colin closely.

"To pack my trunks. I'm leaving for Inveraray."

"Why? To see the duke's daughter?"

Lips set, Colin climbed onto the bench. He set off at a quick pace. "Of course. I must go and introduce myself."

"Is this girl unmarried?"

"I am assuming so."

Her eyes narrowed. "Will you still collect me tonight for Lady Delham's soiree?"

"No."

"Tomorrow?"

"I'm leaving for the Highlands tonight."

A hard gleam entered her eyes. "I've been waiting

a long time for you, Cawdor. You can't leave me now."

Taken aback, he stared at her. He knew she was no innocent. She'd proven herself quite adept at getting her way. But the harsh light in her eyes hinted at something dark in her personality, something he hadn't even suspected. "It's beyond my control."

She lifted an eyebrow. "Do these poems you've written me mean nothing?"

"Amelia, you must try to understand. Duty ranks higher than pleasure, and a duke ranks higher than an earl. I would prefer not to leave you, but I must."

"You're making me very unhappy."

"I'm heartily sorry for it."

"You've used me, and now you are trying to discard me."

Dislike for Lady Helmsgate stirred within him. Thinking that the duke's request might have saved him from a difficult involvement, he retreated behind formality. "Lady Helmsgate, if I've abused your feelings in any way, I apologize. But you must agree, our flirtation has been very circumspect. While our passions might have tempted us to more, common sense has prevailed to date."

"We aren't finished yet, Cawdor," she replied, her tone strangely determined.

"You've many swains draping themselves across your doorway. Will not one of them do?"

"No."

Eager to be done with the conversation, he offered her a small bone, one that he had no intention of ever retrieving from her, but might be enough to soothe her pride. "I don't expect to be gone long. I'll send a note when I return."

She rubbed her nose into her muff. "I'll be waiting."

This time, her gesture hadn't the slightest effect on him. Thankfully, the rest of the carriage ride passed in silence.

❖ 3 ❖

The journey to Inveraray Castle took Sarah from the eastern Highlands, where boulders and wind and heather held sway, to the harbor-rich west coast of Scotland, where the air possessed the sting of salt and the hills and forests formed a rolling green blanket. She, the duke, and Phineas had been traveling for three days now and were due to reach Inveraray before dusk.

As she sat upon the driver's bench and watched new scenery unfold with every mile, she could think only of the life she'd left behind, a comfortable life of independence, filled with the satisfaction of helping those she loved most: animals. Only her fine sense of honor kept her at the duke's side. She had owed the Murphy family for saving her life and raising her, but now that debt had been transferred to the duke.

Thankfully the duke had bought them clothes, food, and farming equipment, rather than give Mr. Murphy more money for whiskey. Obligation now demanded she stay by the duke's side and travel to Inveraray as he'd requested, even though the prospect of being thrust into the duke's alien world terrified her.

"You must tell me again what you remember of the accident," the duke said, seated on the driver's bench with her.

In fact, they were all squeezed onto the bench— she, Graham, the duke, and his driver. Only Sionnach, who had graciously agreed to join her on this trip to the duke's home, remained inside the carriage, his body curled into a little red ball. He apparently didn't mind having his nose clogged with dust while boiling alive.

Sarah closed her eyes. Beside her, the duke suddenly became very quiet, as though he dared not even breathe. She could almost feel his gaze on her face. Not for the first time, she cast her thoughts backward over the years, reaching for her earliest recollections.

The first thing that came to mind was, as always, the white beast, its gleaming coat shining in the darkness. She was atop its back, riding through the Highlands and feeling safe.

Then she remembered sheep. Mr. Murphy's flock, surrounding her. And a keening wind that seemed to bemoan her fate. Of the white beast, she now saw nothing. It had deserted her. A faint dread invaded her body, making her shiver. "I remember being very cold, and the sky dark. Nighttime frightened me. I heard things."

She hesitated, unwilling to tell the rest of her tale. She'd told it before. No one had ever believed her. She might have questioned the memory herself, if not for the animals' occasional sightings of the white beast. And yet, perhaps here, at Inveraray, the white beast was a common animal. The duke might even keep a few white beasts in his stables.

She decided to mention the beast. "Near dawn, a...white beast came. I rode on its back to the Murphy grazing lands."

His eyebrows drew together. "A white beast?"

Sarah shrugged. "Something similar to a horse."

"A white horse brought you to the grazing lands?"

"Aye."

"You must have been delirious," the duke pronounced. "Or perhaps you mistook a sheep for a horse. You were found in a herd of sheep, no? A sheep would look very big to a four-year-old."

"It could have been a sheep," she admitted, discouraged. Apparently the white beast was no more common here than in the village of Beannach. She wouldn't belabor the point and appear irrational. Nevertheless, in her gut, she felt certain that a beautiful white beast with a flowing mane had taken her to safety. "I do recall the herd of sheep, engulfing me like a sea of ivory. That sea brought warmth. It protected me from the biting uplands wind. I slept. I canna remember another thing, until I awoke on the Murphy farm several days later."

The duke rubbed his chin with two fingers. "And you remember nothing of your mother, or the carriage accident?"

"Nay."

"I pray my wife didn't suffer too much in the accident." The duke's shoulder slumped and he frowned, as though the memory pained him still. He stared out at hills clothed in purple heather. "The duchess and my daughter, escorted by Mr. Graham, were traveling in a carriage bound for Dunrobin Castle and the Countess of Sutherland. You may have heard that the Countess of Sutherland has been clearing her lands for years of Sutherland clansmen in favor of sheep. Well, several displaced Sutherland tenants banded together and ambushed my wife's carriage as it approached the castle along the cliffs. The horses panicked and sent the carriage hurtling over the cliffs. Mr. Graham managed to jump off before the carriage went over."

Sarah's frown grew deeper. The duke's words evoked a peculiar feeling of loss.

"We found the carriage the next day," he continued, "in pieces along the shoreline. Apparently it had washed out to sea, then come back in on the tide. We discovered my wife's body on the beach almost a mile away. My daughter's was never found. Naturally we assumed..." The duke broke off and swallowed, his throat working.

"Ye assumed the sea had taken them," Sarah stated baldly.

His faded blue eyes watery, the duke glanced at his man of business. "Phineas, repeat what you saw moments after the accident."

Mr. Graham took a deep breath. "I was fading in and out of consciousness, you understand, and didn't trust my eyes, but I thought I saw a little head moving within the carriage after it had gone over the cliff."

The duke took up the tale. "Although Phineas insisted his brain probably had been fevered when he'd seen movement within the broken carriage, I nevertheless spent days searching the Highlands and the sea for my daughter. Eventually I stopped the search and faced the worst possible truth: that my daughter had died along with my wife and washed out to sea.

"For many years I lived with unimaginable grief. I had no one left. Consequently, it was with great excitement that I received the Earl of Cawdor in my salon one day and examined the ring he'd bought for me from a jeweler. The heart-shaped emerald is a one-of-a-kind piece and cannot be mistaken; I knew it to be my wife's ring, for I had commissioned it myself, and Cawdor had remembered it, too. I immediately sent Mr. Graham to trace the origins of the ring, and he returned with a strange story. We left for the Highlands on the very next day."

Phineas shot a glance at the duke, then studied for a moment, rousing her curiosity. When he spoke, his voice was low. "There were two others in the carriage who were traveling with the duchess: a maidservant and her daughter."

The duke turned a baleful eye on Phineas. "Must you mention this, Phineas? I thought we had already agreed that Sarah is my daughter, my own flesh and blood."

"Don't you think my lady should know all details of her past?" Phineas didn't appear the least perturbed by the duke's obvious displeasure.

"Aye, my lady needs tae know all details," Sarah interjected. "How old was the maidservant's daughter?"

"About your age," Phineas replied.

She faced the duke squarely. "So two girls supposedly died in the carriage accident, not just one."

"Aye."

"What if I'm not yer daughter, but the maidservant's daughter instead?"

"God help me, you are my daughter," the duke

cried out. "I pray for the moment when you accept this. You had the ring, did you not?"

"Perhaps I found the ring on the moors," she suggested. "Or maybe your true daughter gave me the ring, as a token of friendship."

"While you might persuade me that my wife had allowed my Sarah to wear the ring for a time, I cannot believe she would give the ring to a maidservant's daughter to play with, or allow my daughter to give the ring away. And the chances of a four-year-old finding a ring among the heather are slim to none."

"Do I look like yer wife?" She cast a critical gaze over his gray hair, touched with red in places. "I don't look like ye. We haven't even the same hair color."

"My wife had black hair like yours. You also bear a passing resemblance to my grandmother, God rest her soul. I'll show you her portrait when we reach Inveraray."

"Then I must be yer daughter," Sarah admitted, though something inside her refused to believe it. She just didn't feel like a member of the nobility, and wished there was some way to know for sure, one way or the other.

The duke grew very still at her words. Without speaking, he laid his hand over hers. She felt his fingers trembling. Instead of softening her, however, this time his rush of emotion made her angry.

She yanked her hand away from his. "Evidence suggests I'm yer daughter. But ye're missing one important point. I was raised tae tend animals, not prance through drawing rooms. I dinna like fancy dresses, or soft beds, and I have little patience for those who do. I dinna even speak as ye do!" She paused to take a gasping breath, and dash away the tears that had moistened her eyes. "I'll never fit intae yer world, Yer Grace, and by insisting I try, ye'll destroy us both."

Her outburst silenced them all for a moment. The duke's driver coughed discreetly and slapped the reins against the horses' rumps, no doubt wishing he sat anywhere but upon that bench.

Finally, the duke said, "Your blood is blue, Sarah. Breeding always wins out. You will learn what you need to, and when the time comes, you'll step into the role of duchess as your birthright demands."

"I want tae return tae Beannach. My croft stands empty and I have several ill patients who need my attention," she told him. "Let me return home. People know me there. I willna starve. Please dinna ask me tae become something I'm not."

"I won't keep you here against your will," the duke said softly. "Still, I insist you give your new life a try."

Thinking of the money that the duke had spent on her behalf, she frowned. "God help me, I'll stay, at least until ye realize how wrong ye are."

The duke took her hand again. "*I* will help you. So will Phineas. I've also called upon the Earl of Cawdor. The three of us will complete your transformation."

"The Earl of Cawdor? The man who originally found the ring?"

"Aye. He's a distant cousin and well versed in the ways of society. He'll meet us at Inveraray."

"And after I've 'become' yer daughter? What then?"

"In the beginning of September, I plan to hold a ball at Inveraray in your honor, to present you to London society. The season will have ended and your presentation will provide a finale few will forget. Afterward, we'll remain at Inveraray until the season begins again next spring, in London. Eventually you will marry."

"I have three and a half months tae become an aristocrat?"

He patted her hand. "Everything will turn out all right, Sarah. You'll see."

Her movement more gentle this time, she pulled her hand from his. Seeing nothing, she stared out at the hills and meadows passing beside them. Her last hope lay in convincing the duke that he couldn't make a silk purse from a sow's ear. Only then might he release her from her obligation to him, and allow her to return to the place where she truly belonged.

She pulled her panflute out of a pocket in her skirt and began to play. The tune she chose was a mournful one, and she poured her soul into it, her fingers flying across the holes as a melody only partially audible to human ears drifted away on the breeze. Sometimes her playing brought her solace, but on this day, it only reminded her of what she had lost: endless peace among the pinks and browns of the moors, the carefully given friendship of other Highlanders like her, the simplicity and dignity with which she'd lived.

Beneath her, in the carriage, she heard a series of small yips. And yet, she simply couldn't acknowledge Sionnach's counsel: *have patience*. Rather, her playing became more mournful with each passing mile.

"Look ahead, at that deer," the driver suddenly barked, wonder in his voice.

Sarah stopped playing and glanced at the magnificent stag poised only a few feet from the edge of the road. It didn't move, despite their approach. When they grew close enough, Sarah read the concern in its deep brown eyes, along with a simple sort of trust that she'd often found in wild animals who'd heard her song.

The driver slowed the carriage until they were nearly walking. At this pace they passed the deer. "By God, I could grab its antlers and haul it onto the bench, if I'd a mind to," he whispered.

"It must be ill," Phineas offered.

"Drive on," the duke commanded. "I've grown weary of traveling. You may hunt deer at another time."

"Aye, Your Grace," the driver agreed, and spurred the horses to greater speed.

Sarah lifted her panflute and quickly played a warning, telling the stag to beware the driver, who planned to return and hunt him down.

Comprehension in its fathomless eyes, the stag turned and disappeared into the woods.

Even though the stag had gone, its concern for her had raised her spirits a bit. It had risked great danger to comfort her, and in doing so reminded her that these woods around Inveraray would be teeming with wildlife she could make friends with. She would not be completely alone.

Perhaps these animals might even have some new information about the white beast. If anyone could tell her who she really was—a member of the serving class or a daughter of a duke—the white beast could. She'd always known on some primal level that it was an animal of truth. Its purity and selflessness, untarnished by the greed of humanity, continued to call to her. Though she recognized the notion as a childish one, she couldn't help but believe that finding the white beast would set everything aright.

She raised the panflute to her lips again, and this time her song was full of questions:

> *Have you seen a white horse with a*
> *long flowing mane?*
> *It is kind, and gentle of spirit.*
> *And graceful, and sure of foot.*

One of the horses pulling their carriage twitched its tail, whinnied loud and long, and sent one foot backward in a disdainful kick.

Their driver grunted in surprise and slapped the reins against the horse's rump, evidently misreading the gesture as one of high spirits. Sarah, however, understood what the horse had told her: a white horse like the one she'd described was surely useless, and she shouldn't waste her time looking for it.

Other animals heard her as well. She sensed their presence rather than saw them, and heard the confusion in their answers from deep within the forest. Sionnach uttered another small yip from with the carriage, urging her to forget the white beast.

Moments later, a mockingbird flew overhead, chirping excitedly and repeatedly diving for their hair.

Phineas Graham swatted at it. The look he gave the bird was beyond annoyance. "We must be near its nest."

"Aye." Excitement made her voice tremble. She heard what the others could not. This bird, this delightful, wonderful, and smart bird, had seen the white beast. But according to the mockingbird, the beast was hurt.

Some of her excitement turning to worry, she played a little melody that asked the bird if it was quite certain. The bird tumbled in a little circle, expressing outrage at her doubt. Her fingers flying over the holes of the panflute, she demanded that the bird come for her at Inveraray, and then take her to the white beast, so she might heal it.

The bird cawed like a crow in response, talking about its nest. And with that, it flew away.

Her music begged the bird to come back.

But it was gone.

"What is all this panflute playing, my lady?" Phineas asked suddenly. "It seems to have driven off that bird, at least."

Frustrated, Sarah laid the panflute in her lap. "I play because it relaxes me."

Thankfully, Phineas didn't ask any more questions.

Near dusk, they passed over an arched bridge and pulled onto the road leading to Inveraray Castle. A magnificent avenue of beeches led them past a pond before ascending a considerable hill. Sarah noticed the bushes along the edge of the forest stirring. Word traveled fast among the animals. Apparently they'd already heard of her arrival. A glimpse of a black tail with a white stripe down the middle, and a set of antlers, told her they might consent to come out later and meet her.

"We're home." The duke pointed off into the distance.

Sarah gazed in the direction he'd indicated and suddenly, she wasn't thinking about talking to animals anymore. Nor was she thinking about befriending them. The castle filled her vision, a blue-gray edifice surrounded by trees ready to burst with life. Pointed turrets and crenellated towers spoke of knights and jousts and centuries of warfare. Beyond the castle, a fabulous garden of tulips edged a lawn where each blade of grass looked chopped to the exact same height.

Everything about it was a study in sheer perfection.

She glanced behind her. Far below, the little town of Inveraray spread out in neat squares along the bay. A chord of recognition vibrated within her.

The duke sighed. "Ah, a fine sight for these sore eyes."

She said nothing more as they continued on up the carriageway, and pulled around a half circle to stop at the towering front doors. Despite the castle's familiarity, the feeling that she didn't belong here swept over her and urged her to run, to hide in the woods with the creatures who understood her. When the carriage stopped, several footmen rushed forward to help them from the bench. She felt their gazes upon her face and person and shivered. The knowledge that they clearly had more sophistication in their little fingers than she had in her entire body made her wish the ground would open and swallow her up whole.

Sionnach yipped from inside the carriage. He'd grown tired of being jostled around. Concern for his well-being thawed her momentarily. She hurried around to the door and motioned to a footman. "Please, sir, open the door, I must retrieve my pet."

The duke stepped between her and the footman. "Sarah, these men are your servants to command as you wish. You do not need to address them as sir, or even by their first names. Nor do you need to provide explanations. Simply tell them what you want."

Her cheeks flooding with warmth, she focused on the footman again. "Open the door, please."

His expression bland, the footman stepped forward and turned the latch on the door. And while he moved quickly enough, Sarah nevertheless sensed his contempt for her, in the way his lips curled ever so slightly and his gaze held hers a moment too long.

The second the door opened, Sionnach hopped from the carriage and into her arms. He placed a paw on her shoulder, trying to calm her. Even so, she had the sinking feeling that this time, she was on her own.

His attention on the carriages that had stopped before the castle, Colin absently took a sip of claret. He'd arrived at Inveraray Castle only yesterday and had spent most of this afternoon in the study, reviewing the estate workings. Reminded of the days when he'd lived at Inveraray, he'd spent an uncomfortable few minutes thinking about his defection to London. What had he really done with his life over the last decade?

He couldn't come up with a satisfactory answer.

When word had come of the duke's imminent arrival, however, he'd abandoned the ledgers and those negative thoughts in favor of a glimpse of the duke's so-called daughter.

The duke's dogs, two setting spaniels who could scent a pheasant from a mile away, had spent the day lounging in the study with him. Now they had their noses stuck out the window, which Colin had opened earlier for fresh air. Jostling the dogs aside for the best position at the sill, Colin narrowed his eyes as he tried to identify the newest family member.

His gaze passed over the duke and Phineas Graham rubbing their backsides. He studied the driver, who was directing footmen as to the disposition of luggage, before examining a serving wench. He could only see her from the back; nevertheless, he took a second to appreciate her tiny waist and the fine curves, evident through the dirty old rags she wore. Even her tangles of black hair held promise.

Smiling, he decided his forced vacation in the Highlands could prove more interesting than he'd imagined. It wasn't his usual habit to involve himself with a backstairs wench, due to their differences in station, but he'd made exceptions in the past and had invariably discovered that maids take direction rather well, and had an eager attitude no matter what he asked of them.

His mood improving by the moment, his attention veered away from the wench to search the rest of the yard for a "daughterly" figure. Finding no one, he decided the duke's daughter must still be sitting inside the carriage.

Just then, the serving girl turned around. A small red animal stirred in her arms. A fox, he realized. A live version of the muff he'd bought Lady Helmsgate.

"What in hell..." Colin rubbed his eyes to make sure he was seeing properly. The dogs, stationed on either side of him, began to growl.

"Easy Cheltnum, Townsend," he muttered.

Movement in a thicket of gooseberries on the far side of the carriage caught his attention. His eyes narrowing even more, he struggled to make sense of what he saw: antlers, a large brown body...

Christ Almighty, a stag. Standing there on the edge of the carriageway, watching the proceedings just like he was. The stag was mostly hidden, but Colin's vantage point in the library allowed him a view through the thinnest portion of the vegetation. He doubted that the duke or anyone else near the carriages could see it.

Cheltnum, his white-and-red coat bristling, gave one sharp bark before stiffening into a pointer stance, his head faced in the direction of the stag.

"I see it, old boy," Colin murmured. "I wonder what's wrong with it, that it would come so close to the house."

Cheltnum's tail wagged briefly, as if in response.

Colin transferred his gaze back to the carriage. Stag aside, the duke's new daughter had yet to appear. When did she intend on alighting? Tomorrow? What was keeping her?

Townsend, the other dog at his side, suddenly stiffened into a pointer stance as well, but its head faced in a different direction than Cheltnum's. Brow furrowed, Colin followed the dog's lead and discovered another small body hiding in the brush, this one black with a telltale white stripe down its back.

"A skunk," he breathed. "We've an animal convention on our hands."

Townsend whined, long and low.

Mystified, Colin turned toward the door. Were raspberry leaves so tender, that a skunk and a stag would put themselves in danger to munch upon them? He didn't think so. Still, why else would they be skulking around the raspberry bushes edging the lawn? He sat his glass of claret upon a side table.

As he approached the door, the dogs scrambled at his heels, then charged forward. Clearly they were eager to escape outside and chase down the interlopers. He grabbed their collars and hauled them back to the hearth.

"Stay, Cheltnum," he ordered. "You too, Townsend. Stay."

Whining, their eyes very dark and fixed intently on Colin, the dogs sat back on their haunches.

"Don't disappoint me," he warned, then slipped out of the study and closed the door on them. He'd gone no more than five paces down the hall when he heard them scratching on the wood and yipping. Mouthing a few choice oaths at the disobedience of some dogs, particularly spoiled ones, he walked into the main hall and prepared to greet the duke and his new daughter.

The main hall was an imposing room indeed, whose ceiling towered to the full height of the castle and was painted with the shields of all the various members of the Clan Campbell. When he'd walked through this room yesterday, for the first time in over a decade, Colin had felt his Scottish roots keenly, and with it, guilt at how long he'd neglected the Highlands. What kind of Scotsman was he, forgetting his clan in favor of fucking and gambling?

The best kind, he'd told himself with a grin, and promptly dismissed the guilt.

Until now, that was. Guilt had come sneaking back up on him like a wretched cur, making him wish he wore a kilt rather than his fine, tailored, and very English breeches. Before he'd had too long to castigate himself, however, another footman opened the front door and announced the arrival of His Grace, the Duke of Argyll.

Colin promptly rearranged his posture to one of attention and respect, for he did love the duke and all the old man had done for him. When the duke walked in a few seconds later, his face bearing a few wrinkles that Colin hadn't noticed before and his hair a shade or two whiter than Colin remembered, a sense of lost time knotted in Colin's throat like a bitter draught of ale.

"Welcome home, Mac Cailein Mor," he said, using the duke's Scottish name of highest rank.

The duke smiled, but it was a weary, disillusioned smile. "Ah, Colin, I wondered if you would come."

Stung, Colin frowned. "Of course I came."

"Good. I have need of you." Without waiting for Colin's response, he turned toward the door. As if on cue, Phineas Graham walked through the portal with the petite serving wench on his arm. Her dress was even raggedier close up. Fox in hand, she looked as though she'd been hitched onto the end of a plow and dragged through a field.

Disappointment tinged Colin's first thought: *Phineas has already claimed her. More's the pity.*

Surprise tinged his second thought: *He's rather bold, bringing a maid whom he's diddling right into the main hall.* Phineas had always been a fussy man of the utmost sense of propriety.

Shock tinged his third and final thought: *Good God, she's not a serving wench at all!*

"My daughter, Sarah," the duke said, his smile becoming gentle, loving, full of pride...the smile of a doting father. Colin had never seen such vulnerability in the duke's expression before.

He swiveled to look at the girl. She frowned, perhaps resenting his scrutiny, and he saw at once how very dark her eyes were, not black but a strange shade of blue, almost purple.

She was very small, her face cat-shaped and her

nose tip-tilted. Her skin looked brown, the mark of a farm girl. If any lady in London had ever possessed such burned skin, he mused, she would have walked around in a mask. And yet, her complexion did little to hide an odd, unsettling sort of beauty. Aware that he was standing there openmouthed, he attempted a greeting.

"Very nice to meet you, ah...Lady Sarah, the duke has spoken of you—"

A movement near the end of the hall caught his eye. A footman stood outside the study door, his ear cocked. Listening. Seconds later, he grasped the doorknob and turned.

"No!" Colin shouted, but it was too late.

Townsend and Cheltnum barreled out the doorway. They pelted down the hallway with a cascade of enraged howls.

A blur of red flashed by him on the right. The fox, he realized, had jumped from the girl's arms. A quick glance at her confirmed that her mouth was open in an oval of surprise. Or fright. Probably both.

"Bloody dogs," he growled, and lunged toward the part of the hallway that opened onto the main hall, in an attempt to block the dogs' advance. They jumped nimbly around him and skidded into the main hall with all the vigor of two hounds from hell. Their nails made a scratching sound across the marble floor.

"Cheltnum, Townsend, heel," the duke shouted, to no avail.

Snarling and baying, the dogs charged at the fox, sending him straight up the furniture. The fox began pelting around the room like a mad thing, jumping from table, to chair, to shelf, with the dogs hot on its little red heels. The dogs leaped at least three feet into the air, even twisting while in midair to get after their quarry. It was an inspired effort, and if circumstances were different, Colin might have applauded.

The footman who'd allowed the dogs to escape hurried into the hall, wringing his hands and hurling apologies at the duke. "I'm sorry, Your Grace, but they were scratching on the door, and I didn't want any accidents to occur in your study."

"Grab them, then," the duke ordered. "Phineas, help him!"

The girl, her face growing whiter than her brown complexion allowed, suddenly pulled a flute from her pocket. Shocked, Colin watched her lift the instrument to her lips and begin to play. Not only had she little talent—the tune was utterly discordant—but he couldn't believe she chose to play music just as a foxhunt had commenced in the great hall.

Thinking her daft, he circled around in the opposite direction Phineas took, hoping to corral the dogs between the two of them. They were still jumping up on their hind legs and barking viciously at the fox, who had shimmied up to a shelf bearing a priceless Ming vase.

When Phineas, his face a mask of distaste, drew close enough to grab Cheltnum's collar, he lunged at the dog. As the fates would have it, the dog chose that moment to back down and skirt two paces to the left, perhaps to get a better angle at the fox. To Phineas's credit, he realized his attack would fall short and he stretched mightily, elongating his body in midair, despite the fact that a miss would leave him flat on his face.

But the angle of Phineas's attack had unexpected

results. The duke's man of business landed square
on the dog's back, drawing a frightened yelp from
the purebred. Like a squirrel with a piece of tin tied
to its tail, Cheltnum reared away from his attacker
and pelted around the hall, Phineas holding on to
his withers and scuttling across the fine marble
floor.

Colin sprinted after Phineas. The girl continued
to play her panflute. And the duke shouted at the
footman, his voice entering the realm of panic.

"Open the door, for God's sake. Let the fox out,
before the dogs kill one of *us!*"

The Ming vase fell to the floor with a splintering
crash as the fox flung itself toward a wall sconce and
sprawled expertly between its golden arms.

Scurrying, the footman made it to the door and
yanked it open just as Phineas, his arms still locked
around Cheltnum, skidded to a halt at the threshold.
And yet, the entrance was not clear as they'd all expected. A skunk—probably the same one he'd seen
from the library window, Colin realized—had frozen
into a position of outrage on the other side.

The dog stopped short, and Phineas with him.
The three of them stared at each other. Two seconds
later, the skunk had turned around. Colin squeezed
his eyes shut. He had enough sense left to guess
what was coming. Phineas's high-pitched shout,
mingling with the dog's squeal, bolstered his fears.
The stink of skunk spray erased the last of his doubt.

Truly frightened, Colin slowly opened his eyes.

Phineas had dropped to the floor and was clutching his face. Cheltnum began to hop around the
room, shaking his muzzle, circling madly. Colin
tried to lunge out of the dog's way, but he didn't

move quickly enough. Cheltnum bumped him in the legs so hard that Colin nearly fell over.

For her part, the girl played even more loudly on her flute. She wasn't daft, Colin thought wildly, but rather an agent of chaos. The skunk, evidently the wisest of them all, disappeared down the steps and back into the brush.

"Enough, I say," the duke thundered. "Enough!" He strode forward and cuffed Townsend on the withers, drawing a yip from the dog.

Townsend cringed and skulked away from his master.

"Chase that other stinking dog out the door, now!" The duke gestured angrily at the footman, who herded Cheltnum toward the front door with a series of well-placed nudges.

Clearly seeing an opportunity, the fox hopped down from his perch and landed on a display case housing Rob Roy's dirk handle, among other treasures. He made it to the marble floor and started toward the girl's arms.

Both Townsend and Cheltnum froze when they saw the fox. Cheltnum, still shaking his muzzle, glanced uneasily at the duke. The fox froze as well.

"Don't you dare," the duke breathed.

The girl played a quick little melody on her flute. Colin had the odd sense that she was adding her own warning to the duke's. A few seconds passed as they all waited to see if the dogs would obey.

They didn't.

Another volley of baying and growling filled the center hall. Both dogs lunged after the fox, who turned sharply and raced up the staircase. The duke shouted after them, but this time, the dogs were obviously determined beyond the point of reason to have their quarry. Perhaps it had become a matter of pride, perhaps they knew they had nothing left to lose. Whatever the case, Cheltnum and Townsend tore up the stairs and disappeared into the upstairs hallway.

"Great God in heaven," the duke shouted, and moved toward the stairs.

The girl, her flute clutched in her hand, raced past him and followed in the dogs' path.

"Sarah, stop." His face growing an alarming shade of red, the duke started to climb the stairs after her. "The dogs are maddened. They'll bite to kill!"

Colin heard terror in the duke's voice and wondered at it. The duke *never* became hysterical. It underscored how very much he valued this girl of his.

"Your Grace," Phineas warbled, from behind them.

Aghast, Colin watched as the duke's man of business sank into a swoon.

The duke stopped and swung around to stare at Phineas. "Good God, is he dead?"

Growling echoed from above, reminding Colin of the urgency of Lady Sarah's situation. He sprinted up the stairs past the duke. "Help Phineas," he urged. "I'll go after those damned dogs."

He didn't wait to see if the duke had listened to his instructions. Rather, he followed the sound of barking toward the private drawing room, near the end of the hallway. Just as he turned the corner and espied the door to the drawing room, the girl disappeared within and shut the door behind her.

Alarm raced through him. The foolish chit had trapped herself in a room with two dogs who clearly weren't going to rest until they'd tasted fox. Or girl.

A cacophony of enraged baying echoed through the hallway. Colin also heard the discordant notes of a flute. There she was again, he thought as he ran down the hallway, playing her bloody panflute. What did she think the dogs were going to do, give up the hunt to dance a quick cotillion?

Fear giving him the strength of ten men, Colin skidded to a halt outside the door to the drawing room. Inside, the snarling and growling had reached a fever pitch. His heart pounding, he scanned the hallway, looking for a weapon. An old suit of armor stood about two feet to the left of the door, a war hammer placed near the silver boots.

Colin grabbed the war hammer and hefted it to his side. The weapon might prove a bit excessive, but would certainly make his point. The moment he clasped the doorknob, however, utter silence descended upon Inveraray Castle. Gone were the snarls and growls, gone were the sounds of vases breaking and nails scratching across the floor.

Even the flute playing had ceased.

Dread suddenly weighting his limbs, Colin allowed the war hammer to drop to his side. *She's dead,* he thought. The dogs, enraged beyond the point of reason, had ripped her throat out. Slowly he turned the knob, his chest tight with terrible anticipation.

And froze when he saw the tableau inside.

The girl sat calmly upon a fine Aubusson carpet, her tattered skirts spread out around her. She had the fox cradled in her arms. Cheltnum and Townsend sprawled comfortably near her feet. That wild, murderous look had gone from the dogs' eyes. In fact, they reminded Colin of two puppies who'd enjoyed a rousing play but were ready for a nap. If not for the stink of skunk in the room, Colin might even have questioned if the ruckus downstairs had really occurred, or if he'd been having a nightmare.

The girl, who seemed to have frozen solid at his entrance, stared at him with a wide violet gaze. She took a hitching breath, then said unsteadily, "Good evening, sir."

The war hammer dropped from his numbed fingers. He glanced from the dogs, to the fox, and then focused back upon her. Abruptly he saw the tips of bare toes peeking from beneath her skirt. "How did you...I mean, what happened...I..."

He broke off, aware he had come close to gibbering. He hadn't the slightest idea how this kittenish sprite had calmed the duke's maddened dogs, but now that he'd drawn close to her, his trained eye reminded him of her lovely face and even lovelier body beneath all of that grime and ill breeding.

The sight instigated a strange fluttering in his gut.

Colin, a man who had never been at a loss for words, suddenly had no idea what to say. Annoyance rushed through him as he cleared his throat and struggled for composure. Good God, he mused, he'd shown more aplomb before the Prince Regent.

The notion was enough to loosen his tongue. "Welcome to Inveraray Castle," he said gruffly.

❖ 4 ❖

Sarah returned his gaze, a queer nervousness stealing over her. She didn't know what to make of him. Men, in her experience, were rawboned and taciturn, their manner dour and preoccupied with livestock and other farming matters. Their clothes appeared serviceable, their boots worn-out. They took pride in how many sons they'd sired and dogs they kept and fields they'd plowed.

Coarse and old-fashioned, the men she'd known stood leagues from the one in front of her.

She had a difficult time pinpointing exactly what about him had quickened her blood. Other than a full lower lip, he hadn't any remarkable features; straight and regular, his countenance could have belonged to one of the men she'd known. He was of average height and build, and hadn't any physical qualities that she might think of as patrician.

But his eyes, they were dark blue and full of provocation. Coupled with his full lower lip, they gave him a wicked air, as though he were a man accustomed to lavish indulgence. Glittering jewels, fine silk, creamy bonbons…these were things she'd often wondered about but never experienced. This man, she suspected, experienced them regularly and with wanton appreciation.

"Townsend and Cheltnum seem to like you," he said, his gaze assessing. "Should I follow their lead?"

Sarah opened her mouth, and then closed it just as quickly, unable to think of a satisfactory reply. His manner and words implied he expected her to protest innocence, but for what crime, she couldn't say. As she sat there, mute, she realized that each second she hesitated in answering gave him the advantage. The longer she waited, the more he discovered how he'd flustered her.

"Who are ye?" she forced out.

"I am Colin, Earl of Cawdor," he told her, his lips curving lazily upward.

She blinked, unprepared for the sheer power of his smile or the effect it would have on her. Her throat grew even tighter. His hair, she noted helplessly, was a gleaming black with bluish streaks through it, reminding her of a crow's wings.

"Pleased tae meet ye, my lord. I'm Sarah Murphy." She waited for him to flinch at the sound of her accent.

He didn't flinch at all. Rather, his smile gained a touch of concern. "This day must have been very difficult for you, Lady Sarah. I'm certain you'd have preferred a gentler welcome, particularly after traveling. Your nerves must be quite raw."

Underneath the sympathy in his eyes, Sarah noticed an inexplicable glint. She couldn't quite explain why, but the glint seemed at odds with his apparent concern. He was studying her, she thought. Assessing her. Searching for weaknesses?

She shivered. A strange perception took hold of her, one she couldn't shake. Beneath the cool blue of his eyes she saw a much warmer flame, that of a hawk who has sighted his prey. And yet, there seemed to be a gentleness in him that suggested his bite would have more in common with pleasure than pain.

The impression made her wary. "Aye. My nerves are raw. A bed is all I seek."

"You shall certainly have one. Cheltnum, Townsend, come here. You'll spend the night outside for this evening's antics."

The two dogs, their bellies scraping along the floor, inched their way over to his feet. Crouched there, they appeared the very picture of abject misery. And yet, Sarah saw their tails twitching, a fond wag they barely managed to suppress. Listening closely, she heard a rumbling in their throats, one she translated into a plea for forgiveness.

The earl grabbed their collars, hauled them to the door, and handed them over to a footman she hadn't even noticed. Sionnach took the opportunity to jump out of her arms.

Deserter, she silently berated him, as he slunk away.

His smile still intact, the earl returned to her side and offered her his hand. "Let me help you up."

"Thank ye." Swallowing, Sarah placed her hand in his. Considerably larger, his palm engulfed hers with warmth. She flinched at the intimacy of their bare skin touching and, as soon as she'd stood, withdrew her hand. She held the palm he'd grasped in her free hand, feeling as though he'd scalded her.

His smile grew wicked. "You seem to have an uncanny way with the duke's hounds. Are you part goddess, perhaps? Pan's mate?"

Confusion furrowed her brow. Goddess? Pan's mate? She had no idea of what he spoke, but she had enough common sense to distrust his manner. "I'm nae one's mate, my lord."

His eyes widened for a brief instant. "What will you have me call you? Lady Sarah is your proper address."

"I'm nae comfortable being Lady Sarah."

"What would you prefer?"

"Sarah is fine."

"Thank you, Sarah, for the privilege of using your first name. Why don't you call me Colin as well?"

His teeth, she noticed, were even and white in his tanned face. "As ye wish, er, Colin."

"The duke has asked me to teach you the ways of society," he said in an offhand manner. "Has he discussed this with you?"

"Aye," she warbled.

He stepped closer. "How do you suppose you and I will get along, Sarah?"

His lower lip, she saw, was protruding slightly. Its sensuous curve fascinated her. Her gaze dropped lower, to his square chin, then settled on the white neck cloth beneath it. He was sophisticated, imposing...and yet, he smelled quite distinctly of skunk.

"We'll get along fine, if ye dinna ask anything of me and change yer clothes," she replied calmly.

A beat of silence passed between them.

Then, without warning, he chuckled. "I'm afraid I'll have to ask plenty of you. We'll have to work on your language first. Your accent gives you away."

"Then I dinna think we're going tae get along at all, sir. I find nothing wrong with my speech."

"The proper address for an earl is *my lord*, not sir," he told her, in tones she deemed pompous.

"I'll nae have any lessons from ye," she informed him. "I've nae wish tae be here at the duke's estate, and I've nae wish tae become the duke's daughter. The sooner I've convinced him of that fact, the better."

"Then why are you here?"

"Because I'm obligated."

"In what way?"

She looked him straight in the eye. "Ye haven't been listening tae me. I dinna like it here. I want tae go home. I stay only because I promised him I would."

"And you're a lady of honor," he said, his attitude suggesting he didn't think her very honorable at all.

"I'll stay until he tells me tae go."

"Well, at least I know your position." He sighed loud and long, as though she'd wearied him. "Sit down with me, so we might become better acquainted. I'd like to know where you learned to play the flute, and why you keep a fox for a pet."

He offered her his hand, which she took with the slightest hesitation, knowing exactly how warm and agitating his palm would feel against hers.

"This way," he said, his voice low, and led her toward a group of chairs clustered around a table.

She held onto him, wary, trying to suppress the surge of warmth that flooded her every time they touched. When he released her, she couldn't prevent a small sigh of relief. This man, she thought, was a wolf among the flock.

He folded his frame into a fancy little chair. She, too, took a seat, and for the first time noticed her surroundings. Her lips parted as her gaze darted from treasure to treasure.

Everywhere she saw gold. Cream ceilings gilded with golden flowers and intricate oval designs, gold traced across delicate chairs and tables, a golden harp propped up in the corner. And there, amid the gold, were two crystal chandeliers, each a waterfall of clear, faceted jewels that reflected rainbows of color.

Without quite realizing it, she stood. "What is this place?"

Colin stood as well, his attention locked on her.

" 'Tis the private drawing room." A smile began to play about his lips. "Guinon and Gerardi embellished the ceiling, Dupasquier gilded it. The windows were designed by Robert Mylne, who also designed the Almack's rooms in King Street, St. James's."

Unimpressed, Sarah nodded. A faint squeaking sound caught her attention. She wandered in its direction and quickly discovered the origin of the sound: a tiny gray mouse, peeking out between a crack in the baseboards. Reassured by its presence, she pulled out her panflute and played the mouse a quick welcome.

It answered with a vigorous squeak.

Aware that Colin was staring at her with a bemused expression on his face, she concealed her panflute in her pocket and trailed her fingers across the back of a chair, its seat a tapestry of pink roses. " 'Tis sae beautiful here. Sae fine. Sae clean and bright, and soft tae the touch, and sweet smelling. Everything delights the senses."

"Inveraray is a special place," he allowed.

She thought of her croft with its rush flooring and an army of fleas that lay in wait beneath the rushes, and almost scratched her arms in reflex. "Do all aristocrats live as the duke does?"

"Some live better," he said, "and some worse. It depends on their fortunes and their ways of thinking. I know both hedonists and monks, but most of us fall somewhere in the middle."

"And ye? Where do ye fall?"

"I tend toward hedonism."

She nodded, not sure what hedonism meant. "I can't imagine having enough time in the day tae worry about anything but the next meal. All of this is sae different tae me."

"You've lived a life of penury, where survival, rather than stimulation, is the order of the day. Your senses are deprived. The duke and I shall shortly remedy that condition, and I suspect you'll enjoy your treatment immensely."

"What do ye mean?"

"Wait and find out," he murmured, and suddenly, the gleam was back in his eyes, warm and provocative.

She swallowed and walked a safe distance from him. Those imaginary men she'd kissed in her dreams had never possessed a face. They'd been dark shadows, men who could never actually exist. And yet, now those dreams had invaded her daytime hours, and the imaginary man had acquired a face: Colin's.

Trying to divert her thoughts to a less dangerous subject, she studied the drawing room and waited for that chord of familiarity to strike. If she'd lived in this castle, surely she must have visited a room as beautiful as this one quite often. And yet, she knew nothing other than awareness of the earl's attention upon her.

She wandered toward a tapestry hanging on the far wall, her gaze flitting idly across the room. A blur of white among many brilliant colors caught her eye, and abruptly, she froze, her attention locking on the tapestry.

Garlands of roses danced along the edge of the weaving. They encircled a woodlands scene at night. A woman and young girl, bathed in moonlight, stood near a brook. In the background, trees stretched up toward a spray of stars. And there, beside the girl, with one hoof in the water, stood the white beast.

The tapestry's weave was very fine, its colors as stunning as the scene it depicted. Sarah moved close to the tapestry, close enough to touch it, and traced the white beast's horn with a trembling finger. She wondered if the earl had ever seen one, and if so, where.

"The chairs are covered in Beauvais tapestries, as are the walls," the earl informed her, walking a few steps closer.

She looked around and saw that every wall had a rug covering it, each one a brilliant array of colors and depicting scenes of women and children romping in veritable gardens of Eden. But she found no more weavings of the white beast.

She returned her attention to the tapestry in front of her. "This white beast, have ye ever seen it?"

His eyebrows drew together. "White beast?"

"Aye." She touched the weaving reverently.

"Do you mean the unicorn?"

"Is that what it's called?"

"Yes."

Hope sparked within her. She spun around to

face him directly, her hands clasped in her skirts to hide their shaking. "Will ye take me tae it?"

"To see a unicorn?" His expression had grown bemused.

"Aye. Please, I must see it."

"My lady, it would be my very great pleasure to take you to see a unicorn...if one existed. But the only unicorns in Scotland that I know of are painted on the Scottish royal arms. They're the stuff of fables. Legends. Surely you know this."

Her shoulders drooped. Here it was again, that infernal doubt. "Are ye certain?"

"Of course I am."

"What makes ye sae sure?"

"Common sense."

"If ye say sae."

He shook his head. "I've never met a woman such as you. Believing in unicorns, keeping a fox for a pet—" He hesitated, as if a thought had occurred to him. "How do you manage to keep the creature near you?"

"What creature?"

"Your, ah, fox."

"Oh. He's a friend."

"A *friend*? Surely you jest."

"Nay, I'm serious. And I'm beginning tae resent ye questioning my every statement."

Rather than reply, he simply stared at her.

Her cheeks grew warm. She stepped away from the tapestry and moved to the middle of the room. Her attention flitted to the fireplace, a study in white marble. Above it hung a mirror framed in gold, and carvings of two robe-swathed women embraced the hearth from either side.

"The duke acquired those marble chimney pieces

from Bellevue, in Edinburgh. Quite a coup, it was,"
Colin murmured.

Sarah nodded, pretending interest in the house
that supposedly would someday be hers. But her attention was truly upon another woman, this one in
the mirror. Tangles matted her hair and dirt made
brown splotches on her threadbare dress. She was a
blight on the glittering room, a gray pox upon fine
white skin.

She looked away. "I dinna belong here."

"Sarah?" Colin moved behind her. A brief moment passed, and then his hands descended on her
shoulders. His skin felt warm, and firm, and aroused
a tickling sensation deep within her that she'd never
known before, one that was part pleasure, and part
yearning. She became utterly still, afraid that he
might move his hands and end the pleasure, and yet
somehow afraid he wouldn't.

"I'm here to help you," he murmured huskily.
"Trust me, Sarah. Confide in me. Who are you, really?"

She sensed a presence in the doorway and turned
her head just in time to see the duke.

"Thank God you're all right," the duke said as he
hurried into the room. When he espied Colin's
hands resting on her shoulders, however, he stopped
short and raised an eyebrow.

Colin released her. The place on her shoulders
where he'd rested his hands abruptly grew cold. Disappointed at the duke's entrance without quite
knowing why, Sarah frowned, while Colin went to
slouch against the fireplace mantelpiece.

The duke strode to her side. "Has Colin done anything to upset you?"

"Nay," she demurred. "I'm just tired from the journey."

"We all are." The duke's gaze fell upon the spiked weapon that Colin had been wielding when he first came into the room. "Good God, who brought in the war hammer? You, Colin?"

"Yes." Colin shrugged.

"What in blazes were you planning to do with it?"

"I thought I might need to beat the dogs off, and the war hammer was the only weapon I could quickly find."

"You would have wielded it gently, I hope."

"With infinite care."

The duke took a moment to examine the drawing room, then returned his attention to Colin. "Judging by the lack of destruction in the room, and the good health of my dogs, you didn't need to use it."

"No, your daughter had everything in hand before I entered."

The duke's focus swiveled to Sarah. "How so?"

She swallowed. "Well, I talked softly tae them, and petted them, and told them they shouldn't harm Sionnach, for he was my personal friend."

"Really? And this calmed them?"

"Yer dogs are quite reasonable."

"I see." The duke glanced at Colin. "Perhaps they simply needed a woman's touch."

"I heard Sarah playing the flute before I entered," Colin offered. "Cheltnum and Townsend may have a musical bent. We should arrange for lessons."

"Indeed." The duke's lips twitched. "Whatever the case, I'm glad all has turned out well. Phineas is fine, by the way. Smelling salts revived him. He's taken a bath and is now resting comfortably in his room."

Colin nodded. "He had quite a shock."

The duke turned his attention to Sarah. "Sarah, I've brought Mrs. Fitzbottom with me. She is my housekeeper and will see to your needs until I can engage a suitable lady's maid. Mrs. Fitzbottom, please come in."

An elderly lady dressed in gray, with her gray hair pulled back into a chignon, entered the room. Sarah thought she had a kindly face, round and slightly red, with a large bosom and plump figure...the perfect kind of woman to cry upon, whom Sarah guessed she might soon need. With every moment she was feeling more out of sorts.

"Good evening, Lady Sarah," the housekeeper said. "Please come with me. We'll get you into a hot bath at once."

"A hot bath?"

"Aye, in a tub," Mrs. Fitzbottom confirmed, sniffing pointedly.

Sarah became freshly aware of the skunk smell in the room. "Ye want me tae sit in water? Water doesn't get rid of a skunk's spray."

"Water works fine," the housekeeper stoutly assured her, "if you use a little soap to break up the skunk oil, and lemon juice to neutralize the odor."

Sarah drew in a determined breath. "I canna sit in water. I'll catch my death of cold. Bring me a bottle of vinegar, and I'll sponge the skunk spray off."

"We've a *bath* for you, lass. I'll not have you stinking like vinegar. That's nearly as bad as skunk."

The duke, clearly reading the consternation on Sarah's face, moved closer to her. "Please, my dear, you must take a bath. We're all in need of a bath."

Sarah shook her head stubbornly. "I will nae. A

woman died last year of ague for swimming in the River Brora—in the heat of summer."

She chanced a look at Colin. He had propped himself up against the fireplace mantel. "My lord, ye would not allow them tae put me in a bath, would ye?"

"I would rather put you in one myself."

The duke spun around and fixed Colin with a glare. "Watch yourself, Colin."

The younger man grinned.

Sarah felt heat rise in her cheeks. She studiously avoided Colin's gaze.

Mrs. Fitzbottom gently clasped her arm. "Come on, lass, it won't be so bad. You'll see."

"Nay, I'll nae go with ye." She tried to pull free. She wouldn't allow this group of fools to consign her to weeks in bed, ill. "Where is Sionnach? I must show him where we're tae stay."

"Sionnach?" Mrs. Fitzbottom's eyebrows drew together, her grasp on Sarah's arm growing firmer. "Who is Sionnach?"

"My pet fox."

Mrs. Fitzbottom gasped. Just as quickly she regained her composure. "Lady Sarah, you cannot allow a fox to sleep in your room. We are not in the habit of keeping wild animals within these walls."

"Sionnach must sleep in the stables," the duke pronounced.

"In the stables? Never." Sarah narrowed her eyes. "Sionnach stays with me."

"Sarah..." the duke warned.

"And I'm nae sitting in water," she added.

From his corner of the room, Colin murmured, "It seems we have several problems to resolve."

"Where is the fox now?" the housekeeper asked, releasing her.

Sarah shrugged. "He deserted me a while ago."

"Merciful heavens, he's running loose through the house?"

"I suppose so."

Mrs. Fitzbottom threw up her hands in a gesture of surrender. "Lord help us—"

"Sarah must be bathed," the duke interrupted, cutting off what was no doubt the beginning of hysteria. "And the fox stays in the stables."

Sarah stiffened her back. They were going to have to drag her from the room.

"Why would the duke propose a bath for you if he thought you would become ill?" Colin pointed out. "You're his daughter, one recently arisen from the dead. He would no sooner risk your life than his own."

Sarah nodded, albeit unwillingly. She had to acknowledge the logic in his argument.

"Besides," Colin pressed, "aristocrats always take baths. If you're to become Duchess of Argyll one day, you must learn to behave like a proper aristocrat."

"I don't want tae become Duchess of Argyll."

"You promised to try," the duke reminded her from his corner of the room.

"But must I sit in water? I can't imagine anything more uncomfortable."

"Uncomfortable?" A slow smile spread across Colin's face. "You are quite wrong about that. Do you remember me mentioning the fulfillment of the senses a few minutes ago?"

The duke visibly stiffened.

"Aye." Sarah narrowed her eyes. What was he getting at?

"Well, a hot bath may be one of the most pleasurable sensations one can experience. The water is warm and flows like silk across your bare skin. Lavender oil and rose water mingle in your bath and become hot, sending a sweet mist into the air. And if you are daring, and submerge your head beneath the water—to rinse away the soap—your hair will float around you, teasing and tickling in a way that I guarantee you'll find delightful."

Sarah barely suppressed a shiver. "And I won't become ill?"

"I promise you'll not."

She nodded slowly. "All right, then. I'll take this bath, but if I dinna like it, I'll nae take another."

The duke sighed, his relief apparent. "A fair deal, if ever I've heard one."

"What about Sionnach?" she asked the duke. "Will ye allow him tae sleep with me?"

"I won't have a fox in the house," Mrs. Fitzbottom stoutly declared.

Sarah narrowed her eyes. "And I'll nae sleep without him."

Colin and the duke exchanged a glance.

"Thank God we didn't invite Phineas to join us," the duke muttered. "He would have swooned again."

"And then he would have quit Inveraray for good," Colin agreed.

Silence descended upon them. Again, Sarah mused, they'd reached an impasse. Well, she wasn't giving an inch, not where Sionnach was concerned. "I've compromised on the bath. Don't ye think ye should compromise a little as well, and allow Sionnach tae sleep in my bedchamber?"

Colin abandoned his stance at the mantelpiece, and moved to her side, his attention fixed on the duke. "She has a point."

Sighing, the duke nodded his acquiescence. "Keep your fox with you, then, if it pleases you."

"Thank ye, Yer Grace," Sarah murmured, very pleased indeed.

Mrs. Fitzbottom harrumphed, then gestured toward the door. "Let's get you cleaned up, so your fox doesn't have to put up with the skunk smell all night."

She turned to go, feeling a bit guilty for giving the duke such a hard time. He had, after all, only her best interests at heart—or at least what he *thought* were her best interests.

"Wait a moment, Sarah," the duke said, forcing her and the housekeeper to pause. "I'd like to have a word with you in private. Colin, please join me in the salon in an hour or so. I believe I'm in need of a game of billiards."

Colin assented with a bow of his head and, his stride smooth and assured, left the room. Mrs. Fitzbottom eased her way outside as well, and shut the door behind her.

"Please sit." The duke waved to a nearby chair.

For once, Sarah obeyed without comment.

"What do you think of the Earl of Cawdor?" he asked unexpectedly, his stare taking in every aspect of her countenance.

"He is...well, nice."

"He's a bonny lad, no?"

Her cheeks grew warm. She nodded.

"Colin's a distant cousin of mine. Several families

separate us. Nevertheless, he was my successor for the dukedom of Argyll. Until I found you."

"What do ye mean by that?"

"For all intents and purposes, girl, you have cheated Colin of the dukedom of Argyll. In Scotland, women regularly inherit titles, and when I die, you will become the Duchess of Argyll."

"I'm nae a duchess."

"Not now, you aren't. But someday you will be."

A thought suddenly struck her. "Does Colin resent me for taking his inheritance away?"

"No, he doesn't. He has a solid income in his own right, as the Earl of Cawdor. Besides, I've known the lad long enough to know he isn't the type who envies other people's blessings."

"A point in his favor," Sarah murmured.

"He isn't a bad sort," the duke agreed. "But once he was a better man than he is now."

Surprised, Sarah lifted her eyebrows. "How sae?"

"He once had a bit of shepherd in him. That is, he liked to protect his flock. And Inveraray Castle—the estate and the people who live upon its grounds—was his flock. But over time, he's lost his shepherding quality, and mark me, he's also lost a good portion of his honor."

The duke stretched back in his chair, in the manner of one settling down for a tale. "I first met Colin a few years after my wife died. I thought you had died with her and, in my grief, I'd allowed Inveraray to fall to ruin. Later, when I realized that I was headed toward bankruptcy, I consulted with experts. They claimed nothing could save Inveraray.

"Right around that time, Colin came to live with me. By his twenty-second birthday, he'd magically shepherded this estate into realms of profitability rarely seen before. Over a decade he worked on Inveraray, coaxing it back into greatness. Inveraray and its tenants were his life's blood."

Sarah found herself unable to reconcile this picture of Colin with the man she had just met.

"After a time," the duke continued, "I began to think him far too wrapped up in estate matters. I knew he eventually needed to find a wife and start a family. To that end, I urged him to go to town to gain some polish. With hindsight I regret my demands, but at that moment, I thought he needed city experience to round him out and make him attractive to a suitable member of the opposite gender." The duke paused to clear his throat, then admitted, "Colin took very well to society. Too well, in fact. He became something of a...rakehell. Do you know what that is?"

"I have nae idea. But it doesna sound very good."

"Well, to put it delicately, Colin abandoned his nobler values in favor of pursuits I cannot approve of."

Remembering Colin's quick smiles and intriguing banter, Sarah frowned. She was willing to wager that at least one of those pursuits included the fairer sex.

"City life," the duke continued, his lips turning downward in a mournful curve, "has persuaded Colin to forget about Inveraray. I despair that he will ever truly return, even if he is physically here. Given all of this, my decision to have him assist in polishing you must seem faulty to you."

"Aye, a bit," she agreed, though some reckless part of her still trembled with anticipation at the idea.

"I can only say that while he is polishing you, it

is my dearest hope, Sarah, that you will polish him."

"Polish him? Whatever do ye mean?"

"I have brought him back here to Inveraray," the duke revealed, "with hopes that he will remember the years he spent here as a youth. I hope to rekindle some of the better qualities of his personality, qualities he has long since abandoned. You can help him remember."

"Me? How?"

"By being yourself. You lack the wiles and hard exterior that those in the thick of society take pride in. I hope you'll remind him of an earlier time, when he, too, had a gentleness of spirit."

Sarah took a deep breath. "Clearly the earl is a favorite of yers. I would like tae help ye and him. Ye've certainly helped me by paying my debt tae the Murphys. But I'm nae sure I can."

"Just be yourself," the duke counseled. "Don't fear his beguiling ways. I'll protect you from him. You might even think of your time with him as a learning experience, for you must be taught how to deal with men such as he. And once you've entered society, I'll see you happily settled, with an honorable man of your choosing."

Sarah looked away, unwilling to argue with him about her future. As far as she was concerned, they had no future. She would stay at Inveraray only long enough to convince the duke that she could never be the daughter he wished for, and then she would return to the life that she knew.

At her silence, the duke stood and held a hand out to her. "I'll escort you to your bedchamber now, Sarah. I'm certain Mrs. Fitzbottom has already begun to draw you a bath, and we don't want the water to cool too much."

Sarah bit her tongue, lest she start another argument about the bath, and took his hand. With his assistance she rose and allowed him to lead her from the drawing room, feeling all the while like a sheep on the way to shearing.

✦ 5 ✦

Colin selected a wooden cue stick from the wall and examined its tip to insure it would shoot straight. Over the last hour he'd taken two baths and exchanged his ruined clothes for a burgundy silk smoking jacket and breeches. Now, comfortably ensconced in the salon, he gathered up two white balls and a single red one and placed them in their appropriate location upon the billiard table.

The noble game of billiards always had a calming effect on him. It required him to concentrate on how best to pot the ball, rather than chew over the current problems life had dealt him. While playing, the tension simply flowed from his body. Oddly enough, by the time the game was over, he often had a solution to whatever had been troubling him. He supposed his mind continued to work on the problem even though he wasn't aware of it.

Today, though, he couldn't find any peace. Sarah refused to leave his thoughts. He didn't know what to make of her. He'd prepared himself for gross ignorance, vulgarity of manner, and meanness of opinion. He'd assumed he'd find her coarse but re-sourceful, a greedy-guts utterly lacking in morals who knew how to use her feminine wiles. After all, she'd managed to rise from a poverty-stricken farm to the lap of luxury, and only the shrewdest of farm girls could have managed that.

And yet, she was far different than he'd ever imagined. Soft-spoken, attractive beneath the grime of ill breeding, she possessed a certain vul-nerable quality that roused protective feelings in him that he'd thought long dead. Of wiles he'd seen none, and she didn't seem very eager to assume the mantle of duchess. In fact, the idea appeared to ter-rify her.

Colin held the cue stick between his fingers and attempted to pot both the red and white balls into side pockets, without bringing his own ball back across the balkline. None of the balls sank into the pockets. Instead, they bounced against the cushion surrounding the table and rolled toward him, putting him in position for the most difficult shots possible.

He was definitely off his game, and had been since he'd come to Inveraray. He repositioned the balls and prepared for another shot. Just as he drew the cue stick back, the duke walked into the salon. Colin raked the tip across the fabric tabletop, leav-ing a mark.

"You're jumpy today," the duke observed. Also dressed in a smoking jacket and trousers, he picked up a cue stick while Colin retrieved the balls. "Did my daughter rattle you?"

"Not at all," Colin lied. "I simply haven't practiced enough lately."

The duke smiled and withdrew two cigars from his smoking jacket. He held one out to Colin.

Colin accepted the offering and ran the cigar beneath his nose. The woody scent of fine Sumatran tobacco and the smooth firmness of the cigar itself promised a very fine smoke indeed. He sighed appreciatively. Both men lit their cigars.

After puffing a few times, the duke set his cigar on a plate and aimed his cue stick at a ball. "So, what do you think of Sarah?" He tapped the ball, sending it across the table and into another ball, which dropped into a pocket.

Colin considered before replying. "She's certainly different from what I expected. Rather pretty. Almost kittenish. She has an odd way with animals." He, too, set his cigar down and tried to pot a ball, but ending up banking against the cushion again. "I don't understand why she played a flute this afternoon, in the middle of a disaster, or how she had the courage to face down Townsend and Cheltnum. I suppose living on a farm has made her impervious to events that would send another woman screaming from the room."

"Women such as Lady Helmsgate?" the duke asked casually.

Colin winced. The duke and Lord Helmsgate were close friends. He hoped the duke hadn't heard of his dalliance with Lady Helmsgate through Lord Helmsgate. "Lady Helmsgate is an acquaintance only. I don't know her well enough to predict her behavior."

The duke sighed, but didn't respond otherwise.

Colin sought to keep the conversation going in the right direction...and away from his London antics. "How do you think Sarah managed to calm two enraged dogs to the point where they willingly lounged in a room with a fox?"

"I don't know. There are many things about her I don't understand," the duke admitted, taking another shot and sinking the ball expertly. "I thank God she wasn't hurt this afternoon."

Colin plucked the ball from the pocket and replaced it on the table. "It's been a long time since I've experienced chaos on that order. Since my school days, at least. I suppose we are going to have to put up with her fox for some time."

The duke nodded thoughtfully. "From what I've seen, animals seem to take to her like no other."

"What do you mean, they 'take' to her?"

"Oh, I don't know. They won't run away when she draws close to them, and seem to enjoy, well, watching her. Perhaps it has something to do with her panflute. She often plays it for them, though the music doesn't sound like much to my ears. Whatever the case, she's apparently possessed an odd knack for animals all of her life. The Murphys said as much, and Phineas heard an earful about her 'skills' while investigating her story in the village where she grew up."

"Her odd knack with animals may have a very simple explanation. Don't forget, she lived on a farm," Colin reminded him. "Perhaps through her daily contact with animals, and years of observation, she has gained an affinity for them and can interpret sounds and gestures that you and I would dismiss as random."

"How so?"

"She is simply an adept student of the farmyard.

I've seen this effect before, particularly in the horse breeders and traders who frequent Tattersall's. They always seem to know exactly what the damned horses are thinking."

Despite his rationalization, Colin felt an uncomfortable curling in his gut. Something just didn't fit. The flute, and that music she played, it had sounded so discordant, so disturbing. He remembered the moment when her playing had sounded like a warning without words.

He positioned his cue stick and tapped a red ball. This time, he managed to pot it. "Did you know that a stag and a skunk observed your arrival with Sarah from the bushes? They were well hidden, but my vantage point from the study window revealed them to me."

"So?"

"Their proximity to the castle in broad daylight was most unusual. They appeared to have come to, well, welcome your daughter, as if they had read her mind and found a kindred spirit in her. While the breeders in Tattersall's might know what the horses are thinking, the horses certainly don't know what the *breeders* are thinking."

The duke, who'd bent over in preparation for another shot, paused. "What are you suggesting? That she is more than a 'student of the farmyard,' and has cast a spell over them?"

"I'm not suggesting anything. I'm simply stating the facts."

"I think the explanation of Sarah's ability that you originally offered is quite reasonable. The events surrounding her, while odd, have simply been a series of coincidences. Only a madman—or a superstitious old woman—would believe anything else." The duke hit his ball with a sharp *snap*. "Please, Colin, don't start babbling about the dangers of shattering a mirror and the benefits of a pinch of salt thrown over the shoulder."

Colin snorted. "Forgive me for mentioning it." Still, his uneasiness stayed with him.

The two played in silence for a while, until the duke beat him easily and stretched, clearly pleased with himself. "Another game?" he asked.

"It would be my pleasure." Colin took up the balls and put them in their proper places on the billiard table. Unbidden, an image of Sarah formed in his mind as he did so. He thought of those fantastic eyes in her cat-shaped face, her fine bone structure despite those chapped hands and arms. He thought of her ugly dress and glorious hair, her atrocious speech, and the challenging glint that shone in her eyes.

A line of poetry occurred to him. Mentally he filed it. He would write it down later.

"Your daughter is going to clean up nicely," he predicted, taking his first shot and potting two balls at once.

"Good show, Colin." The duke worked his way around the table, looking for the best angle, then positioned his cue stick. "With Phineas's assistance, you'll teach her all of the qualities a lady of her stature should possess, including instruction on how to manage Inveraray Castle."

Colin propped his cue stick up against the table. Their cigars, he noticed, had almost burned down to ash. Not often did he waste a good cigar like that. He was definitely out of sorts.

He moved to the bar, poured himself a finger of whiskey, and drained his tumbler in one brisk move. The whiskey created a path of warmth to his stomach. In fact, his gut burned like fire, and he couldn't help questioning if the sting had more to do with the thought of losing Inveraray than the Macallan's fine whiskey.

"Would you like one?" he asked the duke, lifting his tumbler.

"Yes, thank you."

Colin poured the duke a few fingers of whiskey and handed it over. "Lady Sarah will, of course, inherit the estate and all of the other lands associated with the dukedom of Argyll. How well will it fare in her hands?"

"When I am dead, you mean, and she has inherited the estate?"

"My pardon—"

"No, no, death is part of life, Colin. I don't fear it and I'm not offended at your mentioning it. When I am gone, Sarah hopefully will have learned enough to manage the estate adequately." The duke sipped his whiskey.

Colin frowned. "Do you recall the arguments we just had regarding her bath? She gives the impression that she's an independent sort and, while another woman might lean upon a man's superior judgment regarding estate matters, she clearly can't be relied upon to act predictably. She hasn't been brought up to act predictably."

"Perhaps that's a good quality," the duke observed. "In any case, her husband will likely assist her in managing the estate."

His cue stick gripped in his hand, Colin bent over

and hit the ball on the side, sending it into an accidental spin. The fire in his gut grew stronger. "When she marries, who's to say she'll marry someone capable of keeping a fine estate like Inveraray profitable? Perhaps her future husband will even begin a clearance like the ones practiced by the Countess of Sutherland."

The duke watched him closely. "We all must make choices in life."

"You're beginning to sound like a man of the cloth."

"I can't give you any assurances, Colin. I don't know what the future will bring."

Colin put his tumbler on a side table none too gently. "Christ Almighty, I worked my arse off for nearly eight years to make Inveraray what it is today, while preserving homes for the many branches of the Campbell clan. And now you tell me you're going to let some farm girl throw it all away."

"She may not throw it away." The duke was still staring at him, almost as if gauging his reaction.

Righteousness flared within Colin. "What do you expect me to do, Edward? Marry her, to preserve Inveraray?"

The idea came out of nowhere, preposterous and pleasing at the same time. He'd already acknowledged that she was easy on the eyes, and once she'd been cleaned up, she might even prove quite...delectable. Of course, she had that odd way with animals, but as the duke's daughter, she'd have to give up all of that nonsense.

And wasn't it time he married? He'd turned two and thirty months before. The duke had been after him for a long time now to provide legitimate heirs, and his mother had recently written him from the Continent twice to ask when he would marry. His father was dead, of course, and couldn't badger him, but several elder members of the peerage had cornered him over the last season and demanded he settle down and start attending sessions in the House of Lords. As Sarah's husband, he would not only retain management of Inveraray Castle, all of the dukedom's lands, and its income; but he'd also gain a respite from society's matchmakers.

Yes, when he thought of it that way, Sarah was quite a catch. Her prospective fortune and title would make her a popular commodity on the marriage mart once the duke introduced her to society. He couldn't think of a more obvious, convenient choice for a partner in marriage. Indeed, he saw now that the duke must have had this in mind when he'd summoned him to Inveraray.

"You'll not marry her," the duke said mildly. "Not while I live, and I intend to see her married off long before my body is beneath the earth."

"Pardon me?" Colin had lifted his cue stick, and now he set it down again to focus fully upon the duke.

"I said you'll not marry her."

Colin couldn't believe what his ears were telling him. "Why not?"

"Because you want to marry her for all the wrong reasons: primarily her future title and wealth."

"Since when are *those* reasons wrong?"

"I spent a long time alone, Colin, grieving for my wife and child." The duke set his cue stick upon the table, too. "I ached from loneliness. I still do. For seventeen years, no one has touched me with love. If anything, these dry and dark years have taught me the importance of being loved."

Stung, Colin shook his head. This "love" nonsense was ridiculous. He suspected the duke had used it as a convenient excuse to spare his feelings, and didn't think him good enough for Sarah. But why? He, too, was a good catch, a much-sought-after bachelor whose inheritance—the earldom of Cawdor—was older than the hills and more respectable than the princess's underwear.

More importantly, he knew Inveraray better than any other. The duke *had* to acknowledge the convenience and absolute rightness of his match to Sarah. "After all these years of pleading with me to marry, you choose *now* to insist I remain a bachelor?"

"Every man should marry before thirty years of age. You are long overdue. Still, I won't allow you to court my daughter. You're simply not the man for her."

Colin swallowed back feelings of unworthiness.

"Now that I've regained Sarah," the duke continued, "the last thing I intend to do is force her into a match solely for the sake of convenience. She will marry for love, and with God's help, won't suffer the same sort of life I've led."

"What will you do if I marry her anyway?"

"I'll know that you married her for her inheritance, and I'll make it my life's work to see you ostracized permanently from the society you so love. Don't test me on this, Colin."

Taken aback, Colin stared at him. "You're very serious."

"More serious than you can know."

The two men faced each other. The duke was the first to look away. "I don't mean to suggest I think you unworthy, Colin. If I have abused your feelings, I apologize. You are a favorite of mine. Surely you realize this. But I *will* have a love match for Sarah." He waved to a grouping of chairs near the fireplace. "Come, sit down with me."

Thoroughly disgruntled, Colin walked over to the chairs the duke had indicated and selected one. He sat, the fire within the grate doing little to warm him. "Tell me how, and where, you found Sarah."

The duke collected their tumblers and grabbed a decanter of whiskey before joining Colin by the fire. He poured more whiskey into each glass, and handed one to Colin. After Colin had accepted it, he leaned back in his seat and sketched out the steps he and Phineas had taken to recover her.

"It all sounds very straightforward," Colin observed, when the duke had finished. "But tell me: why is she dressed so poorly? I didn't even realize she was your daughter when you arrived earlier. I thought she was a serving maid."

The duke sighed. "I had a damned hard time convincing her to leave that little croft of hers. Can't blame her, really. It's the only world she's ever known. I needed every ounce of persuasive skill I possessed to bundle her into the carriage, and I drove off in a hurry, before she could change her mind. We had no time for clothes. I have, however, sent for a modiste from Edinburgh, who should arrive within a few weeks."

"Until then, is she to wander about in rags?"

"She may wear my wife's clothes. They look nearly the same size." A suspicious moisture suddenly clouded the duke's eyes.

Colin looked away, giving the duke a moment to collect himself, then refocused on the old man. "Sarah had an odd reaction to the tapestry in the drawing room that depicts a unicorn. She called the unicorn a 'white beast' and thought it really existed. Does this sound normal to you?"

"She does have some strange qualities," the duke admitted. "She also mentioned a white beast to me, on the way to Inveraray, and claims that it rescued her from the moors after the accident. I wish it *did* exist. I could use a little magic in my life."

The two men fell silent, Colin thinking that the duke's desire to believe in magic was yet another instance of sentiment getting the better of him.

"And the fox is her pet?" Colin eventually asked.

"Yes. He's called Sionnach, by the way. She wouldn't leave her village without him."

They both stared into the flames eating away at the wood in the fireplace.

"While I was sitting in the Murphy farm kitchen, waiting for Sarah, Mrs. Murphy told me she'd often thought of Sarah as a changeling," the duke said, his tone reflective. "Sarah came from nowhere. She looked nothing like them, petite and fine-boned where they were tall and stocky. You must admit, Colin, she has none of the stocky peasant build you might find in the lower classes."

"No, indeed," Colin assented, remembering the fine curves he'd noticed beneath her gown.

"Even the townspeople of Beannach have come

to regard her as one of the faerie folk, sent to walk among mortals and charm their animals."

Startled by the closeness of the duke's description to his own rogue thoughts of Sarah's fey quality, Colin shifted in his chair. "She looks made of flesh and blood to me."

"You clearly find her quite attractive," the duke murmured, looking up from the flames to fix Colin with a direct stare.

Colin smiled. "I do."

The duke lifted one gray eyebrow. "Colin, I see something in your eyes that worries me."

"I assure you, you have cowed me quite thoroughly with your threats. I won't bother her."

"Don't think that with age I've grown stupid, boy. I know you're a lady's man, accustomed to hiding your affairs. But don't think I won't catch you."

"You've misread me completely," Colin protested. "I have no illicit intentions toward her. I would not dream of insulting either you or her."

The duke appeared not to have heard him. "And don't even attempt to use your 'bad blood' as an excuse for an ill-considered seduction."

Colin sighed. "Bad blood? Perhaps 'hot' blood might fit better."

His parents, the Earl and Countess of Cawdor, had belonged to a fast set whose exploits had been legendary in the king's time. They'd drank, gambled, put a serious dent into the Cawdor fortune, and sold Cawdor Castle, which had no entailment and therefore no protection. Fortunately, a scandal involving Colin's father and a viscount's underage daughter forced them to leave England before they could completely bankrupt the estate. The earl and countess had fled rather than face the viscount's pistol and society's censure, for even the *ton* had its limits.

But they hadn't taken Colin with them. Instead, they'd sent their ten-year-old son to live quietly in the Scottish Highlands with the Duke of Argyll, who'd recently lost his wife and daughter and rarely left his country estate. The duke had taken Colin, the only living heir to his estate, not because he had any affection for the lad, but because he recognized the fact that someday, Colin would assume control of the Argyll dukedom. As such, Colin needed to learn the intricacies of estate management, something his parents couldn't have cared less about.

Colin, who had up to that point associated only with immoral people and their immoral children, remembered finding the duke's upright code of ethics ludicrous. Inveraray, his new home, had struck him as so far from civilization that he might as well have fallen off the end of the earth. With time, however, he'd come to appreciate the duke and Inveraray—love them, even—though he'd still longed for the days in London where the beautiful people laughed and danced.

Recalling those years of hard work and sacrifice, Colin stared into his glass of whiskey. "Do you realize that you were the one positive influence in my life?"

"Aye, I know. As I've said before, your parents should have been horsewhipped. Have you heard from your mother lately?"

"She's still on the Riviera with that French comte," Colin admitted. He had never missed either her or his father, never wanted them back. His father had died about five years ago, in a riding accident in Italy. Colin hadn't bothered to attend the funeral.

"God keep her safe," the duke murmured. "I wish I could have spared you their mismanagement, boy."

Colin found himself defending them, for in explaining them, he was defending himself. "They didn't mismanage my upbringing. Rather, they were simply living as society demands. Manners and money vie for importance with each other. Gluttony and gambling are fashionable vices. The more wild the behavior and appalling the extravagance, the more successful the gentleman."

"Things never seem to change," the duke observed. "And to think, I'm the one who sent you back into society's clutches, after working so hard to make an honorable man of you."

Colin sighed deeply. "Did you know that in showing me the values of self-control and perseverance, you taught me in some ways to loathe myself?"

"Loathe yourself? What do you mean?"

"When I look back to my days at Inveraray, and compare them with my life now, what I feel most is unworthiness."

"Why did you never come back to Scotland, then?" the duke asked in a grumpy tone. "At Inveraray, you could have embraced these positive influences you speak of."

Colin shrugged. "Even though at times I regret the life I've chosen, I have to admit I prefer it. I enjoy London's vices, its colors and smells and sounds and tastes. I love its women and its intrigues." And yet, even as he stated his partiality for society, he admitted that the odd dissatisfaction he'd felt lately had been growing.

"You loved Inveraray once," the duke reminded him.

"That was very long ago." Shifting on his chair, Colin took a sip of whiskey. He was beginning to feel very unsettled, although exactly why, he couldn't say. "I believe we've spent enough time cataloguing my faults."

The duke took a deep breath. "While I can't help myself from chiding you, ultimately I'm not blaming you for your attitudes. I know they are the attitudes of the day and considered sensible by all. But I repeat, I will not have you toying with Sarah's affections in any way."

Colin stared at him, nonplussed.

The duke finished his tumbler of whiskey, then set it firmly on a side table. "You have only one purpose here: to teach Sarah how to act like the daughter of a duke, and in general what is required of the aristocracy. You have a little more than three months to complete her transformation, after which I will present her at a ball held here. Of course, I'm counting on your discretion. I don't want rumors about her past to surface. Ever."

"In this I am your faithful servant," Colin murmured.

"Good. You and Phineas shall begin with Sarah tomorrow."

Colin shifted back in his seat, thinking that this evening's sleep might prove the last good one he enjoyed for a quite a while. It wasn't in his nature to keep his hands off a woman whom he found both attractive and intriguing. And yet he must, for the stakes were very high.

And while he taught her to dance, and to eat with the proper silverware, and to flirt with the best of them, he would reiterate his promise to quietly investigate her origins. He would make sure that the duke hadn't placed all of his bet on a mare destined to lose the race.

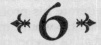

Sarah yawned and stretched, the smell of hay all around her. She smiled as her dream of Colin fragmented, then disappeared from her mind, leaving her warm and achy in its aftermath.

Pieces of straw poked through her nightgown, while early morning sunlight found its way through chinks in the roof to shine upon dust motes floating in the air. Disoriented, she sat up straighter and looked at the polished wooden beams supporting the roof. Herbs and corn hung in sheaves from the rafters.

It took her a moment to remember where she was. This, she realized, was the duke's barn. She looked for Sionnach and found him curled up nearby and almost covered with hay. Her faithful companion, he'd complained not the slightest when she'd insisted on abandoning her bedchamber in the middle of the night.

Heaven knew the bedchamber had been very fine, laden with gilt-edged white furniture and fancy chairs supported by legs so thin she suspected they would break if she sat on them. The bed, full of feathers, had puffed up around her when she'd lain upon it, and enfolded her with a silky embrace.

But after hours of tossing and turning, the feather mattress had become stifling, and the covers too hot. She didn't like the canopy over her bed, either. It turned the bed into a large box, reminding her of a cage. In the moonlight, the white chair legs had looked like glittering bones, and a faint mustiness had pervaded the air, one that made her sneeze. Each sneeze had reminded her that she'd actually bathed earlier, rousing worries that she was becoming ill.

Annoyed, hot, and sweaty, she'd eventually fled her bedchamber and the castle. The stars and cool breeze had reassured her somewhat, for they at least hadn't changed from what she'd known in the village of Beannach. Sionnach had found the hay barn against a wall surrounding the kitchen garden. There, clutching her panflute, she'd managed to gain a few fitful hours of sleep.

She crawled across the distance between her and Sionnach and rubbed the soft fur behind his ears. He opened his eyes and, in their black depths, she could see the same sort of confusion that had plagued her when she'd awoken.

Sarah dug through the straw, and found her panflute. She lifted it to her lips and played a soft, reassuring melody that told him they were in the Duke of Argyll's barn.

The fox's eyes lost that hunted look at her words, and he stood. Yawning widely, he stretched and shook himself, then informed her in no uncertain terms that this barn, like her new bedchamber, was far too hot for anyone to have a good night's sleep, least of all a fur-covered fox.

Sarah wasn't surprised. The hay in the barn had kept them very warm. Now, with the sunshine coming through the roof, the temperature had risen several degrees. She combed through the hair behind his ears, knowing this was the best way to cool him. Sionnach's ears were large and dissipated heat. While she petted him, the fox rubbed against her hand, telling her how much he appreciated her attention.

Usually, petting Sionnach relaxed her and brought her peace. But this time, she couldn't stop wondering how she was going to cope with the day ahead of her, a day in which her every word, thought, and mannerism would surely be criticized as peasantlike. As she rubbed the fox's fur, she tried to imagine how Sionnach would behave in such a situation, and decided he would likely have some good advice for her.

She picked up her panflute and asked him, exactly, what he would do.

He stretched out one last time, then sat up on his haunches and stared at her, his little face earnest. He looked so adorable that she wanted to gather him in her arms and crush him to her, but she didn't dare. Sionnach had told her more than once that he wasn't a toy, or a pet. He was her teacher, and she had better show him some respect.

With a low rumble in his chest, he scratched at the hay with his paw. Sarah translated his gestures loosely. He was asking her what a fox was best at.

Head tilted, she considered for a moment. Sionnach never gave a direct answer to a question; no fox did. Overall, they weren't a straightforward sort of animal. Rather, they worked to blend in with their surroundings, to come and go unnoticed, to move silently about without revealing their intentions, and generally to distract. Even now he was being oblique, not telling her how to cope, but asking her to remember what he'd taught her.

Well, Sionnach had several clever techniques up his sleeve, but her favorite was his charming performance. When he came upon an animal that he thought might make a juicy prize, he would charm it by leaping and dancing about, and rolling over, and chasing his tail. These nonthreatening antics would thoroughly capture his prey's attention. And while he danced, he would draw ever closer without the prey realizing it. At the right moment, he would snap his jaws shut around the unsuspecting prey.

She thought of this technique as camouflaging, or disguising one's real goal behind a series of fake, more pleasant goals. She lifted her panflute to her lips and told him that foxes camouflage and distract, in order to survive.

He yelped in his throat, his tone indicating approval, then rumbled at her again, indicating she should practice camouflage today.

With a quick trill on the panflute, she asked him to elaborate.

His tail wrapped around his body, he stared at her, and in his eyes she could see his frustration. At length, he uttered a series of yelps and rumbles, and buried himself in the hay, only to leap outward a moment later, spreading pieces of chaff everywhere. They both sneezed. The surprise of his attack brought a smile to her lips.

Scratching his paw through the hay and yelping, Sionnach demanded to know if she understood.

Sarah nodded. If she blended in with her surroundings, came and went unnoticed, and moved silently without revealing her intentions, she'd see and hear things that she otherwise could not.

At her nod, Sionnach added that she had to be careful, until she understood better this new world she now lived in.

Her mouth drooped. She felt so out of place, and Sionnach's warning had only underscored how much she didn't belong. "I dinna like it here," she whispered in human language. "Even though I have ye, Sionnach, I feel lonely."

Sionnach gave no indication of comprehending.

She blew on her panflute, asking him if he liked it here.

The fox gazed at her with dark, shuttered eyes. For once, she couldn't tell what he was thinking. Even so, she couldn't imagine that he was enjoying himself any more than she was. Feeling guilty for bringing him here, she urged him to go and explore the woods, rather than feel that he had to stay with her all day. Reminding him to see if any news about the white beast had surfaced, she pointed out that at least one of them could experience some freedom.

Sionnach didn't growl in reply. He didn't twitch a muscle. He didn't even berate her. He just stared at her with his dark eyes.

Curious, Sarah studied him. An impossible idea occurred to her and set her heart to racing. The melody she played him sounded off-key even to her as she asked him if he'd already heard something about the white beast.

Slowly, reluctantly, the fox informed her that the white beast was coming.

"What?" Sarah almost jumped up and down in

the hay. At last, she would see the unicorn. She demanded more details from him, such as when the beast was coming, and where, and if he was still sick.

Sionnach confirmed her worries. The beast, he admitted, was coming to her because he was sick.

"And he wants me to help him," she breathed. Quickly she asked Sionnach when she could expect the white beast.

Growling that he didn't know, the fox then revealed something very strange: he knew little about the white beast's plans, because it couldn't speak. Without explaining further, Sionnach turned on his heels and slipped out the barn door.

Stunned, Sarah watched him disappear across the lawn. The unicorn was coming...and it couldn't speak. Whatever did Sionnach mean? Most of the different species of animals could understand each other, after a fashion. But the fox's demeanor had suggested that the unicorn couldn't communicate at all. Sarah had half a mind to chase after Sionnach and insist he explain more fully. If not for her nightgown, she would have been racing across the grounds right now.

Pots clanged somewhere in the distance, reminding her that the household was awakening. She scrambled through the hay, dragged her dressing gown over her arms and tucked her hair into her nightcap, thinking that she dreaded having to spend the rest of her time at Inveraray wearing clothes that Mrs. Fitzbottom foisted upon her. While they were very soft, they were also numerous and tangled in her legs more determinedly than her old cotton nightgowns ever had; and though the lace hanging from the bodice and sleeves made them pretty, the lace also itched and put her completely out of sorts.

Silently promising to cut the lace off this nightgown at her first chance, she slipped out of the barn and kept to the shrubbery to avoid being seen. She wanted to smile with the knowledge that soon, she'd see the unicorn; still, she was far too worried about the beast's health to give in to the desire.

A quick look at the sun's position told her that morning was already well underway. She had overslept dreadfully. Her movements even more furtive, she crept toward the simple wooden door behind the kitchen, opened it, and stuck her head in. The door opened onto a hallway, which appeared to be empty.

She pulled her nightcap lower over her ears and, breathing fast, hurried inside and through the main hall, past weapons with scythe-like blades and hooks that glinted in the sunlight. She passed a young maid who was dusting a silver shield and made for the grand staircase. The maid kept her gaze on her work; nevertheless, Sarah prayed that the duke, Colin, and Phineas were late risers, and the servants not inclined to gossip.

"Sarah?" a male voice asked in startled tones.

She froze, one foot on the staircase, her hand on the iron balustrade leading upward. Lip caught between her lower teeth, she turned and looked in the direction of the voice.

Colin stared back at her. Dressed in a brown coat with large brass buttons and cutaway tails, he held a leather crop lightly against his thigh. "Sarah, is that you?"

She turned her back to him and raced up the stairs. She didn't want him to know where she'd spent the night. He would surely make her suffer an arrogant diatribe on her ill breeding or, worse yet, give her pitying looks.

"Sarah!"

The sound of footsteps pounded up the stairs behind her, drawing closer until a hand descended on her arm, halting her flight.

Frowning, she turned around and discovered him on the step below her, putting them almost face-to-face. He looked very tanned in a wash of sunlight coming through the second-story windows, and dangerously masculine. She could smell an appealing scent on him—something spicy, beneath a stronger combination of leather, dust, and horse-flesh.

A shiver—part pleasure, and part dismay—ran through her. She pulled the edges of her robe closer together. "Good morning, Colin."

Rather than answer, he stared at her from the tips of her toes to the top of her lacy nightcap, his gaze burning a path across her body and reminding her that two thin pieces of cotton—her nightgown and robe—hid her nakedness from him. She saw something flicker deep within his eyes, and his face tightened somehow. Her own breathing quickened in response.

After what felt like an eternity passed, he reached out and plucked a piece of straw from her hair. "Where have you been? The stables?"

"Tae the hay barn. In the kitchen garden."

"You've been to the hay barn."

"Aye."

"In your nightdress."

She hesitated a moment, then nodded.

Eyes widening, he allowed the straw to drop to the floor. "May I ask why?"

"Ye may ask, but I'm nae inclined tae answer."

"Would you rather I surrender to suspicion?"

"Suspicion?" She eyed him closely. "Explain yerself."

He tapped his crop against his thigh. "There are very few honorable reasons that I can think of for a lady dressed in her nightclothes to emerge from the stables, particularly at this time of day."

"Ye think I'm...I'm..." She stuttered as his meaning sank in, then broke off, unable to think of a delicate way to protest her innocence.

"I think you're...what?" he pressed, an insolent smile suddenly playing about his mouth.

He wanted her to come out and say it, she realized. To speak indelicately, to talk about lovemaking. For some reason, putting her at a disadvantage in this way clearly amused him. She saw the way his nostrils had flared and knew it had excited him, too. But he had sorely underestimated her if he thought he could embarrass her like this.

"Ye think I've been laying in the stables with a man?" She enunciated each word clearly, and spoke loud enough for anyone nearby to overhear.

His smile faltered. "Have you?"

"Ye insult me, my lord. If ye must know, I slept in the stables. I found them more comfortable than my fancy bedchamber."

He digested this news in silence. When he refocused on her, a sharpness had faded from his face, giving him a boyish aspect that Sarah found infinitely more appealing. "My apologies. I didn't mean to insult you."

"I'm nae one of yer fine society ladies tae trade barbs with. I prefer plain language and honesty. If ye canna remember that, then ye and I willna get on at all."

He grinned. "I like you, Sarah."

"I canna say the same tae ye. Yet," she allowed.

"The next time you plan to sleep in the stables, please inform me. I'll guard you."

"I'm afraid I'll need a guard for the guard," she said.

This time, he laughed aloud. "You're a smart lass."

"Are ye going tae tell the duke?"

"How can I not? You *do* need someone to watch over you."

"I need no one. Please dinna tell the duke. He'll insist I return tae my bedchamber."

"Sarah, I must tell him."

Her shoulders slumped. "Do what ye must."

He picked another piece of straw from her hair in a gesture that was strangely possessive. "You had better return to your bedchamber. Quickly. I just passed Phineas in the hall, and he has asked me to attend your first lesson in the dining room at ten o'clock sharp. As it is nine o'clock now, you have only an hour to dress."

"Only an hour?" She shook her head. "I need nae more than five minutes tae dress."

"Here, you'll need at least an hour," he predicted.

"Did Phineas tell ye what we're studying today?"

"Language and dining room manners. I'm sure we'll both fall asleep in the middle of it."

They exchanged a glance, and Sarah saw that his smile had become more than just an expression of amusement. It was an invitation. A painful giddiness gripped her, and as the silence between them lengthened, she imagined Colin kissing her.

Suddenly she wished she were an experienced society lady, one who took lovers on a whim and knew exactly what to demand from a man. Then she could demand what she wanted from Colin with confidence, rather than with insecurity and yearning, two sensations that had become uncomfortably familiar to her.

Waiting for her thudding heart to calm itself, she broke eye contact and spun around. "I must go," she said over her shoulder, and hurried up the stairs, fully aware that his gaze never wavered from her, not until she turned the corner and moved out of sight.

An hour later, Sarah completely believed Colin's prediction that she would need at least an hour to dress. As soon as she'd reentered her bedchamber, Mrs. Fitzbottom had proceeded to layer her with outlandish bits of frilly clothing: chemise, stockings, garters, drawers, stays, petticoat, and a beautiful sky-blue silk gown with lace edging the bodice. Through it all, the housekeeper had plied her with questions as to where she'd gone, and why she had straw in her hair. Sarah had answered each question truthfully, and in short order Mrs. Fitzbottom had been clucking in sympathy.

Now, as Sarah sat in front of the looking glass while the older woman teased her hair into curls, she could hardly credit how much of her breasts the gown revealed.

"Is this proper?" Catching the housekeeper's gaze in the mirror, she gestured toward her cleavage.

"That it is, lass. 'Tis circumspect, even. This gown belonged to the duchess, who wasn't a fast dresser by any stretch of the imagination, God rest her soul."

"I look sae strange," Sarah complained. "My face is dark from the sun, while my...other parts are milk white."

"I would hope they are milk white." Mrs. Fitzbottom began twirling a ribbon through her hair. "Your face will soon be white again. I've a lemon juice mixture we can apply to your skin this evening. Just stay out of the sun, and soon you'll match all over."

The stays biting into her ribs, Sarah took a sip of the hot cocoa the housekeeper had brought up. While her silk dress felt very soft beneath her fingers, she couldn't feel its softness anywhere else. She had too many underthings on to enjoy it. "Must I always wear sae many clothes? These are sae uncomfortable."

"Be glad you didn't live fifty years ago, when hoop skirts were the fashion."

"I'm hot, and I canna breathe."

"There, now, lass. We're almost done."

True to her word, Mrs. Fitzbottom finished coiling Sarah's hair and stepped back to view her handiwork. "You are lovely," she pronounced. "The men won't be able to look anywhere but at you."

Sarah stared into the looking glass and saw a sun-darkened, slightly flushed face over a white bosom that heaved for lack of air. "If ye say sae."

"Oh, now, you must trust me on this. Indeed, think how beautiful you would look if I'd had the proper amount of time to dress you."

"It wearies me tae think of it."

Ignoring her comment, the housekeeper glanced

at the clock on a side table. "I've kept you far too long. Mr. Graham is probably grinding his teeth with impatience. You had better go."

"Where am I going?"

"To the dining room. Shall I ring for a maid to take you there?"

"Nay. I'll find it." She grasped her panflute from off a white bureau edged with gilt and felt around for a pocket. "Is there a pocket in this gown?"

"A pocket? Heavens no. When we picked this gown out for you, we sewed the pocket up."

"Why? Are pockets nae allowed?"

"They're completely out of fashion. You cannot have a pocket on anything but a riding habit."

"Where should I put my flute, then?"

"In a reticule. I believe I have one somewhere." Mrs. Fitzbottom tossed through the underclothes she'd placed on Sarah's bed, then drew out a sky-blue silken pouch on a thin cord. "Here you are, lass."

"Thank ye." Sarah took the reticule and slipped her panflute inside, noting that the little purse hadn't much room for anything else. "I'm off tae the dining room."

"Good luck," the housekeeper called out as Sarah left.

She managed to find the dining room after only two wrong turns. The duke, Phineas, and Colin were already inside, all three involved in newspapers, with steaming cups of coffee on the table in front of them. As soon as she entered, they put their papers down and jumped to their feet.

Hastily.

The duke, his gray hair brushed back neatly from

his forehead, stared at her. An odd moisture gathered in his eyes. For one horrible moment, Sarah thought he might cry. She remembered Mrs. Fitzbottom telling her the sky-blue gown had belonged to the duchess.

She moved forward, wanting to comfort him and yet not knowing how to do so.

"You look delightful, Sarah," the duke said, before she had taken more than a step. Taking a deep breath, he turned to his man of business and wagged a finger. "Are you ready to admit how wrong you were, Phineas?"

A grave smile lightened Phineas's countenance. "Lady Sarah can be nothing but sparkling, Your Grace. She is, after all, your daughter."

Sarah thought Phineas' statement more courteous than heartfelt. Nevertheless, her cheeks warmed up beneath their admiring gazes. She sneaked a glance at the Earl of Cawdor, who had exchanged his riding clothes for a pair of butter-yellow breeches, gray jacket and light blue necktie. More light-hearted than formal, his attire reflected a teasing mood, as did his sly wink.

"Lady Sarah, 'tis a pleasure to see you looking so fine this morning, though I must say, I think I prefer the last outfit I saw you in," he said, a provocative gleam in his eyes.

She swallowed. "Thank ye, my lord."

"Call me Colin."

The duke gestured abruptly for them all to sit down. "Colin, are you mad, preferring Sarah in those rags she was wearing yesterday?"

"She had a certain charm, the last time I saw her." Colin took his seat and leaned back in his chair.

He stretched, muscles bunching beneath his jacket and hinting at the power in his lithe body.

The duke raised an eyebrow. "And when was that?"

"I'm sae happy ye all approve of my gown," Sarah cut in, recognizing danger in the duke's line of questioning. She selected a chair near the duke and sat, trying not to stare at Colin. The more she looked, the more her heart thumped. "I feel strange, wearing such fine clothes."

Phineas, too, took a seat. "They become you, my lady."

Shortly afterward, a servant entered and began to place covered silver dishes on the sideboard. Steam rose from each dish, sending the smells of eggs, ham, beef, and freshly baked bread into the air. A serving girl poured coffee into the cup near Sarah's elbow.

"You will have to become accustomed to many fine things, as the daughter of a duke," Colin murmured, his expression deceptively angelic. "Such as bathing. Did you enjoy your bath last night?"

The duke narrowed his eyes at Colin.

Memories of the warm, silky feel of water sliding over her bare limbs, and the heady lavender mist in the air surfaced in Sarah's mind. She surrendered to indulgence and stared at him. A master of the senses, he was. Nevertheless, she knew he wasn't acting in an entirely proper manner, and she had no intention of allowing him to take advantage of her.

Sarah assumed the most innocent expression she possessed. "Is it nae rude tae inquire after a lady's bath?"

"Yes, it is," the duke confirmed. He sounded annoyed. "I don't know what's come over you, Colin. This recklessness will only land you in trouble."

"Recklessness?"

"All of these veiled…innuendos you throw around."

Colin snorted. "You've been out of circulation for too long. You forget what society is like. Think of my 'style of conversation' as a lesson for Sarah. She will have to learn how to counter such…innuendos at every party she attends. Plain speaking is definitely *de trop*."

The duke nodded. He turned to Sarah. "He has a point, Sarah. His folly is our gain. He will teach you to spar."

Her brows drew together in confusion.

"I'll help sharpen your wit," Colin clarified. "The wittier you are, the better. Indeed, with your fortune, you'll be faced with more than your share of rakes. Perhaps I ought to play the part of rake, just for your enrichment."

" 'Tis a part you play so well," the duke remarked. "Make certain you remember our earlier discussion."

Colin stretched again. He appeared pleased with himself. Like a cat in the cream, Sarah mused.

"Go ahead, Colin," she challenged him. "Pretend ye're a rake. We'll see how ye fare."

A smile curled his lips upward. "Before we thrust and parry, we must refine your speech."

She put a hand on her brow. She was beginning to feel giddy.

The duke leveled a searching look in her direction. "First, let's enjoy breakfast. It's easier to learn on a full stomach than an empty one."

The servants, taking their cue from the duke, began to circulate around the table, offering sliced ham, eggs, porridge, fresh fruits, and other delicacies from their silver bowls. Her eyes wide at the variety, quantity, and quality of the food being offered to her, Sarah indicated for the servant to give her double helpings of everything. Then, her mouth watering, she stared down at her silverware. Forks and spoons of various sizes stared back at her. Which one should she use?

His own plate full, Colin selected a fork and began to eat. Watching closely, she picked up the same fork and tried to scoop some eggs up. Most of the eggs fell off the fork on their way to her mouth. Frustrated, she traded her fork for a spoon and had much more success.

Most farmers she knew eschewed forks for spoons. Only with a spoon could one scrape up every last drop of food from a plate. Forks were just too wasteful, and spoons also allowed one to eat faster. She'd learned early on that those who ate the fastest ate the best.

Sarah glanced around the dining room. Thoughts of home had left her feeling lonely, and never more so than now did she feel out of place. She was accustomed to rough stone walls, but here, delicate paintings of ferns and leaves, exquisite gilding, and geometric plastered designs covered nearly every exposed surface. The windows looked out upon manicured lawns instead of moors, and a crystal chandelier presided over the room, rather than oil lanterns that belched smoke.

"I've secured a French maid for you. She's very accomplished. The Duchess of York has kindly offered to lend her to you. She'll join our staff in a few months." The duke paused in eating to offer Sarah a kindly smile. "Until then, Mrs. Fitzbottom will act as your lady's maid. She knows the latest hairstyles, fashions, and all the other things so important to you women. The modiste, a Frenchwoman living in Edinburgh, will be coming along soon as well. I've already given her your approximate size. She'll bring trunks of fabric along for you to select from."

"Thank ye," she murmured.

"I don't know much about the latest fashions," the duke admitted. "I'm hoping the modiste will outfit you properly. Perhaps Colin can assist."

Colin's attention darted toward her breasts before focusing on her lips. "It would be my pleasure."

Sarah fought the urge to cover her cleavage with her hands. An aura of leashed male passion clung to him, a wickedness that continued to arouse lustful thoughts and desires inside her. Breathing quickly, she glanced downward and confirmed that a rosy blush now stained the tops of her breasts. With that knowledge came embarrassment, and with the embarrassment, an even deeper rosy blush.

"Also, you've received a letter from London." The duke grasped a folded piece of parchment on a silver tray she hadn't noticed before, and handed it to her.

Sarah took the letter, aware that Colin's attention had yet to waver from her. "I dinna know anyone in London. Who is it from?"

"I suspect you will have to open it and read it to find out."

She slipped the letter into her reticule, unwilling to admit that her reading skills were, at best, rudimentary. She knew enough to prevent the storekeeper in Beannach from cheating her, and nothing more. Mrs. Fitzbottom would have to read it to her later.

Fighting for nonchalance, she scooped up a few more spoonfuls of eggs and noticed Phineas watching her eat. She slowed down, her appetite dwindling, and stared at him, hard, hoping he would look somewhere else. He did. His gaze fell to her plate of food, lingering there before focusing on his own.

"Is something wrong, Mr. Graham?" she asked, her voice the only sound in the room other than silverware clattering against plates.

"Not at all," he replied. "I'm simply thinking about our first lesson. Perhaps we ought to begin now. We're all just about finished with our breakfast."

The duke wiped his lips with a napkin and threw it on the table. "In that case, I'll bid you good morning and leave you alone. Colin, would you like to ride with me?"

"No, I'll stay behind and observe Phineas's lesson."

The duke stood. "As you wish. I'll be in the study afterward, if anyone needs me," he said, and strode from the dining room.

Sarah put her spoon down. She wished Colin would leave as well. These thoughts he evoked in her both disturbed and annoyed her. Had she no control over herself? "Well, Mr. Graham, what do ye wish tae teach me?"

Phineas put his silverware down and daubed at his lips with a napkin. "First, you must learn to speak. You say 'tae' rather than 'to,' and 'sae' rather than 'so,' to begin. Try to say *to. Tooooooo,*" he drawled, his lips forming a pouchy circle. "As in *foooooool.*"

"Too-oooo," she repeated, feeling like the fool he'd spoken of.

"And now *so.*"

"Sew, as in mending clothes?"

"Exactly."

"So—ooooo," she drawled, darting a glance at Colin. He was still looking at her with eyes like blue smoke, smoldering yet unreadable.

"Good. You've almost got it. Now you must simply remember not to slip back to *tae* and *sae*. You also say 'ye' instead of you, and 'yer' rather than your. These are both indications of the peasantry. Try to say them correctly, now."

"Ye...or. Yeee...ou."

"That's close. Try again."

"Yeor," she said, a bit more forcefully. "Yeee... ou."

Phineas sighed. "This will take time. Remember to practice."

She shrugged, having no intentions of practicing. She just wanted to go home.

"There are other words that you must relearn as well, such as *isn't* rather than *ain't,* and *of* rather than *o'.* Sometimes you drop your *f's.* And your *h's,* for that matter."

"I *am* a scandal," she murmured.

"Overall," Phineas continued in a dogged voice, "your tone has a kind of nasal quality that declares your farmhouse upbringing for all to hear. Speak softly, melodically, in the manner of a song."

"Won't you demonstrate what you mean, Phineas, and sing for us?" Colin interrupted.

Startled, Sarah met his gaze head-on. He smiled, his intensity evaporating beneath a playfulness she found even more disarming. All at once, she felt an answering chuckle building within her. She bit it back.

Phineas sighed, clearly nonplussed. "I suppose we ought to move on."

Their movements unobtrusive, the servants began to clear the plates.

Colin sipped his coffee. "This is most entertaining. Phineas, when you pronounce *to* and *so* for Sarah, you look as though you're angling for a kiss."

The man of business sniffed and assumed an injured air. "If you're going to have fun at my expense, my lord, I invite you to leave the room."

"I'm sorry," Colin said, with another sly wink in Sarah's direction, which only Sarah could see. "I won't offend you further."

Phineas raised an eyebrow. "Perhaps I ought to put you to work."

The other man shrugged. "I'm at your service. And Sarah's."

Sarah eyed him distrustfully. A lock of black hair had fallen across his brow in a rakish fashion, and his lower lip protruded. Kissing him, she decided, would prove very similar to being swept out to sea by an unexpected wave.

"I dinna mind if he helps," she said, then damned herself for her weakness.

"Good." Colin offered her a smile. "What shall I do?"

Phineas smirked. "I need a hostess. Do you mind?"

"Not at all."

"Follow me out of the dining room, then. Lady Sarah, please come along."

Sarah did as she was bid, and soon they had assembled outside the dining room door. The earl lounged a few feet away from her, his attention traveling from her slippers upward, to settle upon her face. Admiration glinted in his eyes.

"Now, let me begin by saying that only the unknown shakes one's poise," Phineas declared. "If one knows what to expect in these situations, one will remain at ease. First, we'll examine the guest's part in a formal dinner. I will be the host, and the earl, our hostess."

"Colin, a hostess?" Sarah looked from Phineas to Colin. "Isn't a 'hostess' a woman?"

"Today I am hostess," Colin told her, grinning. "'Tis my punishment for impudence."

Ignoring Colin, Phineas cleared his throat. "When it is time to go into dinner, the host offers his right hand to the female guest of honor and proceeds into the dining room."

"Am I the female guest of honor?" Sarah asked.

"Indeed you are." Phineas took her arm. "You and I go into the dining room first. The remainder of the guests follow us, excluding the hostess, who brings up the rear with the male guest of honor."

Phineas glanced over his shoulder as they marched into the dining room. "Now it's your turn, my lady," he told Colin.

Pretending to hold someone's arm, Colin sauntered into the dining room behind them.

"Now, the host and hostess stand behind their chairs—" Both Phineas and Colin took up post near chairs facing each other, at the opposite ends of the table. "—and the hostess indicates where each guest is to sit. Ladies approach their chairs from the left and sit from the left. Gentlemen seat the ladies to their right. The hostess is seated by the male guest of honor, and the host by the female guest of honor. Preferably the hostess should sit near the entrance through which the food will appear."

Sarah pressed one hand to her forehead. She felt the beginnings of a headache. "That is a lot tae remember."

"*To*, not *tae*," Phineas chided. He gestured to a chair next to him. "As the female guest of honor, you must sit here, next to me."

Sarah moved to the indicated seat.

"Now, there are exceptions to this seating protocol," the man of business informed her, confusing her further. "Young engaged girls who are to be feted, dignitaries, people who have come a long distance and are rare visitors to the household...all must be considered on a case-by-case basis."

"For now, why don't we focus on the simplest situations," Colin suggested, earning Sarah's gratitude.

Phineas sighed. "If she is to be presented at court, she must learn all. We'll practice eating now."

"Heaven help me," Sarah muttered.

They all sat down at the dining room table again. Phineas motioned to a footman standing in the corner. "Please bring out a single service, including silverware."

The footman bowed and left the room.

"While he's gone, I'll explain the serving process." Phineas leaned forward slightly. "The butler will take his stand behind the hostess. The only time he moves from his vantage point is to serve wine. In the meantime, servants—one per every four guests—ladle out portions of the course.

"After the majority of the guests are finished with a course, the butler will direct his staff to remove the plates. A good butler displays no sense of hurry at this juncture, and certainly no audible clatter or staff direction."

Sarah could see that matters regarding etiquette were of life or death importance to him. She nodded, feigning appreciation, when in truth she thought these "dinner manners" a bunch of stuff and bother over a basic animal instinct: that of eating.

The footman reentered with a tray containing a plate and silverware before Phineas could launch into another diatribe.

"Set the service before Lady Sarah," Phineas directed.

Silverware clattering, the footman set the plate, forks, knives, and spoons in front of her.

Colin yawned audibly. "Is this the way it's going to go over the next three months, Phineas? If so, I'm afraid Sarah and I will expire from boredom. I demand that we end this lesson soon, so I might take her riding. Remember, she has to tour the property, particularly if she will be managing it one day."

"You are particularly subversive today, my lord," Phineas remarked.

"Might we break the lesson up intae several parts?" Sarah questioned, her head beginning to pound. Phineas had a patronizing attitude about him and had managed to make her feel like a complete dolt. She checked the urge to march away from the older man and his silly lessons.

Phineas sighed. "I suppose I must. Still, there is so much you must learn, and so little time to learn it. I don't know how we are going to teach you properly. Today, at breakfast, you took second portions. You must never take second portions or appear the glutton. You also must never assist in serving food, or smoke at the table, or greet servants, or try to wipe up spilled crumbs. These are but a few of the rules that you must live by or you'll disgrace the duke."

Sarah looked down at her place setting. Resentment burned in her gut. To her horror, she realized that tears were filling her eyes. Blinking rapidly, she forced them away. She'd be damned before she'd show any sort of weakness before this pair. "Sae what do I do with the forks and knives?"

Phineas groaned. "*So*, not *sae*."

"So-oooo," she amended, fighting for calm.

Lips pressed together, the man of business jabbed a finger at her plate. "This fork is for salad, and this one for the main course. This spoon is used for soup, and the other for stirring. You hold them like this, the knife and fork remaining in the same hand, Continental style..."

Sarah tried to mimic him and failed. Her fingers acted like thumbs. "I'll need tae practice."

"*To*, not *tae*."

"I'm sorry."

He appeared not to have heard her. "When you are done with your silverware, place them on the right side of the plate, sharp side of the blade facing in, the fork tines up, to the left of the knife."

A scream of pure frustration built inside her. Although she was able to keep the scream from erupting, she couldn't prevent herself from uttering a few heartfelt words. Hand clenched around a fork, she tried for an even tone. "I dinna understand why ye give trivial details such a high importance. Why should I care if I place my fork with its tines up or down?"

Phineas's face and neck reddened. "My lady, these details are far from trivial. The placement of the fork, among other things, is key in understanding the depth of breeding a person has. You must realize that other aristocrats will be watching your every move, and assessing each one in an attempt to solve the mystery of your past. So, if you do not learn these things *to the letter,* you will forever be branded a peasant and a disgrace to my honored employer, the Duke of Argyll!"

Sarah stared at him, shocked by his disdainful tone and the way his voice had risen during his final sentence. Abruptly she could see how much he loathed this task the duke had given him, and how hopeless a case he thought she was.

Gently she placed the fork she'd been holding next to her plate, pushed back from the table, and stood. "I think I need some time tae think. Please do nae follow me. I'll return when I'm able," she told them, and walked out of the dining room.

❖ 7 ❖

Tears that Sarah had managed to banish earlier now came flooding back to run down her cheeks. As soon as she was out of sight of the dining room, she clamped a hand over her mouth to stifle the sobs and raced up the staircase. Within seconds she reached her bedchamber and locked the door behind her before throwing herself on the bed. She buried her head in a pillow and let go, hoping that the soft down would muffle the worst of the noise she was making.

Almost immediately, recriminations filled her head. She'd been a fool to come here. She was inferior, a peasant who hadn't the slightest chance of learning to act like an aristocrat. She simply couldn't be taught. And she was completely alone.

She wanted to go home.

A fresh wave of gulping sobs shook her. So absorbed was she in her crying, that she almost didn't hear the knock on the door. When she stopped long enough to see if someone *had* knocked, she heard it again, a gentle rapping that demanded attention.

Wiping at her eyes, she climbed off the bed and walked over to the door. "Who's there?"

"Colin. Please open the door. I'd like to talk to you."

"Is it proper for a man tae visit a lady in her bed-chamber?" she asked in bitter tones.

"No, it isn't, but to hell with propriety. I need to talk to you."

Thinking of her swollen, reddened eyes, a sign of her weakness and vulnerability, she told him to go away.

"Sarah, if you don't open this door, I'll go to Mrs. Fitzbottom, retrieve the key, and enter without your consent. I will not leave you alone."

Scowling, she opened the door. "Say yer piece, and then leave."

Eyes wide, his expression uncertain, he assessed her for a moment before coming in and gesturing toward the chairs by the hearth. "Let's sit down, shall we?"

"I don't want tae chat, Colin. What is it ye wish tae say?"

He paused, his black hair falling rakishly across his forehead. She dropped her gaze lower, to those sensual full lips of his that she yearned to touch with her own, and quickly looked away.

"Phineas has handled this situation abominably," he said, his voice husky. "He insisted you learn too much, too quickly. No one, not even the most aristo-cratic lady in all of Scotland, could have kept up with him. His lessons need to be more orderly and thought out, and delivered in smaller chunks."

She wiped at her eyes with her sleeve. "That would help, although ye must see that I'm nae fit tae be a duchess."

He touched her hair, and then allowed his hand to quickly drop away. "Sarah, this has nothing to do with you, and what you are or are not capable of. A student can't learn if the teacher can't teach. Please don't blame yourself."

His sympathy brought a fresh wave of tears to her eyes. Quickly she looked away. Even so, he must have seen them, for suddenly he mouthed an oath and slapped his fist against his open palm.

"If only I had said something to stop him," he growled. "I should have seen what he was doing to you. I should have acted. To me, Phineas is amusing in even his worst snits, but to you…of course you wouldn't find him amusing. Can you forgive me?"

She turned to face him again and attempted a shaky smile. "There's nae tae forgive. Ye didn't realize how badly I felt. And I know Mr. Graham is feeling a lot of pressure also. I guess these next three months will be hard."

"Not so hard, Sarah." He clasped her hand in his own, his grip strong, warm, and capable. "You aren't alone here. I'll stay with you, and help you, and be your friend if you need one."

Sarah fought a desire to lean against him. She'd never wanted to lean on anyone else before in her life. But he'd lifted the worst of her problems from her shoulders, giving her relief at a time when she needed it most. She couldn't help but admit how good it would feel to have this kind of support all the time.

"Will you ride with me?" he asked. "At two o'clock?"

"I would enjoy that very much." Obeying an impulse, she covered their clasped hands with her own free one, earning a questioning look from him that was dark and primal and nearly made her giddy.

"My lady, I beg your forgiveness," a male voice sounded from the doorway, breaking the spell between her and Colin. She released Colin's hand and moved away from him to face Phineas, regretting the older man's interruption but in a way glad for it, because she knew that if she'd spent any more time alone with Colin, she might have acted out one of her dreams.

Phineas stepped forward and positioned himself in front of her, his features schooled into both deference and worry. "I beg your forgiveness," he repeated. "I hadn't realized how hard this is for you, and I'm afraid I make a dreadful instructor. I see that I must think this whole thing through again and try to present the material you need to learn in a more patient and orderly fashion."

Sarah tried on a smile and found that it fit pretty well. "Ye can have another chance, Mr. Graham. We're all struggling, nae just me."

The duke's man of business bowed very low. "Thank you, my lady."

When he rose, he appeared relieved. "We'll continue to work on your speech. We'll also spend the rest of the week talking about manners at formal and informal meals. Hopefully by the end of the month we'll be ready to move on to dancing and singing."

"Dancing and singing?" she asked doubtfully.

"And embroidery." He looked at her with sympathy. "These are the skills a well-bred woman must display. We'll take each day one at a time."

Mrs. Fitzbottom chose that moment to join the fray, bustling into the room with an expression of worry on her face, then shooing the men out of the bedchamber, declaring her charge needed a nap. Phineas exited abruptly, more than happy to obey the elderly dame, and Colin followed after leveling one last smoldering look Sarah's way, which left Sarah weak at the knees.

The housekeeper tried to urge her over to the bed, but Sarah would have none of it. She needed fresh air much more desperately than a nap. Still, the mystery of the letter within her reticule kept her from heading out of the bedchamber. Who could have written her? She knew she couldn't have a peaceful walk until Mrs. Fitzbottom had read it to her.

"Mrs. Fitzbottom," Sarah said, "I am going for a walk. But first, would ye be sae kind tae...that is, to...read a letter for me? I never learned tae...to read properly."

"Are you sure you won't take a nap? You appear a little peaked."

"I won't take a nap," she confirmed.

"Well then, lass, you cannot walk in that dress." Mrs. Fitzbottom hustled over to Sarah's wardrobe.

Mystified, Sarah examined the sky-blue satin wreathing her form. "Why not?"

"Walking requires an entirely new dress. As does riding." The housekeeper yanked an ivory muslin gown from the wardrobe.

"I'll be riding later in the afternoon," Sarah warned her. "With the Earl of Cawdor."

"I can see you'll be keeping me busy." The older woman slipped around behind Sarah, presumably to undo Sarah's buttons. "I forget what it's like to be young. So much energy!"

Sarah moved out of her reach and drew the letter from her reticule. "Please, would ye read the letter first, Mrs. Fitzbottom?"

"Why, of course." Squinting, the housekeeper accepted the parchment from Sarah, walked to the windows, and opened it. She began to read in a matter-of-fact voice:

My dear Lady Sarah,

How pleased I was to hear from my husband, Lord Helmsgate, of your reappearance! My husband and your dear father the Duke of Argyll are very old friends indeed, and we were both overjoyed that the duke's anguish over his loss might finally abate.

The ton *is abuzz with news of your recovery. Let me be the first to welcome you back to your rightful position. I understand you are as yet unmarried, with your debut planned for three months hence. I am writing to offer you both my friendship and advice in dealing with the society in which you will soon immerse yourself. The waters here in London can be very thick with sharks!*

Indeed, my Lord Helmsgate has brought it to my attention that a certain nobleman—other than your dear father, of course—is residing in Inveraray at this moment.

Mrs. Fitzbottom trailed off, her brows drawing together. A slight flush grew on her cheeks. "Oh dear. I don't know if I should go on."

Dismayed, Sarah followed the housekeeper to the window. She knew who the nobleman at Inveraray was. "Ye must. Please, finish. I must know the rest."

"All right, then." Mrs. Fitzbottom cleared her throat and began to read again.

I must implore you, stay away from this no-bleman! By all accounts, he is a rakehell who has made a name for himself among the fairer sex.

The housekeeper hesitated, her cheeks flaming. Sarah turned around and stared thoughtfully out the window. She was starting to get a very clear picture of Colin's personality, and the part of her interested in self-preservation demanded that she keep as far away from him as possible. And yet, remembering how he'd come to her after that terrible scene in the dining room and asked to be her friend, she wondered if goodness in him might outweigh the darker aspects of his character.

"Go on, Mrs. Fitzbottom," Sarah directed.

The housekeeper hesitated, then continued in a resolute voice:

Protect yourself from him, dear Lady Sarah, for he is the worst sort of man, insuring his own immunity by tormenting victims who cannot fight back without ruining their reputations: women.

I hope you find usefulness in my advice, and look forward to meeting you, Lady Sarah. When you are planning your next trip to London, please visit. We would so enjoy your company.

I remain yours, in friendship,
—Lady Amelia Helmsgate

Mrs. Fitzbottom refolded the letter. Her mouth drooping, she handed it back to Sarah. "This letter saddens me. I see Mr. Colin hasn't changed much."

Brow furrowed, Sarah took it from her. "How well do ye know him?"

"I've known the earl since he was a young lad first come to Inveraray. Now, I don't usually talk about the family, mind you, but seeing as you've received such bad tidings regarding him, I feel it's my duty to explain."

"Please do, Mrs. Fitzbottom," Sarah encouraged, all ears.

"Call me Mrs. Fitz." The elderly housekeeper patted her kindly on the hand. "I don't know much about Mr. Colin's mother and father, other than what I heard in the servants' quarters.

"Apparently the duke didn't like the late Earl and Countess of Cawdor much. Called them wastrels who flitted from one scrape to another, and considered their son wild beyond redemption. The lad had already been sent down several times from different fancy schools, and it had come to the point where no one would take him."

"It doesna sound like he had much guidance," Sarah murmured.

"No, he hadn't any guidance at all. And if you ask me, he had even less love. I don't know how your mother raised you, Lady Sarah, but in my book, a child needs to be hugged and paid mind to. Mr. Colin had none of that. No touching, no affection, just a cuff on the cheek for some wild prank or another."

Unbidden, thoughts of her own youth with the Murphys surfaced in her mind. Mr. and Mrs. Murphy had known so many worries that they'd paid her little attention, other than to insure that she didn't starve. In fact, they'd taken her in only because they couldn't have children themselves and needed help on the farm. Sarah had grown up telling herself she shouldn't feel neglected. Such was the way of life in the Highlands, and everyone accepted it.

But now, listening to the older woman talk, she wondered if perhaps she should have expected more as a child. Would her true mother, whoever she was, have loved her and cuddled her? If only she could remember just one scrap of a memory about the woman who'd borne her! That aching loneliness that she'd always known during her nights flared to life in full daylight. She bowed her head, a deep melancholy gathering around her like fog, dulling her senses, making her tired.

The housekeeper grew still. Then, hesitantly, she stroked Sarah's hair. "There, lass," she murmured. "I can see you know a little of what I'm talking about. But you're here now, where you belong, with people who love you. You will always be loved, lass. We'll always take care of you. That's what family is for."

Swallowing back the tears, Sarah looked up and wiped her eyes. She didn't want to talk about her own place in the family, not with the duke, and not with Mrs. Fitzbottom. She didn't want to come to rely upon them—love them, even—when she only planned on staying long enough to convince the duke that she could never be the daughter he wished for.

"Still, the duke took Colin in," she whispered huskily.

"Yes, he took Mr. Colin in because the lad was the only living relative to the Argyll dukedom. And don't you know, I heard Mr. Colin crying in his bed every night for at least a month after he'd come here. His parents' abandoning him hurt him terribly."

Sarah could hear outrage in the housekeeper's voice and knew Colin's suffering had been very real. Still, she had a difficult time picturing that sensuous mouth of his doing anything but teasing.

"I often thought the lad needed something to grab hold of him, to encourage him to feel again," the housekeeper continued. "I credit the duke with putting the only crack into Mr. Colin's shell by prodding him to work on the estate. After a time, Mr. Colin threw himself into making Inveraray a grand estate again with such a vengeance that it was as if God had put him on this earth for that purpose only."

"He did a first-rate job," Sarah observed, remembering the beautiful gardens and perfectly appointed rooms.

"Aye, he did, but Inveraray has been the only thing to ever pierce the armor he's surrounded himself in. I don't mean to suggest he doesn't love women, for he does, in his own safe way. But he's never been *in* love, as far as I know. Indeed, I don't believe he knows *how* to love." Mrs. Fitzbottom shook her head. "That's why Lady Helmsgate's letter saddens me so. I was hoping he might have found someone who'd taught him how to love."

Head tilted, Sarah mulled it over. No longer did Colin appear quite so wicked. Instead, for all he had, he just seemed lost, like her.

"Have you met Lady Helmsgate?" she questioned.

"Not met, exactly. She came to visit a few years ago, after she and Lord Helmsgate had married."

"What did you think of her?"

"She was very young." The housekeeper pressed her lips together, evidently unwilling to say more.

"Do you trust her word?"

"I've heard these things about Mr. Colin through other sources," she admitted. "Still, I stand by my opinion. He may be damaged, but inside, he's a good man. In fact, when you go riding with Mr. Colin, stop and ask a few of the duke's tenants about him, and consider what they tell you."

Sarah nodded thoughtfully. Colin may, indeed, have a good heart beneath that lecherous exterior, but she still had to treat him with care, lest he ruin her in some way. If only the notion didn't bother her so much. Heaven knew she looked forward to every second she spent in his company. He was the most fascinating man she'd ever met.

She had never thought about the feel of silk against her skin, or the sweet taste of honey rolling across her tongue, or the soft whisper of rose water rising off a hot bath, until he had urged her to do so. A sensualist, Colin had clearly devoted a good portion of his life to feeling physically, if not emotionally. And when he looked at her with those smoky eyes of his, she could think of nothing but begging him to teach her every little detail he'd learned.

Mrs. Fitzbottom, who had been studying her, placed a gentle hand on Sarah's arm. "I like Mr. Colin, but I'll still tell you to be wary of him. From what I've heard, he could sweet-talk a woman into almost...anything."

Sarah nodded her agreement, far too aware of Colin's charms.

"Will you be going for your walk?" the older woman asked.

"Aye."

"Let me help you change, then."

While Mrs. Fitzbottom fussed about, subjecting

Sarah to another interminable session of prodding and lacing, this time into a sturdier gown, Sarah remembered the picture of the white beast in the drawing room. A unicorn, the earl had called it. Suddenly the need to find her unicorn almost overwhelmed her with its intensity. She was so confused. She didn't even know her own mind anymore, or where she belonged.

"Please hurry, Mrs. Fitz."

"I'll call a footman." The housekeeper moved toward the silken pull cord.

Sarah stopped her with a soft touch to the wrist. "I want tae go alone."

"But my lady, you mustn't. You could get lost, or run into a ruffian from the village, or—"

"I'm going alone, Mrs. Fitz. I'll see ye in an hour or sae, tae change intae my riding gown. And thank ye for being sae frank with me."

With that, Sarah grabbed her reticule and a woolen shawl, hurried from the room, and raced down the staircase. She walked across the great hall and out into the sunshine, a tapestry image of the white unicorn held firmly in her mind.

Beneath her feet, the grass was springy, and on another day it might have put a lilt in her step. But today, she felt as if a weight hung from her heart, dragging her downward, and she plodded along. A sigh slipped from her lips as she crossed the grounds, then passed the kitchen barn where she'd slept, and made her way into the woods surrounding the castle.

On the whole, she hadn't much experience with woods. She'd spent much of her life standing high on a hillside, the wind rolling down from the mountains to thunder in her ears. Rather than tread down a sylvan path surrounded by trees and emerald bushes, like the one that now led her into the forest, she'd picked her way down a swath of green that wound past crumbling rocks and wiry brush.

Sarah paused after entering the forest, noticing how much darker it was beneath the canopy of green. Mist wound past her face and she shivered a little, growing cold. She pulled her shawl tightly around her shoulders, not certain if she liked this new place. It had the feeling of secrets, the sound of slightly off-key melodies that had hidden meanings. And it was very quiet.

She came to a place where the path forked and, frowning, chose to go to the left. The sunshine had always been clear and bright in the high country, without the haze that the lowlands brought, and it had always warmed her through her cotton dress, even as the wind clawed at the plaid she wore round her shoulders. At home, if she became cold, she merely had to slip into a space between two gray stones and the wind would become a whisper, while the sun grew hot on her face.

Here, though, the mist twined around in spectral shapes and darkness reigned. She could find no safe haven to warm herself. She paused, bumps rising on her arms, as an unfamiliar animal cry echoed through the woods. It sounded like a very small child crying out in fear. Wondering what could have made that horrible noise, she searched the trees and surrounding brush in vain for animals she recognized, but saw nothing.

Abruptly she turned around and retraced her

steps down the path, wishing she hadn't decided to come into these woods. She'd been too hasty in deciding to go off on her own. Trembling, she wondered if she hadn't heard an animal at all. Perhaps these woods were haunted.

Aye, she'd heard a lot about haunts, and faeries who didn't like people. The ghost of a shepherd who'd fallen into a gully and broken his neck had supposedly haunted the moors around Beannach for years, calling for his lost sheep, and everyone knew about the young man who'd fallen asleep in the hills for one hundred and two years, only to awaken with a long white beard and his life nearly over, the victim of a vengeful faerie colony. What sort of ruthless creatures did *these* trees hide?

She came to a fork in the path, the same one that she'd passed by several minutes before, and studied her two choices. Had she gone left earlier, or right? Shoulders tense, she decided she'd taken the path on the right before, and now had to go left.

She began walking again. Stagnant pools of water had gathered on either side of the trail, and little white insects landed on their surfaces. Some of the insects flew about, looking much like snowflakes that refused to settle upon the ground. She might have thought them pretty if she didn't feel so nervous.

Another cry echoed through the woods. Again, the cry remained unfamiliar, but this time it sounded gravelly, threatening. She moved even faster, until she was nearly running. She had to get out of these woods. She didn't know what sorts of creatures lived here, but she didn't fancy meeting up with some angry faerie who could put her to sleep for a hundred years.

Her heart pounding, she pelted forward, not seeing the exposed root until the last second, certainly not soon enough to stop herself from tripping over it and falling into a pile of dead leaves.

The nasty, throaty cry rang out again, this time from only a few feet away.

Nearly sobbing, she scrabbled away from the noise and into the brush, and when she felt a nudge on her arm she squeezed her eyes shut and yelled aloud, afraid the faeries had found her.

Something growled in her ear.

Remaining utterly still, she slowly opened one eye, and then the other. Two small, beady black eyes stared back at her. Swallowing, she pushed herself up until she was sitting, her skirt spread around her, and stared at the little creature. He was gray, black, and buff, with a white stripe from his nose to the back of his head. His claws were curved and powerful looking, suggesting he did a lot of digging. In fact, he reminded her of a large weasel.

All at once she felt like a perfect nitwit. Good Lord, how she'd allowed her imagination to run away with her! She willed her heart to slow down, and her breathing to calm, and soon she felt almost normal.

Curiosity filled her. What sort of creature was this? Avoiding looking directly into his eyes, as most animals viewed that gesture as confrontational, she pulled her panflute out and played the weasel's song, a crafty melody about self-reliance and of the things beneath the earth.

He responded with a throaty growl that she could almost understand, but not quite. Regardless, delight filled her. She knew she'd understand him in time. Here was a new friend, someone to talk to during the lonely weeks ahead of her.

A tiny chattering noise caught her attention. In the nearby brush, a hare stood absolutely motionless, its gaze fixed upon her. Here, again, was another friend. The rabbit's song she knew well, and she played it for him, warbling about fertility and fleetness, drawing the creature from the brush to her side.

One by one, other animals joined the first two, their attitudes both curious and friendly. If she knew a song for a particular animal, she played it, much to the newcomer's gladness. And as she trilled her panflute, and thanked them for their greetings, and listened to their stories, some of the sadness and anger that had been a part of her for weeks began leaking away.

When Sionnach arrived and joined in with a spirited yip, she gave the little fox her first true smile since she'd come to Inveraray and began to enjoy herself. She didn't worry about anyone witnessing her socializing with the locals; she was so deep in the woods that she doubted anyone could ever find her.

Laughing aloud now, she called all of the forest's inhabitants to her, and played so merrily on her panflute that some of them began to dance.

✤ 8 ✤

Already dressed in his hunt coat and breeches, Colin sprawled in a chair and stared moodily out the window. Sunlight painted shadows on the floor nearby and burnished the simple Scottish furniture in his dressing room to a rich mahogany. He glanced at the ormolu clock on the mantelpiece and saw the time had drawn close to one in the afternoon. Another whole hour had to pass before Sarah would meet him in the great hall for their ride.

Leg hooked over one side of a chair, he absently stroked the velvet covering the chair's back. Thoughts of Sarah with her panflute, her violet eyes gazing at him and tilted upward like a cat's, filled his mind. Something in her eyes, some fey quality, continued to haunt him. It stirred an uneasiness in his gut. And yet, he wasn't afraid of her. Rather, she attracted him in some primal way he couldn't quite define.

Many years ago, during a ride here at Inveraray, he'd found a little feral cat who'd caught her paw in a leghold trap. The cat had hissed at first, then looked at him calmly, its eyes fathomless yellow pools that had seemed very wise to him, above the pain of a mortal existence. Why wasn't it screaming? he'd wondered. Didn't it feel the pain of the trap? It was made of flesh and blood...how could it not feel pain?

Naturally, he had freed it. Before he could catch it, it had raced off into the woods. Having witnessed its vulnerability, part of him had wanted to help it, and protect it. He'd always wondered what had happened to that cat, and had checked the barns for it frequently. Had it succumbed to infection, or gone on to enjoy a lengthy life?

The cat's odd introspection, its otherworldly look coupled with vulnerability, had aroused the same sort of uneasiness in him then as he felt now. Perhaps his uneasiness was rooted in the fear that came with not understanding, he mused. Of sensing that the cat had thoughts so different from his that he simply wasn't *equipped* to understand.

Whatever the case, Sarah possessed that same wild, fey quality the cat had shown, and now, ten weary years later, Colin couldn't let this go. He wanted to understand. He needed the faint dread and boredom that had taken over his life to go away. He needed to hope.

A poem came to mind, one of his favorites by William Blake, about a tyger burning bright. He wondered if he could capture Sarah's strange qualities on paper, just as Blake had immortalized the tiger. Frowning, he stood, walked over to his writing desk, and sat down. He slapped a fresh piece of parchment on the desk, dipped his quill in ink, and considered.

What was it about her that had stirred his uneasiness? That fey quality? And why did she intrigue him so? She was beautiful, yes, but something more than that bound him to her.

Unbidden, one of Sarah's panflute melodies came to mind. The hair rose on his arms just from the memory, and he knew in that moment that it had to be her aura of, well, enchantment that had unsettled him. He didn't believe in magic or its possibilities, and yet, more than once she'd displayed a special touch with animals that went beyond the normal. His gut told him she had a bit of the faerie folk in her. Indeed, she was upsetting notions that he'd held close for the majority of his life, and even as the thought made him uneasy, it drew him on like a lodestone.

The verbal explanation that he'd cooked up in his mind hardly satisfied him, however. It just didn't fully capture the intense yearnings and restlessness he experienced around Sarah. His reaction to her was visceral, without logic, and could not be quantified or qualified. Giving in, he put his quill down and stood. Then he moved over to the window and stared out at the lawn, seeing nothing.

A soft knock at the door interrupted his reverie.

"Come in," he said, and turned around to face the entrance.

Higgins, his valet, walked through the doorway, a man unremarkable in dress and appearance in tow. "Mr. Cooper, lately of London, has come to call," the valet announced softly.

The runner offered Colin a smart bow. "Good afternoon, my Lord."

Glad to see the runner at last, Colin answered with a similar greeting and told Higgins to leave them. Cooper had a reputation as being the finest bloodhound in all of England. He'd captured criminals in thieving dens and had, according to gossip, unmasked traitors in the most exclusive drawing rooms of London. Now, he would help Colin discover whether or not a certain kitten was really the duke's daughter.

Once the valet had closed the door behind him, Colin asked Cooper to sit and offered him a brandy. The runner accepted and, with little ado, got straight to the point.

"So who's the girl I'm to investigate?"

Colin fixed him with a stare. "Mr. Cooper, can I rely on your discretion?"

"Of course you can, my lord." Several years older than Colin and sporting a grizzled mustache, Cooper nodded once to emphasize his trustworthiness, then patted a side pocket that no doubt held references.

Colin took the other man at his word. He had no reason to distrust the man. Still, he hesitated. The words almost refused to pass his lips. Unaccountably, he felt like a conniving devil. "I need you to verify the story of a certain young lady who has come to live at Inveraray."

"Do you mean the duke's daughter?"

Colin nodded. "I want you to make certain that Sarah Murphy is, indeed, his daughter. I bear no ill will toward her," he hastened to add, "but I don't want the duke led down a garden path, only to discover that the girl whom he had thought of his own blood is nothing more than a common peasant. Will you do it?"

"Aye, my lord, the assignment sounds interesting." Cooper stretched his legs out and took a sip of the brandy Colin had given him.

"I'll tell you what I know of her. I've also written

down the particulars of her former address and directions to find it. Higgins will give these to you as you leave."

"Very good." The runner put his brandy snifter on a side table. "Tell me everything you can."

Remorse niggling harder at him, Colin explained the circumstances of the carriage accident that had claimed the Duchess of Argyll and her entourage. He told the runner everything that the duke had relayed to him about Sarah's earliest years, and enumerated the events leading up to the duke's discovering Sarah on the moors, including his own role: that of discovering the duchess's unmistakable, heart-shaped emerald ring in a jeweler's collection when he went to purchase a birthday present for Amelia Helmsgate.

One eyebrow raised, Mr. Cooper listened attentively to Colin's entire discourse, and when Colin was through, he leaned back expansively. "I suppose you'll not be wanting the duke to know about my investigation."

"This is between you and me, as are the results. You must tell me, and me only, what you find."

"As you wish, my lord." Cooper stood. "With your leave, I'll head into the Highlands on the morrow."

"Excellent." Colin opened a small trunk pushed against one wall of his dressing room and withdrew a fist-sized velvet pouch. He tossed the pouch, full of gold sovereigns, to Mr. Cooper. "Will this be enough to get you started?"

The older man caught it, loosed the strings, peered inside, and whistled. "Aye, my lord, that's more than enough."

Colin rang for Higgins. The valet knocked on the door less than a minute later and entered.

"Please escort Mr. Cooper out, Higgins."

"Yes, my lord." The valet gestured to Cooper, who bowed in Colin's direction before leaving with the servant.

"I should return within a fortnight or so," the runner said over his shoulder, just before disappearing from sight.

Colin closed the door behind them. He sighed, relieved that the distasteful business was over. He took no joy in the investigation or the hurtful truths that Cooper might turn up, and in other circumstances he wouldn't have bothered to hire the runner. And yet, because the duke meant so much to him, he just couldn't allow Sarah to flit along her merry way without some sort of investigation. He'd seen enough intrigue in his day and knew how damaging it could be.

Then why did that niggling feeling of regret over hiring Cooper keep growing stronger in him? He tried to push it aside, telling himself he was more than justified, but the guilt just wouldn't let go. He remembered that wild, primal look in the cat's eyes. In his mind, Sarah's eyes replaced the cat's and, without warning, he felt her vulnerability keenly.

His dressing room abruptly felt stuffy and closed in. He dragged on his necktie, loosening it, and decided to go for a walk. He had almost half an hour before two o'clock, plenty of time to take a turn about the grounds and let the fresh air clear his head.

He left his dressing room and descended to the great hall, passing Mrs. Fitzbottom on the way.

The housekeeper, upon seeing him, paused. "Are you looking for Lady Sarah, Mr. Colin? Milady mentioned she would be riding with you this afternoon."

"Not at the moment. We're to meet at two o'clock." Alerted by a pinched look around her mouth, he assessed her with a swift glance. "Is there a problem, Mrs. Fitzbottom?"

"Well, no, not really. 'Tis just that milady is walking the grounds alone, and I'm worried that she may become lost."

"Was there not a footman available to accompany her?"

"Milady did not want a footman."

"Did she tell you where she planned to walk?"

"No. She wanted to be alone. But I watched her from a second-floor window," the housekeeper admitted, coloring. "She crossed the lawns in the direction of the Maltlands."

"Of course. With her kinship for animals, I should have guessed she'd head for the stables. Rest easy, Mrs. Fitzbottom. I'll find her and bring her back."

"Thank you, milord."

Leaving the housekeeper behind, Colin strode across the great hall and out the front door. He walked across neatly clipped lawns that were the color of emeralds, skirting around muddy spots that the rain had brought, and finished the half-mile distance to the Maltlands quickly. The smell of dung sharp in the air, he passed through the stone arch leading to the courtyard and surveyed the busiest place at Inveraray Castle.

Arranged in a rectangle around a packed-earth courtyard, barns, carriage houses, a hothouse, and rubble-stone sheds all competed with each other for usefulness. Nectarines and peaches pressed against the hothouse's glass walls, their obvious ripeness inviting Colin to come in for a bite. The sounds of a hammer striking metal and an ax hitting wood emerged from the great barn, where the duke's wrights, smithies, and other craftsmen worked. The horse stalls and carriage barns held numerous varieties of both.

Nowhere did Colin find a trace of Sarah.

He walked across the courtyard and questioned an elderly groomsman polishing the duke's saddles and bridles. The groom mentioned seeing a young woman hurrying past the Maltlands' entrance arch. She'd peered into the courtyard but hadn't actually entered. When Colin pressed him as to which way she'd gone, the old man pointed off to the west.

Colin stared into the large grove of beeches and firs that eventually opened onto fields along the River Aray. He couldn't imagine Sarah becoming lost. While the woods around Inveraray were thicker than in most parts of Scotland, they weren't thick enough for anyone to wander in for any length of time without coming to the river. The river, of course, led to Loch Fyne and the town of Inveraray.

Sighing, Colin left the Maltlands and headed west, into the trees. The day had warmed up considerably and created pools of stagnant water. Tiny, white-winged insects took advantage of these perfect conditions and hatched in the pools, flying upward to weave and dip among the rushes.

He swatted at the bothersome insects and avoided the pools, determined to arrive back at the castle without smelling like a swamp. Gradually, as he explored, he became aware of lilting, flutelike notes. *The panflute*, he thought, and followed the sound, knowing it would lead him to Sarah. After a short trek, he drew close enough to hear the panflute clearly. The music trembled and squeaked in a guttural fashion. It seemed to originate in a clearing just beyond his line of vision.

A soft breeze blew from the direction of the clearing, sweeping past to dissipate in the woods behind him. On the breeze he could smell a hint of flowers. He looked above the clearing and saw an amazing variety of tiny birds flying around. He suspected their chirping had given Sarah's music that squeaky quality. Most likely they were chirping in excitement at the bountiful feast of white insects, but some fanciful part of him wondered if the birds were accompanying her music with a bit of their own.

Smiling at the capricious notion, he stepped around some hedges. Ahead, a tree possessing a girth twice his size blocked his view of her. He didn't need to see her, however...her music drew him on. Soon he reached the tree and peered around its trunk to look into the clearing. Blinking, he squeezed his eyes shut and then snapped them open again. Amazement made him feel light-headed.

Trees filtered the harsh glare of mid-afternoon sunlight, allowing only a soft, golden haze to touch the clearing. White insects flew around in great abundance, their wings glittering gold in the lambent glow and dipping around Sarah like faeries. Sarah sat in a patch of white flowers, her skirt spread out like a blanket. In a loose circle around her, animals of all kinds watched.

What the hell?

Swallowing, Colin stared at the small white hare that held out its front paw to Sarah. An owl perched on a branch above the hare, ignoring what should have been a grand meal in favor of Sarah and her panflute. He swiveled to gaze at the brown goose that honked insistently, and at the red fox sitting quietly next to the goose.

Why wasn't the fox attacking the goose, and the owl eating the rabbit? His heart was beating too fast. He tried breathing deeply to calm down.

A wren was flying circles above Sarah, and the magnificent stag he'd witnessed from the study on the day of her arrival stood just outside the circle. The stag's brown eyes seemed to hold wisdom that Colin could never understand. With a start, he realized that her audience even included an otter, for God's sake…perhaps up from Loch Fyne and the seas beyond to attend her little musical.

He passed a shaky hand across his forehead. This was a trick of hers. Either that or he was losing his mind.

She patted her skirts, as though inviting the rabbit to have a seat. The little animal hopped right over to her and sat where she'd indicated. At the same time, the wren fluttered downward to land on the tip of her panflute, and a ray of sunlight penetrated the treetops above her and settled upon her face, painting her gold.

She laughed, the sound soft, yet full of joy.

Colin gripped the tree trunk. The bark felt rough and crumbly beneath his fingers. He'd been pressing his knee into the trunk, and now he realized it had begun to ache. He welcomed the pain and dug his fingers harder into the bark, reassured that Sarah and her animal friends weren't a dream or a hallucination.

His evaluative side had overcome the shock and was beginning to take over.

Could he be losing his mind? No. He didn't hear voices or smell strange scents, and hadn't suffered the kind of terrible incidents that sometimes drove people mad. Madness had claimed King George III, but it had not claimed him. His stomach rolled with uneasiness.

How could he possibly accept what he was seeing, then? This went far beyond a special touch with animals. She was talking to them, for God's sake. Charming them with her flute in a way any goddess worth her salt could.

Sarah, who had been caressing the hare, turned toward the stag and played a quick little melody on her panflute. In response, the stag lowered his head and bent forward on one leg. Colin had the distinct impression he had just offered her a bow.

He shook his head. He could stand here and deny what his own eyes were telling him, or he could accept it and try to understand. Since he couldn't think of one logical, scientific explanation for her talent, he had to ascribe it to magic. To the fey folk. In the past he had always dismissed tales of Highland faeries with utter contempt, but now, he was seriously reconsidering his position.

She played on her panflute some more, and the stag raised himself. When she stopped playing, the stag embarked on a series of gestures and low rumblings that she listened to with her head cocked to one side. A frown crept across her face. She nodded, her shoulders sagging, then looked at the ground for a few seconds before refocusing on the stag, a tremulous smile replacing her frown.

She'd received some bad news, he thought. He studied her with a new sense of awe, and a strange sense of buoyancy that dissipated his uneasiness.

A skunk meandered across the clearing to sidle up to her. Colin flinched at the sight of it. It evidently didn't have spraying in mind, however. Instead, it growled and scratched the grass with its clawed feet, then fixed her with an expectant, if beady black stare. She replied on the flute, and it scratched some more. Avid curiosity grabbed hold of Colin. What were they talking about?

Sarah pointed at a deeper portion of the woods. The skunk rumbled, then took off in the direction she'd pointed. Colin, watching the skunk trundle off, could stand it no longer. He had to reveal himself and find some answers. He stepped out from behind the tree.

The moment he did so, all of the animals froze. Seconds later they scattered off into the woods, the stag knocking down branches in his haste to get away. Sarah stared at him, panflute in hand, her face very pale. She slipped the flute into her reticule without ever looking away.

"I've spoiled your party," he said, trying to smile, and stepped closer.

"My lord," she breathed. "How long have ye... what did ye..."

"How long have I been standing behind that tree?" Hesitantly he moved to her side. His heart was pounding in his chest. He hadn't felt this off balance in an age. "Long enough to see you chatting with your friends."

A blush stained her cheeks pink.

"You were...chatting, no?" he pressed, hunkering down until one of his knees touched the forest floor. He kept his other foot on the ground, his leg bent. From this position he faced her squarely.

"What of it?" Defiance laced her tone. She challenged him with narrowed eyes.

"What of it? What of it, you say? Are you suggesting I should find nothing...odd in the way you talk to animals?"

"Talk?"

"Yes, talk. I watched you and that stag have a conversation."

She laughed shakily. "Ye're seeing things."

"No, I'm not. Tell me how you do it."

"But my lord, I cannot talk tae animals—"

"I've *seen* you. And you can't convince me I'm hallucinating. What are you afraid of?"

Scowling, she scrambled to her feet and looked down on him. "Am I supposed tae trust *ye*, a rake with an appalling reputation? I've been warned about ye."

Sidetracked, he frowned, and stood as well. "By whom?"

"A friend." She looked away.

"That letter you received. It contained gossip about me?"

She didn't answer.

"Who was the letter from?"

A glint in her eyes, she marched past him. "I'm going back tae the castle."

"Wait a moment." He maneuvered in front of her, blocking her exit. "If you're not going to tell me who wrote to you, at least explain how you learned to talk to animals."

"And if I don't answer, what will ye do? Speak tae the duke about my secretive nature and my odd ability, which hints tae ye of witchcraft? Perhaps then he'll renounce his claim on me and return yer inheritance tae ye."

Taken aback, Colin stared at her. "I'm not your enemy."

"I have no desire tae confide in ye about anything."

"Are you at least going to admit you talk to animals?"

She shrugged. "I'll allow that I have a special touch concerning animals."

"But I saw you conversing with them." He paused to take a deep breath, excitement and awe grabbing hold of him all over again. "What a magnificent talent it must be. What do they tell you? How did you learn? Please, Sarah, you must trust me."

Sighing angrily, she spun away from him and stared into the trees.

"What are you so afraid of?"

Without warning, she whirled back around to face him. "What would people think of a girl who claimed tae talk tae animals? They'd think her mad. Those few who believed the accusation would brand her a witch or a faerie. She would live as an outcast."

"So you keep quiet about your talent."

"Aye, I do." She stopped short, her eyes widening as she realized her admission.

He smiled. "You *can* trust me. I'll tell no one. Won't you satisfy my curiosity, and describe how you came to possess such an ability? Does it have something to do with your panflute?"

She looked away, one hand tightly clasped around her reticule.

"What did the stag say?"

"I asked him about a...friend."

"Ah, another friend. Is there something amiss with your friend? The stag's news seemed to sadden you."

"My...friend is growing more ill with every passing day."

"Can I do anything to help?"

"Nay."

"Will you introduce me to your friend?"

She shook her head *no*.

"Won't you at least tell me this friend's name?"

"I won't answer any more questions."

"I'm a patient man. I'll wait until you're ready to answer." He slung an arm around her shoulder and pulled her close, noting how she'd fit perfectly into his body. "We have three months ahead of us, during which we will come to know each other very well. I must admit, I've never looked forward to the future with more eagerness than I do now. I expect you to tell me all of your secrets. Perhaps I'll even tell you a few of my own."

Visibly swallowing, she sagged against him. Her hand fluttered up to rest upon her breasts, which were heaving with some unnamed emotion.

After all of those stubborn refusals, her surrender and that soft look in her eyes brought a tightness to his loins. Extremely conscious of the soft press of her breast against his ribs, he breathed her scent in, memorizing it. "Are you all right?"

"I'm fine," she muttered.

"You need to rest. We'll ride out tomorrow."

"Absolutely not." She straightened and pulled away from him. "I want tae explore the grounds this afternoon, like we planned."

She sounded so determined that again his thoughts went back to the stag. What had the animal communicated to her? He lifted an eyebrow, intrigued. "Whatever my lady wishes."

❊ 9 ❊

An hour later, Sarah found herself dressed in a
new gown, this one designed specifically for riding,
according to Mrs. Fitzbottom. Chafing at the delays
created by these long dressing sessions, Sarah could
hardly stand still while the housekeeper fussed with
her hat. The stag's revelation had underscored the
urgency of the unicorn's plight. Long ago, the unicorn had helped her, and now he needed her. If she
didn't find him soon, and nurse him through his illness, he would die.

The sunlight streaming through her bedchamber
window had taken on the mellow glow of late afternoon. A quick glance at the clock confirmed that the
hour was well past two. She wanted to spend as
much time as possible exploring the grounds and
looking for the unicorn before dusk fell, but at this
rate, she'd be lucky to have two hours in the saddle.

"Can ye not hurry?" Sarah asked. "Colin awaits
me in the great hall. I'm more than half an hour
late."

"All grand ladies are late," the housekeeper

chided her. "Besides, we need to place your hat at just the right angle, so you look confident."

"Confident? I look like I'm ready tae march off tae war." Sarah glanced downward at her habit of bright green, ornamented down the front and embroidered at the cuffs with military-type golden frogging. The tips of her boots peeped out from beneath her skirt. She lifted her hem a little to admire the green lace and fringe decorating the boots more fully. "Still, I like these little black boots. Even my feet are pampered."

"You appear far from soldierly. If I were to compare you to something, I'd choose a violet. This green habit makes your eyes look purple, and you are small. Even a bit shy, bless you." The housekeeper finally pinned the small riding hat of black velvet onto Sarah's curls. Then she stood back and assessed Sarah with a keen gaze. A smile lightened her face. She nodded. "Perfect, lass. Mr. Colin will hardly be able to pull his attention from you."

"But I don't want his attention," she protested, and felt her face heat at the lie. Mrs. Fitzbottom's earlier revelations about Colin's youth had intrigued her. Now she wanted to know him better...though how much better, she wasn't yet willing to decide.

"I guarantee you will have it regardless," the housekeeper said. "Now go, and remember to ask the duke's tenants about Mr. Colin."

Nodding, Sarah grabbed her kidskin gloves and hurried out of the bedchamber before Mrs. Fitzbottom decided to fuss some more with her appearance. At the second-floor balcony that overlooked the great hall, she paused and gazed downward. Instantly she found Colin, who stood near the door. He was looking at a gold watch fob he held in one hand. As if he felt her stare upon him, he glanced upward.

Their gazes locked. Sarah caught her breath. A fluttering sensation danced in the pit of her stomach. Her cheeks unaccountably warm, she broke eye contact and walked slowly down the stairs. With every other step, she risked a glance at him, taking in his appearance bit by bit.

She'd originally thought his build no better than average, but now she saw that his breeches outlined muscular thighs, and his hunt coat emphasized broad shoulders. His black neck cloth contrasted with a white waistcoat, a combination that reinforced her impression of his dual nature. Was he dark, or was he light? Was he good or bad? At the very least, his powerful build suggested strength and capability. Suddenly he seemed very male to her.

She smiled at him upon reaching the bottom stair. "Good afternoon, Colin."

Blinking, he assessed her for a moment, then murmured, "You never cease to surprise me."

All at once she felt feminine and pretty. Enjoying the sensation, she moved to his side.

He clasped her arm and led her across the hall, toward the front door. "You look like a duchess, you know."

"Not because of any effort on my part. Rather, I think Mrs. Fitzbottom has a bit of magic in her."

"You're not even trying to improve yourself?"

She shrugged. "Nay."

"Don't you want to become a grand lady?"

"I want tae go back tae my home in Beannach." *After I find the unicorn,* she silently added.

He lifted an eyebrow. "Why don't you just leave?"

"Because the duke and I have a deal. He's satisfied my debts with the Murphys, who found me wandering the moors, took me in, and raised me. In return, I've promised tae stay here and pretend to be his daughter. Stay I will, until he realizes I can never be the daughter he wishes for."

Smiling, he closed the distance between them, clasping her hand in his much larger gloved palm. "You're already the daughter he wished for."

Her heart sank. Maybe the duke didn't care *who* she was, he just wanted a daughter to lavish his attention on.

Colin steered her toward a stone carriage path and changed the subject. "We'll walk to the Maltlands. The groomsmen have horses waiting for us there."

They started down the path, which led around a grove of trees. Colin pointed out the sights to her along the way, naming an arched bridge as "Mr. Frew's Bridge" and explaining the history of the area. Beneath his rich, cultured voice, Sarah thought she heard a hint of regret. She remembered the duke telling her that once, Colin had considered Inveraray his home. Perhaps he was now wishing he hadn't forsaken Inveraray's quiet country charm for London and society.

To her right, she recognized the kitchen gardens, where she had wandered last night before stumbling across the hay barn and making her bed. A gardener had recently turned the earth, leaving muddy clumps in his wake. Neat rows of lettuce, spinach, and snow peas marched up and down the aisles. She memorized its layout, so she wouldn't become lost during her next midnight walk through its leafy interior.

When Colin led her past the garden and around the grove of trees, Sarah could see a series of archways in the distance. The archways opened onto a square surrounded by white barns. These were the Maltlands, he told her, containing all of the duke's horses and carriages, as well as a forge and the water-driven sawmill used by the duke's wrights, smithies, and other craftsmen.

Properly impressed, Sarah passed beneath the central arch and stopped in the square. Slatted doors faced her from every direction, suggesting a dizzying variety of carriages. Bales of hay bulged from one barn and a granary spilled oats into a wooden trough. Here, animal feed lay scattered all over the place, unlike upon the farms in Beannach, where every piece of hay was precious. She wondered if the plentiful feed had ever attracted the unicorn.

Moments later a groomsman with two horses in hand walked toward them. Although she'd never owned a horse, she'd learned a fair amount about them through treating their complaints. These horses were thoroughbreds, far above fourteen hands and well pampered, judging by the way they sidestepped and pulled on the reins. The smaller one—a mare—even had little burgundy bows woven through its mane.

Colin turned to her. "Have you ever ridden sidesaddle?"

She assessed the fancy saddle atop the mare, with its red velvet seat and ornate tooling of birds and flowers on the leather skirts. Both stirrups hung down on one side.

"Nay, this is my first time."

"Have you ever ridden atop a horse?"

"Of course," she answered indignantly, stretching the truth only a little. Occasionally she'd brought her patients to her croft for overnight care, and ridden them home once they'd regained their health. "I'm nae that ignorant."

"How did you ride, then?"

"With one leg on either side of the horse's back."

"In a saddle?"

"I didn't have time for a saddle."

"You'll have to use a sidesaddle from now on. Ladies never ride bareback. It's considered very indelicate."

"Why?"

"I suspect some medieval prude declared it so," he murmured softly. "I won't go into any further details; they're too scandalous for your sensitive ears."

Intrigued, she wondered what could possibly be considered scandalous about riding atop a horse's bare back. She hadn't even a guess, but didn't have much time to think about it, either. Colin smoothly continued his riding lesson.

"Today, you will learn to ride sidesaddle. I'll show you how to mount first." He led her over to the mare, who shook her dark brown mane at their approach.

"Now, here is the mounting block," he said, pointing to a rectangular, roughhewn log about two feet high that sat on the ground. "Generally, you'll stand on the block, position your left leg in the stirrup, and pull yourself atop the saddle."

"Before we begin, may I acquaint myself with the horses?"

A bemused smile crossed his face. "Please do."

She left his side and walked across the packed earth until she stood face-to-face with the mare, who scratched a few times on the ground, then neighed softly. Sarah translated with a touch of disbelief. The horse wanted a pastry, and a blueberry one, at that. What a difference wealth made. Many of the people in Beannach could afford pastries only rarely.

The mare blew air out of its nostrils, and leaned close to fill its nose with Sarah's scent.

"What is this mare's name?" she asked the groom, smiling now.

"Sunlight."

"Blueberry is a better name for her. In any case, I have a question for ye. Have ye noticed any animals getting intae the feed at night?"

"Aye, we've had some thievery," the groom said. "Rats. Skunks. Raccoons. Anything that likes oats has had a go at the storage bin."

"Did ye ever see a...white horse come here at night?"

"Can't say that I have. Why? Is someone missing a horse?"

"I thought I saw a white horse out my window last night," she invented. She should have known the unicorn wouldn't prove *that* easy to find. "If ye see it, please send word tae the castle. We should try to catch it. It must be lost."

"Aye, my lady."

She sighed. "I didn't think tae bring a treat for Sunlight. Do ye have something I could give her?"

"How about this, my lady?" The groom pulled an apple from his pocket.

Nodding her thanks, Sarah took the apple and handed it to Sunlight. While the mare chewed, she filed away her penchant for blueberry pastries. The next time she rode, she would bring one for the mare.

"Still looking for your unicorn?" Colin asked, brow quirked.

Rather than answer, Sarah glanced at the other horse, a large, chestnut-colored thoroughbred, and gauged its angry hoof stomping. "How long has it been since ye've ridden yer horse?"

He shrugged. "Almost ten years, I suppose."

She nodded sagely, finally understanding the meaning behind all of that angry bluster. The horse thought Colin had abandoned him, and was also bragging about having unseated Colin so many times that Colin couldn't get the dirt out of his pants anymore. "I guess he's thrown ye a fair share of times."

"How do you know that?"

"Oh, he's obviously spirited."

"That fleabag has a penchant for low-hanging limbs," Colin admitted.

Hiding a smile, Sarah didn't bother to tell him that he'd likely find himself on his arse again today. The horse had promised vengeance against Colin with a determined hoofbeat. "When are ye going tae teach me tae ride?"

"Now." He turned to the groom. "Please leave us."

The groom offered them a bow, then walked across the courtyard and disappeared into a barn.

They were completely alone.

"Come over to the mounting block," Colin urged.

She joined him by the block and examined the sidesaddle. It looked very uncomfortable. "Do I sit facing to the left?"

"No, you face front, your shoulders and hips in the same position as they would be if you were riding astride. Your right leg is draped around the pommel, here, at the top of the saddle, to steady your ride."

She nodded. "All right. Go on."

"Usually, a groom or a gentleman companion will assist you into your seat."

"Assist me? How so?"

At her question, a teasing glint darkened his eyes. He hesitated, clearly thinking something over, then grinned at her, making her breath quicken with anticipation.

"Ladies need help settling into the saddle. However, you must be ready to retaliate against those who touch you in places not essential to the mounting process."

"Retaliate?"

"Sometimes, a gentleman will allow his hands to linger too long. Such gestures deserve a sharp response."

She swallowed. "Ye'll have tae explain more fully."

"When you mount, a gentleman will put his hands around your waist to help you into the saddle." Mimicking his words, Colin put his hands around her waist, grasping her firmly.

She trembled, and fought to hide it, not wishing him to know how effortlessly he affected her. "Go on."

"If his hands wander here, in a supposed effort to grasp your waist, then he has stepped over the line of decency." He slipped firm palms down to her thighs for just an instant before returning them to her waist.

She gasped, the place he'd touched burning as though on fire.

Without warning, he picked her up and lifted her

into the saddle, settling her down gently on the velvet seat. She felt the brush of his hair against her cheek, smelled the musky scent of him just as she settled into the saddle.

She grabbed at the mare's neck, exquisite sensations running through her body.

"Lady Sarah, are you well?" he asked, his hand lingering on her waist.

She glanced at him. His blue eyes veiled, he watched her closely. At the same time, a tiny grin tugged at his lips, as if he knew exactly what he was doing to her and found a great deal of satisfaction in it.

Stiffening her spine, she forced herself to sit up. Beneath his amused stare, she regained control of her breathing. When she was finally able to look at him with a modicum of calm, she raised one eyebrow in what she hoped was an expression of cool disinterest. "Tell me, how do I punish men with bad manners?"

His grin growing to unabashed proportions, he handed her a small leather riding crop. "If he touches your waist too long, you should tap him lightly on the cheek with your crop to make your point. Should his hands wander to your hips, a more severe whack is in order, preferably to the shoulder. For the most flagrant violations, I would suggest two whacks, applied with significant force to any available part of him."

Eyes narrowed, she drew herself up to her full height and lifted the riding crop. Determined to deliver at least one whack to his solid-looking buttocks, she lifted the riding crop. "Let me practice."

With lightning reflexes, he grabbed the crop just as she flicked it downward. "Not on me."

She allowed the crop to drop to her side. "Ye are quick."

He laughed aloud. "Do you know what you remind me of? A kitten with her back up, spitting at me. A very adorable kitten, in fact. You have to learn to growl louder, kitten, and react more quickly. Such experiences are often a part of riding. Men will try to take advantage of you."

"Men like you?"

"I'll admit, I enjoy teasing you. But you needn't fear me. Your London friend may have marked me as a heartless seducer, but the duke has protected you from me well. If I dare toy with your affections, he'll see that I lose all. I'm simply trying to teach you what you may expect from men who wish to court you, and how to defend yourself from their advances."

He mounted his own horse without explaining further and took her horse's reins. Frowning, she put her leg around the pommel at the top of the saddle and faced forward, as he'd directed. They began to walk.

"Carry your weight on your right thigh and seat," he said. "Move your center of gravity forward to encourage more speed, and sit back to slow the horse down."

Heading down the gravel path, away from both the castle and the white barns, they walked into a field of dried grass that hadn't been cut the previous year. Golden in the late afternoon sunshine, it made a soft rustling sound as the horses walked through it and gave up little bits of chaff that swirled in their wake.

Lifting her chin, she glanced off into the fields beyond a hedgerow. "What did you mean by saying you'd lose all if you toyed with my affections?"

He assessed her with a swift glance. "Let your left leg hang naturally in the stirrup, with your heel down. Sit straight in the saddle, your head held high, your back slightly hollowed."

"Answer me, my lord," she countered, after following his directions.

"The duke has vowed to see that I'm permanently ostracized from society if I so much as harm a hair on your head."

"I know the duke thinks very highly of ye. Why doesn't he trust ye?"

"He and I see things differently. In his time, men only bestowed attentions on women they considered marrying. He never entered society and learned otherwise."

"And you attend to all women, and plan to marry none."

He shrugged rather than answer her directly, then added, "Edward wants only the best for you. A love match, he says. He spent too many years feeling lonely and grieving for his wife to force you into a match with a man who didn't love you."

Intrigued by his evasiveness, she studied him. "Is there someone ye wish tae marry, Colin?"

After a small hesitation, he said, "I believe in marriages of convenience. In fact, a match between you and I would make eminent sense."

Her eyes widened at the thought of being *married* to Colin, of sharing his days and his bed. To her surprise, she didn't find the notion at all horrible despite his supposedly wicked ways. In fact, heat filled her cheeks at the thought of them sharing intimacies and she shivered as a powerful yearning unexpectedly assailed her.

They passed through a hedgerow choked with fir trees, birches, and vines, and started into a vast new field. Near the end of the field, perhaps a mile away, she noticed stone cottages. Smoke curled from the chimneys of a few of them, mingling with the cool spring air and scent from the firs to form a fragrant aroma.

"But the duke has forbidden a match between us," she reminded him.

Colin's brow lowered and his mouth grew tight. He looked like he'd just felt a pain. "He cannot believe that I could ever love anyone, and assumes that if I pursued you, my sole reason for doing so would be to regain my inheritance through marriage. He protected you by threatening me with consequences he knew I couldn't live with."

"And sae I'm quite safe from ye."

"Yes. You are. He plans to marry you off to the man of your choice, once you've debuted in society."

"Then if nothing can ever exist between us, why do ye...tease me sae?"

"Because I simply can't help myself, kitten," he told her, his voice low. "There's something about you that pulls at me."

She assessed his sincerity and decided he came up short. "How many women have heard that confession?"

"None other than you."

They both fell silent. Sarah glanced his way. Brow lowered, he didn't acknowledge her regard, instead staring out across the fields. She'd expected a teasing smile from him, but this cool solemnity forced her to reassess his sincerity.

"Would you like to meet some of the duke's

tenants?" Colin asked abruptly, breaking into her thoughts.

Remembering Mrs. Fitzbottom's admonition to do just that, Sarah nodded. With luck, the tenants would shine even more light onto Colin's character. Even more importantly, those stone crofts in the distance appeared very similar to her own home. Suddenly she wanted to be among simple folk who understood and accepted her. She *needed* to be among those who lived rich lives despite their empty pockets.

"When you talk to the tenants, please try very hard to speak as Phineas taught you," he reminded her. "Otherwise, your accent will reveal your humbler origins, which the duke wishes to avoid at all costs."

A little ache tightened near her heart. "I have nae quarrel with my humbler origins. I wish the duke felt the same way."

"The duke is trying to protect you. The less that's known about your past, the easier you'll be accepted by society."

"I dinna care a bit about yer society," she informed him grudgingly, "but I'll go along with ye for the duke's sake."

"Good."

As the afternoon sunshine started to lose its strength, they continued to walk through fields and hedgerows until, at length, Colin stopped his horse and scanned the countryside. Sarah stopped, too, and when Colin apparently made up his mind about the direction they should take, they both headed off toward the south.

"Where exactly are we going?" she asked in the deepening silence between them.

"A farmer I once knew, by the name of McKay,

used to reside in a little croft near the loch. I'd like to visit him and see what has changed. Indeed, I don't even know if he still lives."

"How did ye make his acquaintance?"

"He and I worked together to improve the duke's lands several years ago."

He spurred his horse to a trot. Sarah also began to trot, her backside thumping against the saddle as she slipped around. Certain she would fall off, she tightened her right leg around the pommel, her lips pressed together in a grim, panicked line. Just as she opened her mouth to plead with him to slow down, they stopped before an old byre house.

Slate formed its roof, and moss covered its gray stone walls, which had begun to crumble. Perched on top of the stable, the house had unusually narrow window openings that suggested it might have once been a garrison. Pigs rooted around in the farmyard out front, where manure, mud, and the stink of rotting vegetables reigned. Oxen lowed from the byre below the farmhouse, and a plow sat rusting near a trough of muck-ridden water.

Colin had fixed his attention on the front porch. "I'm still expecting to see old Chiswick," he murmured mysteriously. Then he dismounted and walked to her side.

She eyed him suspiciously. "Who's Chiswick?"

"Nobody important," he insisted, shrugging elaborately.

Unconvinced, she dismounted from her horse with his assistance. As soon as her feet touched the ground, though, she discovered that her legs no longer worked. Unaccustomed to riding, they'd grown weak with the effort to keep her steady on the saddle. She sagged against him, needing his support, and after a brief hesitation he offered it, putting an arm around her shoulder.

He felt so strong, and safe, and warm, that compulsively she moved closer to him and turned slightly to face him. She hadn't planned this, and almost couldn't believe she was acting so recklessly, but she wanted his heat and strength for her own. These last two days had been awful and she needed someone to lean against.

He drew in a quick breath, and slipped an arm around her waist, pulling her even closer. She risked a glance at his face and saw that his eyebrows had drawn together in an expression resembling pain. He buried his nose in her hair and whispered softly, something she couldn't quite hear.

Trembling now, she turned to face him fully, like a flower turning toward the sun. Her gaze dropped to his full, sensuous lips, and she noticed the white lines around his mouth, lines of strain. He held her even tighter, his own attention fastened on her mouth, and she felt him shaking ever so slightly against her, as though he were trying to resist some wild impulse.

And yet, she knew he couldn't resist. Neither could she. As his mouth descended to hers, she could see dark rim around the lighter blue of his eyes. They were so close, she thought, almost as one, but not yet. Her heart pounding, she recognized that there was still time to stop this madness.

Treacherously her arms slipped around his broad shoulders almost of their own accord. She parted her lips and closed her eyes, praying that he would kiss her, and praying equally as hard that he would release her and allow her to remain innocent.

A tortured moan escaped him. Ever so gently, he leaned forward and kissed her mouth.

The pressure of his lips against hers, and the intimacy of it, shocked her. She stood absolutely still. Sensations assaulted her: the smell of his shaving lotion, the firmness of his lips against her much softer mouth, the hard body pressed against hers, the feel of his stubbled chin rubbing against hers.

Heat curled through her thighs and belly. Involuntarily her hips moved against his. A longing was building in her, though for what, she didn't know.

At her movement, he groaned again, low in his throat, and pulled his mouth from hers. Breathing hard, his hair mussed, he turned toward the byre house. "I never meant to kiss you, Sarah. Please forgive me."

Sarah looked away, her lips tingling. Her own breath coming fast, she ran her hands over her skirt, as if by smoothing them she was hiding the marks of his kiss. "Why *did* ye kiss me?"

He swore softly, then turned her until she faced him. "You're like a fire in my blood. I can't think of anyone or anything else." He punched his thigh lightly with a closed fist. "God help me for following my impulses this afternoon. We both risk ruin because of it."

She focused on his shirtfront. She understood very well that the duke would never condone a match between herself and Colin. What was she doing anyway, thinking about a husband? She planned on returning to her village and her animals. Didn't she?

Confusion and a wrenching sense of loss replaced the warmth that Colin's kiss had brought her.

Someone coughed. Colin moved away from her hastily. Sarah realized they'd dismounted behind a screen of trees that concealed them, if not their horses, and was thankful for it.

An old man hobbled out the byre house's front door and down the steps. Squinting, the old man drew close to their horses.

Colin stepped from behind the trees.

"Mr. Colin? Is that ye?" the farmer asked.

"Yes, McKay. It's me."

"By God, I thought ye were dead." McKay turned to Sarah with a questioning air.

"McKay," Colin said, gesturing toward Sarah, "may I present Lady Sarah, the Duke of Argyll's long-lost daughter?"

The old man's eyebrows climbed high as he inspected her. When he'd finished, a smile brightened his face and he offered her an awkward bow. "Pleased tae meet ye, my lady."

Sarah smiled. She knew McKay's type very well. In fact, he reminded her very much of Mr. Porter, the farmer whose lamb she'd delivered the day the duke had come to Beannach.

One of the very old school, she guessed McKay lived frugally, cared for only a select few, and was fond of a few drops of whiskey—perhaps too many. Muscles that had once strengthened his thin frame had long ago gone to flab, and his hair had deserted him as well, leaving him with a gray-fringed pate. Veins crisscrossed his nose and cheeks, but his eyes were penetrating, despite their clouded and bloodshot condition. He was smart, but old, and weary of chasing sheep around the pasture.

Thinking of her accent, she dropped him a curtsy

and greeted him as briefly as possible. " 'Tis lovely tae meet ye."

McKay looked at her with incomprehension in his eyes, and she realized he hadn't heard her. Like many older farmers, he had probably become slightly deaf.

Still, she didn't repeat her greeting; instead, she smiled and nodded.

"Where are ye from, my lady?" McKay asked.

"My lady prefers not to dwell on the past," Colin answered for her. "Rather, she is touring the estate to learn about its present strengths and weaknesses."

"Ye'll find Inveraray more strong than weak," McKay stoutly declared.

Colin smiled. "May we come in and sit for a while, McKay?"

"Of course ye may. The missus would sae enjoy seeing ye." McKay led them across the farmyard, up the steps, and through his front door.

An elderly woman stood near an open-hearth fireplace, tending an iron pot that hung over the fire. She appeared so stout that Sarah suspected she had to go through the door sideways. As soon as the woman saw them, the kindest smile that Sarah had ever witnessed lightened her features, and she rushed over to Colin.

"Oh, Mr. Colin, how good of ye tae visit us. Lord, we wondered what had happened tae ye. Sit down here, and tell us where ye've been." She patted a chair by the kitchen table, a roughhewn affair with many scratches to attest to its years of service.

"Mrs. McKay, it's a pleasure to see both you and your husband are well," Colin said, smiling. A slight flush had risen in his cheeks.

He's embarrassed, Sarah thought.

"Oh, by heavens, I didna see the lady. Forgive me." Mrs. McKay moved next to Sarah and put her arm around Sarah's shoulders. "Good day tae ye, my lady."

"And tae ye, Mrs. McKay," Sarah said, striving to mimic the tempo and resonance of Colin's speech. She knew she didn't sound exactly like Colin, but nor did she sound like a so-called peasant.

Colin gave her an approving nod, clearly pleased with her effort. "May I present the duke's newfound daughter, Lady Sarah."

The ample woman threw herself into a full curtsy, and gushed, "Oh, my lady, what a pleasure. Mr. McKay and I have been hoping tae meet ye."

Sarah smiled and nodded in response. She saw no sense in opening her mouth at every opportunity and pushing her luck.

"Sit down, and let me get ye something tae drink," Mrs. McKay urged them.

Colin and Sarah followed Mr. McKay to the kitchen table, where they all sat themselves. At the same time, Mrs. McKay went back to the iron pot and lifted its lid. The delicious scent of hot apple cider filled the room. "I used the last of my fall apples today. Who would like some cider?"

They all asked for some. Mrs. McKay filled four pewter mugs with hot cider and handed one to each. Sarah took a sip and sighed in appreciation. This was what she missed most—simple fare and simple company.

As they drank, Colin asked McKay to catch him up on estate matters, and for the next ten minutes, the old man regaled Colin with stories about fields and plowing and tenants who resisted agricultural improvements. He praised Colin for his past efforts in Inveraray and told him how much they'd all missed his fine judgment.

Colin listened attentively to everything McKay said and suggested solutions to certain difficulties, displaying knowledge more suited to a farmer than an aristocrat. Once or twice, Colin said nothing, but simply appeared concerned.

Sarah could see that a bond existed between the two men, one that went deeper than usual. She remembered the duke telling her that Colin had once brought the estate back from the brink of bankruptcy, and realized she was seeing the old Colin now, the Colin that the duke wanted back.

Her sense of Colin's dual nature deepened.

This, she mused, was a man to whom others looked to for strength. They trusted him. And based on the comments regarding Colin's long absence, they probably felt betrayed by him, too.

"It's been a long time since we've seen Mr. Colin," Mrs. McKay said softly to her, drawing her into a conversation separate from the men's. "How long ago did he arrive at Inveraray?"

A little nervous at the thought of having a full-blown conversation with Mrs. McKay, she knew she nevertheless had to try to talk to the older woman. This was her first real test as the duke's daughter. She glanced around the kitchen, finding familiarity in the rough slate floor and the scratch-molded shelving. When she saw the tortoiseshell cat curled up on a tattered wool blanket, within arm's reach, she petted the cat, knowing from the soft rumble in its throat that it appreciated her efforts. Gratitude toward Colin, for allowing her to practice being an aristocrat with an audience she felt comfortable with, filled her.

"Colin arrived just before me," Sarah answered. She tilted her head thoughtfully. "Mrs. McKay, who is Chiswick?"

Eyes widening, the farmer's wife pressed a hand to her ample bosom. "Did Mr. Colin mention Chiswick?" At Sarah's confirming nod, she went on, "I didna think he would remember Chiswick. That old dog has been dead for over a decade now."

"Chiswick was a *dog?*"

Mrs. McKay laughed. "A bonny little dog was Chiswick. He used tae chase our sheep around the pasture. For some reason, he took a liking tae young Mr. Colin."

"Colin said he was still expecting tae see Chiswick on the porch when we rode up," Sarah revealed.

"Aye, Mr. Colin took a liking tae Chiswick, too. I still remember the day that dog died. Chiswick got in the way of old man Rindley's pony cart and got dragged half a mile down the road. There wasn't much left to him when Rindley stopped. Rindley couldn't see two feet in front of him, and I'm surprised he didn't kill more than just Chiswick."

Sarah made a sympathetic noise, guessing by the tone of Mrs. McKay's voice that losing Chiswick had been hard.

The farmer's wife sighed. "Mr. Colin found Chiswick's mangled body and buried him on the spot, in a fine wool jacket right off his back. Would ye believe Rindley had the nerve tae complain about it when he discovered the grave on his land a week later? Said it would make his cows give bloody milk.

"So Mr. Colin dug Chiswick up and burned him on a bunch of logs he set aflame." Mrs. McKay's voice dropped a notch. "Superstition aside, I think

the fact that Rindley didn't want Chiswick buried on
his land bothered Mr. Colin terribly. He seemed tae
take it as a personal insult. You see, everyone knew
how Mr. Colin loved that dog, and how the dog loved
him, and for a while the two were inseparable.
When Rindley refused to have Chiswick's body on
his land, it was as though he were telling Mr. Colin
that Mr. Colin was a bad seed and anything that
touched him was corrupt. After that, I never saw Mr.
Colin take tae an animal again."

Sarah shook her head. Again, Colin had opened
his heart and been rejected and pushed aside. "How
terrible for him."

"Aye, it was."

The two women fell into a comfortable silence,
Sarah imagining how the courage to love had been
squeezed out of him inch by inch. After a time, Mrs.
McKay leaned close and murmured, "If I don't inter-
rupt them, they'll go on all night."

She tapped Colin on the arm. "I wish we'd ken yer
visit, Mr. Colin. There are many who'd have liked tae
say hello tae ye."

"Tell them to come to me at Inveraray," Colin offered. He reached into his jacket and pulled out a
small leather pouch. "I'd be happy to see them."

"I didna mean we needed yer help," she chided,
her attention on the pouch.

"I know." Colin took Mrs. McKay by the hand,
pressed the pouch into her palm, and closed her fingers around it.

McKay took the pouch. When he opened it and
peered inside, coins clinked against each other.
Moisture filled his eyes. "Bless ye."

"Ye're a good man," Mrs. McKay pronounced

with another of her kind smiles. "We've missed ye sorely."

"We have at that," McKay added in gruff tones. "When I hear about the treatment some of my friends are receiving at the hands of their chieftains, it makes me verra angry, and sorry fer them, too. Many of them have been driven off their land tae make grazing lands fer sheep."

"The clearances," Sarah murmured, frowning.

"Aye, the clearances. I thank God every day that we have chieftains like yerself and the duke tae watch over us."

Acknowledging the other man's comment with a nod, Colin stood. "Thank you for your hospitality, Mrs. McKay. My lady, we should be going."

"Of course." Sarah stood. "Thank you both."

Colin took her arm just below the elbow. He led her out of the house and over to her horse, where he helped her mount. Then, he swung atop his own horse and they both waved as they rode away from the byre house.

As they headed back to the castle, Sarah spoke aloud what had been on her mind since the moment they'd left. "Does the duke ever intend tae clear his lands like the other chieftains?"

"The duke isn't one to place profit over family," Colin replied. "His tenants will always have homes on his land."

"He's better than most, then." Sarah hesitated, her new position in society becoming even clearer to her. "I can see that being the duke's daughter is more than going tae parties and speaking with a pretty accent."

"It's a great responsibility. When you become the Duchess of Argyll, you'll have many people depending on you for their very lives. One decision on your part could affect an entire town."

"It's not a responsibility. It's a burden."

"It all depends on how you look at it. You once lived in a village and, from your account of it, you lived very poorly. You probably also knew families who had been evicted from their lands as part of their chieftain's plan to turn homes into grazing lands."

"I did," she admitted.

"Well, then, think of your new position this way: the duke has offered you a great gift. As his daughter, you'll be able to end the suffering of others like you—if, of course, you choose to do so."

Sarah felt everything go still inside her. Such a thought had never even occurred to her. Helping sick animals had always brought her such satisfaction; how would she feel if she were able to help whole families as well? A tiny bud of excitement unfurled within her.

"I can see by your silence that I've given you something to mull over," Colin said.

"Aye, ye have."

They both grew quiet for a time, the silence between them a comfortable one. Thinking of the pouch he'd turned over to Mr. McKay, she eventually murmured, "It's amazing tae think how easily a pouch of coins could save the lives of several families."

"The duke keeps his tenants well-heeled. The sovereigns I gave the McKays will buy McKay a new pipe and his wife a lace apron. But there are other clans outside of the duke's in dire need. I've seen such families all over England. The problem is so huge I doubt we'll ever end it."

Intuition told her that he was more generous

than he allowed. "But you help where you can, regardless of the clan name."

"Yes, I occasionally do. So I can sleep at night." He shrugged. "Sometimes a good night's sleep doesn't come cheap. Sometimes it can be the most precious thing in the world. If a couple of gold sovereigns buy me a solid rest, then I consider it a fine bargain. And I haven't been sleeping very well lately."

"Why nae?"

He rubbed his chin with two long fingers. "I'm not certain. I think I've been away from Inveraray for too long."

"Ye surprise me, Colin. I can't understand how someone whose heart is sae generous can lead such an indulgent life."

"You have a distorted idea of both my generosity and wickedness. I can see why you might think I'm Robin Hood in disguise, given McKay's glowing accounts—which were a bit embroidered—but I wish I knew where you had learned of my wickedness. If only you would tell me who wrote you that letter—" He paused, clearly giving her a chance to unburden herself, which she chose to ignore. "But since you will not, let me confess my own beliefs in the origins of my debauchery. The simple truth, Sarah, is that I enjoy sensual things. Things that make me *feel*: fast horses, beautiful women, a rousing game of chance, anything physical. 'Tis a certain weakness of character which I frequently regret but cannot deny."

Sarah noticed his horse twitching its tail in a peculiar manner. A glance up ahead confirmed that a branch hung low. Colin's horse was heading straight for it. The horse was about to have his long-awaited revenge. "And yet you possess this generosity that is anything but weak."

"It's a generosity that I've ignored in favor of other pursuits," he admitted. "Until now. I suspect its rekindling is due to a strong new influence in my life—"

At that moment, his horse plunged gleefully under the branch, catching him across the chest. Air left his lungs in a loud puff. The branch dragged him backward and swept him right off his horse's back. Clearly stunned, he sat in a puddle of mud, holding his backside and staring at his horse, who had stopped to wait for him.

"You mangy, flea-bitten carcass," he finally said, his voice low and threatening. He stood, revealing a pair of breeches stained brown in the seat, and approached the horse with lowered brows. "How would you like a trip to the knacker's? One more stunt like that, my friend, and that's where you'll end up."

The horse's ears twitched in a disagreeable way.

Sarah couldn't quite muffle a laugh. "Yer not just a man of the senses. I'd say yer also a man with dirt on his pants."

❖ 10 ❖

The rest of the week passed in a dreary fashion, with rain pounding at the windowsills nearly every day. Sarah spent little time with Colin during that week. He always had something else to do. She wondered if he were avoiding her. Had she committed a social blunder she wasn't aware of?

Rather, she sat with Phineas in the dining room and went over etiquette, seating arrangements, and forms of address until she thought she would scream. Phineas also drilled her on her speech with all the aplomb of a sergeant major, until finally, at the end of the day, she broke down and called him every awful name she could think of—behind his back, of course.

But her speech improved. Mainly because she wanted it to. She'd been thinking long and hard about what Colin had said. A large part of her was leaning toward fulfilling her role as the duke's daughter. She could accomplish so many good things with the power of the Argyll name behind her. And she'd discovered over the weeks, after spending a great deal of time in the duke's company talking and laughing, that there was much to love in the man who called himself her father.

And yet, despite all of this rationalization, the thought of giving up her croft, her animals, and her freedom and embracing this pampered world still made her uneasy.

Now she sat before the windows with Mrs. Fitzbottom, trying to capitalize on what little light the day offered. Heavy clouds raced overhead and sheets of rain spread across the lawn, adding to her gloomy state of mind. But the nonsensical task to which Mrs. Fitzbottom had set her really bothered her the most. Who in her right mind would sit for hours in front of a petticoat and embroider its hem with colorful thread? No one would ever see the petticoat. Surely her time could be put to better use.

"That's right, lass," Mrs. Fitzbottom encouraged her, a pair of spectacles sitting on the end of her housekeeper's nose. She, too, had an embroidery hoop set up before her. She was putting some flowers on the ends of pillowcases destined for the guest bedrooms. "Your stitches should be close enough together that you do not see the linen beneath, but not bunched on top of each other. The embroidered area should look like satin."

"Satin." Sarah gritted her teeth. Her eyes felt near to crossing. "Mrs. Fitz, I cannot do any more of this today."

The housekeeper sat back from her hoop and looked over the edge of her glasses at Sarah. "You know, my dear, I've just about had enough, too. Why don't we take a short break before you begin your next lesson?"

"My next lesson? Please don't tell me that Phineas

plans to berate me over my sad poverty of language again."

"Didn't I tell you? Mr. Colin has volunteered to give you your first lesson in reading."

Sarah grew still. A few days ago she'd admitted to the duke that she knew enough of letters to get by at the general store in Beannach, but not much more. The duke had immediately pressed Colin into teaching her to read better. Now, she tried to imagine sitting nose-to-nose with Colin, pouring over some dusty tome, and knew very well that her thoughts would be far from bookish. A flicker of excitement stirred within her. "When is he coming?"

"Why, any moment now."

"Where has he been this past week? I've hardly seen him, even at dinner."

"He's been involved in estate matters. I have to admit, it's good to have him back at Inveraray."

Sarah couldn't imagine Inveraray without him, either. She dreaded the moment when he completed her training and returned to London.

A short time later Colin entered, bringing with him a breeze of warm air that smelled faintly of spice. He looked very solid and strong this morning, she thought, in a green coat that outlined his shoulders and tapered down to a trim waist. In fact, a fresh and energetic aura clung to him, and Sarah found herself glancing at the window, to see if the sun had come out. But no, clouds still ruled the skies. The brightness in the room came solely from Colin.

"How have you been?" he asked, his tone offhand, as Mrs. Fitzbottom excused herself.

Sarah watched the housekeeper go with a fluttering in her belly. Would this lesson, like the riding lesson, end in a kiss? God help her, she hoped so.

"Phineas has kept me working very hard," she replied, barely preventing herself from adding that the lessons, without Colin's presence, had lost their luster.

"And your friend, the one the stag told you about. How is he? Or she?"

"My friend is no better," she admitted.

Over the last four weeks, she'd made a point of taking a walk or a ride across the grounds at least once a day, usually with a footman whom she could bully into allowing her some privacy. During these private moments she would talk to the animal friends she'd made, including the stag she'd met on the day she arrived. Always she searched for the unicorn.

In fact, just yesterday she'd walked through the woods and questioned as many of the forest's creatures she could find about the unicorn. The few that had seen the white beast told the same tale: he was sick, and coming to find her. Her worry had grown with each day, and her walks had been lengthening until even the duke had remarked on her love of nature.

"Can I help in any way?" Colin asked, drawing her back to the present.

She shook her head *no*. "I have to find him before I help him."

"I wish you would confide in me."

"If I need help, my lord, I'll ask you first."

A heavy sigh escaped him. "You have to learn to trust people, Sarah."

"Where have you been these last weeks?" The

question was out of her mouth before she could stop it.

He looked away, put his hands in his pockets, and walked over to the windows looking out on the carriageway. "I've been busy, too."

"Doing what?"

"Riding across the estate, and thinking. Trying to forget how you make me feel. And trying to decide what to do with my life," he replied huskily.

At his words, her heart thumped, and she fought the urge to fly into his embrace. Instead, in a small tight voice, she asked, "How do I make you feel?"

He turned to face her then, his brows drawn together and his mouth thinned as if with pain, and she stiffened, knowing that he was about to say something very important.

Instead, though, he simply asked, "Are you ready to learn how to read?"

Deflated, she let out the breath she didn't even know she'd been holding. The need to press him further about his feelings for her burned in her veins like fire, but she didn't quite have the nerve to do so. She was partly afraid of what he might reveal. "I am."

He led her over to a shelf of books about waist high. "This is where the books written solely for reading pleasure are kept. They contain no treatises, nor are particularly useful for anything other than one's amusement. Why don't you select one?"

"All right." She strolled back and forth before the library shelf, until a little book bound in blue cloth, which was nearly hidden behind some other larger tomes, attracted her attention. Judging by the well-worn cover and dog-eared page corners, the book had been read often and was much loved. A quick turn through the pages told her nothing about the story. Shrugging, she plucked the book from the shelf and returned to his side.

He dragged two chairs over to a desk and gestured for her to sit down. She did so, handing him the book as she fluffed her skirts beneath her. Once they'd both comfortably arranged themselves, Colin opened the book and glanced at the title.

Unaccountably, he reddened slightly. A muffled oath escaped him.

Startled by his reaction, she leaned close to examine the page, and saw a gold-stamped title. The wording had nearly worn off. "Obviously this book has been very well read. What is it called?"

He closed the book with a sharp *snap*. "It's a book by John Cleland, called *Fanny Hill*. I didn't know the duke considered it a favorite of his. Regardless, it isn't an appropriate book for *you*."

Her curiosity thoroughly aroused, she stared at him. "Why ever not?"

"It deals with indelicate matters. You're far too young for such knowledge."

"Too young?" She bristled. "Do you think me a child? I'm a grown woman, more than capable of handling *anything* you have to teach me."

"This is inappropriate reading for a lady," he insisted. "It delves into society's more sordid side—"

"Aren't you responsible for teaching me how to survive in society?"

"Well, yes—"

"Then I demand we read this book. I don't want my knowledge of society limited to pretty dresses, balls, music, and bonbons. I want to know the dangers, too."

To Tame a Wild Heart

He shrugged, his eyes glinting. "Very well, then,
my lady. Read it we shall. But don't say I didn't warn
you."

"Fine." Determined to have the knowledge he
would withhold from her, she turned past the title
and to the first page. Immediately she recognized
the form of the writing as similar to the letter she'd
received from Lady Helmsgate in London.

"Why, it's a series of letters," she said.

"Not letters. Memoirs. Recollections of Fanny
Hill's life, given in letter form. Read here, as best as
you can."

Taking a deep breath, she spoke aloud. "Madam, I
sit down to give you an…" She stumbled, not knowing the word.

"Undeniable," Colin supplied.

"Undeniable proof of my…"

He nodded encouragingly. "Considering."

"Considering your desires as…"

"Indispensable."

"…indispensable orders," she finished triumphantly.

"Very good. Now I'll read." he directed. "Try to
follow along."

He bent his head close to hers, the scent of him
reminding her of his masculinity. For the next
several minutes, he spoke of the personal history
of one Frances Hill, born at a small village near
Liverpool, in Lancashire, of parents extremely
poor. For the most part, he skipped around from
page to page, just reading selected passages that
hinted at things Sarah simply didn't understand.
Overall, she thought she and Fanny Hill had lived
very similar lives…until Colin stopped reading at

the part where Fanny, who had gone to London to seek her fortune, accidentally witnesses a lover's tryst.

"I'm going to stop here," he said. "Do you understand what's happened to Fanny?"

Sarah shook her head. "Truly I don't. Why is Fanny's benefactress telling her all of those things about the mysteries of Venus?"

Amusement gleamed in his eyes. "Fanny's innocence has placed her in a very bad situation. The woman who took her in is a madam, and the madam's apartments are a bawdy house."

She swallowed. "Oh."

"Would you like to choose another book?"

"No. I fought hard to have this book read, and now I'm going to read it."

"This is knowledge which you shouldn't have."

"This is knowledge I want."

"I can think of other ways to teach you."

Her gaze flew to his. She saw desire there, smoldering embers that needed only the slightest breath of wind to flare to life. She was unable to look away.

"I want *you* to read, now." He turned a couple of pages, and then pointed. "Start here. I'll correct you where necessary."

"All right." Her voice ragged, she began to read again. She stumbled over several words, requiring Colin's correction:

> As he stood on one side, for a minute or so, unbuttoning his waist-coat and breeches, her fat, brawny thighs hung down, and the whole greasy landscape lay fairly open to my view; a

wide open-mouth'd gap, overshaded with a grizzly bush, seemed held out like a beggar's wallet for its provision.

At the end of the passage, she grimaced. "This reminds me of a sow giving birth."

He laughed aloud. "Yes, it does. Read the rest."

"All right." She focused again on the book.

But I soon had my eyes called off by a more striking object, that entirely engross'd them.

She paused to glance at him. "A striking object?"

His smile slow, he brushed a stray lock of hair away from her temple. "Your reading is improving tremendously, just in this one short lesson."

She bent her head back over the little blue book, which looked innocuous from the outside but in fact was a regular fount of forbidden knowledge.

Her sturdy stallion had now unbutton'd, and produced naked, stiff, and erect, that wonderful machine, which I had never seen before, and which, for the interest my own seat of pleasure began to take furiously in it....

She broke off and fanned herself. "This is quite remarkable."

With a laziness that stole her breath away, he traced a finger across her lips. "Quite remarkable," he confirmed.

Quivering from his touch, she refocused on the book.

*Whilst they were in the heat of the action,
guided by nature only, I stole my hand up my
petticoats, and with fingers all on fire, seized,
and yet more inflamed that center of all my
senses: my heart palpitated, as if it would force
its way through my bosom; I breath'd with pain;
I twisted my thighs, squeezed and compressed
the lips of that...*

She trailed off, embarrassed and terribly overheated. The room was so hot she thought she might
faint. "I can read no more."

"I'll finish it," he offered, his lips brushing against
her exposed ear ever so lightly. She choked back a
moan.

He began reading, his voice possessing an odd lilt
to it, a throaty quality that roused her almost as
much as his kiss had:

*...and compressed the lips of that virgin slit, and
following mechanically the example of Phoebe's
manual operation on it, as far as I could find admission, brought on at last the critical extasy,
the melting flow, into which nature, spent with
excess of pleasure, dissolves and dies away.*

His narrative trailed off, leaving a highly charged
silence in the room. She took the book from him
and closed it, bewildered yet tantalized by many
things she'd heard this afternoon. "What is this critical ecstasy?"

He smiled. "You'll have to find out by yourself."

Eyes downcast, she turned the book over in her
hands, ostensibly studying its cover but not really

seeing it at all. Yearning for him brought a flush of warmth to her secret places. "Perhaps you would teach me," she murmured, her face growing hot with her own boldness.

"I suggest you take *Fanny Hill* upstairs to your bedchamber," he said, "for some private reading instead, in case you can't sleep."

Feeling even more embarrassed at his gentle rebuff, she arched an eyebrow. "You know very well that I won't sleep a second."

"Neither will I, my lady." With one last lingering glance, he stood and made his way to the study door. "Neither will I."

The next four weeks proved torturous for Colin. While he read to Sarah and took her riding and taught her to read, he otherwise did little to satisfy his growing desire for her, one both physical and spiritual. Now he could barely look at her without becoming rock-hard, his body aching for release between her soft white thighs, even as he wished to claim her purity and sweetness for himself...forever.

He recognized that he'd begun to count on her presence beside him every afternoon on their horseback tour of the grounds. Her delightful, and sometimes haunting stories of her past in the Highlands fascinated him, and her practical, if earthy advice often had him laughing, even as he recognized the value in it. At night, he contented himself with merely watching her across the dining room table and later, in the drawing room.

Hour by hour, she was becoming increasingly essential to his existence. Her laughter, her smiles, her soft touch on his arm when he revealed some painful incident from his childhood were a balm to his wounds. Even though it scared the hell out of him, he knew he could stop himself from feeling this way no sooner than he could leave Inveraray itself.

And yet, June had already come and gone. He had less than two months left before she debuted and found a husband, while he returned to London and his old, now unappealing ways. Her debut had now become linked to disaster in his mind. The mere thought of it was enough to send his mood spiraling downward.

This morning, he and Phineas had agreed to meet and discuss Sarah's progress. When the duke's man of business appeared in the study, Colin pushed away from his desk, stood, and invited Phineas to have a seat on one of the chairs clustered in an informal circle near the hearth.

Phineas, the very picture of propriety in his severe black suit and gray hair styled *a la Brutus*, selected a hard-backed chair. Colin sat across from him and engaged him in a few minutes of desultory conversation, chat about the weather and various estate problems. At length, however, they got down to the real business of the day.

"How is she doing, in your opinion?" Colin asked, stretching his feet out in front of him. "Do you think she'll be ready for her debut?"

Phineas observed him with a grave expression. "Her accent is greatly improved."

"Yes, I've noticed. But will people believe she's the duke's daughter?"

"She's coming along quite well with regard to manners at formal meals, and has nearly memorized the various forms of address and standard seating arrangements for members of the aristocracy. We've also discussed the more delicate matters of etiquette, such as dealing with self-invited guests, problem drinkers, obnoxious guests, and the guest who simply won't leave."

"So she might be able to hostess a fete at this point, as long as she didn't have to dance," Colin surmised.

"Yes, it's possible she could."

"You don't sound very confident, Phineas."

"Well, there is so much left for her to learn, such as dancing, and singing, and household management. To make matters worse, she doesn't possess the basic skills upon which these other abilities build. For example, how can she approve Mrs. Fitzbottom's dinner menus if she can't read properly?"

"I've been helping to improve her reading skills. We've had three lessons so far. Her progress is exceptional." Colin didn't add that all of those lessons had been focused on *Fanny Hill*, at Sarah's insistence.

"Thank God for that," Phineas muttered, then shot an apologetic look at Colin. "Pardon, my lord, I did not mean to sound critical—"

"No offense taken. These past weeks have been trying for us all."

The two men fell silent, Colin thinking of their most recent lesson, where the beguiling floral scent of her hair had dared him to press a kiss against the tender spot at the back of her neck.

"And the riding lessons?" Phineas asked after a while. "Has she learned how to ride properly?"

"She looks very natural in the saddle," Colin observed, remembering the way the horses always fawned over her, as though she were the queen of all things equine.

"Her riding skills are good, then?"

"Very good."

Phineas narrowed his eyes. "Have you ever noticed how well she gets along with animals? I've seen her with His Grace's dogs on occasion. They're completely infatuated. Usually the dogs will growl at anyone they don't know from birth."

Colin shrugged, trying to appear unconcerned. "I see nothing unusual in the dogs' behavior toward her. In fact, they're friends with more than a few of the duke's tenants, whom they certainly didn't know at birth."

Phineas's shoulders slumped. "Perhaps it's just me they don't like."

Colin sought to divert him. "I've taken Sarah on several rides across the property. She now has a good grasp of the estate and its tenants."

And he'd had more than an eyeful of her luscious curves and jaunty veil, which whipped him in the face if he came too close. Although he hadn't surrendered to his desire to kiss her deeply, he wondered how much longer his resistance would hold.

Phineas shook his head. "If only she didn't possess such a keen interest in animal husbandry, she should get along very well. It's a most unsuitable occupation for any duke's daughter."

Colin nodded. "Several of our rides across the property have ended in some farmer's barn, with Sarah peering into a sheep's mouth."

"God forbid." Phineas shuddered. "She must give this up."

"The duke has asked her to. She refuses."

"Did you hear that her fox raided cook's henhouse for a third time last night?"

Colin frowned. "I understood she had taken measures to keep the fox from the hens."

"Apparently her measures haven't proven successful. The duke plans to ask her to allow him to cage it."

"I don't imagine she'll agree."

"He'll have a fight on his hands, to be sure."

A knock at the door interrupted further conversation. At Colin's request, a footman bearing a silver tray entered.

"The post has arrived." The footman extended the tray toward Colin.

Colin took the letters. While he idly sorted through them, the footman continued, "Mr. Cooper is here to see you, my lord. Shall I show him in?"

Paying him only half attention, Colin examined a letter to Sarah. Her name and address were written in a feminine hand, with lots of loops and flowery tails. The letter had no return address. He lifted the envelope to his nose and sniffed.

Honeysuckle. He'd smelled that scent before. Perhaps on a woman he'd known? He couldn't remember. Lost in thought, he tapped one end of the letter against his palm. "Lady Sarah's London friend has written again."

"Who?" Phineas asked.

He fixed Phineas with a gaze. "Do you know who Lady Sarah's London friend is?"

"No, I don't, my lord."

He frowned, his mood growing darker. Over the last several weeks he'd grown embarrassed of his hellish reputation and the intimate skills such a reputation demanded he possess. He wanted her to think him honorable, rather than practiced in the art of seduction. One might think, judging by the way he was carrying on, that he wanted to marry her. But he couldn't marry her, not if he ever wished to visit a London drawing room again. The duke would instantly see him ostracized from society.

Colin focused on the footman. "Who did you say has come to call?"

"A Mr. Cooper, my lord."

"Cooper! Bring him in at once. Phineas, can we continue later?"

"Of course, my lord." Phineas rose from his chair and offered Colin a quick bow.

As Phineas exited, Colin asked the footman to show Mr. Cooper in. A few moments later the servant was ushering the Bow Street runner into the chair Phineas had vacated.

"Good day, Cooper," Colin said, once the runner had settled in. "I hope you have some news for me."

"Indeed I have, my lord." The other man's voice held a note of enthusiasm. "I went to the scene of the accident," Cooper revealed, "and investigated the spot where the carriage allegedly went over the cliff. While I was there, I saw a ship not too far out in the North Sea. Apparently, the shipping lanes to Inverness are quite close to shore at that point."

Colin nodded. "Go on."

"I then visited Beannach, the village my lady grew up in. I confirmed her story with the Baron of Beannach and a few other locals."

"Were you able to find out anything else?"

"I have discovered something interesting, but it's a difficult piece of information."

"Difficult? In what way?"

"I had to promise to keep the man's confidentiality before he would speak, and it cost me plenty."

"Expenses are no object. I'll reimburse you."

The runner nodded, clearly pleased. "Will you promise to take no action on what I tell you?"

"I won't make any promises."

"Then I can say nothing, my lord."

"Cooper, for God's sake, explain to me what you've learned."

"Not without your word that this man will remain untouched."

"Is there no other way?"

"I have a reputation to maintain. If I betray my informant, others may refuse to confide in me."

"All right, I give my word. Now who is this man?"

✻ 11 ✻

The Bow Street runner's tone grew confidential. "I've found one of the original brigands who chased the duke's carriage over the cliff."

A hush descended over the study.

His lips thinning, Colin grew still. After a time, he murmured, "I gave you my word, Cooper, but I'm having a damned hard time keeping it."

"You must, my lord."

Jaw tight, Colin clenched his fists. "What did he say?"

"He gave me the particulars of the accident, which we already know. He also confirmed my lady's story, along with Phineas Graham's."

"Did you discover anything new?"

"Only that the man saw a ship at the time the carriage plunged over the cliff. He said it was far to the north and moving very slowly southward."

"Phineas Graham noticed the ship as well," Colin said impatiently. "Why should we care about a ship?"

The runner shrugged. "The ship's crew couldn't possibly have witnessed any details of the accident.

They were too far out to sea. However, I've discovered that the tide was coming in around the time the carriage tumbled over the cliff. Perhaps the tide might have picked up the wreckage from the accident and brought it out to sea, near the ship. They might even have found a body."

"I don't think it very likely." Colin spoke softly.

"But not impossible, eh?"

"No, not impossible. I don't want to leave anything unconfirmed. Do you think you could identify the ship, even after almost twenty years?"

"Most of the larger ports like Inverness keep records of ships' comings and goings for decades. Since I know the approximate time it passed the cliff, I can guess when it made port in Inverness."

"In that case, I want you to go to Inverness and examine their accounting books. Find out where that ship came from, who owned it, and where it was going. See if you can locate anyone who remembers sailing on it."

"I'll go immediately." Cooper nearly quivered with excitement, reminding Colin of a bloodhound who had just caught a fox's scent. He stood up from his chair and started for the door.

"And Cooper," Colin added, just as the other man reached the threshold, "you've done a first-rate job so far. Expect a healthy bonus if you manage to track this ship down."

"Don't worry. I'll find it."

As he watched the runner go, Colin had no doubt that the man would, indeed, locate someone who had sailed on that ship. His reputation as the finest bloodhound in England was well deserved.

Colin's attention drifted back to the letter Sarah

had received from London. Its soft white surface
and flowery penmanship looked innocuous enough,
but Colin had no doubt it contained poison of the
most vicious kind. Silently he cursed the shrew that
kept sending Sarah these notes. Sarah invariably
treated him to days of betrayed looks after one arrived.

Who, he wondered, could it be? Lady Helmsgate,
perhaps? The blond woman had certainly revealed a
fine temper to him on the day he'd left London for
Inveraray. Remembering her vow that she hadn't finished with him yet, Colin could very easily imagine
her sabotaging him in this way.

He picked the letter up, stuffed it into his coat
pocket, and left the study for Sarah's bedchamber.
That tedious French modiste had arrived about an
hour earlier and had asked him to attend Sarah's
final fitting. In her first fitting, Sarah hadn't trusted
the modiste's opinion and had balked at many of her
suggestions. The modiste, at her wit's end, had requested Colin's presence, and thereafter things had
gone much more smoothly. Now he was required to
attend every fitting—a task that tormented him, considering it afforded many opportunities to glimpse
Sarah's ankles and curves.

He heard the modiste in the hallway before he
even reached the bedchamber.

"Please, my lady, you must try and understand.
You cannot wear anything but white for your debut.
It isn't proper for you to wear the yellow gown."

"Why must I wear white? To appear virginal?"
Sarah snorted. "Look at the bodice on this gown.
Good Lord, no one will think me virginal, regardless
of what color I wear."

Smiling at her tartness, Colin knocked softly on the sitting room door. "May I come in?"

"Yes, my lord," the modiste cried.

He entered and shut the door behind him. His gaze went immediately to Sarah and remained there. His lips parted. He thought he had never seen her look quite so stunning...and so very strange.

Her hair was swept upward into a mass of glossy black curls held in place by a gold ribbon. A white satin court gown hugged her curves, its form-fitting nature partially disguised by a matching white silk tunic that flowed around her. Gold bands embroidered with Grecian figures decorated the hem and criss-crossed over her breasts.

"You'd look like a goddess," he observed, "if not for that muck on your face."

Sarah grimaced. "Good morning, Colin."

He walked a tight circle around her, loving everything he saw except for the white paste on her face. "Is that substance on your face the newest trend in lady's fashions?"

"No, it's a skin conditioning cream. Mrs. Fitz insists I wear it for at least an hour a day. She says it will help to fade my skin to white. I can't wait to wipe it off."

"Doesn't it get in the way of the fitting?"

"No," the dressmaker answered. "I am working on her body, and the housekeeper works on her face. You like my creation, then?"

Disconcerted by the feeling of possessiveness that came over him as he looked at her, he nodded. "This gown is perfect. Demure and clean of line, yet subtly sophisticated, it emphasizes her best qualities. And its classical embellishments remind us all that she's the daughter of a duke."

Gratitude shone in the little Frenchwoman's eyes. "Please ask my lady to stand still while I pin the hem," she mumbled, pins sticking out of her mouth.

Colin turned to Sarah and drew the letter from his pocket. "You must remain motionless, or Mrs. Fanchon may stick a pin in you. Here is a letter to entertain you while you wait."

Her gaze flying to meet his, she took the letter and examined the writing. A frown darkened her face. "From my friend," she murmured.

"Would you like some privacy?"

"Yes, please."

Giving her a smart bow, he withdrew to the window, where he studied the lawns. Behind him, he heard the sound of parchment ripping, and imagined Sarah opening the note. He scowled. What scandalous tale would her friend relate this time?

A forceful sigh escaped her.

Despite his promise otherwise, he spun back around. Her frown had grown deeper, he saw. She looked up, marking the fact that he was no longer giving her the privacy she'd requested. Still, she didn't ask him to turn his back to her.

Instead, she kept casting unhappy, considering glances at him as she finished reading the letter. Once done, she regarded him with narrowed eyes. He could nearly feel her disappointment in him, like a palpable aura in the room.

He said nothing. In his mind, he willed her to tell him who had written the letter—Lady Helmsgate, maybe?

The silence between them grew.

She continued to look at him, then dropped her

attention to the letter. In an offhand way, she began to snap the corner of the parchment against one finger.

"More good news regarding my reputation?" he finally asked, when he could stand the anticipation no longer. Once he had surrounded himself with immoral people and had occasionally taken pride in outshining them. At this moment, however, he deeply regretted those days.

She grew still. "I do not understand you, Colin. You can be generous to a fault, and yet, also so terribly wanton."

"I cannot change what I am. Will you consider revealing to me your friend's name, so I might defend myself?"

Sarah set the letter on her bureau. "I'm not being fair to you. I *should* tell you, even though the lady begs me to keep her confidences."

Triumph filled him. "Give me her name."

A knock at the door prevented her from answering. "Who is it?" Colin barked.

"Edward." The duke sounded curiously uncertain. "May I come in?"

"Yes, please do," Sarah invited, offering Colin an apologetic smile.

The duke walked into the sitting room to join them, a burgundy velvet smoking jacket and silk trousers covering his thin frame. Eyebrows lowered, he seemed preoccupied. Even so, he hadn't been in the room for more than a second or so before he stopped to assess both Sarah and Colin.

"Is anything wrong?" he asked.

"Sarah received another letter from her London friend, the one who fills her ears with confidences that Sarah is not allowed to repeat," Colin informed him. "Many of those confidences involve me."

"Oh?" The duke focused on Sarah. "Lady Helmsgate sent you another letter? We must invite her up to Inveraray. I don't know if she'd come—after all, the season is almost in full swing—but it's worth a try."

Lady Helmsgate.

Colin muttered a choice oath. He'd suspected as much. His past had truly caught up with him.

Eyebrows lifted, Sarah regarded the duke. "You knew who was sending me the letters?"

"Of course. Lady Helmsgate sent me a letter, too, informing me that she planned to befriend you. She's been a friend of the family for many years. Her husband and I used to hunt together, before his hip started to hurt him."

"I see that I'm the last to discern Sarah's friend's name," Colin growled.

The duke looked at Colin with wide eyes. "Didn't you know?"

"No, Sarah withheld her identity."

"At Lady Helmsgate's request," Sarah added.

"Ah, the intrigues of the *ton*." The duke nodded sagely. "I don't miss them."

"Should I trust Lady Helsmgate?" she asked, her attention divided between both of them.

"No," Colin barked.

At the same time, the duke said, "Yes."

A pause ensued. The duke cast a sly glance at Colin. Colin choked back a few choice oaths.

"I would say yes," the older man finally repeated. "Lady Helmsgate is very well-informed on society's intrigues."

Colin felt as though the walls were closing in on

him. "You're not really going to invite Lady Helmsgate to the castle."

"I think we should. Sarah needs a female friend her own age." The duke focused on Sarah. "How about you, Sarah? Would you mind if Lady Helmsgate came to visit for a fortnight or so?"

"I'd like a friend," she admitted shyly.

"It's done, then. I'll write Helmsgate immediately and ask him to send his wife to us. We'll even hold a card party after Lady Helmsgate arrives, to give Sarah a taste of society before her debut."

Colin clutched the back of a chair for support. He couldn't even begin to imagine how Lady Helmsgate would cause trouble for him. Indeed, she'd already caused him a lifetime's worth of trouble.

"But I didn't attend you here in your sitting room to chat," the duke continued. "Unfortunately, I have some bad news for you."

Sarah's eyes widened. "Bad news?"

"Regarding Sionnach."

She pressed a hand against her temple. "Is he hurt?"

"No, no, it's nothing like that. Sionnach raided the henhouse again last night and cook's in a lather."

"Oh dear." Her hand dropped to her side.

"I know you love that little fox, but he's keeping the household in an uproar. He muddies clean laundry with paw marks and jumps all over the furniture. Just yesterday Mrs. Fitzbottom saw Sionnach jump off a shelf, knocking a priceless Grecian urn to the ground and leaving it in shards. I've even heard the hens are no longer producing eggs."

Her face had grown quite pale. "What do you suggest?"

"I'm afraid you must make a decision, Sarah. Either you must release Sionnach into the wild, where he can fend for himself, or you must place him into a cage."

"A cage?" Two spots of pink suddenly bloomed in her cheeks. "Sionnach is my friend. I would *never* put him in a cage."

"Perhaps *cage* is the wrong word for what I have in mind. Rather, I would allow him the run of one of the barns in the Maltlands, where groomsmen will feed him only the best of meals each day, and comb his fur, and keep his home spotless. You, of course, may visit him whenever you wish."

"But he could never leave this barn."

"I'm afraid not," the duke confirmed.

"Then it's a cage." She crossed her arms over her breasts and faced them with narrowed eyes, her movements pulling several pins from her gown.

The modiste uttered a small cry and threw up her hands. "How can I finish this fitting if you move about so?"

"The fitting is over for now," Sarah informed her.

Muttering under her breath, the modiste curtsyed and told them before leaving the room that she would return later.

The duke ran a hand down his face, in the manner of someone in a very difficult situation. "My apologies, Sarah. I wish I didn't have to stand firm on this. In fact, I've tried to give you as much free rein as I could. The fox, however, is causing too much difficulty for the entire household. He is made to roam free in the wilds, not skulk about a drawing room."

"May I have time to think about it?" she asked in a small, hard voice.

"Of course. But I must have an answer soon. I'm sorry, my dear."

Colin watched this exchange with an uneasy feeling in his gut, one he couldn't quite place. Keeping her fox out of trouble made eminent sense; and yet, the image of Sionnach roaming a closed barn filled him with dismay.

If the fox ended up in a barn, tamed, he would become the most pampered fox in England. And in losing his wildness, he would lose the one thing that made him a fox. He would, in short, lose himself. Colin knew a little about losing a part of oneself, and he wouldn't wish it on anyone else.

"I'll leave you now," the duke murmured. "I regret that I had to deliver such an uncomfortable choice to you."

Sarah nodded unwillingly. "I understand."

And Colin speculated if she really understood at all.

Sarah found Sionnach near the edge of the woods. He bounded up to her when he saw her, his furry red body standing out clearly against the brilliant green of midsummer. He barked and growled a greeting, clearly excited about something.

She blew a calming melody and asked him what had sent him into the boughs, her thoughts on the difficult discussion ahead of them. How would her friend react to the duke's ultimatum?

Sionnach's revelation, however, quickly diverted her from thoughts of the cage that the duke wanted to put him in. He yipped to her that the unicorn had arrived.

Sarah clutched a sapling to steady herself. Her vision became more acute somehow, focusing in on Sionnach as if he were a lighthouse in the middle of a fog bank. Her fingers gripping bark, she asked the fox if he could take her to the unicorn.

Sionnach jumped in a circle, answering *yes*. When she pressed him for details about the unicorn's health, though, he simply demanded she come and see for herself, then raced off into the forest.

Sarah followed, wrapping her shawl tightly around her shoulders. The sky, which had done nothing but rain on them for the last few weeks, had cleared the previous day, ushering in bright sunshine and warm breezes. Lily of the valley, honeysuckle, and wild damask roses bloomed in that gentler weather, splashing the trees and mulch with color and releasing their delicate fragrances into the air.

She chased the fox over thick beds of moss that squished underfoot and around overturned tree stumps. After a time, the forest opened onto a series of fields. Sionnach urged her through each field, heedless of the grass dragging at her skirt. They managed to cross three fields before a stitch built in her side and forced her to slow down. She estimated that they'd been racing through the woods and fields for almost half an hour.

Barely able to find enough air to play her panflute, she pressed a hand against her side and questioned him on the remaining distance between them and the unicorn. When Sionnach revealed, with an impatient wag of his tail, that they had another mile or so to go, Sarah wanted to flop onto the grass and die.

Rather, she grit her teeth and pressed onward.

The fox led her around a dovecote made of white stone and topped by a slate roof, and up a grassy hill until she stood so high she could see all of Inveraray laid out before her, on the bay. There, she and Sionnach paused. The sound of rushing water made her thirsty. She noticed a fast-moving brook several feet away.

Winded, she spun around and studied the view from every direction. The farmer's fields sprawled to the west, and a tenant's croft belched smoke into the sky far east of them. North, of course, lay the castle. She realized she didn't know what lay south. She and Colin had never ridden in this direction.

Almost as if sensing her disorientation, Sionnach explained that they were now walking far beyond Blackhill, a hillock so named for its thick, rich soil. As he trotted to the edge of a cliff, he added that they'd moved beyond even Water's Edge. Only the knowledge that the unicorn lay just ahead kept her going forward.

Trembling, she picked her way between rocks and boulders and stopped at the cliff's edge. Far below, mist billowed outward like a curtain, hiding the land at the bottom. The sound of rushing water had grown louder. Sarah noticed that the little brook at the top of the hill spilled over the cliff somewhere nearby.

But the fox had disappeared.

Suddenly, red flashed against green. Sionnach stood on a little path about ten feet down the cliff face.

She peered over the edge of the cliff again. The unicorn was down *there?* Without warning, she felt dizzy. Almost sick. Her heart began to pound in her chest. Eyes widening, she backed away and begged Sionnach to lead the unicorn up to her.

The fox refused, saying the beast was too big, and too ill. Barking encouragingly, he insisted she follow him.

"I can't," she muttered in human language.

Again, he offered her another encouraging yip.

Sarah took a deep breath. Her friend was right. If she wanted to see the unicorn, she would have to follow him. She put one foot on the small path that traversed the cliff face. It was so narrow that she doubted a goat could find his way down without slipping. She faltered.

Sionnach glanced around at her and, seeing her hesitation, demanded she come.

She put her other foot on the path and, slowly, inched her way along until the cliff ledge stood even with her waist. Her heart was beating even harder than before. In her mind, she heard a man's deep-throated cry.

Her fingers hooked, she clutched a root that was sticking out of the ground. Mist enfolded her in its clammy embrace, mingling with the cold sweat that had broken out on her brow. Closing her eyes, she recalled bouncing around. Jostling. A little girl's hand holding hers.

A cry built in her throat.

More images assaulted her.

A doll flapping around, as if caught in a terrible wind. Two women screaming. Her free hand hurt. She opened her fist and discovered an emerald ring.

Mother, help me.

A groaning noise filled her ears. Sarah realized she was the one making it. She forced her eyes open. Her entire body shook. But her hand was empty. She wasn't holding an emerald ring.

The accident!

These were memories of the carriage accident. Powerful ones. Slowly she let go of the root she'd been clutching. She lifted her face to the sun and felt its warmth, listened to the water tumbling over the edge of the cliff and allowed its roar to wash her mind clean, touched the silken softness of the clothes she wore.

Slowly, the panic faded.

Sionnach stood about ten feet ahead, his dark eyes watching her without blinking. She saw the concern in his gaze and summoned a nod.

He yipped again, telling her how proud he was of her, then continued on down the path.

Stiffening her spine with resolve, she carefully picked her way after him, the mist swallowing her up and making it difficult to see more than five feet ahead. When at last her feet touched the bottom, she felt Sionnach rub up against her legs.

They stood at the base of a waterfall, in a grotto of sorts. Ivy and ferns grew up around gray stone that stuck out at odd angles and stretched upward on three sides. The fourth side opened onto more woods.

She reached down to scratch the fox behind the ears and wondered how the devil she was going to climb back up. At the same time, Sionnach pointed his nose toward a niche near the waterfall. There, hidden in the mist and surrounded by vines and exposed tree roots, lay a small horse.

Sarah grew absolutely still. Hungrily her gaze roamed across the white beast. He was so beautiful, her heart ached just to see him. His coat was pure white and shining. Tiny droplets of moisture clung to his white mane, giving it a silver cast. A small ivory horn grew from the middle of his forehead.

Pure of heart, and yet so vulnerable, she thought, her throat tight. She heard a soft sighing in her mind, and like a dream suddenly recalled, she realized he was whispering her name, just as he had whispered to her all of those years ago, when she'd nearly died. Indeed, he'd always been with her; she just hadn't recognized his presence.

His head, she saw, was bent downward, touching the mosses and ferns beneath him. His eyes were closed. A mystical aura of calm surrounded him.

An image of him running through the water, his hooves splashing droplets everywhere, formed in her mind. He'd saved her from the water, she remembered. Now she owed him her life.

Sarah took a step toward him.

He didn't stir.

He didn't even twitch an eyelid.

Dismay brought a frown to her lips. Only the sickest animals behaved this way. She pulled her panflute from her reticule, lifted it to her lips, and played a greeting.

The unicorn shifted a little on his legs, which he'd folded beneath his body, but otherwise he paid her no attention.

She took another step toward him, her song becoming more intense. Pleading.

This time, the unicorn lifted its head and opened his eyes a fraction. They were as blue as the summer sky. Still, he remained motionless and uninterested.

She held a hand out toward him in a placating gesture and inched forward. Silently she cursed herself for not thinking to bring something for him to eat. With her free hand, she lifted her panflute to her lips and asked him if he liked apples.

By now, she'd drawn close enough to look into his eyes, and when she did she recoiled at what she saw there. Dull, lifeless, they contained a grievous pain that had evidently broken his spirit.

Urgency laced her music. The unicorn was dying. Fast. She asked him where he hurt.

When he didn't respond, she inched forward until she stood next to him. Frustration and worry replaced her excitement. This was the first animal she'd ever met who didn't understand her. Her gift wouldn't help her at all.

Her hand trembling, she reached forward and touched his withers. He was soft, like kitten's fur. He didn't seem overly thin. Even so, she ached for him. What was wrong?

Her touch growing bolder, she ran her fingers along his legs, checking for broken bones. She examined his ribs, felt his heart, and even pressed her head against his chest to listen to him breathing. She heard nothing untoward. He even smelled good, she thought. Like freshly scythed grass.

Sionnach yipped from a small boulder on which he'd perched, asking her why the white beast didn't talk.

She explained to the fox that she didn't know why the beast remained mute, or what the cause of his sickness might be. Then, frowning, she dragged her fingers through the unicorn's mane, pulling out the knots. Once his mane felt smooth and silky, she ran her fingers around his ears, then touched his nose, still searching for something unusual.

The moment she touched his horn, however, a

strange warmth snaked up her arm, along with a tingly feeling. She flinched and yanked her hand back to her side.

Sionnach barked excitedly, wondering what had happened.

Her attention fixed on the unicorn, Sarah touched the horn again. The warmth flowed up her arm and began to tingle. This time she held on. Slowly, an image unfolded in her mind. She had the idea that it wasn't her own thought—no, someone was putting it there. The *unicorn* was putting it there.

It spoke in pictures, she realized.

She closed her eyes.

The picture grew brighter. She saw a unicorn. Frolicking through a meadow. Another joined the first, this one smaller, more delicate. Daisies swayed in their wake. Pollen floated on fading rays of sunshine, turning everything golden. She sensed deep, abiding happiness. She smiled. The smaller unicorn, she knew, was his mate.

A man was there, too. He had deep-set eyes, chestnut-colored hair, and a long, flowing beard. His hair poked out from beneath a golden helmet he was wearing. A golden breastplate protected his chest, and a plaid hung around his shoulders. He held a claymore in his hand. The sword looked sharp and heavy enough to cut a tree in half with a single swing.

He dazzled the eye. *A warrior,* she thought. From long ago. Or perhaps even a king.

Something made of silver sparkled on his shoulder. It held the tartan wrapped around him in place. She focused more closely, and saw that the silver object was a circlet fastened to the plaid. A blue lion decorated the circlet.

Suddenly, a group of men sporting silver breastplates and carrying nets joined the golden man. The golden man, clearly their leader, directed the others toward the unicorns. In a circle, they fanned out, surrounding the two unicorns. The male unicorn bucked and threw his hooves up, trying to scare them away, but he was too small. They laughed at him and closed ranks.

Without warning, the silver men let their nets fly, and the daintier unicorn became trapped within their folds.

Sarah swallowed against the tight knot in her throat.

The male unicorn, still free, skittered away into the woods and watched from afar as the silver men hauled the daintier unicorn away.

Confusion swirled in Sarah's mind like fog. She sensed fear, betrayal, and abandonment. Then loneliness.

The image faded.

She released his horn. Each of his emotions she'd felt as if they were her own. In fact, they *were* her own, to some extent. How many nights had she lain awake in bed, lonely, thinking that she couldn't remember the last time someone had touched or hugged her in a loving manner? Tears gathered in her eyes. "You're very old, to have these memories. And she's been gone for a long time now, hasn't she?"

Head bowed, the unicorn shuddered.

"You've been looking for her ever since." One by one, the tears slipped down her cheek. "And you can't find her. So you don't want to live anymore."

The unicorn closed its eyes.

She sat down on a boulder. Every part of her body felt cold. "I'm afraid you've made a terrible mistake. You've come to me for help, but I can't mend broken hearts."

Utterly still and motionless, the unicorn almost seemed made of marble.

"He's going to die, Sionnach," she whispered in human language to the little fox, who'd crept to her side. "And I can't do a thing about it."

✦12✦

Sionnach said little on their way back to Inveraray Castle. His eyes were so sad. Sarah felt as though lead had weighted her limbs. What could she do to help? The female unicorn had been captured and taken away so long ago—hundreds of years, perhaps. The people who had taken her were naught but dust now.

As they passed the Maltlands, however, she broke the silence. Already full of grief, her heart pained her even more over what she had to tell Sionnach. She pulled her panflute from her reticule and began to play, reluctantly explaining the duke's objections to Sionnach's hunting, and his determination that the fox stay out of the castle and off estate grounds.

The fox slowed. He turned his head toward Sarah. She didn't detect any surprise in his face. He already knew.

Her heart aching, she told him how much she loved him, for his wildness, thievery, and cunning as well as his loyalty and counsel. She loved everything that he was, and accepted those parts of his person-ality that demanded he root around in cook's henhouse. He was only behaving in a way nature had intended him to. But the duke's household, they didn't understand him like she did, and she needed to make him realize this.

He averted his face and asked her what she wished him to do.

Lips in a grim line, she suggested he return to Beannach.

He told her quite promptly that under no circumstances—none whatsoever—would he leave her; then he questioned if the duke had suggested any other alternatives.

She frowned, feeling more tears coming on. The day had been terrible, all around. Her voice husky, she relayed the duke's bargain: that Sionnach go to live in one of the barns in the Maltlands, where he could roam at will and hunt all of the mice he liked, as long as he didn't leave the barn.

The fox became very still.

She sighed and touched the fur behind his ears. When he didn't move away, she petted him, telling him all the while that she would return him to Beannach or, barring that, he could go live in the wild, free. She could not bear to think of him caged in a barn.

Trembling beneath her touch, he informed her that he would stay in the duke's barn, then spun away toward the brush edging the lane and trotted away.

She hurried to catch up with him, not understanding. Furiously she played on her flute, demanding that he tell her why he was giving up his freedom.

His reply was simple: she needed him, and if he left now, she might die like the unicorn.

The notion that he would sacrifice himself to insure her happiness infuriated her. She yelled at him first, telling him she wouldn't be the reason for his unhappiness, then begged him not to do this thing for her.

Sionnach remained obstinate. He wouldn't leave her, not yet. Rather, he would go to the barn. Picking up his pace, he vanished into the brush.

His disappearance felt like desertion. Her tears flowed even faster. Why did he insist on staying? Didn't he know that the barn, no matter how fine, would be naught but a golden cage?

Another two weeks passed, during which Colin's determination to remain a gentleman toward Sarah had crumbled utterly. He knew their deepening relationship would soon lead to intimacy, and he'd come to the point where he could no longer convince himself to resist. Even thoughts of the duke's threats had little effect on him anymore. Fantasies of Sarah filled his mind both day and night. The ache of wanting and needing her burned like fire in his loins. The only question that remained for him was: when would he hold her in his arms?

He sat before a walnut writing cabinet, facing a blank piece of parchment and holding a quill in his hand. He ran a hand through his hair, then pushed back from the cabinet in frustration. He couldn't seem to come up with a single line of poetry that made any sense.

Behind him, in the drawing room, the rest of the duke's family gathered in a scene of cozy comfort. The duke, ensconced in a Queen Anne wing chair, had his nose in a book. His two dogs, Cheltnum and Townsend, lay comfortably at his feet, close to a small fire which glowed in the hearth and provided just enough warmth to banish another chill day full of rain. Mrs. Fitzbottom and Sarah were lounging on a settee by the window. They'd pulled a mahogany reading stand in front of them and were going over menus for the card party, which was only two weeks away.

Colin stared at the parchment beneath his quill. A recent memory of Sarah, her lips curved in a smile, formed in his mind. They'd taken to walking the duke's dogs lately and laughing over their antics, their heads together like two thieves planning a heist. They talked, and rode, and visited the duke's tenants, her simplicity and gentle manner reminding him of another time, when he hadn't the hard, brittle finish he'd gained in London. To his surprise, he'd discovered they shared several interests despite their disparate backgrounds, such as a love of poetry and folk songs.

She was quick and clever and had learned a tremendous amount over the last month. He was pleased with her, and terribly proud of her. She had blossomed, and never was it more so apparent than today, when she'd presented herself in the drawing room. Dressed in violet and wrapped in a crocheted shawl, her hair black and shining and eyes a deep purplish-blue, she was so beautiful that his throat tightened when he saw her, and he reminded himself that until she debuted in society, she was *his*.

He'd hidden his possessiveness well, of course. He concealed many things when it came to Sarah. When he looked at her now, he didn't see a country girl. He saw a lovely woman who was drawing ever further out of his grasp, and he ached. He didn't want to ever let her go, not to some young upstart lord who would make love to her and take her money and drive the wildness from her heart.

He sighed and began scribbling on the parchment: "The love he bore her lifted him; Into bright and golden skies; Her name, her voice rang on the air; But the choice he made unwise; For fate would keep them far apart; With love's sweetness came regret—"

Furious with himself, he crossed out the words he'd written. He sounded like a lovesick boy. Where was his manly control, his cool composure, his devil-may-care attitude? All he seemed capable of was dreaming about the moment when he would lay her on his bed and make her moan with desire as acute as his own. In fact, with every day that passed, he found himself more willing to take risks—

"Hellfire!" Abruptly he could stand it no longer. He just couldn't sit in the same room with her and stare at her from afar, knowing that the most he might have from her was a kiss; soon, she'd belong to another man. He jumped up from his chair, sending it backward with a loud scraping noise that surprised even him.

The duke glanced up from his book. "Colin, what the devil is wrong with you?"

Mrs. Fitzbottom and Sarah paused in their review of the menus. Sarah pressed her hands against her breasts in an attitude of alarm. "Have you received troubling news?"

They didn't know he'd been writing poetry. He preferred them to think he was going over correspondence from friends. Running a hand through his hair, he cooked up an excuse for his behavior. "The rain has kept me inside for too long. I need some activity. A ride, perhaps."

Sarah glanced at the rain hitting the window. "The weather has been simply awful."

He'd noticed that she looked out the window a lot these days, frowning, her brow puckered. He assumed she worried about her pet fox, who lounged in his barn in the Maltlands. "Have you ever ridden in the rain? It's rather refreshing. Come with me."

"I won't hear of it," the duke and Mrs. Fitzbottom said in unison.

Sarah looked at both of them and chuckled. "Although I'd very much like to go, I don't think they'll allow me out the door."

"You've already been to see Sionnach twice today," the duke reminded her. "Each time you've come back sneezing. Would you risk catching cold so close to the date of our card party?"

"No, of course not."

Colin stiffened. Beyond Sarah, the window allowed him a full view of the carriageway leading up to Inveraray Castle. Two carriages bearing crests were heading toward the front door. "I believe our visitors have arrived."

Mrs. Fitzbottom, the duke, and Sarah swiveled to glance out the window. The duke smiled. "Ah, Lady Helmsgate is here. Shall we go and greet her?"

The housekeeper jumped up from her chair. "I'll see that a serving maid has prepared her room, and have a light repast made up for her."

"Excellent. Sarah, come with me. Let's go meet your new friend," the duke directed and, smiling, Sarah took his arm.

Colin followed them out into the great hall. There the three of them stood, chatting about nothing, until a few minutes later, a footman opened the double doors and announced Lady Helmsgate's arrival.

Lady Helmsgate breezed in, looking as innocent as a newborn lamb with her curling blond locks and delft-blue eyes. If she'd dressed in white and carried a hook, she would have made the perfect Bo-Peep, Colin thought. And yet, beneath that innocent exterior lay a dragon of the first order. He shuddered.

"Your Grace," Lady Helmsgate cried, her smile very wide and appealing. She hurried to his side and curtsyed deeply. "How very kind of you to invite me to Inveraray."

"Hello, Amelia," the old man replied. "I'm so glad you could join us."

She straightened and turned to Sarah. Dimples appeared in her cheeks. "And this must be Lady Sarah. I just know we'll get along famously."

Pulling her shawl more tightly around her shoulders, Sarah regarded her with uncertainty. "I very much would like a friend."

Her voice was so vulnerable that Colin wanted to rush to her side and protect her from Bo-Peep's sharp teeth and fiery breath.

The two women embraced. Then Lady Helmsgate stood back and turned to Colin. One of her brows arched, giving her a snide air that the others couldn't see. "Hello, Cawdor. We've missed you terribly in London, you know. The city just hasn't been the same without you." She held out her hand, for him to kiss.

Groaning inside, he grasped her hand and kissed the air a full three inches above her hand.

If she caught the insult, she didn't show it. Instead, she waved airily toward the door and said, "Your Grace, I hope you don't mind, but I've brought

Lord Nicholson with me. He is young and well-informed. I thought he might be able to offer Lady Sarah some useful advice." Her voice lowered a notch. "He is also heir to the great earldom of Mayfair."

A glint in his eye, the duke nodded approvingly. "I trust your judgment, Amelia. If you think he will prove a beneficial addition to the household, then I welcome him with open arms."

Lord Nicholson? Colin tossed the name around in his mind. He thought he'd heard it somewhere before. "Is Lord Nicholson a member of White's?"

Before Lady Helmsgate could reply, a sturdy young man with curling blond hair, straight Roman features, and startling blue eyes entered. He walked in with a casual stride, all confidence and sophistication, and bowed to the duke with a flourish. "Your Grace, how kind of you to invite me to Inveraray, along with my dear friend Lady Helmsgate."

The duke, to his credit, refrained from pointing out that Lady Helmsgate had foisted him on the household, instead responding with the grace that only men of his stature seemed to possess. "You are welcome here, Lord Nicholson. May I present my daughter, Lady Sarah?"

Lord Nicholson swiveled to face Sarah. His blue eyes widened. He drew in a sharp breath. "Charmed," he breathed, and bowed low before her.

Sarah's cheeks grew pink. "My lord. How nice to meet you."

Colin clenched his jaw at the tremor in her voice. Couldn't she see the overweening self-confidence behind his courtly air? Eyes narrowed, he studied the young man as Lord Nicholson straightened and turned to greet him. A sense of familiarity nagged at him.

"Lord Cawdor, my pleasure."

Colin inclined his head. "Have you and I met before?"

The young man raised one blond brow. "We met at White's some months ago. I would not expect you to remember me."

"Ah, but I do. I just can't remember the circumstances surrounding our meeting," Colin insisted.

The duke shrugged. "I'm sure our guests are tired from their journey, and need their rooms. We'll reminisce more at dinner."

"A capital suggestion," Lord Nicholson replied, his gaze returning to Sarah and staying there. "Lady Sarah, will you be joining us at dinner?"

She smiled, clearly flattered by his attention. "I will."

"May I have the honor of escorting you?" he pressed, his attention veering off toward the duke, who gave a nod.

She shrugged. "I would much enjoy it."

"Fine. Very fine." His smile large, Lord Nicholson glanced around at the rest of the company.

He looked thoroughly satisfied, Colin thought. If several footmen had not arrived seconds later and rescued the young buck, he just might have delivered a punishing kick to the man's buttocks. Luckily for Lord Nicholson, the footmen led him and Lady Helmsgate away.

Colin moved to Sarah's side and placed her hand on his arm. "Would you care to return to the drawing room? We still have a few hours before dinner, and I thought we might try singing."

"Are you going to sing for me, Colin?"

"If you can stand the sound of it." He glanced at
the duke. "Will you join us, Edward?"

The old man shook his head vigorously and hied
off to the study. "No, thank you," he said over his
shoulder. "I have business I must see to."

Colin squelched a satisfied smile of his own.

As they walked back to the drawing room, Sarah
eyed him carefully. "Lady Helmsgate knows a lot of
intimate gossip about you. How well are you and
she acquainted?"

He paused, trying to decide between the truth,
which would hurt his case with her, and a lie, which
could damage his reputation further were it discovered. One look at her guileless face convinced him
only the truth would do. "Her husband and the duke
are old friends. She and I met a year ago through
that connection, and as her marriage soured, she
and I became friends."

"How friendly were you? And how did Lord
Helmsgate view these developments?"

"Why do you care? We are simply teacher and
pupil, you and I."

She looked away.

Abruptly the day seemed brighter to him, despite
the rain. "All right, I'll tell you the complete and un-
adorned truth. Lady Helmsgate and I entered into a
serious flirtation. We even went so far as to kiss. But
then the duke's letter arrived, drawing me back to
Inveraray. We ended our flirtation there. As for Lord
Helmsgate, he isn't adverse to his wife enjoying herself, as long as she's discreet. It's just the way of society, kitten."

Her hand tightened on his arm. "I appreciate

your honesty, though it leaves me with a question. Why did you not tell me about your connection to her before now? I would have regarded her letters with more suspicion."

"I didn't know who was sending them," he reminded her. "And by the time I had discovered the identity of the sender, we'd all agreed that my reputation is utterly appalling. In any case, I've no desire to read her letters and go over the incidents she described point by point, assigning truth or falsity to them. I think it better that we just put those letters out of our minds."

"I agree." She frowned. "Everything about her is sweet and pale yellow. She's very striking. Did you love her?"

"Never."

"Why not?"

"She may be sweet and pale, but so is the honey within a beehive. If you put your hand into a beehive, you'll get stung."

Sarah digested this comment in silence, then asked, "How about her companion, Lord Nicholson? Do you know anything about him?"

"I remember him from White's, though the circumstances elude me."

"He too is pale yellow. But I suppose since neither of us knows him, we cannot vouch for his character, one way or the other."

Colin thought he could safely say that Lord Nicholson had come to Inveraray with specific designs, but he kept his counsel, recognizing that he'd sound ungenerous if he voiced his suspicions so quickly. They arrived moments later at the drawing room and, after they'd entered, he shut the door behind them. He walked over to the harp.

Sarah had paused near the entrance and was fiddling around at the desk where he'd been seated earlier. Something had evidently caught her attention. Curious, he walked up behind her. Still, before he could see what she was up to, she spun around, her cheeks slightly pink.

"Are you coming?" he asked, one brow arching upward.

Smiling, she smoothed her skirts and nodded. They strolled over to the harp that stood in the corner. When they reached it, Sarah positioned herself across from him, so the harp stood between them like a golden chaperone. Their gazes met across its delicate frame. Her eyes were very wide, and dark, and a little line furrowed her forehead.

He strummed his fingers lightly across the strings, evoking a waterfall of tones. "Have you ever played any instruments outside of your panflute?"

"No. I had no time to play music for pure enjoyment."

"Then I suppose we must sing *a capella*. Can you read music, by any chance?"

She shook her head. "Why must I learn to sing?"

He pulled a chair up next to her and sat down so close to her that their thighs touched. She trembled against him, but didn't move away.

At her unspoken invitation, his loins tightened and desire flared like a heady wine through him. He breathed in her perfume, something with rose, but spicier. It seemed like it was everywhere. He thought it the most sensual fragrance he'd ever smelled.

Through heavy-lidded eyes, he judged the length

of her disarmament, and fought back a smile. "The young ladies who possess a knowledge of music are elevated in reputation, status, and desirability among the *ton*. And they often regarded their music lessons with great anticipation. For you see, the music teacher was almost always male. He would often pretend to show his female students the proper fingering of an instrument, but instead would touch them in a forbidden way, creating an atmosphere of desire and excitement usually denied young women."

She leaned forward, and her scent overwhelmed him. It was coming from her skin, not her clothes. He thought of undressing her and exploring every square inch of her. How would the rose scent smell near her more intimate parts? Soon he would know. "While it is considered rude to stare overmuch at any lady, the music teacher has an excuse for doing so, and will often study her intently for minutes on end."

"What sort of instruments do most women play?"

"The harpsichord, the flute, and the harp. Women who sing are using their voices, and their bodies, as their instruments."

She looked down, her lashes dark smudges against skin that had become wondrously milk-white over the months. The heat from her thigh had penetrated thoroughly to his. He felt a little dizzy, like he was losing control.

"How do I use my body as an instrument?" she asked, her eyes wide and innocent. At the same time, her foot pressed against his. A quick glance downward confirmed that the hem of her skirt had partially covered his leg, hiding her actions. Shocked, he felt her run her foot up his leg. It felt so smooth and silken that he knew she'd discarded her slipper and was rubbing her stockinged toes against him.

"Well, you little hoyden," he said softly, "you have to learn to control your breathing, to achieve control of your tone and pitch. Sound comes from your diaphragm. Focus on it, and breathe in and out, deeply."

She began to take slow, deep breaths, her foot rubbing against his leg in a leisurely manner.

"You're not focusing properly." He placed his palms just beneath her breasts and held them there, nearly wincing at the sight of her nipples, which hardened instantly beneath her gown. "Your diaphragm is here."

Her breathing quickened. She twisted beneath his grasp, rubbing the sides of her breasts against his hands. "Are you certain you're pressing the right place?"

"Perhaps not." He dipped his head downward, kissing the tops of her breasts that the gown had left bare, her rose scent intensifying. She shuddered against him and moaned; he held her close, supporting her even as he plundered her softness.

Loins aching, he greedily ran his tongue beneath the edge of her bodice, exploring skin normally hidden from his view. She was so sweet and luscious that she stimulated him beyond any woman he'd ever known. Even so, he was determined not to act like a rutting boar. She was a virgin. She needed him to move slowly.

Her head thrown back, she clutched his hair with her hands, pulling hard. Maintaining a tight rein on his own desire, he loosened her breasts from her bodice and cupped their fullness. They gleamed whitely in his hands, filling his palms easily, their nipples pink, rosebud tips that begged for his attention. But her pouting lips interested him more. Groaning, he pressed little kisses along her neck, making his way to her mouth. When he kissed her, her lips felt very soft, and they opened for him easily, her surrender complete and unequivocal.

"This is the lesson you need most," he murmured against her mouth, as her hands clasped behind his neck.

Moaning softly in her throat, she pressed wild kisses all over his face and chin. "Teach me, Colin, please."

He laughed quietly and, one hand running possessively down to her hip, he savored the feel of her petite body. His fingers tested the ribbon tied beneath her breasts; silently he judged the number of buttons running down her back and knew the gown could be easily discarded.

She slipped her hands beneath his jacket, pressing them against his linen shirt, then sliding downward until her palms rested against the heated fabric at his loins. At her touch, an intense desire to bury himself in her body gripped him.

"Touch it," he urged. "Feel how hard I am for you. This is what you do to me, kitten. You make me forget everything."

At that precise moment, the knob to the study door turned. Colin caught its movement from the corner of his eye and pulled backward instantly. He swooped her shawl up from the back of her chair and wrapped it around her shoulders.

She stiffened, then pulled the shawl over her breasts, which were exposed far more than the gown would normally allow.

Lady Helmsgate entered the drawing room, Lord Nicholson in tow. She'd exchanged her traveling gown for a sheer pink muslin confection, while Lord Nicholson looked every inch the young buck in a brown jacket and fawn-colored breeches, his neck cloth tied in the Oriental style.

Colin forced a taut smile. Sweat had broken out all over his body. He stood and moved away from Sarah. "Amelia. Lord Nicholson. I didn't expect to see you this afternoon. I thought you'd both be tired from your journey."

Eyes narrowed, the blond woman examined Colin first, then studied Sarah. "Have we interrupted something?"

"No, just a music lesson," Sarah murmured.

"Ah, music lessons. Cawdor is a very good teacher, is he not, Lady Sarah?"

"He's very thorough."

Amelia gave a tinkling laugh. She walked to Colin's side and linked arms with him. "Someone should open a window. You look overheated, Cawdor, and Lady Sarah's cheeks are quite pink."

"It is rather warm." Lord Nicholson made his way to Sarah's side. His attention focused on Colin, he occupied the seat that Colin had just left. "What were you teaching her?"

"I was just beginning to show Sarah how to sing scales and arpeggios."

"Scales and arpeggios. What a nuisance," Lady Helmsgate pronounced. A mocking light in her blue eyes, she led Colin over to the harp. "Why don't I play, and you sing, as an example to Sarah?" She sat down before the golden instrument.

"As you wish." Colin thought for a moment,

then met Sarah's gaze from across the room. He began to sing in a deep baritone, "Black is the color of my true love's hair. Her lips are like some roses fair."

Scowling, Lady Helmsgate began to run her fingers over the strings of the harp, the matching notes falling reluctantly from the instrument.

"She has the sweetest smile and the gentlest hands, I love the ground whereon she stands," he sang, holding Sarah's attention, not letting her go. "I love my love, and this she knows. I love the ground whereon she goes. I hope the day it will surely come, when she and I may be as one."

Her expression sour, Lady Helmsgate strummed a flourish of notes, as though she wished to drown out or delay permanently the second chorus. Lord Nicholson, for his part, was watching Sarah closely, obviously gauging her reaction. Nicholson gave no reaction to what he saw, but just as Colin prepared to sing the next line, the young buck cut in and effectively silenced Colin.

"Black is the color of my true love's hair." Nicholson's voice firm and strong, he leaned close to Sarah and looked at her with a puppy's eyes. "Her lips are like some roses fair. She has the sweetest smile and gentlest hands, I love the ground whereon she stands." When he finished, he plucked her hand from her lap and pressed a kiss against her palm.

Jealousy flared in Colin's gut. He waited for Sarah to tell the upstart to go to hell.

Rather, she smiled prettily at him. "Very fine, Lord Nicholson."

"And you too, Cawdor," Lady Helmsgate added. "Your voice is true."

Lord Nicholson smiled and bowed. Colin simply grunted.

"What else would you like to sing, Cawdor?" Lady Helmsgate pressed.

"Nothing." Arms crossed over his chest, he retreated to the back of the room. He wasn't about to compete with the likes of Nicholson for Sarah's attention.

"How about you, Lady Sarah? Do you wish to sing?" Lady Helmsgate asked sweetly.

Sarah shook her head *no*.

"I understand from the duke that you play the flute. Would you care to try now?"

Before she could answer, Nicholson bent down on one knee. A silly grin curved his lips. "Please, my lady, play for me. I long to hear your music."

She tightened her hands around her shawl. "I don't play very well."

Colin realized she'd had little chance to fix her bodice. Dismayed, he quickly scanned the room, looking for something to divert Nicholson and Lady Helmsgate, in order to give Sarah a moment of privacy. A furtive movement by the window caught his attention. He looked closer and detected a tiny gray body. A mouse. Perhaps even the same one who came to greet Sarah on the day she arrived at Inveraray.

"I believe we have a visitor," he informed them casually.

"A visitor? Who?" Lady Helmsgate asked, looking at the study door.

"A mouse. Over there, in the corner." He pointed the mouse out.

Lady Helmsgate grimaced. "A mouse! What a diseased little creature." Abandoning the harp, she stood up and moved as far away from the mouse as possible. "Cawdor, please dispose of it."

Colin nodded at Lord Nicholson. "Will you give me a hand, Nicholson?"

Appearing equally disconcerted, the other man stood and joined Colin by the window. All attention was now focused on the mouse. "Circle around to the left," Colin directed. "I'll go to the right."

Together, the two men came at the mouse from different ends, but the creature was far too wily for them. It crept into a barely discernable hole in the baseboard.

"It got away," Lord Nicholson pronounced with a droop to his mouth. He returned to Sarah's side.

Colin noted that Sarah's bodice was now fixed and her shawl lay casually around her shoulders. *Good girl,* he thought.

"I don't feel like playing anymore," Lady Helmsgate announced. "Can we not amuse ourselves in some other way, before it's time to dress for dinner?"

"What would *you* like to do, my lady?" Lord Nicholson asked, his eyes intense and unblinking on Sarah's face.

"Call me Sarah," she told him, her voice soft. "I cannot stand the formality of 'my lady.'"

Colin saw a flicker of conjecture spark in the younger man's eyes, and knew in that moment that Lord Nicholson had set his sights on Sarah...and her fortune.

"Of course, Sarah," the buck replied. "And you must call me Robin."

A spring in her step, Lady Helmsgate joined them, and linked their arms through hers. "Oh, this is a capital development. Can we not all be on first-name basis?"

Clearly swept away by the other two, Sarah agreed. When Lady Helmsgate approached Colin and tried to convince him to join along, he shrugged. "If you like."

Then Lady Helmsgate reminded them that the duke's grand card party was only a week away, and suggested a game of commerce so that they all might practice, forcing Colin to retrieve a pack of cards. When Lady Helmsgate discovered that Sarah hadn't the slightest idea how to play any card games, she squealed in mock horror and left it to Lord Nicholson to teach her. She then retired to the back of the room with Colin.

"You're being very unsocial, Cawdor," she murmured, standing so close to him that her skirts brushed against his leg. "Are you not happy to see me?"

"Why are you here?"

She lifted one delicate eyebrow. "To befriend the poor, unfortunate girl whom you would have deprived of a fortune, had she not been found."

Not liking the blond woman's tone, he faced her fully, turning his back on Lord Nicholson and Sarah for the moment. "I've heard about the letters you sent her. That wasn't very nice of you, Amelia."

"Oh, so she told you about them? I asked her to keep my confidence. She is evidently untrustworthy."

"She told me nothing."

"Then how do you know my letters were about you?"

"The duke revealed your identity."

"He does have a way of spoiling one's fun with his righteousness."

Colin's tone was cold. "Sarah didn't know me before I arrived at Inveraray, and was not privy to society's poisonous gossip. She knew nothing of my character. But when your letters arrived, suddenly I found her regarding me with bewilderment, unable to reconcile my good behavior with my dastardly reputation. I should have guessed that you were behind the letters, Amelia. You're the only woman I know capable of such a contemptible act."

"Oh, pshaw." Her gaze flickered over his shoulder, then settled back upon him. When she spoke, her voice was deceptively sweet. "I know why you've come to Inveraray, Cawdor. You think you're going to win our dear Lady Sarah over, and regain your inheritance. I only hope Lord Nicholson doesn't make a muddle of your plans. He's quite determined to have her too, you know. Just as he had Lady Rowlandson."

Lady Rowlandson... Colin's eyes widened. Without warning, he remembered where he'd heard the other man's name mentioned before. Two years before, White's had been abuzz with a wager placed between Lord Nicholson and several of his cronies. Lord Nicholson had bet a single gold sovereign that within a month, he would topple Lady Rowlandson, who practically had one foot in a nunnery, into his bed and would procure a letter from her to prove it.

He'd won the wager, much to the amusement of his cronies.

He narrowed his eyes. "Do you seek to destroy Sarah?"

"No, just to marry her off. So your attention returns to me."

"Bloody hell! Amelia, you and I are ill suited. A few months' reflection has convinced me of this."

Her voice became an impassioned whisper. "How could you run off to this...this farm girl and leave me alone, in London? Didn't the times we were together mean anything to you?"

"You're a beautiful woman. I enjoyed your kisses and your company. Nevertheless, we both need to move on."

"But you wanted me once. You loved me once." She clutched his arm. "Your poems tell me so."

He frowned. "I never loved you."

"Do you love *her?*"

Colin stared at Lady Helmsgate. The woman was a termagant, a shrew. He had to get rid of her. But he didn't want to send her after Sarah with claws unsheathed. "Of course not. Don't be silly. I have no intention of marrying the duke's daughter. She's a country bumpkin, for God's sake. Turn your claws elsewhere."

Her eyes wide, Lady Helmsgate looked over his shoulder again. "Oh, my dear," she murmured, her look of horror manufactured and barely masking the satisfaction in her eyes. "Lady Sarah, I didn't see you standing there."

13

Sarah stood frozen in place, the coldness in Colin's voice convincing her that he thought of her as an embarrassment and an easy mark to satisfy his lust on. Wounded and aching, she focused on Lady Helmsgate. The other woman's thin smile pierced her heart like an icicle.

"Do you want to join us in commerce?" Sarah asked lamely, then turned around and fled the room.

Through a corridor and up the staircase she ran, and when she reached her bedchamber, she yanked the door open, entered, and slammed it behind her. Then she threw herself on the bed and surrendered to great, heaving sobs. How dare he speak of her in such a hateful manner! He hadn't a heart, but instead a cold, unyielding block of marble in his chest.

And what a fool she was to have trusted him even an inch. Lady Helmsgate was right. He satiated himself on only the safest victims—women—and then discarded them when he became bored. Her ability to talk to animals had obviously been a novelty to him, securing his interest long enough to make a pursuit of her worthwhile. And when he was done with her? Why, he'd leave her bleeding and broken, and traipse on back to London.

She shoved a fist against her mouth to muffle her sobs and jumped off the bed. Some hard, hurtful instinct reminded her that this afternoon, *she'd* been intent on seducing *him*, not the other way around. She was the one who'd run her bare foot along his leg. Her own desire for him, and the knowledge that he wanted her, too, had made her bold. But she'd forgotten that he was here at Inveraray helping her because the duke had demanded he come, not because he'd wanted to. And when the duke released him, he would go.

Three sharp knocks sounded at the door. "Sarah, open the door. It's me. Colin."

She froze, her heart beating frantically.

"Please," he said, when she didn't respond. "Open it."

"Leave me alone, Colin."

"I won't leave until I've spoken to you."

He didn't sound like he was going to go away. She'd evidently have to face him. She ran to the looking glass and assessed her condition. It wasn't too obvious she'd been crying. She hadn't been at it long enough to make her eyes swollen. She grabbed a piece of linen from a dresser and scrubbed at the tracks that her tears had left on her cheeks.

The doorknob turned. He entered. "Are you all right?"

Nearly strangling on the anger and sense of betrayal that choked her, she tightened her lips and glared at him. Suddenly she didn't want him to know how much he'd hurt her. She wouldn't allow him that satisfaction.

A second passed, and then in a hard little voice she said, "I'm fully recovered, my lord. In fact, I was just going to return to the drawing room and rejoin Lord Nicholson."

He looked at her oddly. "When you ran from the drawing room, I thought you might have misread my comments to Lady Helmsgate. Concern for you brought me to your door—"

"Playing the gentleman, are you? How unusual a role it must be for you."

He held a hand out to her. "I didn't mean what I said, Sarah."

She stepped away. "Then why did you say it?"

"I wanted to turn Lady Helmsgate's attention from you. She can be quite vicious."

Grimly she held on to her simmering temper. "You mean you didn't want me to come between your flirtation with her for a second time."

"I want nothing to do with that woman."

"Just as you want nothing to do with me, outside of the duke's instructions to 'polish' me."

He ran his hand through his hair, leaving it sticking up at odd angles. "God, what a coil I've made of things. Can you forgive me, Sarah, for my idiocy?"

"You need no forgiveness, my lord. You've made it clear from the very beginning that your relationship with me has always been less than desirable, and that I could expect nothing from you."

"You're wrong."

"No, I'm not," she spat. "Or have you changed your mind about risking the duke's disfavor for me?"

"It's you I'm trying to protect," he snarled back. "You're making it a very difficult task."

Outraged that he would try to lay the blame at *her* door, she brushed passed him, wondering wretchedly how an afternoon that had started out so promising had ended so dismally. Her head held high, she reentered the drawing room and found only Lord Nicholson within. He rushed to her side as soon as she entered and clasped one of her hands between his two.

"Dear Sarah, tell me that you've dismissed Lord Cawdor's comments as those of an irredeemable rake," he exclaimed. "Know that *I* have nothing but the utmost respect for you."

Colin entered a moment later. His face hardened when he saw her hand clutched within Lord Nicholson's.

"Had I not the notion that I'd be abusing my host's gracious invitation to visit, I'd call you out, Cawdor," the younger man informed him, his lip curling. "As it is, I'll ask that you keep your tawdry opinions about Sarah to yourself."

His back stiff, Colin looked Nicholson straight in the eye. "My opinions about Sarah are anything but tawdry. But you're another matter. Have a care, Nicholson. If you hurt her, I'll be the one calling *you* out."

Her throat aching with unshed tears, Sarah thought back to the happy moments between she and Colin, the laughter they'd shared and the desire that had nearly seared them both to the core. How had it come to this?

She finally understood that Lady Helmsgate had, from the start, tried to draw a wedge between her and Colin. Unfortunately, the woman had succeeded admirably. Any feelings of friendship she might have once possessed for Lady Helmsgate turned to extreme dislike. She rued the day the blond woman had sent her the first letter.

It wasn't until much later, when Sarah sat upon her bed in her nightgown, that she remembered the pieces of parchment she'd snatched earlier from the writing desk in the drawing room. While watching Colin labor over his "correspondence," she'd been afire with curiosity, for she could see from his furrowed brow and frequently mouthed curses how much writing these letters had pained him. After all that work, he'd ended up crumpling them together, clearly planning to throw them into the garbage.

And so, when the opportunity had presented itself, she'd taken the wadded-up papers and shoved them into her reticule. She remembered how Colin had almost caught her and her heart had responded with a mighty thump. If he *had* caught her, she would have been hard-pressed to offer an excuse. She knew she was being nosy and prying into affairs that were none of her concern.

Guiltily she hurried over to her reticule and pried open the strings holding the top closed. She *had* to know what he'd been writing. Drawing a candlestick close, she yanked the papers from her reticule, sat down, and spread them out on her lap.

What she read made her throat tighten with wonder:

I love, I love thee, kitten,
It is all I can say,

It is my vision in the night,
My dreaming in the day.

She pressed her fingers against her lips, shocked. Colin wrote poetry! She never would have believed it if he had told her. Her gaze focused on the word *kitten*. Could the poem be about her? Could he possibly love her?

Trembling, she shuffled the next poem onto the top of the pile:

One face looks up from every page
From snowy cloud or tranquil sea;
One face that can all woes assuage,
Dearer than all the world to me.
The eyes are violet, the brow is fair,
Her hair is black and glossy curl'd...

Quickly she scanned through the rest. All of them seemed written about her. Had she misunderstood what Colin had said to Lady Helmsgate earlier? No, she'd heard his words correctly. There could be no mistake. Then why had he written these poems about her? Continued perplexity was her only answer. The puzzle remained on her mind throughout the week and into the next.

She hadn't a moment of privacy with Colin over the days leading up to the card party. Both Lord Nicholson and Lady Helmsgate adroitly managed to keep her apart from Colin, and she couldn't find the right moment to ask him about his poetry. Similarly, even if he'd wanted to protest his innocence regarding his relationship with Lady Helmsgate again, he hadn't the chance.

In fact, over the last few days he did little other than stare moodily out the window. Sarah knew from the duke that Colin had been staying up late drinking, and more than one night he'd gone into the town of Inveraray. She consoled herself with the thought that at least he wasn't spending *every* evening in that blonde's bed.

And while she sat there wondering where Colin was and what he was doing, Lord Nicholson stayed at her side, entertaining her with nonsense and teaching her the dances sometimes performed at an informal affair like the card party the duke had organized. His behavior exceeded that of a perfect suitor's, and yet Sarah felt nothing for him beyond annoyance at his relentless pursuit of her.

On the morning before the card party, she went to the stables to visit Sionnach. She'd been visiting him at least once a day, to keep him company and insure that the grooms took good care of him. True to his word, the duke had indeed made the little fox a priority, giving him a large barn all to himself and regularly serving him—of all things—chicken cooked by the duke's French chef. This morning, however, as she lifted the latch on the door to his barn and entered the dim and straw-filled interior, a sense of foreboding gave her pause.

Usually Sionnach bounded up to see her when she entered. So where was he, then? She searched for glimpses of his little red body and saw only the yellows and golds of cut straw and hay.

Pulling her panflute from her pocket, she called to him with sweet, high notes.

He didn't answer.

Frowning, she waded through the straw, gently kicking it up to see if he'd hidden himself somewhere. Her alarm growing, she checked his food dish and discovered the remains of a meal. She was just about ready to go for help when she discovered him lying atop a bale of hay, near the small mullioned window that offered a view into the yard beyond.

"Sionnach!" She rushed to his side and fell onto her knees. Her hand trembling, she ran it over his soft red fur. To her relief, she discovered that his heart still beat strong and he breathed normally.

Blinking, Sionnach opened his eyes and stretched.

He'd been sleeping.

Her brow furrowed. The fox never slept this late. What had he been doing to make himself so tired?

He sat up on his haunches and shook himself. His gaze went directly to the window. Measured yips emerged from his throat. He admitted that he no longer bothered to awaken early, for he couldn't chase rabbits who hopped about in the first rays of dawn anymore. Who cared what time he awoke?

Her spirits sank. She didn't like that disinterest in his eyes. And she could see he wasn't eating. When she asked if he'd caught any mice lately, he said *no*.

Stiff legged, he walked over to the window and peered out, yipping about the day being a glorious one—a glorious one that he couldn't enjoy.

She scratched behind his ears.

Licking himself listlessly, he seemed only half

aware of her presence. Then he lay down in a little ball, evidently ready to go back to sleep.

Growing more worried by the moment, she examined his coat. It looked dull. He hadn't been cleaning himself as he usually did. With an insistent melody on her flute, she demanded Sionnach tell her what was wrong.

He yawned in response.

And yet, when she went on to accuse him of not doing anything to make him so tired, he did the human equivalent of a shrug.

She tightened her lips. She was going to get him out of this barn, and told him as much. This place wasn't good for him. His coat was dull, his eyes blank, and all he seemed capable of was staring out the window or sleeping.

The little fox lifted himself onto his front legs, until he half sat, half reclined, and pointed out in a tired, yet knowing voice that he wasn't the only one who slept the day away. She slept, too.

Of course, she denied it. She'd arisen this morning at eight o'clock.

Even so, her denials meant nothing to him. He asked her when she'd last visited her animal friends in the forest.

Suddenly uncomfortable, she knotted her hands together. When had she last walked into the forest? Not for several days now, at least.

Not finished with her, the little fox demanded that she play as many animal songs as she could remember.

She thought back to the many harmonies she'd learned over the years, each one specific to a different type of animal. The sheep liked flowing songs, and cows, deep staccato marches. Each animal had his own preferences and, together, these melodies formed the music of the Highlands, a song she had once known by heart. She wasn't certain if she could recall it perfectly now, though. Her discomfort grew.

His yips growing quieter, he questioned how many times she'd been to see the white beast.

Defensively she reminded him that she'd gone to see the unicorn twice since their first visit. The beast still sat by the waterfall, and the image he drew in her mind didn't change.

Expecting Sionnach to yip in agreement, she almost drew back in surprise when he bristled angrily and pointed out that so far, she hadn't done a thing to help the unicorn. And when she suggested that the unicorn was beyond the kind of healing she was capable of, he really became furious, and growled in his throat. The fox evidently felt she *could* heal the beast, but chose not to.

Eyebrows drawn together, Sarah wondered how he expected her to accomplish such a feat. How was she to find a female unicorn that had been captured centuries before?

The fox lay his head down on the hay. He yipped tiredly. He no longer wanted to argue about the unicorn. Instead, he reminded her that he was both beauty and ugliness. He possessed grace and valued friendship, and yet killed to survive. And while many aspects of his personality contrasted, they made him a unique being. Without each and every aspect, he was no longer whole.

She caressed him softly behind the ears, her gestures telling him how much she loved him, too, and accepted him for everything that he was.

He placed a paw on her wrist, explaining that on the day he'd allowed himself to be locked in a barn, he had become incomplete. He had lost his freedom, which is essential to every living being, and his music had gone out of tune.

Then he asked her a question that made her catch her breath: *Do you see yourself when you look at me?*

Unconsciously she caressed her panflute. She *had* changed since she'd come to Inveraray. Wasn't that the point of her coming, though? To change her from a simple country girl into the daughter of a duke? Yes, she had forsaken many of the things that had brought her happiness in Beannach, even if she hadn't done so with forethought. Still, her life was different now, with different priorities and goals. Of course she was going to forget certain melodies...

The fox demanded she think on it, then closed his eyes.

She leaned down and pressed a kiss against his side, then backed away. Instinct told her that Sionnach was right. Her friend was always right.

Then why in God's name didn't she leave, and take Sionnach with her?

Because she didn't want to leave Colin.

She'd fallen in love with him.

Numbed by these thoughts, she shambled through the barn and stumbled back into the sunlight. All around her, horses neighed with lazy indolence, birds chirped, and goldenrod prepared to open in deference to late summer. Though warmth enveloped her, she nevertheless stood frozen with icy despair, understanding at last that while she'd fallen in love with Colin, she could never be a wife to him, or the mother of his children. The duke, in an effort to protect her, would forever keep her from the one man she loved.

The sound of horse's hooves against gravel caught her attention. She glanced at the archway leading into the stable yard. There, astride a horse, sat Colin. He was coming her way and, though he appeared the worse for wear, she had to admit he still looked provocatively handsome.

A groom emerged from one of the barns and began walking toward Colin. His face unshaven, Colin caught sight of her and steered his horse in her direction. When he dismounted at her side, his eyes had a shadowed look that reminded her of Sionnach's.

Reeking of whiskey, he handed his horse over to the groom. "I haven't been out whoring, if that's what you think."

She couldn't think at all. Just seeing him was enough to make her heart ache and her body tense with longing for his touch.

When she didn't reply, he offered her a mocking bow. His eyes were hard and merciless. "Here's to you, my lady. You've ruined me so thoroughly that I couldn't lay another woman if I tried."

She shivered. That one glance from him had roused a coiling heat between her thighs. She thought of the poems he'd written about her, and her heart quickened in response. God help her, she wanted him so badly she could hardly think of anything else. Still, the exchange she'd overheard between him and Lady Helmsgate remained with her the strongest, and the only words that came to her lips were angry ones. With difficulty she managed to hold her tongue, instead throwing him a fulminating glance.

He finally was the one to speak. "How is your fox?"

"Sick," she replied shortly.

He nodded, as though he'd expected as much. "Hope he improves. In any case, I wish you the best with that whelp Nicholson."

Her heart demanded she tell him that Lord Nicholson meant nothing to her, that she'd decided within an hour of meeting him that she'd tolerate him only because he might make Colin jealous. Pride, however, forced her to hesitate, and Colin walked away before she could utter a syllable.

She let him go. Why put them both through another nasty round of accusations, particularly with him in such an ugly mood? Rather, she walked over to the groom and asked him to bring her mare around. Sionnach's insistence that she could help the unicorn had puzzled her. She decided to ride out this morning and visit him again.

In short order she was atop her mare and headed off toward the cliff. The groom had insisted on escorting her, as he always did, and had objected mightily to her refusal, but she'd remained firm. No one could know about the unicorn. If word of his existence ever circulated, the poor creature would end up in a menagerie faster than lightning, and she could only imagine a horrible life for him from there on.

Once she reached the cliff, with its swaying grass and boulders, she tied her mare to a sapling and carefully picked her way down the cliff face. Images of the carriage accident assaulted her, just as they did every time, but she noticed with a sigh that they'd grown weaker. She hoped that in time, they'd disappear entirely.

At the bottom of the cliff, mist enveloped her and

clung to her overheated skin. She skirted the rocks and boulders and walked toward the waterfall. There, beyond the worst of its tumbling waters, lay the unicorn, his head bowed. His white coat, gilded with silver droplets of water, glowed in the lambent sunlight that fought its way through the mist.

Despairing at the unchanged picture he presented, she moved to his side and ran one hand along his coat. Soft he was, and unbearably vulnerable. He made no movement to indicate he knew she was near.

"Sionnach says I can help you," she whispered. "Tell me what I must do."

The unicorn took a deep, shuddering breath, shook his head slightly, and then grew still again.

Moodily she studied him. Then, her lower lip caught between her teeth, she grasped his horn.

The same scene as before played out in her mind. A warrior with a golden breastplate, helmet, and plaid slung around his shoulders. A castle in the background. Two unicorns frolicking. And then, silver men with nets. The dainty unicorn being hauled away by these men. *Her* unicorn sinking into a bottomless well of despair.

"You helped me once," she whispered, shaken. "I know you did. Show me how to help *you.*"

All at once, a new image began to form in her mind, of a dry and dusty road. A carriage was hurtling down the road at top speed. Several men atop horses, their pistols drawn, chased it.

Sarah fisted her free hand. Her mouth drew up in a grimace. The vision was powerful. With it came utter panic. She knew two women and two children were huddled together inside the carriage, terribly frightened at the carriage's jostling and breakneck pace, even though the unicorn hadn't shown her the inside of the carriage.

Hurtling over a bump, the carriage careened viciously near the edge of a cliff. When Sarah saw that cliff in her mind, she grew very still, for she seemed to know its every nook and cranny. One might say she was acquainted with that cliff in a *very* intimate way. Abruptly she understood what the unicorn was showing her and a scream built in her throat.

The carriage rushed headlong over the cliff, and at that moment, the full enormity of the vision blasted through the waves of terror fogging her brain. She cried out and fell slumped against the unicorn's warm body. She didn't feel his warmth, however. In her mind, she was weightless, her body tangling first with her mother's, then with Sarah's, and then with the grand lady's. Her head banged against the roof. Then her shoulder rammed into the door. The grand lady's foot slammed her in the stomach. A great concussion rocked the carriage.

"Mama," she whimpered.

And then nothing.

Slowly, the blackness faded. Sarah felt pain in every part of her tiny body. She looked down. Her feet were small, her hands were small...everything was small. She'd become a child again. In the deep recesses of her brain, she understood that she remained within the grip of the unicorn's vision, but for the moment, she couldn't quite grasp that fact.

Her mother's broken body lay across her. She began to cry, great hacking sobs of grief. Where was her friend, Sarah? What had happened to the great lady? Surely even a bump such as that couldn't have hurt the lady.

Sarah lifted her head out of the shattered carriage. There, on the ground, the great lady lay like a rag doll. She fisted her hands and pressed them into her eyes.

She was alone.

Still crying plaintively, she shrugged out from beneath her mother and climbed out of the carriage. Mother was gone. Her friend Sarah was nowhere to be found. Threads of terror invaded her grief. Water had come to lap at the sides of the carriage. Squinting in the sunlight, she glanced across the expanse of blue water. A ship bobbed on the waves far away.

The unicorn came a little while later. It raced through the water that had risen to knee height and stood patiently while she climbed on his back. Just about the size of a sheep, he brought her across the water and carried her back up the cliff. She clung to his mane and discovered a strange toy hanging around his neck.

When she touched his horn, he spoke to her in pictures. She saw herself taking the toy—a panflute. So she took it. And she understood that he would bring her to safety. The panflute, she knew, was a gift, for as another picture of a grown lady near a unicorn filled her mind, she realized that someday, she would help the unicorn just as he'd helped her. Until then, the panflute would remain a constant reminder of the truth of his existence, and his need of her.

The vision faded. Sarah released the horn convulsively and fell to the ground next to him. Her fingers trembling, she examined her face to see if any bruises marred it. Discovering she was still whole, she sat up and hugged her knees to her chest.

"I'm not Sarah," she whispered, her mind still trying to grasp that fact. She felt dizzy with it. "I'm...Nellie. *Nellie.*"

Nellie the serving girl. Not the duke's daughter. Her blood wasn't blue. God above, her blood was as red as a Highlands peat bog. She had no pedigree. She was a fraud, a fake. And the duke had made a mistake. A terrible mistake.

❖ 14 ❖

"Your timing is inopportune," Colin told Mr. Cooper, who had just arrived from Inverness. He glanced at the watch fob that dangled from his waistcoat, not in the mood for pleasantries. "The duke has invited all of the local gentry to a card party this evening. The guests should be arriving at any moment."

The Bow Street runner lifted an eyebrow. "Is this Lady Sarah's first introduction to society?"

Colin nodded, then looked away. A gulf had opened up between himself and Sarah, and he couldn't find any way to cross it. At the same time, that whelp Nicholson drew ever closer to her, flattering her and charming her with his smooth words and handsome looks.

Turning back to the runner, he asked the man in a defeated voice to return on the morrow, after the card party.

"If I may say so, my lord, what I have learned cannot wait, even for Lady Sarah's introduction. And once you hear my news, I believe you'll agree."

Eyes narrowed, Colin heard the excitement in the runner's tone and was intrigued despite his low spirits. He briskly walked the man to the study, where he closed the door behind them to insure their privacy. "Tell me what you've discovered in Inverness."

The other man remained standing, and Colin didn't bother to ask the runner to make himself comfortable. This business about investigating her had become abhorrent to him as time wore on. He preferred to end their meeting as quickly as possible. Still, he wouldn't stick his head in the sand and refuse to hear what Cooper had uncovered.

"All of the shipyards opened their ledgers to me...for a price," Cooper said in that understated way of his. "It took some digging, but I did find mention of a ship called *Nederlander*, which had sailed from the port at Inverness in enough time to place it in the general vicinity of the carriage accident."

"*Nederlander*." Colin rubbed his chin with two fingers. "Dutch, I assume."

"Dutch, indeed. She made port in Marseille a few days later."

"Is that all?"

Sidling closer, Cooper lowered his voice confidentially. "While I was in Inverness, I made my rounds through the taverns. One of the men there, a Frenchman by the name of LeBlanc, vaguely remembered sailing the *Nederlander*. He claimed that on a day he described as Satan's own, when the wind refused to blow and the ship foundered in the ocean for several hours, they plucked some wreckage from the sea: ladies' silk dresses, shoes...and a little girl, clinging to a wooden door of some sort."

Colin stilled. "God's blood, man, are you serious?"

"As a nun," Cooper confirmed.

"Then your reputation as the finest bloodhound in England is well deserved. Did this LeBlanc have any idea who the girl was, or where she had come from?"

"At the time, LeBlanc didn't speak English, and neither did his crewmates, so they didn't understand her babbling. They simply took her to Marseille and dumped her in a convent there."

"How old was the girl? Does the timing fit?"

"LeBlanc's memory is that of an old man's. Fuzzy. From what I can tell, there's a good possibility the girl they found is approximately the same age as Lady Sarah."

Mouth tightening, Colin nodded, then walked over to the window, where he stared out at the grounds which sparkled in the moonlight. He saw nothing, his mind intent on the dilemma Cooper had presented him. If he sent Cooper to France, the runner could return with the serving maid's daughter.

And yet, what if Cooper returned with the duke's daughter? Sarah would be revealed as a member of the serving class.

Obviously the duke wouldn't relegate Sarah to the status of scullery maid, should such a circumstance arise. He would no doubt support her throughout her days. Even so, she would never be accepted as one of the aristocracy. And despite her obvious expectations otherwise, Colin wasn't so sure that the people of Beannach would accept her as one of their own again, now that she'd spent time living as the duke's daughter at Inveraray. She didn't think like them anymore, or speak like them, or even want the same things she did before she'd come here. Her transformation was most complete, thanks to him and Phineas.

She would, in short, belong nowhere.

Of late, however, her very transformation had frequently occupied his thoughts. She was different now, totally engrossed in becoming a lady, and he didn't know for certain that the change had improved her. He remembered the fey, quicksilver sprite that had first come to Inveraray, playing her music and talking with her outrageous accent, and charming everyone she came in contact with, including himself. Now she spoke in measured tones, considered every movement before making it, and flirted like the very devil. Of her panflute he'd seen nothing lately.

She was becoming like him and every other member of the nobility. And in doing so, she was losing something...the same thing he'd lost. Thinking of his own wasted life, he realized he didn't want to see her forsake this part of herself for wealth and the selfishness it brought to the unwary.

Colin turned and focused on Cooper. Another thought occurred to him. If Sarah turned out to be a serving girl, would the duke still object to a match between them? The older man certainly couldn't complain that Colin was marrying a serving girl for her money. In fact, she'd need someone to rescue her from the netherworld that the duke's transformation would banish her to.

Thoughts of Sarah filled his mind: her small, cat-like face smiling, and making him smile, too; her contagious laugh that pealed out like a bell, clear and full of life; the little kindnesses she'd shown others. She was an angel...if one discounted the mistress she held in her soul, the hot-blooded woman who clearly loved to experiment and would no doubt prove unimaginably satisfying in bed. Yes, she was everything a man could dream for.

Bemused by visions of Sarah, he smiled foolishly.

"My lord?" Cooper stared at him with a curious expression.

Embarrassed, he cleared his throat. "We must find out for certain, Cooper. Go to France. Find the convent and the girl. And bring her back here."

The other man nodded. "I knew you would say as much, my lord. I've already booked passage. With luck on my side, I should return within a fortnight."

Colin gave Cooper another pouch of sovereigns, to cover any new expenses, and ushered him out the front door. As he did so, he noticed a carriage coming up the drive to Inveraray, passing between the torches that lit the way. The guests were arriving for the card party already.

Frowning, he stepped back into the great hall and waited for the rest of the family to join him in greeting the gentler townsfolk of Inveraray. Would the card party afford him a chance to speak to Sarah privately? Or would she refuse to listen to him? Now that he'd convinced himself that there was a slim chance for marriage, he regretted the distance between them even more gravely.

Thus it was an entirely changed man who waited in the central hall for Sarah to walk down the great staircase and join him as Lady Sarah, daughter of the Duke of Argyll. And when she appeared on the landing with the duke at her side, dressed in raw purple silk, with her glossy curls piled on top of her head and barely tamed by a violet silk ribbon, his throat ached just to see her. Her breasts rose like alabaster from her dark gown and her eyes were huge and violet in her small face, and her lips smiled so sweetly that he stared, bemused, unable to take his gaze from her.

She reached his side. Visions of her continued to bedevil him, memories of the sweet, rosebud peaks of her breasts and the wicked look in her eyes when she'd rubbed his leg with her foot.

In the silence that grew between, a telltale blush grew in her cheeks and he realized that his continued regard of her was complete, profound, and utterly mannerless.

The duke cleared his throat. "I can see you approve of Sarah's appearance this evening," he said dryly.

Drawn back to his senses, Colin offered her a bow. "You look stunning, Lady Sarah. I hope I can count on you as a partner this evening."

"I'm sorry, my lord, but she's already surrendered that favor to me," Lord Nicholson informed him, arriving in the great hall and moving immediately to Sarah's side. Dressed in a flamboyant black frock coat edged with gold embroidery, he took Sarah's hand and placed it in the crook of his arm.

But Sarah, a spark in her violet eyes, touched Colin on the arm with her free hand. "Please, my lord, feel free to stop by frequently and give me your advice on how best to play my hand."

"He does have a knack for gambling," Lord Nicholson agreed, a sneer on his face.

Jaw hardening, Colin moved to Sarah's other side. "I'll visit you often."

She leaned closer to him and spoke softly. "I want to buy the duke a present, a token of my appreciation, to give to him the night of my debut two weeks from now. Do you have any ideas on what he might like?"

He wondered if she were inventing a reason for them to be together. The thought cheered him. "We'll discuss it in length."

"And here is our lovely Lady Helmsgate," the duke announced loudly, ending their whispered conversation. "You've arrived just in time, Amelia."

The lady in question had dressed in a daffodil-colored gown that, coupled with her blond locks and pale complexion, conspired to make her look like a giant beeswax candle. She walked down the stairs in a stately tempo that reminded Colin just how much she enjoyed being the center of attention.

"Good evening, all," she sang out, smiling. When she focused on Sarah, however, her smile faltered and a cold glint came into her eyes. "Lady Sarah, how lovely you look tonight."

Sarah lifted an eyebrow. "And you, too, Lady Helmsgate."

"The guests are arriving," the duke hurried to say. "After the initial rush is over, we'll retire to our respective tables. Sarah, are you ready to meet your peers?"

Swallowing, she nodded and withdrew her hand from Lord Nicholson's arm. "I'll look to all of you for guidance." Her gaze touched each of them in turn, excluding Lady Helmsgate.

Intrigued, Colin studied the two women carefully. A strong dislike had clearly sprung up between them, more so than expected, given that conversation Sarah had overhead between himself and Lady Helmsgate. He'd been the one to say negative things about Sarah, not Lady Helmsgate. Hadn't Amelia also taken the time to write Sarah all of those letters, and even come to Inveraray to supposedly befriend Sarah? So why did Sarah bear such enmity toward the other woman?

He hoped that Sarah was beginning to place her faith in *him*, and not in Lady Helsmgate.

Lady Helmsgate moved toward Sarah, evidently planning to stand next to her. Colin quickly stepped between them. He glanced down at the black curls wreathing Sarah's head and the luscious breasts that were ripe for his kiss, and wondered rawly how he would ever let her go if Cooper found a maidservant's daughter in France.

A flurry of arrivals rescued him from these stark thoughts and forced him to concentrate on social niceties. He bid hello to Baron and Lady Sundridge of Combe Bank, exclaimed over the fine figure Colonel Lachlan McQuarie made even at eighty-years-old, and welcomed Dr. and Mrs. Campbell to Inveraray. Deacon John Brown viewed him with an outraged expression upon their introduction. His wife, Dorothy, ogled him shamelessly. Amused, Colin suspected the couple had heard of his reputation, and while the deacon clearly considered him in league with Satan, his wife had an entirely different opinion on the matter.

In an endless stream they came through Inveraray's great portal: the Reverend Joseph Renfrew, a widower; Lachlan Campbell, provost and sheriff; and other highly placed townsfolk, many of them young gentlemen whose gazes slid right past him to settle upon Sarah. Indeed, everyone who met Sarah seemed touched by her pleasing, yet vulnerable demeanor and generous smile. To her credit, Sarah held up through it all and assumed effortlessly the role of the duke's daughter, answering in the cultured tones that Phineas had drilled into her.

After the introductions had been made, the duke wandered into the drawing room. Lord Nicholson took Sarah's arm and led her away, leaving Colin with Lady Helmsgate. She fastened her hand onto his arm and held on tightly as he brought her along.

Spirited conversation mingled in the drawing room with the glow from at least a hundred candles, lending the gathering a festive atmosphere. Perfumes from the women scented the air, and an array of meats, cheeses, breads, and pastries decorated a refreshments table. Servants had pushed the chairs and settees against the wall, and arranged six circular tables around the room, each one supplying seats for five people. Couples playing commerce, piquet, and whist had already occupied most of the tables.

Sarah, with Lord Nicholson at her side and three other beaux pressing forward to claim her, wore an impish smile. Pink bloomed in her cheeks and her eyes sparkled brightly beneath the candlelight. Clearly now that she had been introduced to country society she would remain much in demand, with more than one gentleman declaring himself bewitched by her beauty.

When Sarah noticed Colin's entrance, she pushed back from the table and, leaving her admirers behind, threaded her way through the crowd to his side. A provocatively innocent smile curved her lips. "My lord, might I speak with you for a moment?"

Trying not to jump on the opportunity, Colin gave Lady Helsmgate an apologetic shrug. "Amelia, would you mind..."

The other woman's answering *no* sounded more

like a snarl, and it was directed precisely at Sarah. "I'll wait right here for you, Cawdor," she informed him with slitted eyes.

Colin, glad to be rid of his shrewish companion, led Sarah away from the gaming tables and to a corner of the room, where a potted palm lent them some privacy. "Is something wrong?"

Sighing, she knitted her hands in her skirts. "Colin, I don't know what to do. Lord Nicholson has a way of twisting the meaning behind words. I cannot turn him away without appearing surly. Just this morning, he took me for a walk to pick violets in the woods..." She trailed off, one hand fluttering to her throat, looking utterly bewildered.

Too bewildered, he mused. The Sarah he'd come to know was smart as a whip. He had a sense that she was deliberately torturing him.

Still, that didn't stop heat from invading his gut. God knew he'd seduced his share of females, and the thought of Lord Nicholson seducing Sarah made him want to plant a fist in the other man's finely chiseled mouth. "What did he do to you?"

"Nothing objectionable, really. And yet, I felt so flustered. I suspected he wanted to...kiss me. At home, I might have aimed a kick at him, but here, everything is so different. The daughter of a duke wouldn't kick."

Silently Colin wished he hadn't been so successful at making a lady of her. "Nicholson is a rake. He's well practiced in getting what he wants."

"How do I put him off without seeming ill-bred?"

Colin bent his head toward her until their lips were mere inches apart, knowing with something close to despair that he wasn't at all different from

Nicholson, at least when it came to Sarah. "We need to begin some new lessons. Now."

"What sort of lessons?"

"The kind we've both wanted from the start," he said as he gritted his teeth.

"But Lady Helmsgate..." A hint of triumph in her manner, she waved airily toward the blond woman, who was scanning the drawing room, no doubt looking for him.

"Lady Helmsgate can wait."

"Oh dear, I believe she's spotted us." Sadly she ran her fingers along the edge of his jaw, branding him with one touch. "I suppose your *advice* will have to wait." Then, without another word, she left him in the corner with only a potted palm for a companion and a rock-hard erection between his thighs.

Christ Almighty, what a hellcat, he thought. She knew *exactly* what she'd done to him. He'd been a victim of her teasing.

Practically growling, he emerged from the corner and rejoined Lady Helmsgate, who claimed him with a proprietary hand on his arm. She dragged him over to a table with two elderly spinsters, Dorothy and Charlotte Rumble. The Misses Rumble declared they were playing quadrille, a card game that had gone out of favor decades before. He sat down with Lady Helmsgate, and quickly he discovered why she had chosen two deaf and blind old ladies as their partners in gaming, when he felt her fondle the fabric of his breeches at the groin.

Unmoved, he took her hand and placed it back on her own lap. Disgust filled him. "Not now, Amelia. Not ever."

She leaned close, the side of her breast pressing

against his arm. "I'll leave the door to my bedchamber unlocked this evening."

"It's over between us," he repeated, his gaze returning possessively to Sarah. To his shock, he realized she'd been looking intently at him.

Sarah stared pointedly at Lady Helmsgate, the color in her cheeks going from pink to red. A quick examination of the angle at which he and Lady Helmsgate sat persuaded him that Sarah must have seen his blond companion explore his breeches.

His mouth set, he moved his chair a full ten inches away from Lady Helmsgate's.

She gaped at him. "What's wrong with you, Cawdor?"

"Find someone else," he growled. "Lord Nicholson, perhaps."

Eyebrow raised, she nodded meaningfully toward Sarah. "Trying to win over your little milksop? Well, you'll have to work very hard, for Lord Nicholson has quite captured her interest."

"I suppose I had better get to it, then," he told her, and pushed back from the table, leaving her openmouthed with the Misses Rumble for companions.

He went to the refreshments table that bore a cascade of plucked violets, reminding him that Lord Nicholson had almost plucked Sarah, and selected a glass of lemonade. Glass in hand, he wound his way past the card tables toward Sarah.

Her eyes sparkled brighter than before and her laughter wove a spell around all of her admirers. If Lady Helmsgate's fondling him had bothered her, she hid it well, throwing herself fully into the card game and charming the men who continued to exclaim themselves her ardent admirers.

Just as their card game wrapped up and Sarah—
of course—collected her winnings, he arrived at her
side with the glass of lemonade. "You must be
thirsty," he said, offering her the glass. "I've brought
you refreshment."

"Actually, I am rather hot," she admitted. Neglect-
ing his glass, she opened a fan instead and fluttered
it expertly. Silently Colin applauded Mrs. Fitzbottom's fine lessons.

"Allow me to escort you into the gardens," Lord
Nicholson said to her. "It's much cooler there, in the
moonlight."

Instantly three identical offers from the other
gentlemen followed his. Colin lifted an eyebrow, half
of him amused. How easily she had tamed them.
His little kitten had a natural ability when it came to
men. The other half of him, however, wanted to tell
her admirers that if they so much as breathed on
her, they'd answer to him.

She shot Colin a challenging look, then placed
her hand on Lord Nicholson's arm. Amid a chorus of
groans, she allowed Lord Nicholson to lead her out
of the drawing room.

Colin couldn't very well follow without appearing
a watchdog; unfortunately, he had to stay behind
and stew. He took up post by the refreshments table
and helped himself to a glass of whiskey, his attention continually returning to his watch fob. One
minute passed since she'd left. Then two. When five
minutes had passed, Colin began tapping his foot,
and after ten, he could take no more. He slipped out
of the drawing room and made his way to the salon,
which possessed French doors leading out onto a
terrace. The doors were open, and beyond the ter-

race, the finest gardens in all of western Scotland glittered in the moonlight.

Every foot carefully placed, he crept over to the terrace. It was empty. The moonlight, however, provided a very good view of the gardens and the couple within, sitting on a bench. During his boyhood days, he'd discovered many a path leading through these gardens, and now he put that knowledge to use by sneaking behind a hedge and sidling up to that bench. While the hedge concealed him, it also made it impossible to observe what they were doing. Nevertheless, what he heard made his ears burn.

"Though we've only known each other for a small amount of time, you mean more to me than life itself," Nicholson whispered ardently. "Can you not feel it, Sarah? From the first day we met, something sparked between us."

Colin heard the sound of rustling, and then the snap of a vine or stem breaking.

"You are a fine gentleman, Robin," she murmured. "Even so, I'm not certain—"

She broke off suddenly with a little gasp. "How beautiful," she finally exclaimed. "It's almost silver in the moonlight."

"For you," he said. "My love is like a red, red, rose, that's newly sprung in June. My love is like the melody, that's sweetly played in tune."

She laughed softly. "Very clever, Robin. Did you make it up?"

Teeth gritted, Colin waited for Nicholson to ascribe the poem to its rightful creator, Robert Burns. When the other man said nothing, he nearly snorted aloud.

"Won't you take pity on me, beautiful Sarah,"

Nicholson pressed, "and tell me that you *could* love me, even if you don't now?"

"I suppose I could, had I a mind to. But I don't, Robin. I don't plan on marrying."

"Why not?"

"Quite frankly, I don't want to lose my freedom."

A long moment passed, during which neither of them spoke, though Colin could almost feel the other man's surprise. Then Nicholson, his tone becoming intimate, murmured, "With me you shall always have your freedom to do whatever you wish...with whomever you wish."

She drew in a quick breath at his reply, but the sound was cut off at the end. Afire with curiosity, Colin risked pushing aside the hedges to see what they were doing.

Lord Nicholson's arms were locked around Sarah. He'd pressed his lips firmly against hers.

Jealousy flooded Colin's body like acid. Every part of him burned. Just as he straightened and prepared to charge through the hedges at them, Sarah pushed Nicholson away and managed in shocked tones, "Lord Nicholson! I certainly didn't expect... didn't give you leave to..."

Without finishing her sentence, she jumped up and brushed off her skirts. "I'm returning to the card party. Please don't follow me."

Stuttering, the other man grasped her arm. "If I misunderstood you, or gave some offense—"

Sarah shook him off and hurried off toward the doors leading to the salon.

Filled with righteous anger, Colin pushed the hedges apart and stepped through.

Nicholson saw him and jumped. "Good God!"

"Keep away from Sarah, Nicholson," Colin ground out. "Do not *ever* attempt intimacy with her again. If you do, I'll personally beat your brains out."

"Who the hell...Cawdor, is that you?"

The moon threw enough light onto Nicholson's face to reveal the sneer that suddenly curved his lips. "Cawdor. It *is* you. Who do you think you are? Her husband?"

"She is the daughter of the Duke of Argyll, who is also my very good friend and mentor." Colin took a menacing step forward, his hands fisting at his sides. "Call me her watch dog if you wish, but know that I will protect her to the death. A week ago, you mentioned a duel between us. Well, if I ever again discover you attempting to touch her in any way, that duel will become a reality. My aim is very good, you know, and I will aim for your heart. Do you understand?"

The other man took a faltering step backward.

Colin advanced. "Do you?"

"I understand that this is an affair of the heart. You aren't her watch dog, you're her would-be suitor. No doubt you're after her fortune. How fabulously ironic." Nicholson laughed nastily. "She won't have you, Cawdor. You've got a reputation to match Satan's. No honorable woman would have you."

"That's of no concern to you," Colin growled. "Just see that you heed my warning."

Another harsh laugh escaped Nicholson. Then, shaking his head, he turned his back on Colin and walked up the path to the terrace.

A scowl twisting his mouth, Colin watched him go. Nicholson was far too close to the mark for comfort. More so now than ever, he wished that he hadn't garnered such an appalling reputation for himself. How in blazes would he ever convince her that the rake wished to reform? And if he did, what did the future truly offer them?

Brushing wrinkles from her skirt, Sarah hurried back into the great hall. There she paused and pressed her palms against her cheeks. Her skin felt hot, hot with anger over her own foolishness for leading Lord Nicholson on so recklessly, risking her reputation just to see if she could stoke Colin's possessive instincts.

Indeed, her entire life was unraveling right before her eyes, and she hadn't the slightest idea what to do about it. Throughout the entire card party she felt as if she'd had an 'F' emblazoned on her forehead: 'F' for *fake*. She didn't deserve the duke's love or Mrs. Fitzbottom's kindness. She shouldn't be wearing these beautiful gowns or enjoying such wondrous food. Everything they'd given her, they'd done so erroneously.

She *owed* the duke the truth.

And yet, now that she had the means to convince the duke that she didn't belong at Inveraray, she couldn't seem to bring herself to confess, to recall her memories aloud and insist she wasn't the duke's daughter. The fine living hadn't stilled her tongue; she'd never had much use for wealth. A full pocket, as she'd so painfully learned over these past months, did not necessarily guarantee happiness.

Rather, she had remained quiet because of Colin. Always because of Colin. Even as she'd listened to Lady Helmsgate claim him with her nasty words a few weeks ago, she'd stayed. Why? Because some naive, half-baked part of her kept reminding her that she loved him, and hoping that something would happen, something, something...to bring them together.

But tonight Lady Helmsgate had truly convinced her that Colin would never be hers, not even for a time. She'd seen the woman lay her hand directly on him, for God's sake. Who knew how many times he'd visited her bedchamber? No, he wasn't sleeping in a cold, lonely bed as she was. Colin *never* slept in a cold, lonely bed. His bed was always warm. Any woman would do.

Jealousy choked her, leaving her practically speechless. Forcing herself to breathe deeply, she tried for calm. Eventually she felt capable of re-entering the drawing room. Pasting a smile on her face, she returned to the card party and found herself immediately surrounded by gentlemen. A quick glance around the room revealed that Colin had left, however, and flirtation lost its appeal for her. She spoke sweetly to them but didn't encourage them any further.

Lady Helmsgate, she saw, had stationed herself by the harp. She'd have expected to find the blonde missing. After all, Colin had slipped away. To her surprise, however, Lady Helmsgate made no attempt to leave; instead, she motioned to the duke, who joined her and listened to something she whispered in his ear.

When she'd finished, the duke glanced toward Sarah and shook his head *no*. Lady Helmsgate laughed and swatted him playfully on the arm, then stood up and lightly clapped her hands.

"May I have everyone's attention, please," she sang out sweetly. "A few gentlemen have asked me to play the harp for them, and I've agreed, but I must have accompaniment. Sarah, since you've been so *diligently* practicing singing, I thought you might join me."

Sarah felt the heat drain from her face. She couldn't sing worth a damn, and Lady Helmsgate knew it. She and Colin had spent their lesson together doing just about everything other than singing, blast the man and her own wayward desires. The other woman was clearly trying to embarrass her. "No, I couldn't," she said firmly.

Her admirers clustered around her begged her to join Lady Helmsgate. The blonde then assisted them in their harassment by grabbing Sarah's hand and physically dragging her toward the harp. Panicked, Sarah looked to the duke to save her. He shrugged helplessly, reminding her that he hadn't much practice himself when it came to society and its games.

"I'd like to hear Lady Sarah play the flute, rather than sing." The deep, masculine voice, coming from the back of the room, penetrated the din of encouragement. "I've already sent a footman to retrieve your flute, Lady Sarah."

Sarah's gaze locked with Colin's. She understood that he was trying to help her, by suggesting she play the flute, which she felt much more comfortable with. Even so, in his flintlike eyes she saw a dangerous gleam, as if she'd done something to anger him.

Her hackles rose immediately in response. Pride demanded she buck his suggestion simply because *he'd* made it. Still, she didn't want to make a fool of herself in front of all these people by opening her mouth in song, and furiously she convinced herself that she would rather take his suggestion than embarrass the duke.

Acquiescing graciously, she seated herself by Lady Helmsgate and accepted her panflute from the servant who appeared by her side moments later. "What shall we play?" she asked the blonde.

Lady Helmsgate lifted one mocking eyebrow. "Play whatever you wish, Lady Sarah. I'm certain I'll be able to accompany you."

Her stomach coiling tight, Sarah turned the flute over in her hands. What, indeed, would she play? The sheeps' song? The cows' song? Or perhaps she ought to trill her flute like a nightingale. The truth was, she didn't know any *real* music on her panflute.

Brows knitted, she felt the pressure from all of the eyes watching her. She gazed at the tapestries and the mirror and the little mouse hole in the corner in the way of a vixen seeking to escape a trap. She had just begun to feel giddy when suddenly, it came to her. Just like that. She had a few friends in this room that Lady Helmsgate didn't know about, and she would call on them now.

"May I have a moment to practice?" she asked those closest to her, and they all nodded eagerly.

"Take as long as you need, Lady Sarah," a gentleman said.

Barely hiding her smile, she lifted the panflute to her lips and began to play, one note at a time—high, squeaking notes that pleaded to her friend the mouse for assistance. She pointed out her foe, the lady in yellow, and begged him to hurry, all the while promising to provide him fantastic snacks for weeks to come if he helped her.

Its snout twitching, the mouse came out of its hole. A blur of gray, it raced across the floor, weaving in and out of shoes and chair legs, until it reached the hem of Lady Helmsgate's dress. Sarah blew a few more encouraging notes on her panflute.

"Are you ready yet?" Lady Helmsgate asked, unaware that the mouse was creeping up her skirt.

Into her hair, Sarah played, then lowered her panflute from her lips. "Yes, I'm ready. I'm going to play an old folk song, 'Black Is the Color'. You know which one I'm speaking of."

"Yes, I do," the other woman snarled, then strummed an opening flourish on her harp.

The mouse had crept around to the back of her dress and was making its way to her hair, Sarah noted. She lifted the panflute to her lips and played the first few notes.

"There's a mouse in her hair."

Someone in the back of the room, an elderly voice, spoke quite matter-of-factly.

Sarah stopped playing.

"Look, there's a mouse in her hair," another voice said loudly, this one male.

"Who's got a mouse in her hair?" Wide-eyed, Lady Helmsgate looked all around the room. "Who?"

The mouse finished its climb and sat upon the very top of her curls, its whiskers twitching.

Paling visibly, Lady Helmsgate pressed a hand against her bosom. "Why are you all looking at me?"

"Good God, that's not an ornament. That's a real mouse."

Someone squealed.

Her lips opening in a round *O,* the blond woman patted her curls. The moment she touched the mouse's body, she screeched aloud and jumped up, knocking the harp over. She began dancing around and tearing at her curls. "There's a mouse in my hair! Someone get him, get him off!"

Her antics dislodged the mouse, who fell to the floor. Sarah immediately scooped him up, her action going unnoticed in the melee that broke out, with Lady Helmsgate screeching uncontrollably and everyone else looking around the carpet. Whispering her thanks to the furry creature, she swiped a large chunk of cheese off the refreshments table on her way back to the mouse hole, and placed him safely in his hole with the cheese.

By this time, servants with brooms had entered and most of the guests had rushed out of the drawing room. The duke, moisture beading on his brow, bid them to remain calm and stay for more card playing. The more sensible guests, however, realized that the card party was over and bid him good night in return, with many apologies for leaving. Soon, everyone had left and, with Lord Nicholson's help, Lady Helmsgate had retired to her room.

The duke watched Lady Helsmgate struggle up the stairs, then shook his head apologetically at Sarah. "I'm sorry, my dear, to have your first party end so dreadfully. Who would have thought that a mouse would climb into poor Lady Helmsgate's hair?"

"What a terrible thing to happen to her."

Wiping at the moisture over his brow, the duke frowned. "I just can't understand it. A mouse, of all things, in Lady Helmsgate's hair. Well, all of this excitement has exhausted me. I believe I'll turn in. Are you coming, Sarah?"

"I have to collect my panflute. I'll be along in a few minutes."

"Good night then, and please don't worry about

your debut. I cannot imagine such a thing happening again. At the very least, I'll make sure that Lady Helmsgate's toilette contains nothing to attract vermin the next time." The duke turned toward the stairs and, still muttering and shaking his head, took himself off to bed.

Sarah stifled a chuckle as she made her way back to the drawing room. Servants had already righted the chairs, swept up the spilled food, and removed most of the extra tables from the room. They'd also extinguished several of the candles. Shadows hid in the corners and dulled the tapestries. The room, she thought, had gained an oppressive air, making her want to tiptoe. Or perhaps guilt was just getting to her. The trick she'd played had frightened Lady Helmsgate far more than she had imagined it would.

Sighing deeply, she collected her panflute from the floor. She had just turned to go when she heard clapping from somewhere behind her.

She spun around and came face-to-face with Colin.

"Brava, kitten. Your playing was, shall we say, inspired?"

✸ 15 ✸

"My lord." Sarah smiled tightly. "You must be angry with me for sending Lady Helmsgate up to her bedchamber overset. Surely she will bar her door to you tonight, and you'll be forced to sleep between cold sheets. My humble apologies."

Colin abandoned his casual slouch by the fireplace and closed the distance between them. Steely-eyed, he flicked a finger across her cheek. "And what of Lord Nicholson? Will he warm *your* sheets tonight?"

"Don't be ridiculous. I'm not the one who goes through lovers more quickly than stockings," she ground out, painfully aware of his hard, lithe body so close to hers.

A disturbing smile lightened his face. "I do believe you're jealous, kitten. Still, you're wrong. I haven't been making love to Lady Helmsgate."

"Do you think I'm blind? I've seen what you and that…that blond baggage have been up to."

"You've drawn the wrong conclusions."

Righteous indignation brought her simmering temper to a full boil. "I suppose this is how a man manages to keep two mistresses at once: by lying to each of them, to keep them docile."

"I'm not lying."

"You always lie."

"Name one instance where I've lied."

Glaring, she poked him in the chest with one finger. "All right, you say you aren't making love to Lady Helmsgate. Then why did she fondle your...your..."

His smile widened to a lazy grin. "My what?"

"You know very well what I mean."

"Oh, that. Well, Lady Helmsgate fondled me without my permission. Didn't you see me remove her hand?"

"No, I didn't," she haughtily declared. "And I don't believe you. All you are is between your legs."

"I'd very much like to show you what's between my legs. We can even put a name to it, if you'd like."

His gaze held a wicked gleam, one that made her heart race and her cheeks flush with heat. Ignoring the tumult inside her, she narrowed her eyes at him. "How dare you."

"You pretend to be the proper little lady, but we know differently, don't we, kitten?"

At this, the final insult, her tongue nearly twisted with fury. "You son of a bitch," she breathed.

He affected a look of hurt. "Kitten!"

She recalled the worst term she'd ever heard used and hurled it at him. "Whoremaster!"

"Lady Sarah!"

Eyes narrowed, she put all of the feeling she was capable of into her voice. "You bastard."

He placed a hand over his heart. "Now you've cut me to the quick."

The frustration and jealousy that had filled her

for days exploded. Determined to do him serious harm, she flew at him, fists clenched. He sidestepped her easily with a laugh and trapped her body against his, crushing her. "A truce, little cat. Please."

Ineffectually she pummeled his chest with her fists. Already the traitorous urges were taking over inside her. Angry at her own weakness, she nevertheless gave in to the inevitable and went limp against him.

Gently he stroked her hair. "Do you realize what your anger tells me?"

"No," she stammered, unaccountably possessed by a desire to cry.

"That you care." Shuddering, he pulled her tight against him. "You have no idea how much I've tortured myself, thinking my horrible reputation had made you indifferent to me."

"I could never be indifferent to you."

"I see that now. Sarah, you have to believe me. There's nothing between Lady Helmsgate and me. Nothing."

"I want to believe you," she told him through brimming eyes. "I want to so badly."

"Then allow yourself to believe. I won't hurt you. I'd never hurt you."

She gazed at his beloved features, his blue eyes with the soft light shining in them, his unremarkable nose, and the soft lock of black hair that fell over his forehead. Something inside her twisted unbearably, something halfway between pleasure and pain. She knew he would never be hers; the duke and their positions in society would always work against them. Still, she needed to hold him, if only for a time. And after he'd loved her and she had fixed his countenance and deep voice in her memory forever, she could return to Beannach.

She sighed softly against him. "You mentioned some new lessons earlier."

A fire leaped into his gaze, one so strong she nearly ran from the room. "Go to your bedchamber," he murmured. "Dismiss Mrs. Fitzbottom as quickly as possible, and leave your door unlocked. I'll come to you as soon as I can."

Ignoring the rapid beat of her heart, she nodded. "Please hurry."

His mouth frankly sensual, he released her. "Go. Now."

Sarah needed no further encouragement. Throwing him one last yearning glance, she hurried out of the drawing room and up the stairs. When she entered her bedchamber, she discovered Mrs. Fitzbottom already waiting for her.

"My lady, I was wondering what had happened to you," the housekeeper exclaimed. "The duke went to bed several minutes ago and said you were right behind him. Well, no matter. What did you think of Inveraray's high society?"

Muttering something unintelligible, Sarah presented her back to Mrs. Fitzbottom for unbuttoning.

"Quite a crowd, aren't they? The Misses Rumble had to be the oldest guests, and they hail from a very good family..."

While undressing her, the housekeeper chatted on about the histories of various guests who'd attended. Sarah watched in the looking glass as the clothes fell from her body. Critically she examined her reflection for signs of freckles and patches of sun-darkened skin, things that Mrs. Fitzbottom had once declared undesirable in a lady. Would Colin find her attractive? Suddenly she couldn't imagine him seeing her naked. She couldn't imagine *any* man seeing her naked.

Dressed only in her shift, she sat on her bed, her feet dangling to the floor. Mrs. Fitzbottom shuffled through her wardrobe and brought out one of her old nightgowns from her Beannach days. When the modiste had suggested sewing her new nightwear, Sarah had firmly refused, preferring to sleep in soothing clothes that reminded her of home.

Now she regretted the decision. She didn't want to appear frumpy tonight, of all nights. Frowning, she examined Mrs. Fitzbottom's choice this evening, a flannel plaid nightgown with a high neck.

"Is something wrong, lass?" the housekeeper questioned.

"I wish I had something prettier to wear," she admitted. "I should have allowed that modiste to sew me some new nightgowns."

The older woman patted her hand. "I know those old nightgowns were your last hold on your old life, and I'm glad to see you want to relinquish them. Why don't I go and ruffle through the duchess's wardrobe? She had some very pretty things."

"Do you think the duke would mind?"

"Heavens no. He's forgotten they exist. I'll be back in a moment, dear," she pledged, and left the room on swift feet. True to her word, within minutes she had returned, a filmy black creation over her arm. She frowned as she laid it out on the bed. "I'm afraid moths have gotten into most of her nightgowns. This is the only one I could find fit for wearing. It's not really suitable for an unmarried lady, though."

Sarah allowed the flimsy gown to slide through her hands. A single ribbon, tied at the neck, held the gown in place. She trembled at the thought of Colin untying it. "I suppose I'll have to wear one of my old nightgowns. Leave this one here, though. I'll put it in my wardrobe to keep it safe until I've married."

"I'd hate to see it ruined," Mrs. Fitzbottom agreed. "It's very pretty."

Feigning several yawns, Sarah rushed the housekeeper along, agreeing to a quick bath but drawing the line when the older woman suggested Sarah coat her hands with salve and wear gloves to bed that evening, to soften her skin. As soon as she managed to hustle Mrs. Fitzbottom out the door, she raced to her wardrobe and pulled out the forbidden nightgown.

She dragged her old flannel one over her head and then replaced it with the black gown, its soft, tullelike fabric settling down over her skin with a whisper, the sensation like a soft caress as it molded itself around her breasts. Her nipples hardened and, shocked at its sensuous feel, she walked to the looking glass and stared at herself.

A different woman stared back, a seductive woman whose soft lips pouted and breasts heaved with excitement, their pink nipples barely hidden beneath a gauze of black. A dark V between her thighs marked the place that ached the most for Colin. Her arms glowed whitely through its folds, she saw, and it flared out in a pretty train behind her as she walked. Her fingers shaking, she tied the ribbon at her neck into a neat bow, then returned to her bed and sat nervously, waiting.

When she saw the doorknob turn, her heart jumped into her throat and she nearly bolted from her bedchamber. But then he was inside, dressed casually in a smoking jacket and trousers, his hair damp and curling at the ends, and she knew she could no sooner leave than she could tell him to go.

His lower lip protruding sensually, he studied her boldly, from head to toe. A flame of possessive desire flickered in his eyes. Otherwise, his face remained dark and unrevealing as he held out his hand to her.

She stood and walked to his side, so conscious of him that everything else in the room faded from sight. A finger of anticipation slid down along her spine to settle deep within the part of her that begged the most for his touch. Moisture slicked her thighs and her breasts ached and she almost moaned as their fingers touched, then intertwined.

"My pretty little kitten," he murmured, drawing her closer through their intertwined fingers. "You have no idea how often I've dreamed of this moment."

Throat tight, unable to speak, she gazed at him beseechingly.

Lazily he brushed his free hand across the tips of her breasts, which jutted through the gauze, as if pleading for his caress. "I'm going to touch you—everywhere—and you'll learn to touch me likewise."

Still, he held her only through their intertwined fingers. Desire for him to do more was nearly driving her wild. She lifted her hand and ran her fingers along the side of his jaw, then traced his mouth, her touch as light as a butterfly's wings. "Is it always like this?"

He laughed deep in his throat and wrapped an arm around her waist, pulling her to him and crushing her against his muscular length.

She felt the hot hardness of him pressing against

her midsection, and her gaze flew to his loins, wondering what his trousers hid. Then he was kissing her, his lips spreading hers relentlessly, demandingly, until she relaxed against him and allowed him free rein. His tongue slipped into her mouth and explored at will, then began teasing hers, the sensation exquisite and unlike any other in the world.

Her total and complete surrender and her lawless desire for him startled her. All of her inhibitions were disappearing. In another moment, he could do anything with her and she wouldn't even know how to voice an objection, let alone want to. Fear suddenly coursed through her. She couldn't stop herself from stiffening.

He raised his head and studied her with heavy-lidded eyes. "Easy, Sarah. I'll try to be gentle. Don't fight the pleasure. Let it overtake you."

Firmly he held her close and did nothing more than run his hands over her body for the next several seconds, cupping her buttocks and smoothing his palms over her arms and skimming across her breasts. Sarah relaxed bit by bit against him, but it wasn't until a tiny moan emerged from her that he tipped her head back with one finger and kissed her again.

His kiss was gentle, questing. She could feel him holding back. And yet, she didn't want him to rein himself in; no, she longed to feel the full force of his desire. Sionnach had told her that a fox was both counsel and cunning, and would be less of a fox without both. Likewise, Colin was a creature of passion, of sensuality, and she wanted to experience him at his most primal, complete level.

Trembling at her own boldness, she found his

waistband and slipped her fingers inside, downward, until she touched the core of him, the hard, thrusting erection that would show her what it meant to be a woman, to be possessed.

He grew still.

Her heart pounding wildly, she wrapped her small palm around him and explored his silken length and warm tip. A hungry, throbbing pain built deep between her thighs.

Passion hardened his kiss. His touch became more insistent, more demanding. Involuntarily she moved her hips against him. Groaning low in his throat, he scooped her up into his arms and carried her to her bed, untying the nightgown's ribbon as he did so. The fabric fell away from her in a flowing black wave, and then he deposited her gently against the mattress. He sat back to study every inch of her, his face tight.

Sarah swallowed. Several candles burned, throwing enough light into the bedchamber to reveal her nakedness to him, and abruptly she became conscious that no man had ever seen her naked before. Embarrassed, she managed to shield both her breasts and the curls between her thighs with her arms and hands.

He took off his jacket and unbuttoned his shirt, and let them both drop to the floor. His trousers joined them an instant later. "Are you shy? You shouldn't be. You have a gorgeous body."

She sucked in a breath at the sight of his naked form. A soft mat of hair covered his chest and tapered off below his stomach, then grew thick again lower, between his legs. Heat filled her cheeks as she stared at the part of him that she had only imagined previously.

Apparently at ease with his own nakedness, he walked slowly to the bed and sat down next to her. Gently he pushed her arms and hands aside and leaned down to enclose one nipple with his lips, while his fingers gently explored her silken triangle, slipping past the outer folds to caress some secret, hidden part of her.

Unprepared for the sheer delight that tore through her, she arched her hips against his fingers, even though she wasn't quite sure what that would accomplish. She only knew that deep inside, she ached with emptiness, and instinct told her he could ease that emptiness if he wished.

At her untutored response, his face hardened with an urgent look. Slowly he slipped a finger-tip inside her, making her cry out at the strange and exquisite sensation. She began to writhe against him, the emptiness inside her somehow only worsened by this intimate exploration. Mean-while, he kissed her body wherever he pleased, nuzzling her neck and swooping down against her mouth, then traveling back to her nipples to tease them gently.

She moaned and frantically explored the muscles that defined his back.

"Touch me," he encouraged in a thick voice. "Feel it."

Eyes closed, she lifted her face to his and opened her lips beneath another demanding kiss; at the same time, she curled her palm around his hard length and pulled, gently.

His low groan of pleasure was nearly her undo-ing. His kisses became more urgent, hungrier, mov-ing from her lips, to her neck, then down to her breasts, leaving a hot, wet trail that made her tremble with increasing need.

When his mouth trailed to her stomach and lower, however, she stiffened, shocked, and pushed at his shoulders. "No, don't, not there..."

He sighed raggedly. "I keep forgetting you're a virgin. We'll save that for another night."

Not allowing the tension in her to ease, he began exploring the dark curls between her thighs with his fingers again, caressing and rubbing in a lazy circular motion until her insides seemed to swell and she thought she might die from it.

"Colin, please," she gasped, shuddering.

Something in her tone must have communicated itself to him, for suddenly he was on top of her and poised between her thighs.

"Wrap your legs around my waist, kitten," he murmured against her ear, all the while licking it gently and making her shiver. "And stay very still."

Her body shaking and jerking with the need for release, she held him tightly around the waist with her legs. The hot, moist tip of him pressed down where before his fingers had explored. The pressure wasn't unpleasant; no, she welcomed it, for it partially eased the emptiness that had grown nearly unbearable.

He bent his head to hers. "I'm sorry, Sarah," he murmured against her mouth, then ground his lips hungrily against hers, robbing her of her breath. Seconds later, he thrust forward, hard, and pierced her deep inside.

Unprepared for the agony, she screamed and pushed away from him. His mouth captured her cry and muted it. Stunned, her most tender parts coursing with pain, she became absolutely still and stared at him with tear-filled eyes. She felt as though he'd just thrust a knife inside her and turned it.

"You said you would never hurt me," she choked, when finally he released her lips.

"I'm sorry," he whispered again, then kissed her more gently. Ever so slightly he moved within her.

Panicked, she pulled her mouth away from his. That swollen feeling, the sensation that intense pleasure would soon be hers, had dissipated almost entirely. She could only imagine what fresh pain awaited her. "Don't move, Colin. Please don't move."

"Shh, kitten, it's over now. The pain will ease."

Despite his words, he did remain motionless, shifting his big body to create a tiny space between them. He propped himself up on one elbow, his blue eyes glinting in the candlelight, and slipped his hand between their bodies. His lower lip full and sensual, he began to caress her between her thighs again, touching with unerring precision that small nub of flesh at the core of her pleasure.

Frightened, she resisted the delight his practiced fingers aroused, preferring to stay still rather than move and risk more agony. He didn't ask anything from her; instead, he kissed her leisurely. As the seconds lengthened into minutes, his slow and easy pace calmed her fear even as insidious waves of delight washed through her, helping her forget the pain.

"Relax, my little love," he encouraged.

Swallowing, she could feel her guard dropping inch by inch, caress by caress. Again, that swelling of pleasure grew between her legs and soon it became too potent to deny. Stunned at how quickly he'd secured her abandonment after hurting her so badly, she twisted beneath him, wanting him to caress her faster and harder.

His gaze searching, he brushed her hair back from her forehead and stared deep into her eyes. "Are you ready?"

"Yes, Colin, please..." she begged.

He laughed low and thrust deep within her, then retreated and thrust again. This time, there was no pain, and the sensation of him inside her was such a blessed relief after the emptiness that she wrapped her legs around his waist and held him tightly, determined to keep him there forever.

Slowly he moved in and out of her, his pace increasing as he swept her along to some unknown height of pleasure. The sensations he'd aroused within her had heightened and combined to form one hard, unbearable ache between her thighs. In a frenzy, she ran her palms up and down his back, clutching his muscles, digging her nails into his skin, and meeting each thrust of his hips with her own.

Just when she thought she could cry from the pleasure he gave her, her body tightened and the swelling inside her burst, then washed her along in a wave of ecstasy that shocked her with its intensity. Whimpering, she clutched him to her tightly and felt his thrusts grow quicker until he, too, shuddered and jerked against her.

The pleasure took several seconds to ebb away and left her feeling like a wrung-out dishrag, her emotions in complete disarray. An inexplicable urge to cry sneaked up on her, and suddenly, she discovered tears running down her cheeks. She choked back a sob and buried her nose in the hair covering his chest.

"There, don't cry," he murmured, his voice holding not the least bit of surprise. "The first time is always difficult."

Sniffling, she snuggled against his chest. "I don't know if I should slap you or kiss you."

"I'd prefer the kiss," he replied, stroking her hair, his voice so tender that fresh tears sprang to her eyes.

"Why didn't you warn me?"

"I told you it would hurt."

"You didn't mention it would feel like someone sticking a knife into my vitals."

A smile crossed his lips. "If I had, would you have made love to me?"

"No," she admitted, her tears drying up. She wiped at her eyes. "Probably not."

He traced a teasing circle around her breasts, then allowed his fingers to drift lower, to her silken triangle, where lazily he stroked her. "What you experienced today is only the very least of the pleasure a man and woman can bring each other. There are so many other things we can do, so many different ways to make love."

Remembering the way his lips had nearly traveled to the curls between her thighs, she trembled. "Will you teach me these things?"

"I want to. God knows I want to."

She waited for him to say more, but he grew quiet. His refusal to speculate on what their future could hold nagged at her. "I know our respective positions in society will ultimately keep us apart," she ventured after a time.

His arms tightened around her, but otherwise, he remained silent.

She trailed a finger across the curls masking his

chest. "I know our intimacy hasn't magically erased the difficulties between us, but after making love to you, I can't imagine us being apart."

"Neither can I. Christ Almighty, what a coil we're in."

"What are we going to do?"

"For now, we're going to finish preparing you for that debut ball of yours," he told her, his voice raw.

"And afterward?"

"Afterward, you're going to marry me," he told her with a deep sigh.

The matter-of-fact nature of his statement squashed any excitement it might have aroused in her. He made marrying her sound like a distasteful task. She narrowed her eyes. "We're not marrying, Colin."

"Oh yes, we are. I've taken your honor, and now I must restore it."

"I don't want you to sacrifice yourself to me."

He sat up on one elbow. "I may be a wretch, but at least I have my honor. We *will* marry."

She, too, pushed up on an elbow. "I absolutely refuse. Our marriage could never be a happy one. If we defy the duke and earn his enmity, we'll be shunned by society. Besides, you don't love me."

A queer look crossed his face. He stared at her for several seconds, mouth twisting as if he'd felt a pain, his eyes glittering with some emotion she couldn't identify.

"Colin?"

Finally a groan broke from him. "I don't understand women. Not at all. They never seem to want what you expect. Always I'm sadly mistaken."

She frowned, thinking again of Sionnach's words:

The fox is both cunning and counsel, and cannot exist otherwise.

"I won't marry you, Colin," she repeated. "You were born into the aristocracy and raised by society. You could give it up, yes, and live quietly at Inveraray with me. But would either of us ever be happy?"

"We could be happy," he insisted.

"Do you know what frightens me most?" she pressed, her voice soft. "The notion that you might come to resent me if you have to give up everything for me. I don't ever want you to resent me, because love requires acceptance."

He didn't deny her logic, and somehow, that hurt even worse than his insistence that they marry. She pulled away from him and fixed her gaze on the canopy above her bed. She felt cold inside. Wounded. "Perhaps you ought to go now."

Quietly he sat up. "Would you like me to help you change the linens?"

"No. Just go."

Pausing long enough to press a kiss against her forehead, he stood, shrugged on his clothes, and left. As soon as the door closed behind him, Sarah hugged his pillow to her and surrendered to tears that lasted almost until daybreak.

When the sun finally did reach its bright fingers into her bedchamber, she groaned aloud. Her head aching and her nose completely clogged, she managed to wake herself up enough to climb out of bed, don a fresh nightgown and change the blood-speckled sheets. She threw them along with the black nightdress into the bottom of her carpetbag, the one she'd brought with her from Beannach, and fell back asleep.

Later, Mrs. Fitzbottom roused her with a cup of hot chocolate and a scone. The older woman studied her for a short time, then clucked sympathetically. "I know your first party didn't go so very well, but don't despair, lass. I've seen the preparations the duke has already made for your debut, and I promise you, no one shall ever forget it."

Sarah drew a cover over her head and groaned.

"Come now, lass, it's time to get up," the housekeeper remorselessly informed her. The older woman managed to coax Sarah out of her bed and into a pretty sprigged muslin.

Feeling ragged and unattractive, Sarah left her bedchamber at Mrs. Fitzbottom's insistence and went downstairs to the drawing room. It was in this ugly mood that she ran into Lady Helmsgate, who looked as fresh as a spring rose in pink satin.

"Good morning, Lady Sarah," the blonde greeted her, her brow arching. "Did you sleep well?"

Sarah muttered a reply and grasped her embroidery hoop, determined to put a few stitches into the damned thing.

Her head tilted, Lady Helmsgate moved past Sarah to study several books upon a shelf. "Perhaps you can help me," she said to Sarah, her attention remaining on the books. "I'd like a book on...*poetry*. Are you aware of any?"

Sarah's fingers stilled, her needle poised just above the fabric. Colin's poems came to mind. "What sort of poetry?"

"Oh, I don't know. Love poems, I think."

"I can't help you," Sarah informed her abruptly, then dropped her gaze to her embroidery. She pushed the needle into the fabric.

"Did you know that Lord Cawdor writes poetry?" the other woman asked, her tone arch.

Sarah gave up all pretense of embroidering and focused fully upon Lady Helmsgate. "No, I didn't."

"He writes love poems."

"Do tell."

"He's written me several."

Sarah's insides twisted painfully. "Oh?"

"Would you like to see them?" Lady Helmsgate dug into her reticule and produced several pages of parchment. She sauntered to Sarah's side and dropped them into her lap. They covered her embroidery like a funeral shroud.

Sarah stared at them. "I don't want them."

"Can't you read?" the other woman prodded.

"Of course I can. I'm simply not interested."

"Quite frankly, my lady, I think you need to see them. He's not very good at it. But it's the sentiment that counts, no?" With that, the other woman left the drawing room.

Her lips tight, Sarah picked up the poems and glanced through them. They all praised Lady Helmsgate's beauty, talked of love, or spoke about some other intimate nonsense. An ache stabbed into her heart. She wanted to rail at Colin, to accuse him of being a heartless seducer who used every means at his disposal, even poetry, to conquer his victim. But how could she admit to knowing of his poems about her without revealing her own bad behavior? After all, she'd stolen the poems from the writing desk.

She crumbled the parchment into a ball and wadded it into her reticule. She knew Lady Helmsgate was deliberately egging her on, but that didn't change the fact that Colin had used poetry to seduce both her and Lady Helsmgate. And though he'd offered to marry her, saying it was the gentlemanly thing to do, he hadn't told her that he loved her when she'd asked him directly. So why should she think that in her case, the verses he'd written about her had been designed for anything but seduction?

Regardless, she would see that Lady Helmsgate and her blond companion were sent packing. She'd had enough of their antics. Her chin firm with purpose, she marched off in search of the duke.

✳16✳

Colin left Sarah's bedchamber and went straight to the study. He knew sleep would prove impossible. Instead, he settled down in front of the fireplace, brandy in hand, and brooded. How had it happened? When had it happened? He couldn't guess. He knew only that thoughts of her had plagued him unmercifully from the first day they'd met, and now he finally understood why. He loved her. He loved everything about her—her quick wit, her smile, her generosity, her sensuality...everything.

Generally, he mused, everyone experienced at least a few defining moments in life, when some simple truth finally became clear. And when that truth surfaced, it often felt like a revelation, shockingly powerful and driving all other thoughts from the mind. Well, he'd experienced one of those moments in Sarah's bedchamber. When she'd said she wouldn't marry him, bells had damned near rung in his head, leaving him in a fog.

He still felt in a fog. So far, the brandy and the fire had done little to burn it out of his mind. Yes, he loved her. But if they married, the duke would see that they had each other, and no one else. She'd been very wise to suggest that love might not be enough.

She was wrong, though. For him, love was enough. He was determined to marry her.

Of course, he had no idea what she felt regarding him. She probably didn't love him at all. He had to admit that he hadn't behaved very honorably toward her. A true gentleman would have taught her what she needed to know without trying to kiss her at every opportunity. But he hadn't been able to keep his hands off her, no matter how many threats the duke threw at him.

Frowning, he set the brandy snifter on a side table and rested his head against the back of his chair. At the moment, he wasn't very happy with himself. Indeed, what a fool he was! One would think that a man of his sophistication could polish an innocent young country girl without falling in love. But look at him now, moping about like some moonstruck calf.

Well, he had a difficult piece of work cut out for him this time. He had to convince Sarah that he was a man of honor, one more than capable of remaining faithful to her and madly in love with her. By the time Mrs. Fitzbottom served breakfast in the dining room, he had an ache in both his head and his heart and an uncertainty that he could do either.

The duke observed him with a raised eyebrow when he entered the dining room. "Good God, man, you look as though you haven't slept a minute. Is something wrong?"

Colin scanned the room and found no sign of

Sarah. "I've a bit of a headache, nothing more. Has Lady Sarah recovered from last night's festivities?"

Just then, Sarah paused in the doorway to the dining room. Purplish shadows had gathered under her eyes. "Yes, I've recovered," she said, directing a cool glance in Colin's direction before she sat near the duke, leaving him alone on the opposite end of the table.

Startled, he studied her closely. Their discussion after they'd made love hadn't been the happiest, but neither did it merit such a cold reception. What bee had gotten into her bonnet this time?

Throughout the following hour, he tried several times to engage her in conversation. Each time, his gambit was met with disinterested answers. The atmosphere in the dining room went from cool to frigid. Even the duke began to shift uncomfortably on his chair and took to reading a correspondence, the letter lifted in front of him like a shield.

Colin's blood heated in contrast. He was starting to feel angry. What in hell was wrong with her? Did she resent him for making love to her, despite her assurances otherwise last night? She'd called him a rake and a seducer more than once. Maybe upon reflection she felt he'd dishonored her. At the very least, she had come to regret their intimacy.

His own speech becoming tense and clipped, he asked her to join him in the drawing room for another music lesson. She refused. Then he reminded her that they'd agreed some time ago to review formal dining etiquette with Phineas before her debut. She said no. At his wits' end, he finally asked her to meet him in the study, to discuss a private matter.

"A private matter? Of what sort?" the duke asked, putting his correspondence down.

"Sarah needs my advice on a certain...purchase." Colin shot a meaningful glance at Sarah, hoping she would remember her request for ideas on what to buy the duke, as a token of appreciation.

Sarah patted the duke's hand. "I'd completely forgotten about asking the earl for his advice. He's quite correct, however. I do need to speak to him privately."

The older man looked unconvinced. "I don't like secrets."

She smiled. "And I suppose you always spoiled the yuletide by demanding to know in advance what people had bought you."

His cheeks growing ruddy, the duke smiled, too. "My pardon, dear, for acting the part of a nosy old codger. Of course you must speak to Colin."

"Before I go, however, I would like to speak to you about our houseguests. Privately," she added, her gaze flitting to Colin.

Her use of "the earl" rather than "Colin" not lost on him, Colin stood and left the dining room. Once in the study, he sat down and waited for her. She joined him in less than five minutes, a frown on her face. He didn't know if the frown was a result of her conversation with the duke, or a reaction to the sight of him. Judging by her mood in the dining room, though, he'd wager on the latter.

After she'd perched herself on a hard-backed little chair, Colin closed the door to the study and selected the closest chair to her. For a moment, they stared at each other, saying nothing.

Her eyes had no sparkle in them this morning, he mused, and her mouth had a pinched look about it.

"You seem bothered," he said after a time, breaking the silence between them.

Turning to look out the window, she shrugged.

"Is it about last night?" he ventured.

"No."

"Has something happened, then?"

She didn't answer.

"Obviously something *did* happen." He rubbed his jaw with two fingers, casting about for possible scenarios that would have put her nose out of joint so thoroughly. Then a thought occurred to him. "May I assume Lady Helmsgate lies at the heart of it?"

"Lady Helmsgate lies at the heart of all misfortune," she said, turning around without warning to face him. Her lower lip trembled and moisture shone in her eyes.

Sighing, he settled more easily into his chair. This, he could handle. "What did she say, or do?"

"She gave me these." She flung a wad of paper at him. It struck him in the chest, then fell to the floor.

He snatched the wad up, unfolded it, and read. When he realized he was staring at his own poems, written for Lady Helmsgate, he grew very still. The heat just seemed to drain out of him. "She dared give you these?"

She supported her forehead with a trembling hand, her attitude one of confusion and deep hurt. "Why, Colin? Why did you write these for her?"

"God curse that woman," he snarled, furious with Lady Helmsgate for hurting Sarah so terribly, and furious with himself for contributing to that hurt, however unintentionally. He crumbled the poems up again and hurled them into the fireplace. "Sarah,

I know you have no reason to believe me given the evidence, but I swear to you I never loved her."

"Then why did you write what you did?"

Shoulders slumping, he knew if he ever wanted to gain Sarah's trust, he would have to be honest, regardless of how it might ruin his chances with her.

"I wrote them to seduce her," he admitted baldly.

"You selfish bastard," she muttered, her gaze fixed on her hands, which she'd folded in her lap. A tear dropped on her wrist.

Raw pain clawed at his gut. He'd done this to her. The Earl of Cawdor, great rake and seducer, had broken the heart of perhaps the most gentle and beautiful woman in England, and now, when he had come to believe that he just might not be able to live without her, she would never have him.

"Were the poems about me written to seduce me, too?" she asked, another tear falling onto her hand.

He drew in a quick breath. "How do you know about the poems I wrote about you?"

Her voice almost faded into nothingness. "I...I found them on the writing desk in the drawing room, the day Lady Helmsgate arrived."

Startled, he cast his mind back to that fateful day. He remembered struggling at the writing desk with a few poems that refused to take form for him. Had he thrown them out or left them there by accident? He wasn't certain. Still, he *did* recall Sarah fussing around the writing desk later on, just as he was about to start their first music lesson. "If you found them, you weren't supposed to. I had no intention of showing them to anyone."

She looked up at him suddenly, revealing dark,

wounded eyes. "Are the sentiments contained in your poetry about me true?"

Caught in the hurt that her gaze revealed, Colin found himself at a loss for words. The declarations that had come so glibly to his lips for other women had deserted him, now that he actually meant them. He hadn't the slightest idea how to best tell her that he loved her outside of a bald assertion that she had no reason to believe, and her attitude toward him certainly didn't encourage him to unburden himself.

"I don't think this is the time for a declaration of love," he murmured.

"Love? You don't know how to love," she cried. Surprising him completely, she jumped out of her chair and raced into the great hall.

"Sarah, wait," he shouted, and started after her.

By the time he made it to the great hall, she had already sped through the front door and was running across the grounds. Just as he reached the front door, a footman from outside opened it.

The duke walked in, his eyes very wide. "Colin! Good God, what did you and Sarah talk about? She just ran past me, and when I asked her what was wrong, she began sobbing. Is she upset that I refused to send Lady Helmsgate packing? Lord Helmsgate is a very old friend of mine, and I didn't want to insult his wife by refusing to allow her to attend my daughter's debut into society."

"Sarah and I have had a misunderstanding," Colin growled, and started past the duke.

The older man grasped his arm, stopping him in his tracks. "What sort of misunderstanding?"

Colin shrugged out of the duke's grasp. "That's between Sarah and myself."

"Oh, now wait. It is most certainly not between you and Sarah. Do you remember my warning all those weeks ago?"

"How could I ever forget it?" Colin snarled. "In just that one breath, you condemned me to misery for the rest of my life."

The duke frowned. "Misery? Calm down and tell me what you mean by that."

"Haven't you guessed it yet?" Colin threw caution to the winds. "Bloody hell, I'm in love with her. Somehow, she made me love her, and now I can never marry the woman I love, thanks to you."

"You? And Sarah? In love?" The duke's eyebrows crept upward to meet his hairline.

"I *do* love her," Colin declared. "But because of my damned reputation and Lady Helmsgate's machinations, I can assure you she will never love me. Don't worry about it, Edward. I won't soil your daughter by marrying her. She won't have me."

"I didn't know," the duke spluttered. "I had no idea. When did this all happen?"

"Gradually. It happened gradually. Now, if you'll excuse me, I have to find her and apologize for my latest mishap."

Still looking amazed, the duke nodded dumbly.

In the back of his mind, Colin noticed that the duke had seemed more shocked than outraged over his declaration. He wondered if the duke would truly stick to his threat if the old man felt certain that the love he bore Sarah was genuine. Filing the thought away for later examination, he hurried out the front door, then paused. Where had she run to? The kitchen gardens? No, she'd been wearing a riding habit, he remembered. She'd probably gone to the Maltlands.

He ran down the gravel path toward the large complex of barns that glowed whitely in the afternoon sunshine. A breeze sprung up behind him and seemed to be pushing him toward the barns, while the trees, caught in that same breeze, pointed their leaves in the identical direction. He almost felt as though it were a sign from above to find her quickly. His pace increased.

The sound of hooves pounding furiously gave him but a few seconds' warning before a horse and rider came pelting out from beneath the central arch leading into the courtyard. Shouting, he jumped out of the way and got a good look at the rider. Sarah, riding without a saddle, bent low over the horse's mane. Astride, her skirts bunched up around her thighs, she spared him nary a glance as she galloped past. He didn't even think she'd seen him. She raced off into the fields, heading south.

Alarm for her safety left him with a tight sensation in his throat. The little idiot was going to get herself killed, riding so wildly without even a saddle to hold onto. He ran into the courtyard and practically bumped into an openmouthed groom.

"Bloody hell, man, what's wrong with you?" Colin shouted. "Are you insane, to let my lady ride off without a saddle? I'll see you sacked for this."

"I didn't even see her enter." The groom, a mere youth judging by the peach fuzz coating his chin, had gone completely white. "I heard her horse whinny. When I ran to see what was the matter, she was astride her horse like a…like a man and riding away."

Colin swore loud and long. "Get my horse, now. If you saddle and bridle him in less than a minute, I'll see you're kept on. Go!"

Flying into action as though a shovel full of hot coals burned in his pants, the groom called out to his cronies, and a team of men saddled the large, chestnut-colored thoroughbred that clearly delighted in unseating him at every opportunity. Colin eyed the horse grimly as the grooms ran him over to Colin's side.

"Unseat me now, you bastard, and I'll shoot you myself," he vowed.

The horse snorted and sawed on the reins in response. Nevertheless, he stayed uncommonly still while Colin mounted. Colin pulled the reins to the left and jabbed his heels into his mount's side at the same time, and the horse took off like a shot, charging through the archway. Directing him southward, Colin held on as they cantered wildly through the grasses where he'd last seen Sarah.

When he reached a hedgerow, he pulled his horse up and scanned the brush for a trampled area that would reveal her passage. Quickly he discovered an area of broken gooseberry branches and clods of dirt from a fast-galloping horse. He plunged through and emerged in a field of waist-high straw. Crushed grasses formed a path through the field, and Colin followed it, aware that they were gradually riding uphill, in a direction he'd never traveled with Sarah during their rides together.

At the next hedgerow, he paused again. The bush wasn't very high here, and another field stretched uphill for almost a mile. There, at the top of the hill, he saw Sarah, her black hair completely undone and flying out behind her like a banner. A shout built in his throat. He choked it back. She would never hear him.

The wind picked up, ruffling through his hair and

whispering urgently in his ears. Spurring his mount forward, he charged after her, his worry growing more acute with each passing moment until it felt like iron bands tightening around his chest. The smell of salt tinged the air, reminding him what lay beyond this latest field: a cliff that dropped directly down to the cold, swirling waters of Loch Fyne. Did she know she was heading for a bluff?

An image of Sarah trying to pull her mount up at the last moment, unsuccessfully, ached in his mind like a canker. He could almost see her sailing over the cliff, only to be broken like a rag doll on the rocks below. He kicked the big thoroughbred beneath him to even faster speeds, aware that if the horse happened upon a single rabbit hole, he would be jolted off his mount and would likely die of a broken neck.

He didn't care.

"Come on," he gritted his teeth, leaning forward into the horse's mane. The horse galloped so quickly now that the wind tore at him and made his eyes water. At last he crested the hill, and brought his mount to such an abrupt halt that the horse neighed in alarm and reared.

Stunned, Colin stared at Sarah's abandoned mount.

Where was she?

His horse pawing nervously at the ground and dancing around beneath him, Colin scanned the surrounding countryside. There, far below, the town of Inveraray spread out in orderly fashion. Smoke drifted from a few chimneys. Beyond the town, two single-masted ships lolled in the harbor. He twisted around in the saddle, searching to the left, right, and behind him for Sarah's slender form. He saw nothing remarkable other than the small stream several paces north, which plunged over the edge of the cliff to land in the valley beneath.

She seemed to have disappeared. Unless...

His heart giving one mighty thump, he dismounted and walked over to the cliff edge. He peered over the edge, almost afraid of what he might find. But she hadn't thrown herself over. In fact, to his utter amazement, he espied her working her way down the cliff face. Mist obscured the valley below and had nearly swallowed her, too.

What in bloody hell?

Sighing raggedly, he found the starting point of the path she'd taken and, clinging to dew-covered rocks and exposed roots, started down as well. Too soon, Sarah disappeared into the mist, leaving him alone to find his way. Anger at her built in him yet again, for risking herself so needlessly. Mouthing silent oaths, he climbed into the mist swirling upward from the valley, the roar of the waterfall growing louder.

Everything was gray and moist, and smelled of earth. He couldn't see much more than ten feet in front of him. But he knew he was close to the bottom, for the ferns grew thicker and more lush with his every step, and soon bushes and trees stretched up around him.

A faint sound beneath the waterfall's roar teased his ears. It grew louder, then ebbed away as he followed it. He couldn't identify the noise; still, it had rhythm and cadence, and he knew it had to be human in origin.

Sarah, he thought.

The sound filled out as he closed in on it. Soon he

identified the blurts of noise as sobs. Remorse choked him. He walked more quickly, caring little for the exposed roots and boulders that sought to tangle his feet. The mist grew heavier, and the waterfall crashed and gurgled somewhere in front of him. He found a small path and strode toward the sounds of her sobs.

Slowly, as he grew closer, the mist cleared around a small figure with long black hair, dressed in a bottle-green riding habit. With a start, Colin discovered she was crouched by a small creature of some kind. Her small body blocked most of the creature from his view. Nevertheless, he guessed she'd found a recently shorn sheep, judging by the creature's short white coat.

And yet, something about the scene gave him pause. The creature's coat wasn't really the dull whitish pink of a sheep's skin. No, this animal glittered white and silver, reminding him of a spray of stars against a velvety black sky. He transferred his attention to one of the creature's hooves, which poked out from beneath her gown. It, too, looked silvery. The hairs at the back of his neck prickling, he slowed down. Then stopped.

The creature neighed softly.

A pony then, he thought, not certain why he was growing more uneasy with every moment.

Mist swirled around Sarah and the creature, alternately revealing and obscuring them. She was murmuring softly to it now, her hand lifting to brush a soft, white-gray nose. Then she shifted, revealing the creature's face.

His mouth dry, he stared. His uneasiness solidified into fear.

The horse had an ivory horn poking out of its forehead.

He began to tremble. Childhood tales of faeries invaded his mind. For one startling moment, he felt sure that Sarah wasn't human. No, she was one of the fey folk, sent to walk among mortals and tease them. Maybe she even stole their hearts and took them back to the place of the fairies, leaving only husks behind.

His hand shaking, he lifted it to his own forehead and touched it softly, as though he were the one possessing the horn. Chill after chill began to race through his body.

My God, she'd found one.

A *unicorn*.

He squeezed his eyes shut, then popped them open again.

The unicorn hadn't disappeared. Sarah still cried over it and murmured to it like an old friend. Just then, a shaft of sunlight pierced the valley, settling unerringly upon Sarah and the unicorn. The mist swirling around them turned gold, each tiny droplet of moisture reflecting with light, until it seemed magic surrounded them and blessed them with brightness.

Colin staggered over to a boulder and held on.

As if sensing Colin's movement, the unicorn opened its eyes and looked at him. Hardly breathing, Colin returned the white beast's stare, losing himself in intensely blue eyes darkened with mysteries, wise with ancient knowledge, and wearied by terrible pain. Even as his throat grew tight and his heart raced, something inside him loosened in some strange way. His mind grew fuzzy. He found himself remembering his past, times in his boyhood when he'd cried, in his early adulthood when he'd helped someone in need, and later, as a man, when he'd indulged in sensations of the flesh.

These memories seared his gut with an almost physical pain. They reminded him of what he'd once been, and what he'd become. He tried to force them away, but they kept coming at him relentlessly. Just when he thought he might cry out, the memories came slower, then dissipated, leaving him with the sight of Sarah crying.

Colin's shoulders slumped. He'd often heard that the unicorn was a creature of truth, and sensed that the beast had looked into his soul and judged him. He'd made many wrong choices. Was he beyond redemption?

The unicorn closed its eyes and lowered its head.

His emotions shredded, Colin struggled back to his feet. "Sarah," he murmured huskily.

Visibly starting, she spun around and squinted at him, as if she couldn't believe her eyes. "Colin?" Without waiting for his reply, she slowly got to her feet and walked toward him, her hand outstretched. "Colin?"

Aching with the need to cry out, to rail at fate for revealing the unicorn to him and destroying him in the process, he walked toward her and grasped her hand. "Thank God I've found you," he managed, and before she could object, dragged her into his arms and squeezed her so tightly that she gasped. "Please don't run away from me ever again."

Unwillingly he released her and stared at her.

Lips trembling, she returned his regard. Then her

attention drifted behind her, to the unicorn. "He's dying," she murmured.

Colin linked hands with her and approached the unicorn hesitantly. It was so beautiful, and pure, and true that he ached to touch it. But he didn't know what the beast would do if he dared. Jaw tight, he kneeled down by the beast's side and placed a gentle hand on its chest. A heart beat sure and true beneath his palm.

"How do you know he's dying?" he asked, fighting a sense of unreality. They'd left so many things unquestioned, so many things unsaid.

"Sionnach and I found him here almost two months ago, right after I came to Inveraray," she whispered, like a physician who doesn't want his patient to overhear bad news. "He hasn't moved since I first discovered him."

"Are his legs sound?" he whispered back.

"As far as I can tell." She paused, fixing him with a searching gaze. "There's something else, Colin. When I touch his horn, I see things in my mind. I believe that's how he communicates."

"Your panflute doesn't work?"

"I've tried using it, without success. I cannot talk to him. I can only see the pictures he creates in my mind."

Brow furrowed, Colin moved his hand from the unicorn's chest and gently caressed its nose. Then, his fingers shaking ever so slightly, he touched the horn.

Nothing happened. Nothing formed in his mind.

He grasped the horn more firmly. "Do the pictures come to you immediately?"

She nodded.

"Then he chooses to speak to you alone, for I see

nothing." Colin released the horn, something inside him rejecting the notion of the unicorn's death. He couldn't allow a creature as magnificent as this to die. "Perhaps we should carry him back to the Maltlands," he ventured. "With expert opinion, proper care, and medicine, he might heal."

"Think for a moment what would happen to him, once his existence became common knowledge," she pointed out. "He'd instantly be placed in the regent's menagerie."

Colin considered Sionnach, who was slowing wasting away in the barn. Then his thoughts centered on Sarah herself. Society had taken something away from her. Every time he thought about it, he ached deep in his gut. And if society had done that to her, it would *kill* the unicorn.

"Anyway, I don't think medicine would help him," she added. "The pictures he creates for me are almost always the same. I see a castle, and a man, and, well, a female unicorn. The female unicorn was captured many centuries ago. He's been longing for her ever since. You might even say he's dying of a broken heart."

Her voice gaining intensity, she described in great detail the scene where their unicorn played with his mate. He asked her to repeat it many times, and as she did so, an odd sense of familiarity nagged at him.

"Tell me about the man in the vision again," he insisted.

"I've already told you everything I remember."

"Tell me again. Please."

Sighing, she repeated her description of the warrior's face—his deep-set eyes, chestnut-colored hair, and flowing beard. His dazzling golden breastplate and helmet suggested to Colin that not only had the man lived several hundred years before, but also had been very wealthy.

"I can almost see this man in my mind's eye," he said. "What colors formed his tartan?"

"It has a red background, with green checks, and yellow and white stripes."

Colin frowned. Something lurked around the edges of his consciousness, teasing him. He just couldn't grasp at it. "The unicorns ran freely in his presence?"

"I had the odd impression the unicorns considered him their pet," she confirmed.

"Describe the castle again."

She told of its trio of arched windows looking out onto a gently rolling hillside.

Frustrated, he sighed. "By God, I feel like I've visited this castle before. If we could discover where it's located, we would stand one step closer to finding the female unicorn."

They both fell silent. Colin absently rubbed the unicorn's velvety coat, reassured by the steady beat of its heart beneath his hand.

Without warning, Sarah tensed. "There's something else. I've just remembered it."

"What?"

"A silver circlet secured the man's plaid. It bore the figure of a blue lion and the word *fumerus*, or *fuimus*, maybe."

His mind racing ahead, Colin turned to face her. "The circlet most likely represented the man's clan. I'm not sure which of the Scottish clans feature lions on their crests, but I do know that the duke keeps a few books on the topic in his study."

He stood and held his hand out to her. "Come

with me. We'll look through the duke's books together."

Sarah wiped her face with her fingertips, then took his hand. "Do you think we might be able to find his mate?"

"We're going to try, Sarah. We're going to try very hard."

Wasting little time, they climbed up the cliff face, hand in hand, and remounted their horses. They arrived back at Inveraray shortly afterward and discovered that the duke had gathered a few grooms about him and gone off looking for Sarah and Colin on horseback. Colin sent another groom to intercept the duke and inform him that they'd returned safely, then drew Sarah to the study. There he selected several books from the shelves and set them on the desk.

"Look through these," he directed, pointing to the two topmost books. "I'll take the bottom ones. Between the two of us, we'll figure out which clan the man in your vision belongs to."

As he paged through hand-painted sketches of plaids, Colin tensed with excitement and hope. The unicorn, he mused, had presented him with the perfect chance to redeem himself in Sarah's eyes. If he could reunite the white beast with its lost mate, then surely she would be willing to trust him again, to believe in him, and forget the poems that he'd so foolishly written for Lady Helmsgate.

"Here it is, Colin," Sarah informed him without warning, a quiver in her voice. She pointed to a page in the book she'd been looking through. "This is the tartan I saw the man wearing."

Colin examined the sketch, then transferred his attention to the caption next to it.

" 'The House of Bruce,' " he breathed. Grasping her hand tightly within his own, he turned the page and found a sketch of the Bruce crest badge. "Here is our blue lion, and even the word *fuimus*—'We have been.' "

"The House of Bruce?" Sarah repeated, eyebrows scrunched together.

"It says here that the unicorn first made its appearance as the sovereign emblem of Scotland in the thirteenth century," he told her. "The prestigious Order of the Unicorn, which carried the Grail motto 'All as one,' was also founded at this time...*by Robert the Bruce.*"

Excitement twisted in Colin's gut. He flipped a few pages, coming to rest upon a description of the House of Stewart. "Back in the thirteenth century, the men who served as stewards to the Bruce eventually became the Stewart clan, and ascended to the throne, becoming the Royal House of Stewart. Would you care to wager what they chose to display on their badge?"

"A unicorn," she murmured, her eyes wide.

"Correct. And there's more. James IV of Scotland, when he ascended to the English throne in the seventeenth century, created a royal arms picturing both England's lion and Scotland's unicorn, representing the joining of the two countries." He snapped the book shut decisively. "Do you know what I think?"

She shook her head *no*.

"I think that through luck, or magic, or a bit of both, Robert the Bruce found the unicorns. They entranced him so that he made them the sovereign emblem of Scotland and created the Order of the

Unicorn. I can't even guess why he tried to capture them, or where he put the female unicorn, or even if she's still alive." He thought of the three high, arched windows in the castle she'd described. It all fit. "Even so, I know where to look for the female—in the Highlands where Robert the Bruce once lived. I believe Kildrummie Castle was the Bruce's family seat, and Kildrummie has three arched windows like you described."

"Where is Kildrummie Castle?"

"Along the east coast, near Inverness." He grasped her hands. "I'm going to go there, Sarah. I have to try to find the unicorn's mate."

"You'll never find her."

"I'm going to try. Nothing is worse than having to live your life without the one you love the most."

For the first time, she entwined her fingers within his. A glow entered her eyes. "You would do this for him, Colin?"

"I'm doing it for you. It's only the second of August, leaving me a month before your debut. I'll try to return in time for the ball." He released her fingers from his grasp, plans already whirling in his mind.

She touched his cheek. "Take Sionnach with you. I'll explain the situation to him and I know he'll go. He can help you."

He caught her hand and kissed it tenderly. "Save a dance for me."

✦ 17 ✦

Colin wrapped his tartan more tightly around his shoulders, for the nights in the Highlands still got cold, despite late summer's heat. Sighing, he settled his arse into the dew-moistened heather and focused upon the ruins of Kildrummie Castle. The moon cast a pale glow over walls that, battered both by the weather and by local farmers seeking to build rock walls defining their property, had crumbled years ago. Only the three high, arched windows that Sarah had seen in her vision remained standing above waist height.

He'd been gone from Inveraray for almost three weeks now. The journey to Inverness he'd accomplished without difficulty, but the road from Inverness to Kildrummie Castle was ill-used and had nearly disappeared into the moors at times. He'd navigated the road until, exhausted and questioning his own sanity, he'd stopped at an inn some five miles away from the ruins.

Colin hadn't lasted long at the inn. As the days had passed, and he'd had no luck finding her, he'd

decided that he couldn't afford to spend *any* time
away from the ruins. What if the unicorn wasn't
trapped anymore but hiding somewhere, and only
came out of her lair infrequently? He knew he
needed to be at the ruins all the time, or possibly
risk missing sight of her. So he'd bought some simple provisions and made camp near the old castle.
Daily he wandered the local countryside, looking for
signs of the female unicorn, who was proving as
wayward as all females, regardless of species.

Sionnach had kept him company through it all.
The little fox's coat had gradually regained its luster
during their journey, and at this point, Colin was
damned glad to have him along. The fox had proven
his hunting skills several times over, and now they
were both living off his kill. Sionnach hunted, and
Colin cooked.

The days of active searching, and the nights of
lying wet-arsed in the heather and scanning the
countryside for her, had given him plenty of time to
think. For the first time in many years he discovered he actually felt good about himself, really
good. He was doing something that mattered, for
someone else, and the knowledge filled him with
hope.

He didn't care that he was eating cooked hare and
sleeping with only a tartan to cover him. He didn't
miss his bath, his shave, or clean clothes. The moon
shone brightly over his head, and the stars glittered,
and the smell of a wood fire got into his nose and
oddly enough, peace came to him. With every passing hour, layers of civilization were falling from
him, leaving him more alive than he'd ever felt before. In fact, he'd come to realize that his senses,

which he had so cultivated over the last decade, had become dulled by society.

But time was running short. He had only a week left and wanted—no, *needed*—to get back to Inveraray before Sarah debuted, so he might be there to support her, and win her love. This time alone with Sionnach had convinced him that he didn't need society and all its enticements. Society would never bring him the contentment he craved. Hadn't he spent the last several years wondering why he felt so empty?

No, he didn't need society. He needed only Sarah and the love she would bring him. He didn't give a good god damn what the duke did to him, he was going to win Sarah back and marry her. If he never set foot in Edinburgh or London again, then so be it.

Scratching his jawline, which had become thick with a beard, he silently willed the unicorn to make an appearance. While he couldn't understand Sionnach like Sarah did, he nevertheless sensed the fox's excitement growing in the way he moved and sniffed the ground. Lately, Sionnach had kept drawing him back to a field riddled with cairns that held the bones of ancient Celts. Colin had the distinct impression that Sionnach had caught the female unicorn's scent and was closing in on her.

A cloud passed over the moon, throwing the moors into darkness. Tensing, Colin heard the bushes to his left moving. Without warning, Sionnach appeared, his red coat nearly black in the night. His eyes shining, he yipped, then turned on his heels and ran onto the moors. At about ten feet away, he stopped, spun around, and yipped again.

Colin needed no further encouragement. He grabbed a lantern and started after Sionnach.

Quickly he discovered the fox was leading him back to the field with the cairns. Trying not to twist an ankle in the occasional hole, or trip over a clump of heather, he followed Sionnach to one of the small cairns on the far end of the field and climbed into it, the hard-packed earth beneath his feet crumbling in a small landslide.

Sionnach raced to the opposite side of the cairn and began scratching furiously on one of the walls, throwing up clods of dirt. Brow furrowed, Colin stood hunchbacked within the cairn, for its ceiling was only about shoulder height, and lifted the lantern high.

Hard dirt walls interspersed with rocks surrounded the ten-foot space in which he and Sionnach stood. If the walls had been decorated, the decorations had long since washed away, leaving the tomb unremarkable. Nevertheless, Colin felt a chill at the thought that the people who were buried here had likely lived thousands of years before.

An earthy smell invaded the air as Sionnach dug.

"What are you doing, my little friend?" he murmured. "We've explored this one in daylight. There's nothing here."

The fox kept digging.

Shrugging, Colin began to dig as well, using both a stick and his cupped hands as a digging tool. He'd spent enough time with Sionnach to have learned to trust the fox's instincts. Obviously something of interest was buried here. A secret chamber, perhaps?

For several minutes, Colin scooped out great handfuls of earth and pushed it behind him. He noticed the dirt felt silky and desert dry. Just as he began to think he was going to bury the passageway out, the dirt wall they'd been digging began to crumble.

Sionnach dug faster. Wonder building in his gut, Colin dug faster, too. Once they'd created a hole big enough to see through, Colin angled the lantern to shine light through the hole, and peered inside a cavern. A gasp escaped him.

"How did you know where to find her?" he breathed.

Obviously proud of himself—and deservedly so, Colin thought—the fox yipped, then nearly turned a backflip.

There, in the middle of the cavern, a skeleton lounged upon a marble slab. Earthenware pots surrounded the marble slab, which bore intricate carvings. The skeleton wore a golden breastplate and helmet, and a silver cross lay on top of the breastplate. Near the top of the marble slab, by the skeleton's head, loomed a marble effigy of a massive warrior; and there, at the effigy's feet, crouched a white creature, its coat touched with silver, its eyes closed, and its chest utterly still.

The morning of Sarah's debut dawned clear and warm. Mrs. Fitzbottom declared the good weather an omen for a fabulous debut and busied herself with preparing Sarah's gown, the white creation edged in gold ribbon. Lounging in a bath of scented water, in preparation for the evening's festivities, Sarah couldn't agree with the housekeeper.

Colin should have returned to Inveraray by now. Indeed, she'd done nothing this past month but worry about him. Where was he? Why hadn't he sent word? Was Sionnach all right? Had they found the female unicorn? These questions plagued her both day and night until she nearly screamed with the frustration of not knowing.

Despite Colin's absence, the month leading up to her debut had passed quickly. Phineas continued to drill her on etiquette, and the duke took over for Colin, teaching her dances and songs she feared had gone out of style decades earlier. Lord Nicholson assiduously pressed his suit with her, earning her annoyance and nothing more. Lady Helmsgate, for her part, had chosen to loll about Inveraray and henpeck all of the servants until Mrs. Fitzbottom declared her the spawn of the devil.

Judging by the frequent scowls the duke threw Lady Helmsgate's way, even he regretted his decision to allow her to stay, despite Sarah's pleading otherwise. He'd also been intrigued regarding the difficulties between her and Colin, but she'd deflected his questions. If she didn't know where she and Colin stood, then how could she discuss it with the duke?

Still, the duke speculated. The letter that Colin had left him, explaining his absence, had stirred up his curiosity even more. Colin, he'd insisted, had no business in Inverness that could have taken him away for an entire month.

"Come on, lass, let's have you out of that bath before you're wrinkled," the housekeeper admonished, now that she'd finished fluffing out Sarah's gown to smooth out a few tiny wrinkles visible only to her.

Sarah stepped out of the water and allowed the housekeeper to enfold her in a soft white towel. "Am I to stay in my bedchamber all day?"

"Aye. We've guests arriving already. You won't see any of them until you make your grand entrance at your debut. Occupy yourself with reading and embroidery. I'll bring up a tray of hot chocolate for you. Before you know it, night will be upon us and I'll be up here preparing you for your entrance."

"I don't know if I can wait that long." Sighing, wrapped only in a robe, she trailed over to her window and looked out across the grounds. "I wish he would return."

The housekeeper didn't bother to ask who she was referring to. Rather, she placed gentle hands on Sarah's shoulders. "Did he say he would return in time for your debut?"

"He did."

"Then trust him. You'll see him tonight."

Sarah frowned, thinking she should have trusted him weeks ago, when he'd insisted he had no feelings for Lady Helmsgate. She'd had plenty of time to reflect on everything he'd said, and all that she'd learned from others who knew him, and had come to the conclusion that she'd been too hasty in her condemnation of him.

She had no direct evidence that he'd ever toyed with Lady Helmsgate once he'd come to Inveraray. Lady Helmsgate had striven to give that impression, but Colin had denied it to the end and now she wished she had believed him. He'd always been brutally honest with her. She may not have agreed with him, but she knew she could trust his word.

The thought that the poetry he'd written about her, Sarah, also represented his true sentiments made her feel warm and wonderfully soft inside. He loved her, he'd declared it in writing, and now she wanted to give him a chance to declare it to her face-to-face.

She knew his past was full of women and might come back to haunt her more than once, but she couldn't blame him or chide him over that. Indeed, his appreciation for the feminine gender was part of his charm for her, and he wouldn't be the man she'd fallen in love with without it. Like Sionnach, who was both cunning and counsel, Colin was both sensuality and masculine strength.

Come back to me, she silently begged, her plea falling unheard on a soft summer breeze. Together they would overcome any difficulties they might face.

She spun away from the window. "My nerves are in shreds."

The housekeeper clucked in sympathy. "There, lass, I know this is an important day for you. Just sit down in that chair over there, and I'll bring you hot chocolate."

Sighing, Sarah went to the chair and sat. She drank Mrs. Fitzbottom's chocolate and had a few pieces of dry bread to absorb the nervousness fluttering in her stomach. She paged through a book, and then fixed her attention on her embroidery before drifting back to the window again. The sun had moved far to the west by now, and carriages continued their steady parade up the drive to Inveraray's front door. Sarah could hear unfamiliar voices raised in laughter and loud conversation both inside the castle. Shivering, her mouth dry, she sipped more of Mrs. Fitzbottom's hot chocolate.

"It's time, lass," the housekeeper finally announced, entering Sarah's room just as Sarah picked up her embroidery hoop again. "All of the guests who've had to travel a distance have arrived, and the rest of them will arrive in about an hour. We need to start dressing you."

"Did Colin return yet?"

The older woman frowned. "No, not yet. Have faith in him. He'll come."

Chewing her lower lip, Sarah allowed Mrs. Fitzbottom to dress her in the lightest cotton chemise possible and a gauze petticoat, in deference to late summer's heat. The housekeeper also insisted Sarah wear a whalebone corset, which extended downward to cover her hips. Padded, cup-shaped supports protected her breasts from the corset's stiff bodice, which pushed her breasts upward relentlessly.

Thus dressed, Sarah moved to the dressing table, where the housekeeper began the laborious task of curling Sarah's thick hair into corkscrews, which she then fastened atop Sarah's head with a gold ribbon. By now, Sarah's cheeks had become quite flushed and her breathing heavy, in part from the corset, in part from the heat, but mostly from the knowledge that in less than an hour she would have to descend into the great hall and play the part of the duke's daughter, something she *knew* she wasn't.

At last Mrs. Fitzbottom finished, though for once Sarah found herself wishing the older woman would never finish and spare her the task of debuting. Downstairs, the strings of a small orchestral ensemble shivered through the air and the sound of conversation had grown very loud.

"Is everyone here?" she asked the housekeeper.

"All are here, lass."

"How many people are down there?"

"At least two hundred. I expect word of your discovery has teased the *ton* for months now, and they came to have their curiosity satisfied. They came to see *you*, lass."

A peculiar giddiness grabbed hold of her. She clutched Mrs. Fitzbottom's hand. "I can't do it. I can't go down there. I'm not..."

"You're not what?"

Swallowing, Sarah squeezed Mrs. Fitzbottom's hand tighter. She'd almost told the housekeeper that she wasn't the duke's daughter. Still, the time for such revelations had passed. For now, she had to go down there and play the role she'd prepared for.

"I'm not ready," she clarified.

"Oh, lass, you're ready. You look beautiful, and your manners are as polished as glass. The duke will be so proud to claim you as his daughter." Mrs. Fitzbottom urged her toward the door. "Come on, now. It's time to go."

"Where is Colin?" she muttered, dragging her feet as they walked to her bedchamber door.

"Maybe he's down there now, waiting for you to descend the staircase. Go and see."

The housekeeper opened her bedchamber door and gently pushed Sarah into the hallway. Her heart thundering in her chest, Sarah paused. The laughter, music, and conversation had swelled to unbelievable proportions. She imagined a sea of faces, all of them turned to study her.

"Go ahead, lass," Mrs. Fitzbottom hissed.

Squaring her shoulders, Sarah started down the hallway. She felt as though she were walking to the gallows. When the top of the staircase came into view, her stomach clenched with fear, and when she saw the tops of some coiffed, bejeweled heads, she slowed down to a snail's pace. Somehow she found the strength to keep going until she reached the top of the stairs, when the entire vista became visible and stunned her with its grandeur.

The great hall had been cleared of all furniture for dancing. People in every corner laughed and conversed, glasses of champagne and ratafia in hand. Candles blazed in chandeliers and sconces, throwing their light upon the womens' bejeweled necks and their pastel silk gowns. The men, for their part, were more richly dressed than Sarah had ever imagined they could be, their shoes, jackets, and waistcoats all bearing gold and satiny accents.

The orchestral ensemble, hidden in the corner, strummed gently on their instruments, as if waiting for some hidden cue. Hardly able to breathe, Sarah scanned the crowd for a familiar face. The duke, she saw, stood near the bottom of the stairs talking to a distinguished-looking elderly gentleman. As though he sensed her scrutiny, he looked up and smiled encouragingly. Then he waved to the orchestra, which struck up an attention-getting flourish.

The partygoers all quieted down. The duke moved to the bottom of the stairs and faced them all. "I thank each and every one of you for coming to Inveraray, and celebrating this splendid occasion with me. As you know, I recently recovered my daughter, and today I present her to you, and to society, as the future Duchess of Argyll." He swiveled around to face Sarah and held his hand out to her. "Come down, my dearest daughter, and meet my friends."

The music began to play again, this time a stately processional melody that made Sarah want to sink instantly into a curtsy. Somehow, she remained standing and began to walk down those stone steps.

Time froze for her, and her vision focused entirely
on the duke. The satin of her gown brushed against
her gauze petticoats with a soft sighing noise, and
her heels clicked against stone, and her heart
pounded so loudly she felt certain the entire assemblage could hear it.

Smiling tremulously, she finished the walk down
the staircase and took the duke's hand. His skin startled her with its warmth. Her own hand must have
been ice cold, she thought inanely.

Applause broke out through the great hall. Men
and women alike surged forward to greet her.

"This is Lord and Lady Jersey," the duke murmured as a brilliantly dressed woman and her
dour-looking husband pressed forward for an introduction. "And this is the Duke of Bedford."

Her throat tight, Sarah exchanged a few pleasantries with them, and then they moved on.

The duke leaned close to her ear. "How are you
doing, my dear?"

"Fine," she managed, her voice shaking.

"Good. Here are the Marquesses of Ely and
Downshire, and their lovely wives," the duke continued, in what would prove to be an endless parade of
aristocrats eager to meet her.

Her face aching from smiling, she chatted with
all of them and allowed the gentlemen to fill up her
dance card as they wished. Lady Helmsgate hovered
nearby, her demeanor growing more sour as time
went on, until Sarah felt as though a poisonous mi-
asma had spread from the other woman to sur-
round her.

When, at last, a curious expression transformed
Lady Helmsgate's face and she walked toward the

study, Sarah nearly sighed aloud with relief. She didn't care what had attracted Lady Helmsgate's attention; she was just happy to be free of her noisome presence.

At length, the parade of aristocrats began to dwindle and someone pressed a glass of champagne into her hand. Sarah gulped the bubbly liquid, which added to her giddiness, and glanced around the room for Colin. Hoping to see his tall form, she instead noticed Lady Helmsgate near the study with a man and a woman, both of them dressed in somber, middle-class clothes.

Her own curiosity piqued now, Sarah stared.

Lady Helmsgate had grabbed the man's arm and was urging him toward the duke. Just as vigorously, the man was shaking his head *no*. The girl, her head a mass of flaming red hair, looked frightened, her eyes very wide and her face almost as white as her dress. Pressed against the wall, she clung to the man's side.

Upon seeing the girl, a chord of familiarity resonated within Sarah, and with it, a strange sense of foreboding.

"I will not allow you inside, sir." The butler's outraged tones penetrated to the farthest corner of the central hall, drawing Sarah's attention to another commotion near the doorway. "I cannot imagine you were invited."

"Don't you recognize me, man?"

The butler sniffed. "Most certainly not."

"Move aside, Whiton," their newest guest growled. "I'm not staying, I just want to see Lady Sarah."

Sarah's heart flipped over in her chest. Those masculine tones more familiar and dear to her than anything else, she left the duke's side and hurried to the doorway.

A large form pushed its way through the throngs of people lingering about. All heads turned in that direction. When Sarah saw him, she nearly gasped aloud.

Colin had returned, but it wasn't the Colin she'd been expecting. A beard and moustache darkened the lower portion of his face. His hair was mussed and his raggedy clothes had patches of dirt and mud all over them. A dirty tartan hung around his shoulders, and Sionnach lay cradled in his arms.

He looked like she had when she'd first come to Inveraray, she mused. But it was his eyes that caught her attention. While they still glittered with blue fire, they seemed strangely at peace.

Her mouth fell open.

"I'm back, Sarah," he announced, "and I've brought what I promised."

Shocked conjecture began buzzing around the room. Lord Nicholson pushed his way through the crowd and strode up to Colin, his lip curled derisively. "What's happened to you, Cawdor? You look like a field hand. At the very least, you need a bath."

Someone in the crowd tittered. Another titter joined the first. Soon, outright laughter filled the great hall. The duke strode up to him, his mouth twisted. "What in God's name do you think you're doing, Colin?"

Colin smiled provocatively. He placed Sionnach gently on the floor. "I've come to claim my woman."

"Your woman? You don't mean my daughter?"

Colin stared lovingly at Sarah. He held out his hand to her. "I do mean your daughter. She's mine and always will be so."

The shock inside her giving way to joy, Sarah took a step toward him.

"Come with me, Sarah," he encouraged, his face gaining an unexpectedly somber air. " I have something to show you."

She took another step. Her gaze never left his.

A nearby ruckus in the crowd stopped her advance. Lady Helmsgate emerged from the sea of bodies, the man and girl Sarah had noticed before in tow. "Just a moment. I want you all to meet someone."

The man wore heavy sideburns and nondescript city clothing. He threw Colin a look that Sarah translated as apologetic. The girl at his side kept her head down, obscuring her features.

Lady Helmsgate's voice rang out triumphantly through the great hall. "Tell them who you are, sir."

"I'm Mr. Cooper, lately of Bow Street, and this... this is Sarah."

"Lift your head, *Lady Sarah*," Lady Helmsgate demanded of the girl, who obediently raised her head.

The second gasp of the day went through the crowd. The girl bore an exact resemblance to the duke.

Recognition sliced through Sarah like a knife. As though in a dream, she lifted her fingers to her lips. The girl was older, yes, but if she concentrated hard enough, she could remember how the girl had looked when younger—at only four years old, in fact.

She swallowed, her hand dropping to her side, a rush of happiness at seeing her childhood playmate quickly squashed by the horrific implications of her appearance. Suddenly she felt hot. Terribly hot. Sweat broke out on her brow and gathered along her spine.

Eyebrows drawn together, the duke stepped forward. "What is the meaning of this? Who are you? And who is this girl?"

"Look at her, Your Grace," Lady Helmsgate urged. "Do you not know who she is? You might as well stare into a looking glass."

His expression wondering, the duke took hesitant steps toward the girl, until he stared her directly in the eye. "Who are you, child?"

"Oh, Papa," the girl breathed and, her eyes glistening with unshed tears, she threw herself into the duke's arms. "I didn't know who I was, but I never forgot your face."

Clearly bemused, the duke closed his arms around her awkwardly and patted her on the back.

Lady Helmsgate marched over to the duke's side. "You should thank the earl for reuniting you with your true daughter," she said, drawing a few shocked exclamations from the avid onlookers. "Mr. Cooper reluctantly informed me that the Earl of Cawdor hired him months ago to investigate the other Lady Sarah's claims, to insure you had recovered your true daughter and not the serving maid's daughter."

Everything inside Sarah went from hot to frozen.

"I'm afraid this woman," Lady Helmsgate sneered, pointing at Sarah, "is not your daughter. She is Nellie, a common serving maid."

Her head ringing with Lady Helmsgate's words, Sarah placed her palms against her ears. Panic invaded her limbs, making them feel tight as bowstrings. She stared at the haughty faces around her, the gazes that all now seemed accusing, and her vision grew fuzzy. Finally her attention rested on Colin.

He dropped his hand to his side. His face had grown white beneath his beard.

Again, she thought with a snarl, he'd betrayed her. He'd been investigating her from the very start, no doubt trying to oust her from Inveraray to secure his inheritance. He'd never loved her. He'd probably never even liked her. He'd only been trying to draw information from her, maybe with the hope that she might inadvertently reveal something incriminating.

The duke put the red-haired girl firmly to one side and faced Lady Helmsgate. His brow looked heavy with disapproval. "Your actions this evening are ill considered, Amelia. Look at the pain you've caused Sarah."

"She isn't Sarah," Lady Helmsgate screeched. "She is Nellie, a serving wench."

"We may have her name wrong, but she *is* my daughter. By embarrassing and hurting her in such a manner this evening," he continued remorselessly, "you have shamed and hurt me equally. I see now how mean and pitiful your character truly is. You are a small woman, Amelia Helmsgate, and I wish you gone from my home immediately."

A hushed silence descended over the crowd.

Lady Helmsgate, her mouth open, stared at the duke.

Very deliberately, he turned his back on her.

Murmurs rippled through the partygoers. Then, without warning, Lady Jersey turned her back to Lady Helmsgate as well. Lady Jersey's husband swung around seconds later. As the moments passed, each of the aristocracy followed the duke's example and turned their backs to Lady Helmsgate, until the entire assemblage had shunned the blond woman with an implacable thoroughness.

"I...I..." Lady Helmsgate, her face crumbling and her hand at her throat, fled up the stairs, nearly tripping on her skirt in the process. Lord Nicholson followed her.

Sarah took little joy in the other woman's downfall. Her own downfall had been just as complete. She'd been full of hope these past few weeks, but now, like a crystal flung against brick, that hope lay shattered in pieces at her feet. She clenched her hands into her skirts and walked up to Colin until she stared him directly in the eye. "You lying son of a bitch."

Colin flinched. "Sarah, please listen to me—"

"I don't ever want to see you again," she spit, and picked up her skirts. Her heart pounding, she hurried to the front door. A startled footman opened the door for her. She raced out into the night, the cool air slapping against her cheeks, which felt afire with shock and embarrassment. She didn't know where she would go or what she would do, she just wanted to be anywhere but Inveraray Castle.

A sudden flood of light behind her indicated that the front door had opened again. At the same time, Sionnach sprinted ahead of her, then yipped urgently.

"Sarah, stop!" Colin shouted.

A cramp in her side, she focused on Sionnach. She saw immediately that he wanted her to follow him. He started to run in the direction of the Maltlands.

Hand pressed against the cramp, she pelted down the drive after him. Her breath wheezed in and out of her throat. Tears pressed against the back of her eyes. The weight of hurt and betrayal she carried made her hunch over, her shoulders stooped. She felt crippled.

WALDENBOOKS

SALE   0543   103   1391   09-27-01
            REL 7.3/1.01   50   11:32:03

01 0743412788   6.50
PREF NO. 742185267   EXP 12/01
PREF DISC   6.50 10% OFF   0.65-
               SUBTOTAL   5.85
INDIANA 5.0% TAX   .29
               TOTAL   6.14
               CASH   20.00
               CHANGE   13.86-
               PV# 0031391

   PREFERRED READERS SAVE EVERY DAY

===========CUSTOMER RECEIPT===========

Footsteps crunched along the gravel drive. Colin was following her. Afraid she might scratch his eyes out if he caught up with her, she picked up speed.

Panting, she stopped at the arched entrance to the Maltlands. Sionnach shot through the arch and raced over to the door on his barn. Doggedly she followed him, drawing the ███ on the door and letting them both inside.

A lantern, hung ███ ███ rafters, cast a soft glow on hay b███ ███ ███h of water. A pile of blanks███ ███ ███ttention. Sionnach ███ ███ ged the blankets ███

Sh███ ███nkets and pushed ███ ███oat glistened in ███ ███ swift breath and ███

He'd foun███

She pushed ███ ███fe-male looked m███ ███ little more delic███ ███very-white coat an███

She ran her hand ███ neck, and head. Its c███ ███neath, its body cool ra███ ███ she pressed a hand again███ ███ pulse, detected no rising ███ ███chest. Her fingers shaking, she touc███ ███

Her mind remained blank.

"Sionnach, is she dead?" Sarah whispered in human language. Her hands fell to her sides and her shoulders grew even more stooped. "Are we too late?"

"I don't know." The deep male voice came from the doorway. Colin entered the barn, his shadow dancing on the wall behind him. "I found her in a secret burial chamber near Kildrummie Castle. Our golden man was there, too, although he was naught but dust and bones. The Bruce was a great warrior, but even he couldn't withstand the ravages of time, like our unicorns can."

She stared at him, unable to speak. Conflicting emotions were roiling around inside her, making coherent thought impossible for the moment.

At her lack of a response, he continued, "On the way home from Inverness, I thought about why they might have buried her with the Bruce. My guess is that the female became listless and deathlike in captivity, just as the male is now. They might even have thought she was dead. In any case, they probably buried her with the Bruce when he died to honor her."

For some reason, he looked very powerful and masculine in his tattered, earth-stained clothes and tartan. The blood in her veins quickened. She fought a traitorous urge to throw herself in his arms and tell him it didn't matter what he'd done, as long as he remained at her side from now on.

Angered by her own weakness, Sarah jumped to her feet and regarded him with narrowed eyes. "Get out of my sight, you lying bastard."

He lifted his hands to his chest, palms outward, as if to ward her words off. "Please, kitten, if you'd give me a chance to explain—"

She clenched her fists at her sides. "I'm not your kitten. Now get out."

His eyebrow flew upward. "Since you're clearly too angry with me to listen to even a word I say, perhaps you'll agree to a bargain."

"A bargain?" She snorted. "I'm not going to bargain with you!"

"Yes, you are."

"Are you that sure of yourself? Your arrogance is disgusting."

"Don't you even want to hear my bargain? It has to do with the unicorns."

Her anger faltering, she looked at the immobile body of the female. A sudden wave of grief made her throat ache. "What is there to do? The female is dead. The male will soon follow."

"I'm not certain she's dead."

"She's not breathing, her heart's not beating, and her body is cool."

"Why hasn't she begun to decay if she's dead?" Colin pointed out. "Clearly unicorns have very long life spans, if the male unicorn can remember the Bruce. So she's probably not expired from old age. Maybe she's just sleeping a very deep sleep. Hibernating, if you will. We need to take her to someone who knows how to take care of her: the male unicorn. And therein lies my bargain. If I help you take her to the male, then you must agree to talk to me, until the sun comes up if need be."

Eyes still narrowed, Sarah nodded. "All right, I agree to your terms. However, I remind you that talking doesn't imply listening."

Unaccountably, he smiled. "Where else in Scotland could I find such a woman, who spits at me with claws unsheathed, then draws my very soul from my body with her sweet kisses and playfulness?"

She crossed her arms over her breasts. "I don't want to hear *anything* from you until we've reunited the unicorns."

"It's a deal." Giving her a satisfied grin, he left the barn and called for a groom to bring out one of the pony carts.

In short order, the grooms hitched up a pony cart, and Colin settled the female unicorn, whom he'd rewrapped in blankets, into the back. He helped Sarah aboard, took up the reins, and they started off down the path that skirted the perimeter of the field. Sionnach jumped on, too, and settled himself near the female unicorn.

Since they had to use paths or get the cart's wheels stuck in mud, the journey to the cliff's edge took much longer than it had on horseback. Sarah sat upon the simple wooden bench, with Colin by her side. The moon shone its gentle light down upon them and a cool summer breeze tugged at her curls, bringing with it the smell of freshly cut grass. Neither of them broke the silence.

When she trembled, he took his tartan off and slung it around her shoulders. She snuggled within its folds, the smell of him thick in her nose. How easy it would be, she mused, to pretend they were a happily married couple returning from a party. But the sick feeling that rose in her stomach, when she thought of returning to Inveraray to face the duke dispelled that notion.

After about an hour of traveling, they reached the cliff face and climbed down from the pony cart.

Colin assessed her white gown uneasily. "Do you think you can climb down the cliff dressed like that?"

"Do you think you can climb down with a unicorn in your arms?" she countered.

"Point taken." He offered her a quick grin. "We'll move slowly and carefully, my feisty little kitten."

"I'm not your kitten," she insisted. This time, there was no weight behind her words.

His grin widening, he picked the unicorn up and slung it over his shoulder. "Let's go. Sionnach, you lead the way. I'll go next."

Raising an eyebrow at his easy camaraderie with the fox, Sarah waited for Sionnach and Colin to precede her, then started down the cliff. As always, memories of the carriage accident assailed her, making her momentarily dizzy. She gripped an exposed root and paused.

Colin continued on for only a second or so before he noticed that she'd stopped. He stopped, too. "Is anything wrong?"

She frowned. "Everything is wrong."

"I mean, can you continue down the cliff?"

"Yes, I can continue." She began climbing downward again, thinking, why not? She might as well tell him about her memories of the accident. He already knew she wasn't the duke's daughter. "The first time I climbed down this cliff, I almost swooned. Do you know why? Because I recalled the carriage accident."

"What did you remember?"

"Just an overwhelming sense of panic, and tumbling through space. Later, when I grasped the unicorn's horn, I actually saw the accident in my mind, as from the unicorn's point of view."

"The unicorn saw the carriage accident?" He sounded surprised.

"The unicorn rescued me. He brought me to the top of the cliff. I believe the tide had already taken...the real Sarah out to sea."

"How did the unicorn know to rescue you?"

"I'm not certain. The unicorn seems to see things...even things in the future. He knew that someday I would help him, and so, he helped me. The panflute was a gift from the unicorn," she added. "Because of him, I can understand the animals who live in the Highlands."

"You've been touched by magic from the very beginning," he mused. "I've wanted to bring magic back into my life for years now. Thank God I've found you. You are magic to me, kitten. Wondrous, incredible magic that I certainly don't deserve. Even so, without you I have nothing."

She glanced at him, and such a warm, loving flame danced in his eyes that she looked quickly away. "Sweet words will get you nowhere. Don't think I'll forgive you for this latest betrayal."

He shrugged. "Tell me, then, what the unicorn showed you of the carriage accident."

"He showed me everything. He even told me who I am. My true name *is* Nellie." She lifted her chin, daring him to respond.

"Nellie. I don't know if I'll ever get used to it. I prefer kitten, anyway. Why didn't you tell anyone you'd remembered your real identity?"

She hesitated. "I wasn't ready to return to Beannach yet."

"Why not?"

Her lips pressed together, she said nothing. She wasn't about to explain that she hadn't had the strength to leave him. Anyway, they'd nearly reached the bottom and her stomach was twisting into knots. Would the male unicorn know some way to rouse the female? Or would he simply allow himself to die, once he realized his mate was dead?

Sighing at her continued silence, Colin worked his way past saplings and boulders and approached the male unicorn, who lay in his customary location, just beyond the waterfall's mist. Moonlight illuminated the mist with a soft glow and settled upon the unicorn, burnishing him with silver-gray. Ever so carefully, he removed the blankets he'd wrapped the female in and set her down next to the male, so that her body curled as much as possible around his. Then he stood next to Sarah and they both watched.

At first, the male didn't move. He seemed unaware of their presence. Sarah pressed a hand against her breast. Convinced the male unicorn had died since she'd last seen him, she began to tremble. "Oh no, we're too late."

"Maybe not. Look," Colin directed. "His nose is twitching."

Sarah squinted through the pale wash of gray. She tensed with excitement. One of his nostrils moved. Then the other. She almost clapped aloud when his blue eyes opened and he pushed up on his forelegs. Whinnying, the male turned around to face the female and licked her tenderly on her face and nose.

Colin's hushed whisper drifted through the mist to her. "Is he growing brighter, or am I imagining things?"

"No, he's growing brighter," she agreed breathlessly. The male unicorn's coat seemed to shimmer in the darkness. Moonlight wasn't reflecting off his coat, she realized. The glow was coming from *beneath* his coat.

Suddenly afraid, she clutched Colin's hand. "What's happening to him?"

"I don't know." Colin stepped in front of her, shielding her with his body.

The unicorn's blue eyes began to sparkle, too, like a spray of a thousand stars at midnight. Shaking himself, he climbed to his feet and turned to face the female. Growing brighter with every second that passed, he whinnied loudly. Triumphantly. His brightness formed a silvery-blue aura around him that also encompassed the boulders and the ground.

Awestruck, she huddled against Colin.

"It's like a cloud of magic," he murmured, his eyes very wide.

The unicorn's horn rippled with ivory sparks, and the mist around him began to steam, as though heated by the beast's aura. Blue eyes unblinking, the unicorn slowly lowered his head toward his mate's. Their horns touched, and the ivory ripples that had encompassed the male's horn transferred onto the female's. Like loving hands those ivory ripples caressed her, spreading from her horn to touch the rest of her body. The silvery-blue magic grew brighter, and larger, until it held both unicorns within, and the female began to gleam with that same inner fire as the male.

The female twitched.

Sarah clutched Colin's arm. Fear and joy warred inside her. Joy won. "My God, she's alive. She's awakening."

Glowing with the strength of a hundred candles, the female unicorn lifted her head. Her eyes opened, revealing irises as blue as her mate's. She whinnied softly in her throat, and stood shakily, reminding Sarah of a colt newly born. The male immediately nuzzled her nose with his own and sidestepped so his body pressed against hers. Then he looked at Sarah, and Sarah felt all of the fear drain out of her at the gratitude and happiness she saw in his gaze.

Startled, she realized that her cheeks were wet. She was crying and didn't even know it.

Colin urged her toward the unicorns. "He wants us to come closer."

"How do you know?"

"I'm not sure. I just do."

Trusting in him, Sarah allowed him to draw her closer to the unicorns, until they stood within the magical aura, too. She tingled all over, and when she looked at her hands and Colin's face, they were colored light blue. Instantly a vision began to form in her mind. She saw Colin close his eyes and knew he was seeing it, too.

She allowed her own eyes to close. A gray castle came into view. Pine forests surrounded it. She understood that she and Colin had enjoyed many rides through that clean-smelling forest, and even a few secret trysts. Smiling, she entered the castle and stopped to view the scene within.

As if she was a spirit watching from above, she saw herself with Colin, in a rustic drawing room with tartan for curtains.

"That's Cawdor Castle," she heard Colin murmur.

He was rolling about on the floor with a little boy with very black hair. She was sitting on a chair, scolding them, her belly big with child, when suddenly she joined them in their wrestling. Colin promptly trapped her next to him and began to kiss her even as their son jumped happily on his exposed side, shouting, "I won, I won!"

Even though she was watching a dream-Colin

kissing her dream-self, desire built in her body until her blood was clamoring with it and her senses swam and she needed him to take her into his arms so badly she almost sobbed with the force of it.

She snapped her eyes open, and watched as Colin opened his a moment later. Startled, she looked around the valley. They were alone. The unicorns were gone, and the magic had dissipated.

"We've seen the future," she whispered, her eyes wide. "They've shown us what is to be. Oh, Colin, did you see it?"

"I saw," he answered huskily, his arms going around her. "Please don't ever leave me. I want that future for us."

Then, a ragged sigh escaping him, he sat down and pulled her down with him, propping his back up against a rock and drawing her into his lap. "I think I owe you an explanation."

"Not now, Colin," she demurred, wishing this perfect moment to last forever. "Explain it to me later. Or don't explain at all."

"This is the last obstacle between us, and I *will* clear it," he insisted. "First, you must understand that though the duke isn't my natural father, I look at him as such. I love the old man, in my own way, and I didn't want to see him hurt. When I first heard about you, I thought you might be out to play upon his grief and insinuate yourself falsely into his life, for monetary gain."

He played with one of the curls hanging against her shoulder. "Then, after I met you, I realized that you hadn't the slightest interest in his wealth and stayed on only because you felt you owed him. And as time went on, I became concerned at the changes

I saw in you. Like Sionnach, you were losing what had made you complete, and I didn't want you to become like me...selfish, hedonistic, and utterly lost. And so I kept Cooper on, determined to pursue the truth and almost wishing he discovered you weren't the duke's daughter."

As he explained, the weight that had borne down on Sarah became lighter and lighter. She snuggled into the hard contours his body offered her and sighed contentedly.

"I had planned to keep whatever Mr. Cooper learned to myself," Colin continued, "at least until I figured out what to do with the information. Unfortunately, Cooper showed up with the real Lady Sarah at the very worst time, and Lady Helmsgate, who has always had a nose for trouble, exploited him and the girl to the best of her ability as soon as she saw them."

His voice shaking, he tightened his arms around her and buried his nose into her hair. "I love you, Sarah. Can you ever forgive me?"

Blindly she turned her face to his, so that their lips almost touched. "How could I not? I love you so much that it almost hurts inside. Never stop loving me, Colin. I don't think I could ever bear the uncertainty and agony of knowing that I might lose you."

He pressed a light, questing kiss against her lips. "Magic has helped me find a woman who means more to me than life itself. You'll never be rid of me, no matter what happens."

"You promise to be faithful?"

"I can't even think of touching any woman but you," he breathed against her lips, and then he kissed her again, his mouth becoming hard and demanding.

She became unbearably conscious of the thinness

of her gown and the chemise beneath it as he ran his hands up and down her back, and hunger for him to take her as fully and deeply as he could knotted in her belly. Her hands shaking, she pushed his coat from his shoulders even as he pulled the tartan from her and exposed her shoulders to the night air.

Groaning, he lowered his head and nuzzled first her neck, then the tops of her breasts. Eager for more of his sweet caresses, she freed her breasts from the gown's silken bodice, her nipples hardening in the cool mist from the waterfall. He swiftly covered first one nipple, then the other with his mouth, the warm sensation of his tongue at such odds with the mist's coolness that desire exploded in her.

His erection pressed against her buttocks, a hard, hot reminder of his need for her. She twisted on his lap, drawing a groan from him, then rolled off his lap and onto her back, pulling him down with her. Moss covered the stone beneath her, cushioning her back and growing warm with her body's heat like nature's very own mattress.

He pulled off his shirt, then covered her with his big body and spread her legs with his knee. Her swollen nipples brushing against his chest introduced another delicate, sensual delight that left her gasping. The silken triangle between her legs began to ache with sheer animal need for him.

Moaning his name, she strained against him, and when his hand slipped beneath her skirt and explored her most tender parts brazenly, she moved her hips against him with equal boldness, certain she would swoon if he didn't soon fill her.

He still had his breeches on, some sane part of

her pointed out. That was a situation she'd have to remedy immediately. She played with his waistband, finding the button and undoing it, then dragged his breeches down around his hips with his eager help. She found his navel with her fingertips, then dragged them lower, scraping his skin lightly with her fingernails.

He shuddered at her caress, and his body tensed as he clearly waited for her to touch him intimately. But an imp of the devil got hold of her, and she allowed her fingertips to roam all around the pulsating core of him, almost but not quite touching what he wanted her to explore the most.

"You need a new lesson," he growled, and brought her hand to his hard length.

Smiling, she gripped him and reveled in his husky moan.

"This is how to please me," he whispered, and showed her what to do. Taking great interest and delight in this new lesson, she practiced enthusiastically until he stilled her hand with his own. Again he began to stroke her between her thighs, circling and skimming her flesh and penetrating the emptiness inside her with his finger until she cried out for him to take her.

Wasting not a moment, he merged his body with hers. His thrusts started out slow and gentle at first, but quickly grew more urgent as passion flamed through her veins and the swelling inside her grew to unendurable levels. Just when she thought she could stand it no more, her senses shattered with pleasure and she began to shake with the force of it, aware on some primal level that Colin was shuddering as well, his seed spilling into her.

Afterward, they lay contentedly in each other's arms, Sarah knowing with an unshakable certainty that they'd just created their first child. A boy.

They would have to marry quickly.

Still needing reassurance, she pushed herself up on one elbow and traced his lips with her finger. "You don't care that I'm not the duke's daughter?"

"I don't give a damn if you're a pauper who was born in a brothel," he growled, catching her finger between his lips and biting softly.

She squeaked and pulled her finger from his mouth. "I never wanted to be the duke's daughter. I wasn't made for such a role."

"Sionnach taught us both to be true to ourselves," he pointed out.

"And the unicorns taught us to love. But what will society think when you marry a serving maid?"

"Society can think what it likes. I have no use for it anymore. I have you, and you're all I need."

"Where will we go, Colin?"

He, too, sat up on one elbow and pressed a swift kiss against her lips. "To Cawdor Castle, of course. I've heard that its current owner has neglected it, and has nearly gone bankrupt. We'll buy it back from him."

"It sounds almost like Inveraray Castle used to be," she murmured.

"I feel like I've come full circle," he agreed. "Only this time, while I'm pulling an estate from the brink of bankruptcy, I'll have my beautiful, luscious wife by my side."

He folded his arms around her then, and pulled her against him. Sarah gripped him in a fierce hug, her heart brimming with happiness. Magic, she knew, was often illusive and insubstantial, like a cloud of gold dust that dispersed on a summer's breeze. But their love, though surrounded by enchantment, had become as real and enduring as the Highlands itself, and would weather any wind that fate might blow their way.

✦ Epilogue ✦

"Oh, Sarah, I hope some day I find a man who loves me as much as the Earl of Cawdor loves you." A little lace cap atop her red curls, the duke's true daughter fussed around Sarah, rearranging the silk folds of Sarah's wedding gown.

A smile curved Sarah's lips. She fixed one of the other girl's curls to fall more attractively against her neck. "You will, my dearest friend. The duke wouldn't have it any other way."

Mrs. Fitzbottom hovered around both of them, plucking imaginary pieces of lint off their dresses and smoothing wrinkles only she could see. "It's been a long time since these walls have witnessed a wedding. I don't think I've ever seen the duke happier."

Sarah clasped the other girl's hand. Their gazes met in the looking glass, and Sarah felt the warmth of friendship in her childhood playmate's regard. She'd never really had a friend while she was growing up, and now regretted it sorely. How wonderful it felt to know a kindred spirit.

Only a month had passed since Sarah's debut, and in that time she'd grown to know her old friend very well. Memories of their shared past surfaced almost daily now, and at last Sarah felt as if she truly belonged. She had a history, a family. No questions remained unanswered. And with Colin at her side, she knew such happiness that at times she felt unworthy of it.

Her worry that the duke might find out about the child growing inside her had been the only blemish on her happiness. The night she'd spent with Colin after they'd reunited the unicorns had proved fertile indeed. But now that her wedding day had arrived, that worry had finally dissipated. They would marry, and their son would be born a month early—not an uncommon occurrence for first babies. No one would ever know about her delightful transgressions with Colin.

Unconsciously she pressed her lower abdomen.

Someone knocked on the door.

Mrs. Fitzbottom sighed. "Come in, Your Grace."

Smiling sheepishly, the duke walked into Sarah's dressing room. "You knew it was me, eh, Mrs. Fitzbottom?"

"I told you not to bother us," she chided, "but I knew that wouldn't stop you. I only hope Mr. Colin shows more sense."

"Mr. Colin has no more sense than the duke," a male voice announced, and Colin also strode into the room.

"You're not supposed to see the bride before the vows are exchanged," Mrs. Fitzbottom said. "It's bad luck."

"I place no faith in luck," Colin declared, his gaze

settling upon Sarah. "Not anymore. My gambling days are over."

Sarah returned his stare hungrily. His tall form made her dressing room seem so small and feminine. She left the redheaded girl's side and went to his.

He grasped her hand. "Any regrets, Sarah? Are you going to run from the altar before the clergyman can priest-link us?"

She lifted his hand to her lips and kissed it gently. "I love you, Colin. How could I have any regrets?"

Palm tightening around hers, he bowed his head, resting his nose in her hair.

Self-consciously, the duke looked away. His daughter moved to his side, placed an arm around his waist, and urged him toward the door.

Mrs. Fitzbottom, picking up on her cue, grabbed the duke's arm and started to haul him toward the door. "This dressing room isn't big enough for five people. Let's leave Sarah and Mr. Colin alone for a bit."

Between the two of them, they managed to get the duke halfway across the room before he broke free. "Just a minute, ladies. I came here for a reason: to tell Sarah that I've just completed a certain purchase, and plan to give this purchase to her and her new husband as a wedding present."

Sarah reached up to caress Colin's cheek. "Don't you want to surprise us?"

"I've had enough of surprises," the duke declared. "I've already told Colin, and I must say, he approves most enthusiastically."

Her mystification growing, Sarah lifted an eyebrow. "What sort of present did you buy us, Your Grace?"

"He wouldn't allow me to buy Cawdor Castle," Colin revealed, his voice very near her ear. "Rather, he bought it for us himself. We can move there as soon as you're ready."

"Aye, you both have a lot to do," the duke added, his voice brimming with satisfaction. "Cawdor Castle is in worse shape than Inveraray was all those years ago, and I hear its tenants are some of the poorest in Scotland. Do you think you can help them, Sarah?"

She pulled from Colin's grasp and walked slowly toward the duke. Then, impulsively, she finished the last few feet separating them in a rush and threw her arms around his neck. "Oh, Your Grace, I don't deserve such kindness."

"Aye, you do, lass, and more. You've brought so much happiness to me and to us all that I thank the day I first set eyes on you. Tell me you'll never change, no matter what happens," the duke implored, his face tight.

Sarah released him and returned to Colin's side. She grasped his hand in her own and smiled lovingly at each of them. "I promise you, I'll never change."

Spellbinding paranormal
romance from

TRACY
FOBES

Daughter of Destiny

Forbidden Garden

Heart of the Dove

Touch Not the Cat

SONNET BOOKS
Published by Pocket Books

3108

**Visit the Simon & Schuster
romance Web site:**

www.SimonSaysLove.com

**and sign up for our
romance e-mail updates!**

Keep up on the latest
new romance releases,
author appearances, news, chats,
special offers, and more!
We'll deliver the information
right to your inbox—if it's new,
you'll know about it.

POCKET BOOKS

2800.02

ROPE

ASIA

RICA

INDIAN
OCEAN

AUSTRALIA

N

W   E

S

OCEAN

Sir Francis Drake was first and foremost a great seaman, whose courage and daring may have been equalled but have never been surpassed to this day, four hundred years later. He was other things too: a swashbuckling adventurer; a cultured gentleman; and a man who enjoyed magnificence in spectacle and gesture. His story is both colourful and human.

Sir Francis Drake

by EDYTH HARPER

with illustrations by FRANK HUMPHRIS

Ladybird Books Loughborough

SIR FRANCIS DRAKE

One day, just over four hundred years ago, an Indian guide and an Elizabethan sea-captain toiled to the top of a ridge on the Isthmus of Panama. Climbing a tree to gain a better view, the Englishman gasped in amazement. Behind him lay the Caribbean Sea. In front blue water sparkled in the heat. It was what is now called the Pacific Ocean, seen for the first time by English eyes.

Brought up as a Puritan, he 'besought Almighty God of his goodness to give him life and leave to sail once an English ship in that sea.'

The man was Francis Drake. Other sailor adventurers such as Raleigh and Hawkins, Frobisher and Sir Richard Grenville knew him well. For Drake was one of the most famous of the sailor-explorers of the Elizabethan age. His father Edmund Drake was a clergyman. Francis was born about 1541 (the exact year is not known) in a farmhouse near Tavistock not far from the port of Plymouth.

When he was 15, the family moved to Upchurch, Kent, to avoid religious persecution. Many ships of the Royal Navy were laid up in the Medway. While Edmund Drake preached among the sailors, Francis and his eleven brothers explored the estuary. They learned to handle boats, using Upchurch steeple as a landmark. It still aids navigators as it did in Drake's day.

Francis Drake
Sights the Pacific Ocean

5

Francis decided to become a sailor, and was apprenticed to the Master of a small coastal trader sailing around the Kentish and the north French and Dutch coasts. In time he learned the tides, currents and shoals of those waters. When the Master died, he left his ship to young Drake.

Everywhere Drake heard exciting tales of adventure at sea. Spain was England's enemy, and English seamen continually raided the Spanish ships returning with treasure from South America to Spanish ports. They captured or sank the ships and brought back rich cargoes to England: silk, spices, gold and silver.

Officially Queen Elizabeth turned a blind eye to her buccaneers but she was secretly delighted with the treasures they brought back, especially with the gifts she received. Drake longed to sail to the west. When he was twenty, his chance came. He set out to cross the Atlantic, and had his first taste of the Spanish Main, Guinea and the slave trade. A just man, slavery sickened him. He refused to take part in it. Instead he fought the Spaniards, for their need for slave-labour furthered the slave trade which he condemned.

In 1567 he became Captain of the 50-ton *Judith*, one of a small fleet of ships commanded by his relative, Hawkins. Treacherously attacked in San Juan de Ulua harbour, Drake and his men fought bravely although they were outnumbered, but only *Judith* and one other ship – the *Minion* – returned to Plymouth two years later.

The fight in San Juan de Ulua harbour

7

That summer (1569) Drake married a Cornish girl, Mary Newman of St Budeaux. Poor Mary saw little of her husband during the thirteen years of their marriage; Drake was now dedicated to destroying as many Spanish ships as he could and spent most of his time at sea.

He was becoming well known, but as well as being a brave, daring seaman, Drake had his faults. A writer living then described him as having 'an aptness to anger and too much pleased with open flattery.' His anger was directed against the enemies of his country, the Spaniards.

For the next five years Drake sailed as often as he could to the Spanish Main. There he carefully spied out the enemy's weaknesses, noticed the strength of their forts,

8

The treasure of silver ingots

the number of their guns and the defences. All the time he was planning how to defeat them.

In 1572 he was ready. He decided to attack the Spanish port of Nombre de Dios in the Isthmus of Panama. There all the rich treasures brought from Peru and Mexico were kept until they could be shipped to Spain.

With only seventy three men and two ships, the *Pasha* and the *Swan*, commanded by his brother John, Drake sailed boldly into the harbour, landed and beat off the attacking Spaniards. Taking some of his crew to the Governor's house, he showed them a pile of silver bars.

'I have now brought you,' he told them, 'to the Treasury of the world.'

Soon, Drake was badly wounded in the fierce fighting. He fainted and his men withdrew, carrying him back to his ship. They valued their leader's life more than hoards of silver. However, Drake had captured a long convoy of mules laden with gold before he attacked the town. Using two captured Spanish ships, he sent this gold back to England.

Recovered from his wounds, Drake sailed on. He burned Puerto Rico, captured many enemy ships and reached the Isthmus of Panama. It was while his men lazed in the sunshine there that Drake, always eager to explore, climbed with his Indian guide to gaze on the Southern Seas. The time had not yet come to sail on them. Now he had to take his men, ships and treasure back home.

They reached Plymouth in August 1573, on a Sunday 'at sermon time'. The Mayor and Corporation as well as most of the citizens were in church when the news came that Drake was back. The townsfolk quickly ran down to the quayside, for all wanted 'to see the evidence of God's love and blessing towards our gracious Queen and country by the fruit of our Captain's labour and success.'

What treasure lay in the holds! Ivory, spices and hides, wood from Brazil, jewelled swords, gold, precious stones, silver, silks and velvets. No wonder all Plymouth rejoiced and the thrifty Queen was delighted.

Drake's homecoming

Drake spent most of the next two years fighting with the army in Ireland but he was always thinking about those Southern Seas and planning how to sail on them. In 1577 he was ready for his great adventure. On 13th December he sailed from Plymouth in the *Pelican*, with *Elizabeth*, *Marigold*, *Swan* and *Christopher*.

Ships in those days were small, short and by modern standards, looked clumsy. *Pelican* was 100 tons, *Elizabeth* only 80 tons. Made of wood, usually oak, they were seldom longer than three times their width. Ship-builders constructed two types of ships. The smaller type had no superstructure.

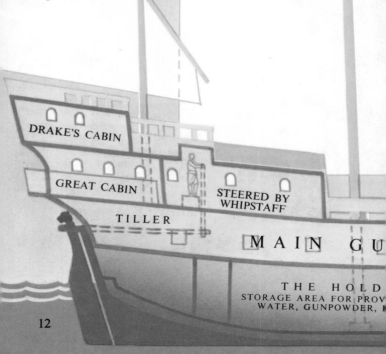

DRAKE'S CABIN

GREAT CABIN

STEERED BY WHIPSTAFF

TILLER

MAIN GU

THE HOLD
STORAGE AREA FOR PROV
WATER, GUNPOWDER,

The bigger ships had a high, built up bow called the fore-castle and a high stern structure known as the poop. The open space in between was called the waist. The poop was built out over the sea, with sleeping quarters for the Captain, a space for steering gear and a great cabin below it. Here the Captain had his meals and entertained guests. A stern walk was reserved for his use.

The fore-castle contained some of the crew's quarters, and some stores. Below the upper deck were more stores, berths for men and batteries of guns. The galley was so low in the ship that its fires caused intense heat which sometimes ruined the stores.

Nearly all ships had a figurehead carved on the prow, painted in bright colours.

FORECASTLE

E C K

ALLEY AREA
BRICK
IREPLACE

Elizabethan fighting ships carried long guns, carronades (short wide cannons) and other types of guns. Calivers and arquebuses (types of guns) fired shot and arrows, while bills, pikes and bows and arrows were also on board. The crew supplied their own swords and daggers but were given morions and corselets (a kind of armour) to wear.

It was to be three years before Drake saw Plymouth Hoe again. Troubles came early in the voyage. A seaman called Thomas Doughty tried to stir up mutiny among the crew. No doubt his task was not difficult, for conditions for sailors in those days were not easy. The voyage ahead was long and dangerous. The crews consisted of volunteers and *pressed men* (men rounded up and put aboard whether they wanted to go to sea or not). There was no lack of volunteers for a voyage with Francis Drake, for some of the prize-money from captured ships went into the crews' pockets and there was plenty of treasure to loot.

There was usually enough food but the quality was poor, especially the beer to drink. As long as the beer lasted, however, the store of water went untouched, except for the sick. Biscuit, salt meat, salt fish, butter, olive oil and cheese were the usual rations.

Romantic as these little ships may seem to us, they were dark, badly ventilated, wet and foul-smelling below decks.

Golden Hind

Often when far out at sea, men suffered from scurvy, typhus and dysentery. Discipline was stern. It had to be, for in an over-crowded ship, obedience to orders was the only way to survive.

Flogging, being ducked from the yardarm or kept in irons were common punishments for disobedience. It may seem hard to us but life at sea and on land *was* hard in those days. Survival at sea depended on an efficient, disciplined crew and on a good leader.

Although Drake was popular, he needed all his authority if he was to succeed on this voyage into the unknown. His little fleet was heading for an ocean the other side of the world, and though one of Magellan's fleet had sailed round the world, many sailors were still not too sure. For all they knew, they might sail over the edge of the world.

Drake had picked his chief men carefully. As Captain he was supreme on board. Not every Captain in those days was a sailor. Some were rich men who left the sailing of their ship to the Master or his lieutenant. The gunner had charge of the guns and the men who fired them, while the master-at-arms looked after muskets and ammunition. A surgeon, a chaplain, a boatswain and a coxswain were some of those who gave orders to the crew.

Trouble with the crew

17

Besides these, a purser who kept the ship's accounts and issued provisions, quartermasters in charge of the hold, a cook, a carpenter and a cooper to care for casks aboard were all necessary.

One member of the crew was never overlooked. He was the trumpeter who stood on the poop and blew his trumpet before going into a fight. Dressed in a brightly coloured tabard, his trumpet hung with a similar cloth, he 'sounded a point' to attract the enemies' attention.

In Drake's ships, everyone had to work. Drake insisted, 'I must have the gentlemen to haul and draw with the mariner and the mariner with the gentlemen.'

Doughty's mutiny failed and he was executed. By the time Drake's ships reached the Straits of Magellan, the *Swan* and *Christopher* had been left behind. In the Straits, he changed the *Pelican*'s name to *Golden Hind*, a compliment to Sir Christopher Hatton who had given much money to equip the ship. His crest had a golden hind (deer) in it.

They left the Straits on September 6th 1578 after sixteen long days of struggle against gales and bad weather which soon blew them off course. *Marigold* was lost with all hands. *Elizabeth* sailed back to England.

Now Drake needed all his powers of leadership and determination, but he was undaunted. He would sail on and take his men round the world.

The Golden Hind *battered by storm*

Soon they were in calmer waters. They sailed up the coast of South America, landing to seize treasure from Spanish settlements or, as at Valparaiso, to re-provision with captured Spanish stores. Many Spaniards were easily captured, since they mistook the *Golden Hind* for a Spanish ship, because no English vessel had ever appeared off these coasts.

The Golden Hind *strikes a reef*

The crew forgot their troubles as the rich goods poured into the holds. At Tarapaca, Drake's men quietly took silver bars from the side of a sleeping Spaniard. At another landing, they removed loads of silver from a train of eight llamas.

On they sailed, with little opposition. From one great vessel, the *Cacafuego*, Drake took thirteen chests of silver coinage, eighty pounds of gold and twenty six tons of silver. They could have sailed home with honour, but Drake had other ideas.

They reached Callao, then the coast off San Francisco, before Drake headed westwards again, across the unexplored ocean that he knew he must cross on his way round the world. For sixty eight days the little *Golden Hind* sailed on with never a sight of land. At times even Drake must have been worried, but all leaders have to hide their fears. On and on they sailed until at last (no doubt to Drake's secret relief) they reached the Moluccas (sometimes called the Spice Islands), in Indonesia. Then the *Golden Hind* struck a reef. A cargo of six tons of cloves and some guns had to be thrown overboard to free her.

Imagine how glad these sailors were to feel firm land under their feet again! Now they could drink fresh water, eat ripe fruit or laze in the sun. Wisely, Drake gave his men a rest ashore for three weeks. They stayed at Ternate, cleaning ship, recovering from illness and the strain of their long voyage into the unknown. Then, when all were fit again, Drake sailed for Java.

Before making the rest of the journey home, the ships too needed a refit. Ahead lay the Indian Ocean where storms could blow up suddenly and fiercely. With so much treasure aboard, Drake took every precaution. Although he had a reputation for great daring, he never took foolish risks, which was the reason for much of his success. He knew the power of the sea too well to set out on any voyage badly equipped.

Soon they were sailing home round the Cape of Good Hope, up the west coast of Africa into the Bay of Biscay and the English Channel that they knew so well but had not seen for three long years. On 26th September 1580, *Golden Hind* came safely to Plymouth.

Mary Drake, escorted by the Mayor, was rowed out to her husband's ship. Drake had kept back the cargo from a Chinese vessel specially for her: beautiful soft silks and Ming porcelain – some reward perhaps for her lonely life. She died childless about three years later.

Resting on a Pacific island

There was plague in Plymouth, so Drake took his treasure of gold and silver on to Deptford on the Thames. This was a handier port for unloading, since most of the treasure would go into the Queen's coffers.

There was work for all. The crew were paid off and given their share of the spoils. Sorting and valuing the cargo took many weeks but some of the treasure was sent to Elizabeth, with a promise of more to come.

It was not until the spring that she went down to Deptford to see for herself just what her gallant sea-captain still had aboard for her.

Drake, of course, was told of her coming. Both he and Elizabeth enjoyed a public spectacle. The *Golden Hind* was scrubbed and painted as never before. Drake wore his most magnificent slashed velvet doublet with jewelled pinpoint and lace ruff and short, gold-embroidered cape. Jewelled rings flashed on his fingers. Drake awaited his Sovereign.

The finest jewels were laid out in the Great Cabin, ready to give to the Queen, as well as a banquet for her majesty. Drake showed her not only gold-dust and silver ingots from Potosi, but pearls, emeralds and diamonds captured from the great Spanish galleons that left Lima each year to carry wealth back to Cadiz. How the Queen's eyes must have sparkled as she saw and graciously accepted Drake's gifts. She had some of the jewels put into her crown, to be worn in proud defiance of Spain.

Queen Elizabeth in the Great Cabin

Half-a-million pounds' worth of treasure was worth a reward. The splendid banquet over, Elizabeth went up to the quarterdeck and bade her Captain kneel. Then lightly touching his shoulders with a sword she said, 'Arise, Sir Francis Drake.'

The lad from Devon was now a knight and one of the most popular men in Britain. In vain Philip of Spain raged and demanded the return of his wealth. The Spanish Ambassador, Mendoza, wrote to his King that when he told Elizabeth 'matters would come to the cannon, she replied quietly in her most natural voice that if I used threats of that kind, she would fling me into a dungeon.'

Sir Francis Drake had his new coat of arms painted on his drum that had been with him all round the world. You can see a replica of it at Plymouth in Armada Way. The drum itself is kept at Buckland Abbey, Devon.

Not only was Drake the first English Captain to sail round the world, he was the first commander of a fleet to do so, for Magellan died before reaching home.

Golden Hind was laid up by the Palace at Deptford until she began to rot. A chair in the Bodleian Library at Oxford, and a table in the Middle Temple Hall, London were both made from her timbers.

Now there was time to rest at home but not for long. Drake was restless and missed sea-life.

Drake is knighted aboard the Golden Hind

After a few years 'Francisco Draque', as the Spaniards called him, crossed the Atlantic again. This time he brought home a hundred disappointed settlers from Virginia, a colony founded by Sir Walter Raleigh. With them, they brought two strange new plants: potatoes and tobacco. On this adventure, Drake had twenty five ships in his fleet and became the terror of the Spaniards along the coasts of the Caribbean.

Home again, Drake was worried. He knew better than anyone that the Spanish fleet was powerful and a threat to England's safety. Philip of Spain was planning an invasion of England. While Elizabeth tried in every way to keep peace, Drake urged action against the enemy.

In 1587 he 'singed the King of Spain's beard', as he put it, by daring to enter Cadiz Harbour. The Spaniards never expected to be attacked in their fortified port but there Drake showed his finest seamanship. He sailed in, sank thirty three ships and escaped unhurt before the Spaniards could rally.

He quickly followed up this raid by an attack on the Azores (Spanish islands in the north Atlantic). Here he captured the *San Felipe*, the world's largest carrack or merchant ship, with her cargo worth £100,000.

While most of this treasure, as usual, went into the royal coffers you can be sure that some of the taffetas, silks, velvets and jewels were given to Lady Drake, for Sir Francis had married again in 1585.

The attack on Cadiz

29

This time his bride was no humble Cornish lass, but an aristocratic and wealthy lady, Elizabeth Sydenham. Drake had also bought Buckland Abbey, formerly Sir Richard Grenville's Devonshire home. He lived in great style in a fine mansion, only a few miles from the rough walled farm house where he was born.

Pewter and silver plate, carpets and rugs, carved staircases and wall-panelling were in his home. Glass windows let in the sunlight to shine on beautiful china and furniture, while well-kept gardens added to the view. Drake was very rich indeed.

Comfortable as he was at home, Drake was not entirely happy. Those who ran the country's affairs were uneasy. While the Queen was anxious not to provoke a war with Spain, she was also against spending money, although men like Drake urged her to equip and keep a strong fleet.

He said he 'must seek God's enemies and her majesty's where they may be found.' Elizabeth refused to listen to his plea 'to encounter them somewhat far off and more near than our own coast which will be the better cheap for your majesty and much the dearer for the enemy.' He thought her dislike of spending money might make her agree to his plans. But though Elizabeth would not act, Drake did.

31

He and Hawkins, who was 'Treasurer of the Queen's Marine Cause', prepared and kept the fleet ready to fight. Drake was the Vice-Admiral in command of the *Revenge* with Admiral Lord Howard of Effingham in the *Ark Royal*. Drake impatiently put to sea to attack the Spanish fleet at anchor in Spanish harbours again, but storms blew him back and he waited with the fleet at Plymouth.

Not for long however, for the wind suited the Spaniards. The Spanish Admiral of the Ocean Sea (they had resounding titles in those days) was the Duke of Medina Sidonia. He decided to sail, to invade and conquer Britain.

It was a wet, uncertain summer. On Friday, 19th July 1588, Thomas Fleming, Captain of an English pinnace, sighted the Spaniards off the Isles of Scilly, sailing up the Channel to join the Duke of Parma's forces at Calais.

Drake was playing bowls when Fleming's messenger arrived. It is said that he remarked calmly, 'There is plenty of time to finish the game and beat the Spaniards too.'

He knew that the wind was against him, and his ships would have to be towed out on the ebb tide later that evening. The game over, Drake gave his orders.

Warning beacons, already prepared, blazed from hilltops and church towers as the fleet put to sea.

Lighting the beacons

33

Next day was airless and misty. Sixty five Spanish galleons, red crosses painted on their sails, moved in a crescent-shape formation, seven miles across. Their Captains, Don Juan Martinez de Recalde, Don Alonso de Leyva, Don Pedro de Valdez had fine names but the English sailors cared little for them.

The galleons were 'very stately built', so high they looked like great castles. Their thick walls were bullet-proof, while cables were twisted round the masts as protection against cannon-shot.

There were also galleys, galliasses, armed merchantmen and pinnaces in the Armada. On board were 8,000 seamen, 3,000 slaves and 29,000 soldiers besides mules, horses and provisions. Each galliass was rowed by 300 slaves pulling on great oars. They seemed more like mansions than ships for they had turrets, rooms and even chapels with pulpits inside them.

The English ships were better built, swifter, and (unlike the Spaniards) carried more sailors than soldiers aboard. They were in a position to send ashore for more water, ammunition and food, so that they sailed lighter than the heavily laden enemy ships. The largest English ship was Frobisher's *Triumph*.

English Captains included Sir Walter Raleigh, the Earl of Oxford, and men of lesser rank such as Masters Thomas Gerard and William Harvie, as well as the famous sailors Hawkins, Frobisher and, of course, Drake.

The Armada is sighted in the Channel   35

Every English ship flew the flag of St George. Although
only four of them were as big as the smallest Spanish
galleon, what they lacked in size they gained in speed and
easy handling. Besides, the men aboard were defending
their own land in water they knew. Every sandbank, rock
and current was a hazard to the Spanish fleet, but the
English knew how to avoid such dangers.

There were four squadrons of the Queen's naval ships
supported by armed merchantmen, small pinnaces and
local boats such as *Grace* of Yarmouth, *Robin* of Sandwich,
John of Chichester and *Frances* of Fowey.

'Out of all havens of the realme resorted ships and men
for they alle with one accorde came flocking thither.'

The English attack

Ashore the army waited, ready to fight any Spaniards who landed. At sea, the sailors were determined to prevent such an invasion. For days, the battle raged. Towards the end, Drake wrote to Walsingham (Elizabeth's Secretary of State),

'There was never anything pleased me better than the seeing the enemy flying with a Southerly wind to the Northward. The Duke of Sidonia shall wish himself among his orange trees.'

Early in the fighting, Don Pedro de Valdez' ship *Rosario* collided with another galleon and lost her masts off Portland. Drake sent his pinnace with a demand for surrender.

At first Valdez tried to bargain with the Englishmen. Drake told him that 'he had no time for arguing but if he would yield himself he would find him friendly.'

Valdez, on learning that Drake was his captor, surrendered. He came aboard *Revenge*, humbly kissed Drake's hand and told him he had decided to die in battle but by good fortune they had been captured by a 'right courteous and gentle man who was known to be merciful.'

Valdez went on to make a long speech praising Drake, who loved flattery. He gave the Spanish nobleman 'very honourable entertainment, feeding him at his own table and lodging him in his cabbin.'

But Drake was clever. He found out all he could of the plans for the Armada. Valdez told him the strength of the Spanish fleet, how at first they had planned to take Plymouth and were surprised that the smaller English fleet had dared to engage them in battle. Having learned all he could, Drake sent his captives ashore. He took guns and ammunition from *Rosario* into *Revenge*. There were 55,000 gold ducats aboard too, 'which the soldiers and crew merily shared among themselves.'

Valdez became a prisoner in England, in the household of Richard Drake where he lived comfortably until, some say, he was ransomed for £3,000. Other accounts say he was exchanged for another prisoner held by Spain.

Don Pedro de Valdez surrenders

39

That night Drake's ship carried the signal lantern for the fleet to follow. He suddenly chased after five vessels dimly seen in the dark, only to find they were merchant ships. Quickly he sailed back into position but Frobisher, always jealous of Drake, never forgave him for this.

During the next five days, the English harried the Spaniards furiously. Lord Howard wrote, 'Their force is wonderful great and strong and yet we pluck their feathers little by little.'

There were very many brave actions. Hawkins and Frobisher were knighted aboard Lord Howard's ship. Hawkins in *Victory* was always in the thick of the fight.

Fire-ships attack the Armada

Frobisher had shown great daring and had saved *Triumph* by superb seamanship.

Sunday 28th July was a day of rest. Both sides, Protestant and Catholic, held services. The Armada had anchored off Calais where 124 ships were counted by the English, anchored a short distance away. On board *Ark Royal*, a plan was formed to send in fire-ships. Small boats such as Drake's *Thomas* and even smaller ones like *Elizabeth of Lowestoft* were piled with firewood, pitch and gun-powder. The crews had only ten minutes to escape in dinghies after setting fire to their ships.

The English plan needed knowledge of wind, tide and current and here Drake was the expert. This was the coast he had learned in his apprentice days to sail along with no charts or lights to guide him.

At midnight a signal gun was fired from *Ark Royal*. The fire-boats sailed swiftly towards the enemy. The crews lit the fuses, but still sailed on, steering for the Armada until the last minute.

The Spaniards seeing men in the fire-ships thought they were devils from hell. In a panic they weighed anchor and made out to sea – straight into Drake's fleet off Gravelines.

From nine in the morning till six at night they fought ship to ship, and not one English ship was boarded. Drake's cabin was twice hit by cannon-balls. Dusk came and with it a wind that first blew the beaten Armada into yet more danger, on the sandbanks, then changed to drive it out to sea northwards round the Scottish coast.

Although the English fleet had run out of ammunition, it still gave chase, driving the terrified Spaniards through the North Sea. Spain was beaten, and England was safe.

It had been a long hard fight for the English sailors. Drake scribbled a report to Walsingham ending, 'Your now half-sleeping, Fra. Drake.'

The fight off Gravelines

43

A year later, with 180 ships, Drake sailed to help the exiled King of Portugal regain his throne, but illness struck the expedition, which was not very successful. On his return, Drake was not welcomed at Elizabeth's court.

In the eight years following the defeat of the Armada, he worked to help Plymouth citizens. He had already been Mayor of Plymouth in 1581, and had been Member of Parliament for Bossinay, near Tintagel, in 1584.

His greatest gift to the town was to bring in fresh water. Even the bigger houses relied on wells and streams for their water supply. Drake had a 'leat' or ditch cut to bring fresh water from the River Mewe and Dartmoor into the town over a distance of twenty five miles, which not only

helped the citizens but made it much easier for ships in the harbour to lay in a supply of fresh water.

There is a tradition that as Drake rode into the town, the water followed him. He may well have planned a dramatic spectacle timing his ride to gallop ahead of the water on its last lap into the town.

Whether it is true or not that the water followed Drake, it is certainly a fact that a procession rode out to meet it as it flowed in. Trumpeters went before the Mayor and Corporation with their wives, and food and wine was provided for all the onlookers.

Drake owned one water-mill, but now he built six more, all turned by water in the leat. They provided many people with work. He was paid £352: 16 shillings for his services and gradually, Elizabeth received him back into favour.

Plymouth's water conduit

He became Member of Parliament for Plymouth, went to Court and served on committees to help wounded sailors or settle disputes over money, property and other matters. Once more a well-known public figure, he decided on yet another expedition.

Though in his fifties, he was still fit and active. Spain was showing signs of building up a new Armada. Drake persuaded Elizabeth that attack was the best policy.

On August 18th 1595, Admiral Sir Francis Drake went to sea again, this time in the *Defiance*. Sir John Hawkins, now an old man, shared the command with him. As the twenty seven ships sailed out from Plymouth, drums beat, flags waved and citizens cheered their beloved admiral on his way.

The voyage ended sadly, however. Apart from the fact that Hawkins was ill, he was far too cautious for Drake's liking. They could not agree on what to do or where to go.

Gales blew up, and unexpectedly the Spaniards attacked them. Hawkins' illness grew worse. When the fleet anchored off Puerto Rico in the West Indies, he died. That night, the Spaniards attacked again. A round-shot crashed into Drake's cabin, smashing the chair he sat on. Unable to capture treasure, he sailed on for Nombre de Dios but before he could reach it he became ill with dysentery. He grew steadily weaker and died near Porto Bello, Panama, on January 28th 1596.

His sailors 'buried him at sea amid lament of trumpets and a roar of cannon'. Then they hastened back to England to bring the sad news to Elizabeth and folk at home.

Sir Francis Drake is buried at sea

46

47

A Spaniard who led the last attacks on Drake, when told of his death, described him as 'One of the most famous men that have existed in the world, very courteous and honourable with those who have surrendered, of great gentleness.' That was a fine tribute from his enemies.

Another Spaniard described Drake as 'of medium stature, rather heavy than slender, merry, careful'. He said Drake 'commanded imperiously'. He was 'sharp, ruthless but not very cruel' as well as 'boastful, ambitious, well-spoken and generous'.

The Spaniards, though afraid of Sir Francis, obviously had a very high opinion of him.

Pictures of him show an alert man with well-groomed beard and moustache, wavy, almost curly hair, wearing fine clothes. He looks plump, short and active with a kindly face.

Drake had no children, but his home – Buckland Abbey – has been occupied to this day by members of the Drake family. There you can see many reminders of this great seaman. His drum, legend says, beats whenever danger threatens England. Sir Henry Newbolt wrote a famous poem called 'Drake's Drum', in which he tells the legend that Drake will come back in time of peril to drum his enemies 'up the Channel as he drummed them long ago'.

This drum must have been one of Drake's most treasured possessions. You can also see his sword at Buckland Abbey, as well as some of the gifts he received from his Queen, and the Bible he took round the world.

Drake's drum (*now at Buckland Abbey*)

SIC PARVIS MAGNA

49

On Plymouth Hoe, there stands a fine bronze statue of Drake; a copy of the statue that is to be seen at Tavistock. The word 'hoe' means a high place and Plymouth's Hoe gives a good view of the surrounding district, as it did in Drake's time. There was a windmill there then, as it was open land with few houses nearby.

So well loved was Sir Francis Drake that many legends grew up around him. Some people believed that when he threw pieces of wood into the sea, they burst into flames and blazed like the fire-ships he sent against the Armada.

But Drake needs no legends to add to his fame. He was the first of the British admirals to show that it was best to attack the enemy well away from our coasts. He also showed his countrymen that the English could explore the world as well, if not better, than any Spanish or Portuguese navigators.

He is remembered most, though, for his daring, his bravery and his skill in seamanship. Among all the Elizabethan sea-adventurers he had no equal, for 'Frankie', as the ordinary people called him, achieved more than any of them.

Drake may lie in foreign waters but his example lives on to inspire generations of seamen who have come after him.

51

INDEX